W9-CLA-355

WITHDRAWN

THE
HOLDOUT

Center Point
Large Print

Also by Graham Moore and available from Center Point Large Print:

The Last Days of Night

This Large Print Book carries the Seal of Approval of N.A.V.H.

THE
HOLDOUT

GRAHAM MOORE

CENTER POINT LARGE PRINT
THORNDIKE, MAINE

This Center Point Large Print edition
is published in the year 2020 by arrangement with
Random House, an imprint and division of
Penguin Random House LLC.

The Holdout is a work of fiction.
Names, characters, places, and incidents are the products
of the author's imagination or are used fictitiously.
Any resemblance to actual events, locales, or persons,
living or dead, is entirely coincidental.

The text of this Large Print edition is unabridged.
In other aspects, this book may vary
from the original edition.
Printed in the United States of America
on permanent paper.
Set in 16-point Times New Roman type.

ISBN: 978-1-64358-623-6

The Library of Congress has cataloged this record
under Library of Congress Control Number: 2020932636

For Caitlin,
the best part of L.A.

THE
HOLDOUT

CHAPTER 1

TEN YEARS IN L.A.
NOW

Maya Seale removed two photographs from her briefcase. She held them face-in against her skirt. This thing was all going to come down to timing.

"Ms. Seale?" came the judge's voice, impatient. "We're waiting."

Belen Vasquez, Maya's client, had suffered terrible abuse at the hands of her husband, Elian. There were extensive ER records to prove it. One morning a few months back, Belen had snapped. She'd stabbed her husband while he was sleeping and then cut off his head with a pair of garden shears. Then she'd driven around for an entire day in her green Hyundai Elantra with the severed head mounted on the dash. Either nobody noticed or nobody wanted to get involved. Eventually, a cop had pulled her over for running a light and she'd managed to stuff the head in the glove compartment.

The good news, from Maya's perspective, was that the prosecution had only one piece of solid physical evidence to use against Belen. The bad news was that the evidence was a head.

"I'm ready, Your Honor." Maya placed a

reassuring hand on her client's shoulder. Then she walked slowly to the witness box, where Officer Jason Shaw sat waiting, his Distinguished Service Medal displayed prominently on the lapel of his blue LAPD uniform.

"Officer Shaw," she said, "what happened when you pulled over Mrs. Vasquez's car?"

"Well, ma'am, like I was saying, my partner remained behind Mrs. Vasquez's vehicle while I approached her window."

He was going to be one of those cops who did the "ma'am" thing with her, wasn't he? Maya hated the "ma'am" thing. Not because she was thirty-six, which she had to admit was probably "ma'am"-worthy, but because it was such a transparent attempt to make her seem stuck up.

She tucked her short, dark hair behind her ear. "And when you approached the window, did you observe Mrs. Vasquez sitting in the driver's seat?"

"Yes, ma'am."

"Did you ask her for her license and registration?"

"Yes, ma'am."

"Did she give them to you?"

"Yes, ma'am."

"Did you ask her for anything else?"

"I asked her why there was blood on her hands." Officer Shaw paused. "Ma'am."

"And what did Mrs. Vasquez tell you?"

"She said that she cut her hand in the kitchen."

"And did she present any evidence to support her claim?"

"Yes, ma'am. She showed me the bandage across her right palm."

"Did you ask her anything else?"

"I asked her to step out of the vehicle."

"Why?"

"Because there was blood on her hands."

"But hadn't she given you a perfectly reasonable explanation for the blood?"

"I wanted to investigate further."

"Why did you need to investigate further," Maya asked, "if Mrs. Vasquez had given you a reasonable explanation?"

Shaw looked at her as if she were a hall monitor sending him to the principal's office for some minor infraction.

"Intuition," he said.

Maya actually felt sorry for the poor guy right then. The prosecutor hadn't prepped him well.

"I'm sorry, Officer, can you describe your 'intuition' in more detail?"

"Maybe I saw some of the head." He was only digging himself in deeper.

"Maybe," Maya repeated slowly, "you saw some of the head?"

"It was dark," Shaw admitted. "But maybe I subconsciously noticed some of the hair—like, the hair on the head—sticking out of the glove compartment."

She glanced at the prosecutor. He silently scratched at his white beard while Shaw single-handedly detonated his case.

Time for the photographs.

Maya held up one in each hand. The two photos showed different angles of a man's head stuffed inside a glove compartment. Elian Vasquez had a buzz cut and a thin, unkempt mustache, crusted with blood. There was a streak of crimson across his cheek. The head had clearly bled out elsewhere, and then later been stuffed into the compartment, on top of the worn Hyundai manual and old registration cards.

"Officer, did you take these photographs on the night in question?" She handed them to him.

"I did, ma'am."

"Do they not show the head entirely inside the glove compartment?"

"The head is in the glove compartment, ma'am."

"Was the glove compartment closed when you asked Mrs. Vasquez to exit her vehicle?"

"Yes, ma'am."

"So how could you have maybe seen the head if it was entirely inside the glove compartment?"

"I don't know, but I mean, we found it in there when we searched. You can't tell me the head wasn't in there, because it was."

"I'm asking why you searched the car in the first place."

"She had blood on her hands."

"Didn't you say, a moment ago, that you 'maybe' saw hair poking out of the glove compartment? I can have the court reporter read that back to you."

"No, I mean—there was the blood. Maybe I saw some hair. I don't know. Intuition, like I said."

Maya stood very close to the witness box. "Which was it, Officer? Did you perform a search of Mrs. Vasquez's vehicle because you saw some of a severed head—which you could not have—or did you perform the search because there was blood on her hands, for which there was a perfectly legal explanation?"

Shaw stewed angrily as he struggled to find an acceptable answer. He'd just realized how badly he'd screwed up.

Maya glanced over at the prosecutor, who was now rubbing his temples. He looked like he had a migraine.

The prosecutor made a heroic attempt to pin Shaw down to either one of his two stories, but the damage had been done. The judge ordered both sides to have briefs filed by the following Monday, at which point he'd make a final ruling on the admissibility of the severed head.

Maya sat down beside her client and whispered that the hearing had gone very well. Belen mumbled, "Okay," but didn't make eye contact.

She wasn't ready to celebrate yet. Maya appreciated the cautious pessimism.

The bailiff escorted Belen out of the courtroom, back to lockup. Then the secretary called for the next hearing.

The prosecutor sidled over. "If you get the head excluded, I'll give you man two."

Maya scoffed. "If you lose the head, you lose the body in the kitchen and the shears in the drawer. You won't have a shred of physical to connect my client to the death of her husband."

"Her husband, who she killed."

"Have you seen the ER records? The broken ribs? The broken jaw?"

"If you want to argue self-defense, be my guest. If you want to argue that her husband deserved to die, you might get a jury on board. But suppressing the head? Really?"

"She's not doing time. That's nonnegotiable. Today, you can have reckless endangerment, time served. Or else you can try your luck next week after the ruling." Maya nodded toward the judge. "How do you think that's going to go?"

The prosecutor grumbled something into his tie about needing his boss's sign-off, then slunk away. Maya slid the photographs back into her briefcase and shut the clasps with a satisfying snap.

The hallway outside was crowded. Dozens of conversations echoed off the domed ceiling.

Courthouses were among the last places where all strata of society still brushed shoulders—rich, poor, old, young, people of every racial and ethnic background in Los Angeles walked across the marble floor. Hurrying to make it back to the office, she enjoyed being temporarily enveloped in the democratic crush.

"Maya."

The voice came from behind her. She recognized it instantly. But it couldn't be him . . . could it?

Forcing herself to breathe, she turned. For the first time in ten years she found herself face-to-face with Rick Leonard.

He was still thin. Still tall. He still wore glasses, though the silver wire frames he'd worn as a grad student had become the thick black frames of a sophisticated professional. He still dressed formally, today in a light gray suit. He must be in his late thirties now, just a bit older than she was. The decade's wear had, cruelly, made him handsomer.

"I'm sorry," Rick said. His voice sounded smooth. Assured. "I didn't mean to sneak up on you."

Maya remembered Rick's awkward hesitancy. Now he carried himself like a man who'd finally settled into his own skin.

She, on the other hand, was flushed with anxiety. "What are you doing here?"

"Can we talk?"

There had been plenty of times, over the past decade, when she'd been *sure* she'd seen him: in grocery stores, restaurants, and once, even more improbably, on a flight to Seattle. Each time she'd felt her skin go cold before she'd been able to reassure herself that she was imagining it. What would the chances have been that she'd just bump into him in a Walgreens? But now he was really here. In the courthouse. This was happening.

She dumbly repeated her question: "What are you doing here?"

"I tried email, phone. Your office. But I never heard anything back. I came to talk to you."

She hadn't received any messages, but of course, she wouldn't have. Her assistant was under strict instructions to hang up on anyone who called asking about the case. Maya kept a spam filter on her email that redirected any incoming messages containing the names of the case's key figures. Her street address was unlisted. She'd purchased her house under an LLC to keep her name off the property records.

Maya had achieved the precise level of infamy at which total strangers knew exactly one thing about her. Sometimes she imagined what it would be like to be an actress embroiled in scandal, or even a politician in the throes of disgrace. Those people's misdeeds were catalogued, public, keyword-searchable. They were open books of iniquity. But all of Maya's sins remained blessedly private—with one exception.

Whenever anyone realized who she was, it was the only thing they'd want to talk about. Prospective paralegals had alluded to it during their job interviews. Prospective boyfriends had dropped hints about it on first dates. Maya avoided corner seats at birthday dinners so as to never again end up trapped at the table's end, fake-laughing off some joke about it made by a friend of a friend. She had done everything she could to put it behind her, and it had not been enough.

Evidentiary hearings were public. Her name would have been on Belen Vasquez's court filings. Showing up here had been Rick's best way to find her.

"What do you want to talk about?" she asked, pretending not to know the answer.

"The anniversary is coming up," Rick said.

"I hadn't thought about it," Maya lied.

"On October nineteenth, it will have been exactly ten years since Bobby Nock was found not guilty of murdering Jessica Silver."

Maya noticed his careful use of the passive voice. But she knew all too well that *someone* had found Bobby Nock not guilty of Jessica Silver's murder. Actually, twelve people had.

Maya and Rick had been two of them.

17

• • •

Ten years ago—before she was a lawyer, before she had ever seen the inside of a courtroom—Maya had answered a summons for jury duty. She'd checked a box and put a prepaid envelope in the mail. And then she'd spent five months of trial and deliberation with Rick and the others, sequestered from the outside world.

None of them had been prepared for the controversy that greeted their verdict. Only after they'd emerged from their sequester did Maya learn that 84 percent of Americans believed Bobby Nock had murdered Jessica Silver. Which meant that 84 percent of Americans believed Maya and Rick had let a child-killer go free.

Maya had searched to find another issue on which 84 percent of the population agreed. Only 79 percent of Americans, she'd discovered, believed in God. She'd been grateful to learn that at least 94 percent believed the moon landing was real.

Under the hot glare of public condemnation, Rick had been the first of the jurors to recant. He'd gone on all the news shows and apologized. He'd begged the forgiveness of Jessica Silver's family. He'd published a book about their experience, claiming that their unjust verdict had been entirely Maya's fault. He accused her of bullying him into acquitting a man he'd always been sure, deep down, was a murderer.

A few of the others had joined him in renouncing their decision. Most, like Maya, had stayed quiet. Hoping to wait out the storm.

Sometimes she still wished she'd chucked that jury summons in the trash like a normal person.

"All the news channels are planning retrospectives," Rick continued. "CNN, Fox, MSNBC. Plus *60 Minutes*, some of the other magazine shows. Of course they would, given all the attention the trial received at the time. Given what's happened since."

Over the years, she'd talked about the trial with her parents. She'd talked about it with her friends, of which, since her notoriety, there were fewer. She'd talked about it with a parade of therapists. She'd provided the broad strokes to her senior partners and recited anodyne details to some of her clients. But in ten years she had never, not once, discussed the case publicly.

"I'm not talking about what happened," Maya said. "Not to CNN. Not to *60 Minutes*. Not even to you. I'm done."

"Have you ever heard of *Murder Town*?" Rick asked.

"No."

"It's a podcast. It's very popular."

"Okay."

"They're making a docuseries for Netflix. Eight hours. Adapted from the podcast."

Maya thought about all the hours of her life that had been swallowed up by the Jessica Silver case. Four months of trial, followed by three weeks of heated deliberations. During the sequester, every waking hour of Maya's life had been, in a sense, given over to the case. When she thought about the suite at the Omni Hotel in which she'd slept every night—how well she could recall every strip of fleur-de-lis wallpaper in that room, every inch of beige carpet—it seemed the case had consumed her sleeping hours as well. Sometimes, back then, to pass the time she'd done the math in her head. *Twenty weeks times seven days a week times twenty-four hours a day was* . . . She still knew the multiplication by heart.

"Who," she asked, "wants to spend eight more hours going over what happened to Jessica Silver?"

"A lot of people. And I'm one of them."

"You're involved in this podcast?"

"It's a docuseries. I'm helping the producers. Getting us all together. All of us. The jury."

Maya felt sick.

"We can share what we think about what happened," Rick said, "after all this time. And knowing what we know now . . ."

Rick paused as if they were already on television.

". . . would you still vote 'not guilty'?"

Maya was suddenly aware of the crowds

pushing past them in the courthouse hallway. All these strangers who'd come to this building for justice, absolution, or revenge.

"No thanks," Maya said.

"I've talked to the others," Rick offered. "They're coming."

"All of them?"

"Carolina died. I don't know if you knew that."

Maya didn't. Carolina Cancio had been in her eighties during the trial. Still, Maya felt a sting of embarrassment at being so out of touch after everything they'd been through. *Twenty weeks times seven days times twenty-four hours . . .*

But Maya hadn't spoken to Carolina, or any of the others, in years.

"How?" she asked. "When?"

"Cancer. Four years ago, her family said." Rick shrugged. "And Wayne told the producers no. Actually, he told them 'fuck no.' "

Wayne Russel. Maya wondered whether he'd ever been able to get himself together. She hoped so. But if he was the same man she'd seen at the end of their deliberations, it was best for him to stay away.

"But all the rest," Rick continued, "the other eight . . . they're coming."

"I hope you all have a good time."

"I came here to ask you to join us."

"No."

"We were wrong," Rick said.

Maya couldn't hold back a sudden flare of anger. "I read your book. You have every right to torture yourself with as many regrets as you like, but leave me out of it."

A few strangers glanced over, then quickly went about their business.

"A girl died," Rick said with an earnestness that Maya recognized all too well, "and her killer went free because we made a mistake. Doesn't that bother you? Don't you want to do something—anything—to make up for it?"

"Even *if* I thought Bobby was guilty—which I do not—there's nothing we can do about it. We have to move on."

Rick looked around the courthouse hallway. "You're a criminal defense lawyer. You work in the same building that Bobby's trial was in. You've 'moved on' all of two floors away."

"Goodbye," Maya said.

"I found something."

"What?"

"I've been investigating."

She wasn't surprised. She knew better than most how obsessive he could be. Once he became fixated on something, especially if it concerned unfairness or injustice, he never let it go. But when it came to the Jessica Silver case, he wasn't the only one. Jessica Silver's parents, Lou and Elaine, had been worth three billion dollars. Hell, Maya thought, by now they were probably worth twice that. Lou Silver owned some meaningful percentage of the real estate in Los Angeles County. His daughter's disappearance had been investigated by the very best.

"Dozens of LAPD detectives worked this case," Maya said. "The FBI. Journalists from all over the world descended on the city, PIs worked nights and weekends for the family, teams of lawyers on both sides of the trial, armies of amateur bloggers and conspiracy theorists with YouTube channels and . . ." Maya stopped herself. She couldn't allow herself to get sucked back in. "There is no more evidence left to be found."

"Well, I found something."

"What?"

"Come to the taping."

"What did you find?"

He stepped closer. She could feel his warm breath on her cheek. "I can't tell you now."

"Bullshit."

"It's complicated. It's a delicate . . . Look, just come to the taping and I'll show everyone—all of us—incontrovertible evidence that Bobby Nock killed Jessica Silver."

Maya looked into his pleading eyes. She could see how much he needed this. He believed, to the core of his being, that they had made an unforgivable mistake.

Maya didn't know if Bobby Nock had killed

Jessica Silver. That was just the thing: She'd never known. That's why she'd acquitted him. Not because he was innocent, but because there simply wasn't enough evidence to ever know for sure. Better, she'd argued, that ten guilty men go free than that one innocent be wrongly punished.

Maybe Rick genuinely believed that he'd found elusive, definitive proof. But Maya had long since given up any hope that it existed. She had spent ten years learning to live with her doubts. And Rick, if he was ever going to get free of this, would have to do the same.

Rick had once been someone she'd cared about. His was not a face that should cause the sick clenching feeling that was now in her stomach. He was a good person. He deserved a happiness that she knew would never be found amid the detritus of Jessica Silver's death.

"Good luck," Maya said quietly. "I hope you get what you want from this. But I can't be a part of it."

She turned and walked away.

She did not look back.

Maya's office at Cantwell & Myers was on the forty-third floor of the firm's downtown skyscraper. She sat at her desk, a midcentury modern piece that her assistant had picked out from a corporate furnishings catalogue. She was finding it hard to focus.

She turned to the windows and took in the skyline of the new downtown, a fleet of sleek skyscrapers cresting into the air. Half of these buildings weren't even here a decade ago. How many of them were owned by Lou Silver?

The blue skies over Los Angeles looked eternal, even primordial—the same color today, the same color tomorrow, the exact same shade of blue as they had been ten years ago on the afternoon a teenage girl vanished. It had happened only a mile from this very spot. People always said that L.A. had no sense of history, but Maya had learned that precisely the opposite was true. L.A. was a time capsule of itself, wrapped up and preserved forever in an immutable sky-blue shell.

"Got a quick sec?"

Craig Rogers stood in the open doorway. He wore a dark suit, perfectly tailored. His close-cropped hair was sprinkled with white at the temples. When she'd first started working for Craig, she'd had to consult his CV to figure out how old he was—was he closer to thirty or to fifty? It seemed impossible to tell. She'd finally found his year of college graduation and did the math: He was fifty-six years old.

In his youth, Craig had been a civil rights attorney. He'd been one of the crusading black lawyers bringing civil suits against the crooked LAPD officers of the Rampart Division, back in the eighties. In the nineties, he'd worked with the NAACP Legal Defense Fund on *Thomas v. County of Los Angeles.* Now he was a senior partner at Cantwell & Myers.

Had Craig sold out? Maybe. But he hadn't come cheap. At Cantwell & Myers, he had unparalleled resources to devote to the cases he deemed important.

"Of course," she said.

He shut the door and took a seat. If the prosecutor on the Belen Vasquez case had gone over Maya's head and delivered a plea offer straight to Craig, she'd bury that asshole.

"Our PR department," Craig said, "has been contacted by the producers of something called *Murder Town.*"

She should have known that Rick Leonard wouldn't be put off so easily. Of course he'd reach out to her boss.

"They're doing an eight-hour docuseries on the Jessica Silver case," she said, "and they want all the former jurors—me included—to participate."

"So they've spoken to you?"

Maya briefly described her run-in with Rick that morning.

Craig seemed pleased. "This is excellent. You'll do the show?"

"I said no."

Craig frowned. "May I ask why?"

"I don't believe there is meaningful 'new evidence' left to be found. Even if Rick has

26

fashioned himself into some kind of amateur sleuth. The facts are long established: blood, DNA, security cameras, cell tower logs, the ambiguous text messages . . ." She still remembered it all. "The bones have been picked clean."

"I thought they never found the body."

"Metaphorically."

Craig leaned back in his chair, as if to suggest that these "bones" might be more than metaphor.

"There is no way," Maya said, "that Rick Leonard has found Jessica Silver's body."

"Amateur or professional, if you spend ten years digging . . . But this is precisely why I would suggest that you attend."

"Define 'suggest.' "

"It's your choice," Craig said. Which was something people only said when it wasn't. "You're free to do whatever you like." Which was something people only said when you weren't. "The firm is with you."

Maya was well aware that her role on the Bobby Nock jury had been among the reasons that Cantwell & Myers had hired her. Had it helped her to sign clients? Of course it had. It was part of her sales pitch. Many criminal defense attorneys had been former prosecutors, but Maya had been a former *juror*—and in one of the most infamous trials of all time. She hadn't just been on the other side of the aisle—she'd been on the other side of the courtroom. Who knew better than she did how a jury decides? What defendant, guilty or otherwise, would not want the counsel of the woman responsible for the acquittal of Bobby Nock?

Yes, the verdict had helped Maya get her foot in the door. But the verdict hadn't finished eleventh in its class at UC Berkeley Law. The verdict hadn't guided three dozen clients through intricate plea bargains and won acquittals in all four of her cases that had gone to trial. The verdict hadn't made partner in three years. And given everything else that the verdict had done *to* her over the years, she refused to apologize for the few things that the verdict had done *for* her.

"Everyone already thinks Bobby Nock did it," Maya said. "Who cares what Rick Leonard says—for the thousandth time—on a TV show?"

"You're a partner now," Craig said. "Which means that anything said about you— *personally*—reflects on all of the other partners. We support you one hundred percent on issues of character. Which is why I would encourage you to support yourself."

Craig's ability to frame everything he wanted as if it were in her own interest was impressive. What he really meant was that the firm would defend itself from being tarnished by Maya's role in a case from which they had not earned a dime.

"It's one thing to have stuck to my guns for a decade out of principle," she said. "But it's another thing altogether to be an idiot clinging to a stupid decision even after new evidence proves me wrong."

"We all endeavor to learn from our mistakes, don't we?"

The twisted part was that if Rick Leonard really did have new evidence that definitively incriminated Bobby Nock—and Maya publicly apologized—she'd be in a better position, PR-wise, than she was in now. Some defense attorneys might be recalcitrant apologists for killers, but not Maya. She'd be someone who could claim to have followed the evidence wherever it led her, even if that meant changing her mind. She'd walk into courtrooms ever after with the presumption that she was a straight shooter.

All she would have to do, after hearing this mysterious new evidence, would be to admit that she'd been wrong.

Maya didn't say much as Craig handed her a memo with the details. The reunion would take place in a month. Once again, the jury would be invited to spend the night at the Omni Hotel, on Olive Street. The same hotel at which they had originally been sequestered.

Maya never actually uttered the word "yes" at any point in the conversation. She just nodded and listened, trying to ignore the twitchy feeling of being trapped.

Finally, Craig stood. He glanced at her desk and grimaced.

"Is that Belen Vasquez's husband's head?"

She'd set the photographs out earlier. "Yeah."

"I heard they're giving you reckless endangerment. Well done."

After he left, Maya remained seated, tapping her fingers against the smooth surface of the grim photographs.

What would she have made of these ten years earlier? The earnest, naïve, twenty-six-year-old girl who'd first entered the courthouse—that was a different person, one whom Maya dimly recalled, like someone she'd once met at a party.

Sometimes Maya still got angry. There were so many people to be angry with: the judge who'd kept them sequestered for too long, the attorneys who'd manipulated them, the talk show hosts who'd turned them into punch lines. She wanted to shout at all of them: *She* hadn't killed Jessica Silver.

Jessica's face was forever submerged just beneath the waterline of her memory. At any moment it could resurface. She'd be standing in line at a coffee shop and suddenly there it was. Jessica's blue eyes, her smooth cheeks, her incandescent smile. The famous image of a beautiful young girl who'd simply been wiped off the face of the earth. Whoever had murdered her was the monster who deserved all of Maya's rage, and everyone else's too.

And yet, sitting at her desk, the killer was not the person at whom Maya directed her anger. No, the present inheritor of Maya's bitterness, the person most responsible for putting her in this position, was Juror 272.

CHAPTER 2

RICK
MAY 29, 2009

"Who the fuck can't get out of *jury duty?*" was how Rick Leonard's roommate, Gil, put it that morning. They were in the kitchen of their two-bedroom apartment.

Rick was a twenty-eight-year-old grad student. He'd never been called for jury duty before, though he remembered his dad receiving a summons when he was young. Plus a few teachers in grade school who'd been replaced by substitutes. If Rick was being honest, jury duty sounded like a high-class problem. Even complaining about it—"Ugh, can you believe it, I got stuck with jury duty"—carried an air of sophistication.

"If you want to get out of jury duty, dude," Gil said, "you can a hundred percent get out of jury duty."

Rick shrugged. "Might as well get it over with."

It was May. He was between semesters. He was doing part-time research for a professor over the summer, on the city-planning failures in Brasília that had produced the ungovernable *favelas*. He had the time. Plus—not that he'd say this to

Gil—wasn't there a chance that he might actually be able to do some good? The justice system could use jurors who took their service seriously. And whatever his faults, he was definitely a guy who took justice seriously.

Rick straightened the blue blazer on his slim shoulders.

"Come on," he said. "One day, two max. In and out, done. What's the worst that could happen?"

Rick arrived at the Clara Shortridge Foltz Criminal Justice Center to find a scrum of press outside. He figured the reporters and camera crews were an everyday thing—there to cover movie stars fighting speeding tickets, or DJs pleading out to community service for possession. He'd feel stupid later, as the days became weeks and weeks became months, for not connecting the press presence to the fact that Bobby Nock was about to go on trial for the murder of Jessica Silver. What better story would those reporters be interested in covering?

A few minutes before 9 A.M., Rick walked into the juror holding room. The uniformed court-house administrator checked his name off on a clipboard and handed him a slip of paper that provided him with his new identity: Juror 158.

"For your personal safety and privacy," the administrator said, "you will be addressed by your juror number *and only* your juror number for the duration of your time here. You understand?"

"Okay."

"That means no real names. Not with us, not with each other."

"Each other?"

"Other jurors." And with that, the administrator turned to the next one in line.

Rick took a seat. He observed the few dozen people waiting with him. He took in their clothes, their magazines, newspapers, puzzle books, and occasional paperback thrillers.

Who the fuck, he thought, *can't get out of jury duty?*

He wondered which of these people would offer easy falsehoods to get themselves excused. Small children, sick parents, financial hardships, mental impairments—any one of these could be used as a reason to get sent home. All you'd have to do is testify to it in front of a judge. The court would have little means to check.

All you'd have to do is lie.

Which meant that the people who'd stayed, whatever else they might be, were honest.

A girl took the seat next to his. She was white, with short dark hair and soft features that at first made him think she was a lot younger than he was, before the poise in her posture made him realize she was probably about his age. She wore a navy skirt, a bright and formal top. Most of the

34

other jurors were in jeans and untucked shirts, but she had dressed as professionally as he had.

He thought about saying hello, but figured, *Then what?* He never knew what you were supposed to say after hello.

They sat in silence until the girl took the final swig from a paper coffee cup and set it down on the floor next to his.

He stood. "Are you finished with that?"

It seemed to take her a moment to realize what he was talking about. "Oh . . . yes."

He plucked both cups off the floor and carried them to the recycling bin.

"That was nice of you," she said when he'd returned to his seat.

He pointed to a placard of rules on the wall. *Please dispose of trash appropriately* was item number two. "Just following the rules."

She gave him a once-over, taking in his khakis and ironed shirt. "I'm guessing you're not the rebellious type."

She lifted up her backpack and plopped it on her lap. Rick noticed a large Obama campaign button pinned to one of the pockets. The button was square, with H-O-P-E in red, white, and blue.

Rick held up his own backpack, revealing the same button pinned to the front.

"He's been in office for four months," she said, smiling. "I guess it's time to take these off." She had a great smile.

"Save it. You can put it back on in three years."

"God, can you imagine going through all that again?"

"Yeah. I can." He felt as if she was already bringing out something embarrassingly earnest in him. "Did you volunteer?"

"I knocked on doors in Pennsylvania for a couple weekends. I was living in New York then."

"Nevada," he said. "I mean, the doors I knocked on were in Nevada. I was living here."

"Ladies and gentlemen," the administrator called out. "Thank you for your service to the city of Los Angeles. If you will direct your attention up here, I'm going to play a short video explaining your duties and responsibilities to this court."

He dragged a black metal cart from the corner of the room, on which sat an old television. He struggled to turn it on, smashing his thumbs against the remote control with ever greater annoyance. Finally, the screen filled with the image of the actor Sam Waterston.

"This is . . . unexpected," Rick said.

"Is that . . . the guy from *Law & Order*?" the girl said.

"Hello," said Sam Waterston on the TV. "And welcome to your jury service."

They both watched the actor explain their solemn responsibilities over the course of a

36

ten-minute introductory video. Sam Waterston informed them that not every country, or even every democracy, guaranteed a criminal defendant a jury of his or her peers. In France and Japan, for example, judges did the finding of fact. In Germany, a three-person team of one judge and two politically appointed laypeople played the role. The use of juries was what made our system so unique, and so precious to the American experiment. Serving on a jury was one of the most profound acts of citizenship one could perform.

Rick didn't let the girl see that he actually found the whole thing sort of inspiring.

After the video, the administrator began the lengthy process of calling them up one at a time to be assigned to a courtroom. "Juror 110! Please approach the desk." The juror was an older man, Chinese, who didn't say a word as he was assigned to a courtroom.

"Why do you think he's doing it?" the girl said, nodding toward the newly christened Juror 110 as he shuffled to the door.

"Doing what?" Rick said.

"Jury duty. It's easy to get out of. Everybody who isn't making up an excuse must have a good reason for wanting to do this."

"Maybe they feel, I dunno, a responsibility to serve."

The girl observed the older Chinese man

thoughtfully. "Or . . . maybe he's a career bank robber. Never been caught. Loves testing the limits, teasing the police, pulling off ever more risky heists. So when he got the summons for jury duty, he couldn't resist a trip to the courthouse that could never put him away."

"Maybe," Rick added, "he'll be assigned to the trial of one of his former associates. Maybe it's all part of his plan."

"That wouldn't be a very good plan."

"How would you know?"

"The statistical likelihood of getting yourself assigned to the exact trial you want . . ."

"Ah," Rick said. "Now I know why you're here."

"Why?"

"You're planning a robbery."

She threw back her head and out came a deep laugh, straight from the gut. A few people nearby turned to look at her.

Rick really liked her laugh. He had to remind himself that it was against the rules to ask her name.

A few minutes later, the administrator called for Juror 111 and duly dispatched an annoyed-looking white man to his assigned courtroom. Rick and the girl agreed that he must have come here to enjoy a day off work from a job he despised, hoping to sit and read his *Sports Illustrated* in peace.

For the rest of the morning, they kept up their game, concocting motivations and histories for each of the jurors as their numbers were called. She was funny. More surprisingly, Rick felt like he was funny, which didn't happen every day. He was trying to figure out a way to ask if she wanted to get lunch when the administrator called for Juror 158.

"That's me," he admitted.

"Good luck delivering justice."

"Juror 158!" barked the administrator.

"Good luck with your robbery," Rick said as he walked away.

Man, did he wish he could have gotten her name.

Twenty minutes later, Rick realized he was in deep shit. He and eight other prospective jurors had each been handed a black pen and a dozen-page questionnaire. There were hundreds of questions, but the very first one clued Rick in to the situation at hand.

"Have you ever personally met, or had any dealings with, Robert Nock?"

Damn. Was he about to be screened for the Jessica Silver case?

Question #2: "Have you ever personally met, or had any dealings with, Jessica Silver?"

Rick vaguely knew what Jessica Silver looked like. He and Gil didn't have a TV, but he'd seen her face dozens of times on screens at Mohawk Bend or any of the other spots he went to read when he wanted to get out of the apartment. She looked like so many of the pretty white girls whose disappearances filled twenty-four-hour news cycles: blond, blue-eyed, ever smiling, the epitome of well-appointed innocence. She looked like she could be the daughter of any of the suburban parents who were the target audience for those broadcasts. They were the real victims of all those shows that existed to terrify comfortable, decent people into believing that their well-ordered lives were under constant threat of attack. Never mind that the likelihood of a white kid from a wealthy family and a good neighborhood suddenly getting murdered was minute. The news shows never mentioned that a kid like Jessica Silver had a higher chance of being struck by lightning. Instead of explaining the rarity of such events, the message was always, *This could happen to you.* They broadcast it every hour on the hour. *This could happen to your children.*

Had Rick ever met Bobby Nock or Jessica Silver? No. But he knew that Jessica Silver was white and rich and Bobby Nock was black and had no money and that the guy was going to be eaten alive.

This is when a reasonable person would lie on the form and go home. Answering a jury

40

summons was one thing, but serving on the Bobby Nock trial would be something else. If Rick was selected, he'd be here for weeks. Half the summer, maybe. Was he really up for that? There were so many easy lies he could tell: Say he knew someone who'd been murdered, or that he hated cops so much that he couldn't ever believe a word they said. Or he could just say something nuts so they'd think he was a crazy person.

He looked down at the sheets of questions. And then, with a sigh, he realized he couldn't stop himself from answering them truthfully.

Shit.

Ninety minutes later, Rick was ushered into a courtroom. The judge told him to take a seat in the jury booth, alone, while the prosecutor and the defense attorney each looked over his answers to the questionnaire. Rick was surprised to see a young black guy seated at the defense table. Was that Bobby Nock?

For the first time, Rick got a good long look at him. In person he looked like a teenager. He was definitely younger than Rick, and it wasn't just that the suit hanging from his shoulders was too big; the dude was scrawny. His eyes were cast down at his folded hands. This kid was supposed to be a murderer?

The judge was balding and white, with a voice

41

so close to a whisper that Rick had to strain to hear as he explained that Rick was about to undergo something called *voir dire.*

"It's Old French," the judge said, "for 'to say what's true.'" The prosecutor and the defense attorney would take turns grilling Rick about the answers he'd put on his questionnaire.

The prosecutor was a heavyset, jowly man named Ted Morningstar. He had the arrogant air of hard-won experience. When he asked Rick if he knew of any reason why he couldn't be impartial in this case, Rick answered no. When he asked Rick if he'd developed any opinions about the defendant's guilt up to this point, Rick answered honestly that he hadn't.

But Rick wasn't blind. There were four black people in the courtroom. They were the defendant, Bobby Nock; an assistant prosecutor, a woman who didn't say a word as she perused questionnaires at the prosecution table; a uniformed police officer providing security; and Rick.

What did Rick know about the defendant? Only that they were both black men in Los Angeles. If the lawyers thought that meant that Rick couldn't be fair, then that was on them. Rick stared at Bobby. The kid's face was unreadable. It was like looking at an old TV, tuned to static.

Morningstar continued to dance around the question that Rick knew he really wanted to ask. The question that was formed by the legacies of all the trials that had taken place in this room, and in so many others just like it.

Can you, Rick Leonard, a black man, fail to consider that Bobby Nock, currently on trial for the murder of a white girl, is also a black man?

Can you, Rick Leonard, just let all that shit go?

More than anything else, Rick wished that the prosecutor would simply say it. But he knew that wasn't going to happen.

Pamela Gibson, the defense attorney, was younger than the prosecutor, thin and angular. She cut across the courtroom floor like an athlete running a well-practiced play. If the prosecutor's tone was one of *We all know what's really going on here, don't we?* then hers was more like *Who's to know what's ever real?*

After Morningstar was finished, it was the defense's job to find a way to not quite ask Rick how that whole "being black" thing was going to impact his decision-making.

Will you, Rick Leonard, give Bobby Nock the benefit of the doubt because you and he share— well, you know?

In the forty-five minutes of questioning, Rick made eye contact only once with Bobby Nock. Gibson asked Rick to list the people he knew who'd been victims of violent crimes—it was a short list—and as he explained that his mother had gotten mugged once, when he was nine, Bobby Nock looked straight at him.

"It wasn't really a violent crime, though," Rick clarified. "The guy just grabbed her purse and ran." And then he was staring into Bobby's eyes, the scared eyes of this poor kid who everybody thought had killed a teenage girl. Was Bobby's look, in that moment, a plea for help? Was it some kind of signal? *Can you help me out here?*

Rick didn't have a clue, and he realized that he didn't care. The only people who thought that he and Bobby Nock had anything in common were people who didn't know either of them. Rick meant what he told the lawyers: He would be fair. Impartial. He would follow the evidence, wherever it led.

"Juror 158?" came the judge's voice, interrupting his thoughts. "You have been admitted to the jury."

The judge instructed him not to use his real name in the courthouse or give any personally identifying information to other jurors. He would be required to show up every day by 8 A.M. and would be allowed to go home by 5 P.M. every evening. But he was expressly forbidden from reading any news reports about the case. Nor was he permitted to discuss the case with anyone *outside* the court—not his family, not his friends, not any prying journalists. The court would shield his identity from the public—they had a procedure for handling his safe arrival and departure every day—so that intimidation and harassment should not be concerns.

Did Rick understand everything the judge had told him?

"Yes, sir," said Rick. And that was that.

The bailiff escorted Rick into the jury room. There was only one other person there. An older woman, she had to be at least eighty, sitting quietly by herself. Rick walked over and introduced himself.

"Juror 158," he said.

"I am 106," she said. She had a thick Spanish accent.

She wore dark pants with wide legs and a bright long-sleeved top. A black canvas tote bag rested by her feet. On the bag, white capital letters spelled out THE HOUSE OF TAROT.

"Are you a fortune-teller?" Rick asked.

Juror 106 looked at Rick like he was crazy. "No."

He gestured to her bag. "The House of Tarot. It's on Sunset, right? I've walked by there. I figured it was a fortune-teller shop?"

She looked unhappy. "We're not supposed to know anything about each other."

"Right, I wasn't asking for your name or anything, I was just . . ." He stopped himself. He hadn't meant to upset her.

He sat down a few chairs away.

"I don't believe in fortunes," she said as she immersed herself in her Sudoku book.

• • •

The day was almost over when the door opened and the bailiff led the third juror into what was to be their new home. Rick laughed. So did she.

"Statistically speaking . . ." Rick said.

"What do you think?" the girl said. "Is this all part of my devious criminal plan?"

Juror 106 looked at Rick and the girl suspiciously. "Do you know each other?" she said.

"We're old friends," Rick said.

Juror 106 looked alarmed.

" 'Old' as in 'from this morning,' " the girl explained.

Rick turned to her and reached out his hand. "I'm Ri—" He stopped himself. "Sorry."

"Do we really have to keep up this whole thing? No real names?"

Rick was committed to what they were doing, and if that meant abiding by a few extra annoying rules, so be it. Justice deserved at least as much.

"I'm 158," he said.

"Nice to meet you." She took his hand. Her fingers felt soft against his. "I'm Juror 272."

CHAPTER 3

H-O-P-E
NOW

"I'm Maya Seale," she said to the production assistant who met her in the lobby of the Omni Hotel. "Juror 272."

"Yes, you are!" the energetic PA said without consulting the clipboard nestled in the crook of her arm. "Everyone is thrilled that you're here! I'm Shannon!"

Maya surveyed the lobby. It was late morning on a Wednesday, a month after Rick had appeared at her evidentiary hearing. The wall art had changed in the past ten years. So had the furniture and the staff uniforms, though their aesthetic was still the sort of timeless, placeless, generic hotel style that you could find in any city, anywhere in the world. It was just a different shade of bland.

Avoiding this place for the past decade had not been difficult.

Shannon gestured to the elevator banks. "Why don't I take you to your room so you can get settled? The hosts will call you in for singles. Today and tomorrow morning."

"Singles?"

"Interviews. One on one. Just the hosts and you."

"That's two on one."

Shannon looked like she was trying to figure out whether she'd done something wrong. "It looks like . . ." She consulted her clipboard. "Your single will be in the morning. But whoever isn't being interviewed at any point is invited to get together in the restaurant. It'll be informal. We reserved the back room. We'll do the official re-vote tomorrow."

"Have the others arrived?"

Shannon nodded.

"What about Rick Leonard?"

So much for nonchalance. It had taken her all of twenty seconds to reveal both that she was anxious and why. But then, why should she care what a PA thought about her anxiety level?

Shannon didn't seem to find the question noteworthy. "I don't think he's arrived yet."

Maya had googled Rick thoroughly since he'd appeared at the courthouse. But she could find no recent information about him. Nothing about where he worked, what his job was, where he lived. He wasn't on any social media that she could find.

There were only old photos. Old vitriol directed at her. Watching pixelated YouTube clips of old interviews surrounding the release of his book, she'd once again felt stung by what he'd said about her and the other jurors.

"When will I have an opportunity to see his new evidence? If I'm going to respond to it, I need to have time to examine it."

"All I know is that he wanted to be interviewed last. And then you'll all hear what he has to say before you re-vote."

Maya looked at her watch. It was going to be a long day.

Shannon removed an electronic keycard from a manila folder and handed it to Maya. "We're really glad you're here."

Room 1208 was *exactly* the same. The paintings, the desk, the chairs, even the coffee table appeared to be the very same ones that she'd lived with, every day and every night, for five months. She imagined that this was what an escaped zoo animal felt when returned to captivity.

She walked across the familiar patterned carpet. She touched the polished wood of the chairs. She stared at the paintings on the walls, the depictions of what looked like English fields. She used to imagine herself running through those fields. Being outside, feeling wind against her cheeks. Being anywhere, anywhere at all, other than where she was then . . . and, now, again.

Instinctively, she squeezed the key in her hand. Unlike last time, she could leave whenever she wanted.

"Pretty cool, right?" said Shannon. "Accuracy—historical accuracy—that stuff is really important to us."

Maya ran her fingers along the desk. The wood had a well-oiled shine. But something was off. The surface was too smooth. She felt for the pockmark on the front ridge of the desk. She'd made it with a pen one long, frustrating night. The mark wasn't there.

"We found hotel suppliers who had older models of the furniture," Shannon offered. "We brought everything in last week."

"These are copies?" Maya's fingertips brushed the leather frame of the desk blotter.

"Same make, same model, same year. We got them from a hotel in Atlanta."

Maya was standing inside a simulacrum of her old life.

The bedroom was identically furnished. There was a basket of fruits and chocolates on one of the side tables and a card that read "Thank you for joining us." It was signed *"Murder Town."*

That's when she saw it, right beside the basket.

Maya had to step back.

"H-O-P-E" read the small, square button, its red, white, and blue lettering smudged and worn.

"What the *fuck?*" Maya said.

Shannon hurried into the bedroom. When she saw what Maya was staring at, she relaxed. "That was yours, wasn't it? We thought it would be another fun reminder."

"I used to have one of these on my backpack," Maya said.

"Yes! I totally remember seeing it when you left the courtroom, after the verdict. That image of all twelve of you, walking away . . . I mean, that shit was iconic." She paused. "Sorry."

Maya couldn't take her eyes off the button. "I still have this. I still have *mine.*"

"For saying 'shit,' I mean."

"You got this online or something?"

"eBay. They're collector's items now. That was fifty bucks."

It occurred to Maya that what once had been her actual life had been reduced to collectibles. Her memories had become memorabilia. They'd been commodified, boxed and traded, sold at a healthy markup.

She cringed.

She was complicit, wasn't she, by being here? She was selling her past, or at least the only part of her past that anyone cared about, which was the part devoted to someone else's tragedy. She'd watched in horror, over the years, as other people made fortunes off what she'd done. The networks, the memoirists, the journalists with "access." How many people had gotten rich off the murder of Jessica Silver? There was the *New York Times* reporter whose book contextualized Jessica's death within the nationwide epidemic of sexual violence against women—for a two-million-dollar advance. Who could doubt that reporter's good intentions? And who wouldn't be envious of her new brownstone in Cobble Hill? Or what about the famed documentarian whose six-part HBO examination of the case took such pains to highlight the LAPD's long history of racial discrimination—surely his two Emmys and expanding production company were but the by-products of his honest convictions? There wasn't a cause in this world so pure that someone couldn't figure out how to make it profitable.

Maya had considered them all grave robbers. But now, standing inside the television re-creation of her former life, how could she claim to be any better? The fact that she'd given away her fee for being on this show, anonymously, to a Skid Row charity, did not absolve her of guilt. If the faded button in Maya's hand proved anything, it was that her youthful good intentions had been worse than useless. The button was a reminder of the dangers of believing yourself to be better than you were. Salvaged, it had become a curiosity, like a rusted spoon recovered from the wreckage of the *Titanic*. It was now an object to be studied by scholars of a once-promising history.

What she missed the most about the person she'd been, Maya realized, was her hope for a coming world that turned out never to have been possible. She was nostalgic for an imaginary future.

Maya looked at Shannon, trying to guess just how young she was. Twenty-three, maybe. "Did you follow the trial?" Maya asked.

The girl brightened. "Oh my God, follow it? I was in junior high but yeah, I was *obsessed.* I still am. I begged for this job. To be assigned to you. I hope you don't mind my saying . . . I mean, I don't want to . . . If it's unprofessional or whatever . . ."

"What?"

Shannon took a breath. "You're my hero."

Maya had no idea what to say in response to something so absurd.

"Why would I be your hero?"

"Because you took a stand. If everything Rick Leonard said is true . . . Well, you believed something, and you stood up for it. Maybe you were wrong. But you believed that Bobby Nock was innocent. And because you believed it, you talked all the others into seeing it your way—you fought not to let an innocent man be convicted and you *won.*" Shannon became suddenly embarrassed. "You know . . . right or wrong, you won. Fair and square."

"I won," Maya said. "Yeah . . . look at what I won."

She gestured to the re-creation of a mid-priced corporate hotel suite around them. This wasn't a canonization; it was an embalming.

Shannon frowned. The Maya she'd met had clearly not lived up to her expectations.

53

Then it was Maya's turn to feel embarrassed. She ran her thumb over the smooth edge of the H-O-P-E button. "Some advice?"

Shannon crossed her arms in front of her chest. "Never meet your heroes?"

Maya smiled. Maybe this girl was tougher than she'd thought. "That shouldn't be a problem," she said. "If you can manage never to have any in the first place."

The first time Maya had debated the evidence in the case of *The People v. Robert Nock*, she had been without legal training. Now, she had the advantage of both law school and four years as a practicing criminal defense attorney.

After ushering Shannon out, she performed a familiar pretrial ritual. She'd printed each major point of evidence out on a separate sheet of paper, and now she laid them across the coffee table.

She'd had a month to gather it all together. Not that she'd needed so much time. She'd been amazed by how little of it she'd forgotten. Looking over the actual, concrete physical evidence, she felt more confident than ever that Bobby's acquittal had not only been just, it had been necessary.

At just after 3 P.M., Maya pushed open the double doors to the hotel restaurant's private dining room and steeled herself to confront the timeworn faces from her former life.

There was Cal Barro standing with Peter Wilkie by the bar. Kathy Wing, Yasmine Sarraf, and Fran Goldenberg sat at a table against the far wall, picking at crudités. Trisha Harold and Lila Rosales were at a separate table, sipping from glasses of beer.

Rick wasn't there yet.

Maya's initial reaction was relief.

There was a little boy too, maybe five years old, pushing a toy truck across the floor, coming right for Maya's feet.

"Aaron! Careful!" Lila Rosales chased after the boy as he scurried along with his truck. "Sorry," she said to Maya as she passed. "That's Aaron." She whispered something in his ear, pointed at Maya, then took his hand and led him back toward her, his truck trailing behind him.

"Aaron," Lila said, "say hello to Mommy's friend."

The boy extended his hand formally. "My name is Aaron."

"Nice to meet you, Aaron. My name is Maya." She gave his hand a good shake. "You know what they say about a man with a firm handshake? He's honest."

Lila laughed. "He likes trucks." They watched him propel the toy across the room again. "In case you couldn't guess." She leaned in to give Maya a warm hug. "Hi, by the way."

Nineteen years old at the time of the trial, Lila

Rosales had been the youngest member of the jury. She had been in beauty school back then, and Maya had once marveled at how much effort it must have taken to prepare her immaculately made-up face every morning. Now, Lila looked worn. Her dark eyes seemed tired. The lines on her pretty face were not as well kept, or perhaps kept so effortfully that the labors showed. The pint glass in her hand was empty.

"He seems very mature," Maya said. "Is his dad here?"

Only after asking the question did Maya think to check Lila's finger for a wedding ring. There wasn't one.

"Who knows where his dad is," Lila said. "Things didn't work out."

Maya felt embarrassed as Lila explained that her babysitter had fallen through, and then Aaron's grandfather was supposed to watch him, but then he couldn't, and so eventually Lila decided it would be okay to just bring him to the hotel for the night, let him watch TV. That was okay, right?

Lila may have aged, but her need for assurance was still there. She had always been the kindest among their ranks. The most compassionate. When their deliberations became loud, angry, painfully acrimonious, Lila had always reached out to the person most viciously attacked by the others. Her instinct had always been to comfort whoever needed it most.

She asked Maya about her own life. No, Maya told her, she wasn't married either.

"Hello!" Jae Kim appeared at Maya's side and embraced both women in a three-way hug.

"How about that kid?" he said to Maya. "Lila did pretty good, right?"

Maya had to agree. Aaron seemed impressively confident, especially at that age.

"Yeah, yeah, yeah," Lila said. "How're *you?*"

Jae told them that his retirement was going just great. Maya remembered that he'd worked in construction—and that he'd lost his job after the verdict. Nobody had said he'd been fired *because* he'd been on the jury, but they'd each found, in their own way, how impossible it had been to go back to their normal lives. He was probably only approaching sixty now.

Maya thought back on the late-night talk show host who'd referred to them, in a running bit, as "the twelve dumbest people in America." There was one *Saturday Night Live* sketch in which they were portrayed as mouth-breathing lunatics who were literally drooling on themselves.

What must it have been like for Jae to try to return to work? Who wanted to set drywall alongside somebody who thought that Bobby Nock was innocent? What company wanted that much distraction over a worker making $17.25 an hour?

But talking to Jae now, he seemed to have made his peace with it.

No, she told him when he asked. She didn't have a boyfriend.

Maya saw Trisha Harold and Fran Goldenberg glancing back at her from across the room. Trisha's dislike—and eventual outright condemnation—of Maya ten years ago had been searing.

Maya marched right over. "Trisha! Can you believe it? Ten years . . ."

Trisha didn't hesitate to give Maya a hug. "Would you believe me if I said that it's good to see you?"

True or not, Maya appreciated the olive branch. "It's good to see you too."

Trisha was African American, tall but somewhat awkward about it, as if despite being middle-aged she was still getting used to her height. She explained that she'd taken an early retirement from her job as an IT tech in City Hall. Having worked for the government for so long, Trisha had always seemed the most comfortable amid the bureaucracy that had consumed their sequestered lives. She'd taken her three-quarters pension and moved to Houston to be closer to her kids and hadn't been back to L.A. since. She didn't miss it much.

If possible, Fran Goldenberg seemed even smaller than Maya remembered her. She had always been a maternal presence in the deliberation room. Every week she'd ordered a

58

tin of cookies for the group and watched to make sure everyone ate at least one. She'd collected their black Sharpies after each excruciating vote. Maya had been grateful that at least someone was trying to keep things orderly.

Fran still lived in L.A., she said. Same place. And yet she hadn't seen any of these people in ages! What was wrong with the lot of them, they couldn't get together once a year or something? What silliness, that they should act like strangers! Half of them still lived close enough it was a wonder they hadn't bumped into each other at Trader Joe's.

Maya looked around: still no Rick.

"I haven't seen him yet," Trisha said pointedly, as if reading her thoughts.

"Who?"

Trisha raised an eyebrow. She deserved better than Maya's coy bullshit, didn't she?

"They told me everyone is coming," Maya said. "Except Wayne."

"He had a hard time after the trial," Fran said.

"We all had a hard time after the trial," Trisha said.

"Yes, of course," Fran said. "But you know Wayne. . . . He's a sensitive man, and after everything he's been through . . ."

Maya would never have described Wayne as "sensitive," exactly. She'd have gone for "unstable."

Trisha did not appear sympathetic either. "Okay."

"He's a good person," Fran protested.

She had always seemed closer to Wayne than the rest of them had. Maya had never quite understood why. Maybe it was just that their rooms had been next door to each other's. Or maybe the web of allegiances and rivalries that had developed between the twelve of them had been more complicated than she could possibly have known.

A few minutes later, Maya found herself on the other side of the bar with Cal Barro. He had to be near eighty, and was bone thin. L.A. born and raised, Cal had been the Eastside lifer among them, full of colorful stories from Silver Lake's most debauched decades. A few of the stories had been a little too colorful for Carolina, Maya remembered. And now Carolina was dead.

Cal hadn't gone to the funeral, he told Maya. Apparently none of them had.

Who was that coming over? It took her a second to recognize Peter Wilkie, delivering a glass of wine that she hadn't asked for. Peter's hair was starting to gray at the temples and it was shaved at the sides, the same length as the perfectly even stubble across his cheeks. The most white-guy of all the white guys, he acted like the tab was on him. Even though they all knew it was on the TV show.

He'd done something in finance that Maya had

never understood. Now, Peter was in weed. Not in the sense of smoking a lot of it, he assured them. He meant professionally. He casually—or perhaps conspicuously—puffed from a hot-pink vape pen. His company made them. He handed her a business card.

It said, "Peter Wilkie. President and CEO. WEEDZ."

"I have clients still in prison for marijuana distribution," she said.

He nodded sympathetically. "It's a travesty that legalization took so long. The opportunities out there right now are killer."

A glass of wine later, Maya realized that she'd been here for two hours and still no sign of Rick.

She let herself hope that he might not show up for this part. He was coming for justice, after all, not happy hour.

Maya huddled for a bit with Kathy Wing and Yasmine Sarraf, listening to them compare notes on their respective children. Kathy had left her husband shortly after the trial, she said. "So at least *something* good came out of all that mess."

Yasmine sympathized. "That was the hardest part, afterward . . . Trying to explain to David— my husband—what it was like. What do you even say?"

Maya knew the feeling. At some point, she forgot about the cameras in the corner. At some point, she got a drink she actually wanted. At some point, she got another. She stopped glancing over at the doors for Rick.

Time, Maya thought, had the strangest technique for smoothing old rivalries. Rather than gestating apologies, the years fomented a false nostalgia. It made them wistful for what had likely been the most miserable time of their lives.

The effect was pleasantly intoxicating. Maya was not immune to the brew. Whatever else you might say about these people, at least they'd known her when.

Then Rick walked through the door.

He wore a blue suit this time, and he entered the room with the same quiet assurance she'd observed at the courthouse.

Maybe she was feeling sentimental. Or maybe she'd just had more wine than she'd thought. But she found herself, somehow, glad to see him.

She watched Rick say hi to the others, one by one. He shook Peter's hand, patted Fran on the back. He dropped to his knees to introduce himself to little Aaron, Lila hovering above them.

Finally, he caught Maya's eye.

She made a face of exaggerated shock, raising her palms to the air like "What the hell?"—as if deeply offended that he hadn't yet greeted her. He frowned in exaggerated regret—as if to show that he was saving the most momentous hello for last.

By the time they spoke, they'd already shared a private joke.

"Hi," he said. "I'm really glad you came."

"I should hope so."

"Are you? Glad you came?"

"I'll let you know in a bit."

Maya could feel the eyes of the others watching them. They must all have been dreading bloodshed. Instead they saw smiles.

"I'm sorry about the courthouse. Showing up like that."

"It's fine." She realized that she meant it. "I'm sorry I just ran off."

"It was important to me—really important— that you were here. I didn't handle it well. I hadn't meant to start an argument, but I did. You came anyway. So . . . thank you."

He never would have apologized with such grace a decade ago. The effect was disorienting.

She had certainly changed over the past decade, but maybe he'd changed even more. The last thing she wanted now was another fight. She didn't want to talk about Bobby Nock. She didn't want to know what Rick's mysterious "new evidence" might be. All she wanted was to enjoy being in the presence of one of the few people on earth who had shared the most intense experience of her life.

"So," she said. "What do you do?"

He shook his head. "Did you ever think, ten

years ago, that one day you'd be asking me 'What do you do?' Like a stranger?"

"If you'd asked me ten years ago whether this would be any of our lives, I'd have said you were crazy."

"I can't believe you're a lawyer."

She took a sip of wine. "Guilty as charged."

He winced at the bad joke. She found herself hoping that he wouldn't use this mention of the law to bring up the case. *Don't spoil this lovely moment.*

"If there's one thing you know," he said obliquely, "it's the inside of a courtroom."

She chose to deflect with honesty. "I learned a lot from our trial. Some law. But mostly, how a courtroom really works. How twelve strangers work together to decide the fate of someone they've never even met." She took a breath. By talking honestly about herself, she could avoid talking about anything more controversial. "I was an expert in something, for the first time in my life. I wanted to apply what I knew. After the trial, law school was a snap."

"Maya Seale," he said quietly. "For the defense. You've come a long way from planning a robbery."

"Right! That first afternoon . . . I'd been trying to remember."

"If you thought I forgot . . ."

Then, in a flash, they both looked anywhere but at each other.

"Your doctorate," she said, staring at her shoes. "Did you finish?"

Her Google searches hadn't turned up any mention of his completing a PhD.

He gestured around the room. "Do you think any of us were allowed to go back to real life?"

Maya didn't think of herself as a lonely person or a misunderstood one. And yet being around him, here, made her feel as if she'd spent a good number of years being both. "Did you want to?"

He thought for a moment. "Probably not."

She knew what he meant. There was no point in pretending that any of them had left that courthouse unaltered on some molecular level.

Suddenly she became aware of the cameras surrounding them.

She reminded herself that she was not inside their old hotel restaurant. She was inside the TV re-creation of it. She thought about the few—two? three?—glasses of wine she'd had already and hoped she hadn't said anything stupid.

"This is pretty weird, isn't it?" Rick said, nodding toward the nearest camera.

"Do you want to keep talking somewhere . . . *not* on camera?"

"Yes please."

Her first thought was to go to the restaurant's main area. But then she realized they'd still be within sight of all the others, not to mention stray employees of *Murder Town*. The hotel lobby would pose the same difficulties.

"My room?" She said it instinctively. It took an instant for her to realize how it must sound to him. "Not like that."

"Not like what?"

She looked up at the perfectly crafted curiosity on his face and realized that she was being teased.

"Oh, for God's sake," she said.

He smiled. "I know, I know, calm down. I remember what you're like when you're flirting with someone, and 'my room' isn't it."

"At least you've remembered my virtue."

"I was more thinking about your subtlety, but sure."

"Are we going?"

He set down his glass. Then seemed to catalogue the remaining jurors left in the room. "I know we're not *actually* doing anything scandalous, but if we leave together . . ."

Maya saw Trisha out of the corner of her eye. She was talking to Yasmine and Peter; none of them *seemed* to be paying Maya or Rick any attention.

Maya adopted an absurd English accent. "To avoid even the mere whiff of scandal, good sir, why don't I head upstairs now, and you'll follow in five?"

"M'lady," he replied, mock-tipping his hat.

She set down her glass beside his. The two glasses made a light clink as they touched.

She approached each of the others one by one to say goodbye, feeling silly for working so hard to make sure everyone saw her leaving alone.

Inside her room, she was pleasantly surprised to find the minibar fully stocked. This had certainly never been the case during the sequester. She remembered opening up the minibar that first night, hoping to find at least a few bottles of something—anything. If only. They'd even taken out the candy.

Maya poured herself a vodka soda, then another for her guest, before she heard a knock.

She opened the door to see Rick standing there, backlit by the hallway lights.

"You didn't forget my room number," she said, leading him inside.

"Some things a man doesn't forget." He took the glass she extended toward him.

"Careful."

"Of?"

"No flirting."

He shook his head. "When I'm flirting with you, you'll know it."

She sat on the sofa. He took the seat beside her. She could feel the cushions sink with the weight of his body.

Instinctively, she glanced at the bed in the next room. She wished she'd thought to shut the bedroom door. Then she felt stupid for noticing, for even letting her thoughts drift in that direction.

Why was she being so dramatic? Nothing was actually *happening*.

He took a sip. "Vodka soda?"

She nodded.

"Funny thought," he said. "We've never had a drink before."

"Wow. That seems . . . nuts."

"Right? Now I can't stop thinking about all the normal, boring stuff we never did together."

"We never took a walk."

"We never made dinner."

"I've never seen you drive a car."

"I've never seen you purchase anything."

"We've never been in a store together!"

"We never used money back then," he said. "The most fundamental exchange of capitalism. 'Here's some cash in exchange for that thing.' "

She smiled. Of course he took this thought to the most theoretical place possible.

"What do you think that means?" she asked. "About the way we all knew each other? How specific it was. How . . . protected from the real world."

"I have absolutely no idea."

She laughed. She set her hand down on the sofa and let Rick place his hand on top of hers. It seemed perfectly natural—both the gesture and the feeling of his warm skin.

What was she doing?

He leaned forward. She felt their knees touch.

He set his glass down on the coffee table. A damp ring of condensation bled out beneath the glass onto a white piece of paper.

"Is that . . . ?" Rick asked. His eyes had gone to the cover sheet she'd prepared on the evidence against Bobby Nock.

"Is that the DNA analysis?" Rick asked.

She squeezed his hand. There was nothing she wanted to think about less than the DNA analysis.

But Rick's hand didn't squeeze back.

He moved his glass aside and picked up the packet. It was full of tables, percentages, summarized conclusions presented in bold type.

"You brought this with you," he said, "for the show."

"Yes."

"To debate me. After everything, you still honestly believe that Bobby Nock is innocent?"

She pulled back her hand. "Not guilty beyond a reasonable doubt. What I'd always believed. Some of us have managed not to change our mind about this six times."

"People *should* change their minds when presented with new information," he said. "That's a good thing, not a bad thing."

"Is condescension a good thing or a bad thing?"

"Come on. You're telling me that none of the facts that came out after the trial—all the stuff we hadn't heard about Bobby—none of it changed your mind? And if not—well, does that say something about the case? Or does that say something about you?"

She wished she hadn't had that last drink. She stood, crossing her arms in front of her. "You are *obsessed*."

"Shouldn't I be? Bobby Nock murdered Jessica Silver. And because of us, he went free."

"You mean 'because of *me*.'"

Rick stood too. "You think that I blame you for the verdict."

"I think you wrote a whole book blaming me for the verdict."

"I blame myself."

"For losing an argument?"

His voice grew soft, almost tender. "I was the one who let you trick me into voting not guilty. I was the one who let you use me. In a moment of weakness . . . I was the one who caved."

"What, I coaxed a vote out of you with my feminine wiles? Please. That's insulting to us both. We had an argument. I won."

"Yes you did. And when I gave up, I betrayed everything I believed in. That shame? I've got to live with that for the rest of my life. If it wasn't for my failures, Bobby Nock would be in jail. So yeah, I am obsessed. I am obsessed with my responsibility to put him there."

"How? There was a trial. He was acquitted. That's it."

"Maybe."

"Double jeopardy. The state can't try him again."

"Yes, you're a lawyer now. Criminal defense. But I'm the only one who's obsessed?"

She didn't know how to explain to him that she hadn't become a lawyer to avenge Jessica Silver or exonerate Bobby Nock. She'd done it for herself. She truly didn't care about the case anymore. She was so sure of it that she was seething.

"This amazing new evidence you're supposed to have," she said. "What is it?"

"I can't talk about it right now."

She scoffed. "You couldn't talk about it before, you can't talk about it now. . . ."

"It's complicated," he said. "I have to wait for . . ." Why was he being so damned cryptic? "On the show. Tomorrow. I promise I will tell you everything then."

"So let me get this straight. . . ." She paced the carpeted floor as if it was a courtroom. "You've spent years obsessively researching this case, and while you're not going to share your earth-shattering findings with *me,* you will share them with a bunch of TV cameras?"

"What are you afraid of?"

"I'm not afraid."

"Doesn't sound that way to me. It sounds like deep down, you're terrified that I'm right. That

I was always right. That's why you came. Not to drink with our old buddies downstairs and not to flirt with me. You came because you are petrified that you might be forced to admit that maybe, just maybe, you were wrong."

She couldn't believe his gall. "Right? Wrong? You think that we're ever going to know what really happened to Jessica? We're not. Some sort of grand, definitive answer—it doesn't exist. We're never going to know for sure."

He shook his head. "I'm telling you, I *know*."

"Okay," she said. "Let's say you *know:* Bobby Nock did kill Jessica Silver. And we let him off. For the first time in history, a black guy in L.A. *wasn't* convicted for a crime he actually committed. The opposite happens every day. But *this* is the injustice you want to spend your life railing against? Really? This one?"

He stood motionless in front of her. "Fuck. You. Because I'm black, I'm supposed to be okay with a child-killer getting off—because that murdering asshole happens also to be black? No. *No.* There are *rules* in this world. I don't mean the law—fuck the law. I mean rules about being a human being. Bobby Nock broke them. He did an unforgiveable thing. But you want him to go free because other black guys were unfairly convicted? You want to talk about injustice? You want to pretend you're so racially enlightened because you invite me up to your room and

72

consider fucking me but then, in the next breath, you tell me that because I'm black I have to let a killer go free? Fuck you."

Maya had no idea what to say. She felt her fingers tremble and her eyes begin to water.

Rick saw what his words had done. He sighed. "I didn't mean to . . ."

"Leave," she said.

"Calm down."

"I said fucking leave."

The momentary guilt he appeared to feel had vanished. "Don't do this again."

"Do what again?"

"Bail the first second the conversation gets difficult."

That was not how she would have described what happened between them ten years ago. But she had no interest in re-litigating what had gone on the last time they were in this room. All she wanted—had wanted—was to spend time with the Rick that she'd first met. The Rick who'd made her laugh on day one of the trial. Not this person in front of her who hated her—maybe really, truly hated her—in a way that she simply could not bear.

"Leave," she said.

He looked furious. As if he'd been holding a well of anger just below the surface and now it was finally ready to erupt.

"No," he said. "I'm not letting you do this

again. I'm not letting you cut me out because you're too chickenshit to have a conversation about what I look like, and what you look like, and what Bobby Nock and Jessica Silver look like, and that conversation isn't polite."

She moved to the door and opened it. "If you won't leave, I will."

"Stop," he said.

She stared him straight in the eye. She tried to think of some last, pithy insult. But nothing came.

She walked into the bright hallway and slammed the door shut behind her.

The lobby was busy, so she kept her head down. She didn't want anyone to see the tears that she was unable to hold at bay.

She walked quickly down the sidewalk, not sure where she was headed. She just needed to get as far away from that terrible room as she could.

What had she been thinking, inviting him upstairs like that? She was as angry with herself as she had been with Rick. He was probably pacing around her hotel room right now, waiting for her to come back so he could tell her again how she'd ruined his life.

What tactical martyrdom! *Oh woe is him.* She didn't think he even meant the worst of his accusations; he was only trying to dig the knife in deeper.

She was forced to stop at a traffic light. She brushed away her tears and felt the calming cool of the night air.

Downtown after dark. When she'd first arrived in L.A., no one she knew would ever have ventured here so late. This neighborhood had been a desolate collection of half-empty office towers bordered by the razor's edge of Skid Row. The lawyers and accountants who worked in the glass skyscrapers fled as soon as night fell, drawn like moths toward the distant glow of the Valley.

Now, only blocks from the Omni Hotel, Maya found a crowd gathered outside the Silver Museum. This area had been a derelict stretch of concrete, a no-man's-land between the on-ramps to two different freeways. Now, thanks to a $400 million donation by Lou Silver, it was home to the finest modern art museum on the West Coast. Free to the public, though you had to sign up for tickets months in advance. Every piece of artwork inside the three-story museum came from Lou Silver's private collection. City Hall had given him the land for one dollar, and he'd built a monument to his own civic generosity.

Some sort of concert seemed to be happening on the lawns. A band was playing, something synthy and shimmering. The crowd swayed along. Maya continued down through the darkened areas beneath the nearby off-ramps. The highway construction had created so many of these non-places, as if there were so much land to go around that there was no need to be efficient about its use. The cityscape was dotted with stretches of unkempt grass and concrete without addresses, without owners, without function other than to be between something and something else. Walking in the dark beneath the ramp, Maya thought that sometimes Los Angeles felt like it was half liminal.

Jessica Silver had disappeared just blocks from here. There'd been some highly technical evidence about where her cellphone had gone, some difficult mathematics having to do with cell tower triangulation. But the gist was that she'd almost certainly been near here, the rough wilds of downtown, before her phone had been switched off. And she was never seen again.

Since then, a half dozen new skyscrapers had been erected. Now they gleamed into the night; the Korean Airlines building cut a blue arc the shape of a shark's fin into the black sky. Twelve years ago, Lou Silver had been on his way to becoming the savior of Los Angeles, personally rebuilding the city's long-desolate historic center, when the city had swallowed up his only child. Whatever had happened since—whatever had happened to Maya, to Rick, to the other jurors, to the Silvers, to this country that had doomed itself to bad decision after bad decision—Los Angeles was now thriving.

The world had begun to feel like a zero-sum game. Rising tides had never lifted all boats, she knew that; but now, to the extent that one rose, another seemed to roll off and crash on the shore. It was the unsparing physics of cause and effect: The wake of one boat became the wave that dashed another.

Lou Silver was doing all right for himself. But then, he'd lost a child.

What about Maya?

By any objective standard, Maya's life was better now. She had a well-paying job. Even better, she had a real profession at which she was talented. She owned a house above the reservoir and kept a Roth IRA. If the winners and losers in American life were separated further and further apart, wasn't Maya among the winners?

But she never felt like one. She'd once dreamed of helping to usher in a more just world. Now all she had was a Lexus in a half-empty two-car garage.

Maybe, of all the decade's ironies, that was the cruelest. Not even the winners were feeling good about the score.

Maya walked back to the hotel. The lobby was sparsely populated, and thankfully she didn't see anyone she knew. She hoped she'd been gone long enough for Rick to have gotten fed up and left her room. If he was still waiting for her, she didn't know what she'd do.

She opened the door to find her suite quiet and dark.

Thank God.

She walked down the short hall to the living room and found the switch by memory.

In the light, she saw a body on the floor. Somehow she stopped herself from screaming.

It was Rick. His arms were splayed out at unnatural angles. His white shirt was stained with blood. A dark red halo pooled around his head and in the palm of his hand was a button with the letters H-O-P-E.

CHAPTER 4

WAYNE
JUNE 1, 2009

Wayne Russel needed to be the first one in the jury room on the first day of the trial. He got there way before anyone else so he could grab the seat right next to the windows.

He had to be by the windows. No excuses. This was the top trick he'd learned from his therapist, Avni. He wasn't going to let the walls start closing in so tight that he couldn't breathe. Avni had taught him to get out ahead of those types of feelings.

Sometimes he'd start to feel boxed in, trapped, like he was buried alive. Things could go downhill pretty fast once that happened. Which is what got him sent to Avni in the first place. It was just a stupid misunderstanding in a Denny's, when he'd had to piss but then he'd started to lose it a little waiting for some guy to finish up in that tiny john that smelled like ammonia. He'd bolted out onto Sunset, trying to find someplace else to go, and the waitress called the cops on him. Saying he'd run out of the Denny's without paying. She told the cops that he was banging on a lamppost outside, like he was a crazy person.

The cops had been pretty chill. But they made him go see Avni after that, in her cramped office in the big hospital complex on Wilshire.

He had *not* wanted to see Avni, that was for sure. Just closing the door to her little room with the desk and the couch made him twitch. What could this pint-size Indian lady teach him? She'd never been through what he'd been through. She hadn't been building a pool for a rich guy in Los Feliz and then fallen off the frame, down the hill, impaling both legs in the rebar mesh. It had taken the paramedics eight hours to figure out how to pull him out. His legs were so messed up that he hadn't been able to walk for six months. But he'd been adjusting pretty well since, except for the thing at the Denny's. And a couple of other incidents like that. And then Avni was saying "PTSD" like he'd been to fucking Fallujah or something?

He'd been totally wrong about her.

The way she explained it, it wasn't "therapy" like "My mom was a mean drunk, so now I'm a sad sack of shit." Avni was all about tools. Tricks for getting the most out of every day.

Like how when you were going to be in a tight space, you sit by the windows.

The jury room windows were frosted, for security, but he could still feel the warmth of the sunlight on his arms. Avni had said sunlight was good, warm was good, those sensations placed

80

you inside your body, inside the actual physical feeling of being you. He could hear the sounds of the city outside. Trucks rumbling across the pavement. The growing clatter of the reporters and camera crews and spectators crowding the street. The trial of the century was about to get going, and somehow here he was, right in the guts of it.

Wayne closed his eyes, just for a sec, and took a deep breath. He was managing the jury room great. The courtroom was bigger than he'd expected, with high ceilings that must have been a pain in the ass to put up.

All he had to do was remember his tricks, be smart, and then all good.

"Knock knock," were the first words that Morningstar, the prosecutor, said in his opening statement. He looked over at the jury box.

Wayne didn't make a sound. Neither did any of the others. Fifteen jurors in total, including three alternates who'd get picked at random, once the trial was over, and dismissed. They sat in two rows in plastic office chairs that Wayne wished were more comfortable.

"Who's there?" Morningstar went on, his eyes searching the jurors for a reaction.

"Bobby Nock," he continued.

Another real weird moment of silence.

"Bobby Nock who?"

Morningstar locked eyes with Wayne and directed the punch line right at him.

"Welcome to the jury."

It was crickets in there. The only sounds were the squeaks of people shifting in their seats.

Morningstar lamely tried to keep smiling. "Nobody's gonna laugh?" He turned to the judge and shrugged: *tough crowd.* The judge definitely did not look like he thought this was funny.

A part of Wayne had to admire the balls on this prosecutor. Even if he seemed like a guy who'd never told a joke before. Like jokes were things he'd read about in books and this was the first time he'd tried one out in real life.

"Well," he said, turning back to the jury box. "So much for lightening the mood. I wanted to start with a joke because this case is going to be hard on you. There's going to be a lot of testimony for you to consider. It's a solemn duty that lies before you. In our system of law, the jurors are called the *sole arbiters of fact.* Do you know what that means?" He paused for emphasis.

"It means," he went on, "that you are going to hear two stories. I'm going to tell you a story, and then Bobby Nock's lawyer over there is going to tell you a story. I'm going to point at a bunch of facts and say, 'Look at these.' She is going to point at a bunch of other facts and say, 'No, no, you gotta look at these.' But what I say, what she says, those are just interpretations. Stories. Being the 'sole arbiters of fact' means that only *you* can say what the salient facts are. Which ones are important, and which ones are noise. So this case is going to come down to one question and one question only: Who do *you* believe?"

Everyone—positively *everyone*—turned toward Bobby Nock right then. The implication was plain as day: That young man over there was not a man you could trust.

Wayne took a hard look at Bobby Nock. Young, black, kinda small, sitting still, eyes straight ahead in a thousand-yard stare.

Was he the kind of guy Wayne could trust?

How the hell was Wayne supposed to know?

Next, Morningstar unloaded the facts in his arsenal like shotgun blasts on the range. *Boom.* Cock. *Boom.* Wayne could almost hear the sounds of clay pigeons bursting as each one hit.

Fact #1: Twenty-four-year-old Bobby Nock had been a part-time English teacher at Jessica Silver's school in the '08–'09 school year.

Fact #2: On more than one occasion, Bobby Nock and Jessica Silver spent unsupervised time together after school.

Fact #3: Jessica Silver's texts—retrieved from "the cloud" after her disappearance by the FBI's cyber division and Verizon—included messages and photographs of a sexual nature between her and Bobby Nock.

Fact #4: If anyone found out about what Bobby and Jessica were doing, Bobby would be fired. And he would never be able to work in education again.

Fact #5: Bobby initially told the police that he was at the LA Public Library on the afternoon of Jessica's death. But library security cameras subsequently revealed this to be a lie.

Fact #6: After this lie was uncovered, Bobby could not provide the police with a verifiable alibi.

Fact #7: That afternoon, a call was placed from Jessica's cellphone to her family's landline. No one picked up, and the caller did not leave a message. Triangulation of that cellphone position indicates that when the call was made, the phone was downtown. Jessica's school was in Santa Monica and her home was in Brentwood—but Bobby Nock's apartment was downtown, right in the area where the call originated.

Fact #8: Hairs matching Jessica's DNA were discovered in the front passenger seat of Bobby's car.

Fact #9: A bloodstain matching Jessica's DNA was also discovered in the front passenger seat of Bobby's car.

Fact #10: A bloodstain matching Jessica's DNA was discovered in the *trunk* of Bobby's car.

When the facts were nailed in like that, one after another, end to end, the story they told seemed tight as a drum.

• • •

Gibson, the young lady defense attorney, had a stern, chilly vibe. She did not look like she was here to fuck around and tell jokes. Wayne could sum up her whole speech in one word: "Doubts."

She paced across the courtroom floor as she explained that there were doubts about every single point in the prosecution's case. Every "iron-clad fact" was really much more ambiguous than at first it seemed. Once you noticed the ambiguity—how these "facts" didn't necessarily mean what the prosecutor said they did—you wouldn't be able to look at the case the same way again.

To Gibson, doubts were like mold in old drywall. Once the rot got in, it was never coming out. Not ever.

Wayne wasn't some kind of dumbass. He knew what she was up to. By the time she was finished, none of these jurors would be able to swear 100 percent to their own mother's name.

But as she wrapped up her opening statement, there was one point that lodged itself in his head. Gibson said that she intended to repeat this last one, with some frequency, throughout the trial.

"You are going to think I'm a broken record," she said to the jurors. "But I'm going to say it again and again because it's important: Jessica Silver's body has never been found."

Not only were there doubts about whether

Bobby had killed her—but there were reasonable doubts about whether or not she was even dead.

The judge wouldn't let them keep pen and paper to take notes. Juror 272, the perky white girl with the dark hair, raised her hand to ask about it on the second day. How were they supposed to remember all this stuff—DNA particulates and parts per million and down-to-the-second timelines—if they couldn't take notes? But the judge said that pen and paper could be a distraction. They should do their best to remember, and if they had questions when the time came to deliberate, they could ask the court reporter to read back portions of the transcript.

Wayne thought this was nuts. But then, after a week or so, it started to make a certain sense. If they each wrote stuff down, what were the chances that they'd each write down *different* stuff? Juror 106, the nosy old Mexican lady, she might write down that the DNA man said one thing. Then Juror 429, the Latina girl who'd baked cupcakes for everybody one day, she'd write down that the DNA man said something else. And then they'd be in an even worse position. Not only unable to agree on a verdict, but unable to agree on what they'd been told in the first place.

The first weeks went pretty well, all things considered. They wound up getting kicked out of the courtroom for a few hours every day while the lawyers argued about what the judge called "matters of law and procedure"—but Wayne left a bag or a jacket on the chair by the window when they went into court, so no one else would take his seat when they got back.

The bailiff complimented Wayne on being an early riser. Steve—the bailiff asked them all to call him by his first name—said he liked to get up early too. Bailiff Steve was white, probably in his forties. His mustache was old-school, and it had just a few streaks of gray. He seemed like a straight shooter.

And then, three weeks in, the judge called them into the courtroom one morning and by the look on his face Wayne could tell that something was messed up.

"Ladies and gentlemen of the jury," the judge said, "I'm afraid I have some bad news. I have to apologize. We have extensive, time-tested systems to make sure things like this do not happen, and I can assure you, the State of California will not rest until we determine how it has. Your names have been reported in the press."

Wayne could hear the air get sucked out of the room.

"I have already sent police officers to your homes, to check on your loved ones. But let me be very clear about this: We do not believe that anyone is in any danger here."

Wayne figured that if police officers were getting sent to their homes, then *someone* was definitely in danger.

"I am faced with a choice that no judge ever makes lightly. But I must prioritize both your safety and the sanctity of these proceedings. You will be sequestered for the rest of the trial."

It took Wayne a second to process what this meant for him. The others seemed too shocked to react. But as the judge went on, Wayne could feel a collective panic setting in. Like they were rats trapped on a sinking ship. Instinctively he looked for the nearest window. But of course there weren't any in the courtroom.

The judge said, "I believe that it would be unsafe to send you home each night, including this one. Relatives will be permitted to bring you clothes, toiletries, any personal belongings you require this evening. And then we'll work out a visitation schedule."

Visitation. As if they were the ones in jail.

"I know this isn't good news for any of you," the judge said, almost sympathetic. "I know that you have lives. Families. Accommodations will be made."

Wayne lived alone. He wasn't back to work yet, since workers' comp was still paying out. He kept his own company and was comfortable with it.

"I promise you that by law," the judge went

on, "no one can lose their job because they were attending to jury service. And you've all already signed statements that you have no dependents for whom you are the sole caregiver."

Juror 272, sitting next to Wayne, was pale. She looked like she was folding up inside. Wayne wanted to reach out, to touch her hand, tell her it would be okay, but he didn't really know her.

He looked back at 429, the Latina girl. Her cheeks were already streaked with tears.

"Bullshit."

Wayne didn't think he'd said it loud enough for anyone else to hear. But the word seemed to echo out through the courtroom like a rifle shot in a canyon.

The judge banged his gavel. "All right now. All right. I have the authority to hold you in contempt of court. That doesn't just mean fines—that means jail time. Please don't make me use this authority."

The room was silent.

But their fury grew when they were told that the bailiff would confiscate their cellphones and laptops. They would be permitted a few calls that night, to make arrangements, and then at least one call each day. All calls would be monitored by the bailiff.

And what could they do about it? Not a damn thing.

Wayne knew full well that this was not Bailiff

Steve's first rodeo. Wayne imagined him listening in on everyone's phone calls. All the jurors on all the trials he worked . . . the shit he must hear.

They were led in silence back to the jury room to wait again. Soon a van would come and take them to the Omni Hotel.

Their new home. God only knew for how long.

Wayne didn't have anybody he needed to call. He thought about telling Avni, but she already knew he had jury duty, that he wouldn't make his appointments for a while.

The others, though, they were freaking out. Juror 429 was in a bad way. The older Jewish lady was trying to comfort her, but not doing a good job of it.

Everybody was scared. And that would not do.

"Well, fuck that shit," he said.

"Yeah," said 513, the older gay one with the leather vest. "This is bad."

"We could all just walk out of here," Wayne said. "Right now. All of us. Just fuck it, you know? What would they do?"

The suggestion of open rebellion seemed to shock the others.

"We'd go to jail," said the black guy in the glasses, 158.

"Trading one kind of cage for another," Wayne said.

He didn't really think they would. But they

weren't animals, and they weren't going to be treated like they were.

"What else can we do?"

Wayne wasn't sure who had asked, but it felt like everybody turned to him. He didn't like the feeling. He could be a rebel sometimes but that didn't mean he was the guy who was supposed to lead a rebellion.

Everybody's eyes on him just made him more pissed off.

"Well, first," he said, "all these numbers are confusing as shit. If our names are already out there anyway, I don't see why we can't use them in here. I'm Wayne Russel."

They all looked at each other. Like they were waiting to see if someone was about to punish them, right then and there.

"The judge was pretty clear," said 158. "We're going to get in trouble."

Juror 158 was dressed up in his preppy sweater and tie. He was a bookworm, Wayne had noticed, always burying his head in a book during their breaks. He'd become friendly with the lively girl, 272. They'd had lunch just the two of them nearly every day so far. But she was way out of his league.

"The judge isn't here right now," Wayne said. "We are. So when it comes to taking care of the people in this room, who do you want to listen to? Him? Or us?"

Before 158 could respond, the guy in the leather vest stepped forward. "I'm Cal Barro." He reached out and shook Wayne's hand. "It's a pleasure to meet you, Wayne."

They went around the room, one at a time, speaking their real names. Wayne tried to remember them all: Cal Barro, Carolina Cancio, Maya Seale, Trisha Harold, Lila Rosales, Kellan Bragg, Peter Wilkie, Jae Kim, Fran Goldenberg, Kathy Wing, Yasmine Sarraf, Arnold Dean, Enrique Navarro.

And Rick Leonard. The preppy guy went last. But even he participated with the rest of them in this, their first act of mutual defiance.

The minute they finished saying their names, there was a knock on the door. It was Bailiff Steve.

"You folks ready to go?"

They all went silent. They looked down, they looked away, they looked anywhere but at the authority figure in the room. Like they were kids caught doing something they knew they weren't supposed to; like each and every one of them was a guilty party.

CHAPTER 5

A FOOL FOR A CLIENT
NOW

Maya sat on the edge of the hotel bed, trying to take up as little space as possible. A team of cops were snapping photographs all around the room. So far, they'd been nothing but polite, quiet, and calm. She was grateful that one of them had already laid a plastic sheet over Rick's body.

"Are you hurt?" asked one of the uniformed cops. He was tall, heavyset, with a big-cheeked baby face. He looked way too young to be a cop. He gestured to her hands, which were balled up on her lap. That's when she noticed that they were covered in blood.

She felt sick. "No. It's his blood. I touched him."

"You touched who, ma'am?"

"The . . . Rick. I found him. This is my room."

"You told me that already."

"Right. Okay. Sorry." She steadied herself. "I touched him. I put my hands on his neck. I felt for a pulse. I wanted to see if I could help him. . . ."

"Did you help him?"

"No he was . . . I mean he wasn't . . . There was nothing I could do."

93

"Was he still alive when you touched him?"

"No."

"How could you tell?"

"Because he didn't have a pulse." She stared at her bloody fingers. Then she stood and turned toward the bathroom.

An older cop, his white hair in a buzz cut, blocked her path.

"Pardon me," he said. "If you'll just wait here for a minute."

"I'm just . . . The blood, I need to wash my hands."

Her whole body felt filthy.

"We're going to need to test that," said the baby-faced cop.

"It's Rick's blood," Maya said. "Why would you need to test . . . ?"

Only then did she recognize the deceitfully friendly look on the young cop's face. This was a crime scene. She was a suspect. The realization was clarifying. Maya forced herself to wall off the image of Rick's bloody head and lifeless body. The scene around her was no longer a surreal horror show that she could barely comprehend. Instead, it was work.

The cops would do their job. She would have to do hers. Ms. Seale arrived to represent the defendant. Ms. Seale knew that her client had already said far too much. What Maya had to do now, above all else, was shut up.

She used a clean finger to tuck her dark hair behind her ear.

"Am I being detained?" she asked.

"The detectives will be here in a minute," Buzz Cut said.

"Ellen!" the baby-faced cop called to the technician who was crouched over the body. "Can we get a swab over here?"

Ellen approached cautiously. "Why don't we get you cleaned up, ma'am?"

"If I'm not being detained," Maya said, "then I'd like to leave."

"Let's just get that blood off of you."

"If you are detaining me," Maya said, "which you have the right to do, I'd like to speak to my lawyer. If you're not, then I do not consent to a search. Have a good night."

She walked toward the door. The baby-faced cop stepped in front of her. Wearily he removed the handcuffs from his belt. "You're not really gonna make me use these, are you?"

Maya eyed the handcuffs. They were the old, metal kind. They looked like they'd been sitting on the cop's leather belt for ages.

Perfect.

She extended her arms in front of her, exposing her bloody wrists.

Come on, she thought. *You know you want to put those cuffs on me. . . .*

With a sigh, the cop snapped the handcuffs

onto her wrists. "Ma'am, we are detaining you in connection with our investigation. We're going to bring you to the station now. Please don't make this difficult."

He kept the cuffs loose. He didn't really think she was a threat, he was just going through an annoying formality.

He waved Ellen off, letting her know that they could take samples at the station. Maya used the opportunity to surreptitiously rub the blood on her hands onto the metal cuffs. She was corrupting any sample of blood they would take. Who knew who else's DNA was on these handcuffs? Any forensic data gathered from her hands would now be useless in court.

Her training had taught her to start laying the groundwork for a defense as early as possible. By the time of an arraignment, the cards have been dealt. She hadn't been charged yet, much less accused, but this was the window of time in which to stack the deck.

She looked up at the cop. "I have no intention of resisting, Officer. I'd like to call my lawyer, please, when we get to the station." She nodded toward the doorway. "After you."

Wired, alert, and conscious of every passing second, Maya sat alone in the station house interrogation room. When another technician came in to wipe and preserve the blood on her hands, she knew she was winning.

She imagined what must be going on back at the hotel. All the other jurors would be rousted from bed, questioned about what they'd seen. She pictured their groggy faces as they opened the doors to their rooms. Had one of them been involved in Rick's death?

The only other people in that hotel who would have even known Rick was there were employees of *Murder Town*—who, whatever one might say about television producers, could not conceivably have wanted to kill their star interview subject. But whatever bad blood had passed between the jurors ten years ago, would any of them really have wanted to kill Rick?

The maddening thing was that the person with the most reason to want Rick dead was her.

After 1 a.m., two plainclothes detectives arrived. A man, Hispanic, and a woman, black, a bit older. Maya could tell the routine they were about to enact by the expressions on their faces. Part of her almost wanted to let them go ahead with it, if just to see whether they were any good.

"I'd like to speak to my lawyer, please," she said before the detectives even got a word out. They exchanged a look.

The woman ignored her request. "My name is

Detective Rhonda Daisey." She wore fashionable black jeans and what looked like a man's blazer. There was a sweetness in her voice, like she was getting ready to dish gossip about their mutual friends.

"Martinez," the man said gruffly. He would be the Bad Cop.

Maya remained silent.

"You don't remember meeting me?" Detective Daisey said.

Maya shook her head.

"Belen Vasquez," Detective Daisey said. "Lady who cut off her husband's head. I did her interrogation. You're her lawyer."

Maya nodded. "I'd like to speak to *my* lawyer, please."

"We found Ms. Vasquez in possession of the head," Detective Daisey went on. "It's not like a big whodunit, you know?"

Maya was impressed. This was textbook strategy, but Daisey was executing it well. She was trying to get Maya talking about something unrelated. She was trying to get Maya's lips moving, hoping that she'd be dumb enough to consider this topic neutral ground.

Maya knew there was no neutral ground when it came to cops.

"I'd like to speak to my lawyer, please. I gave his number to the arresting officer."

"Whoa there," Daisey said. "You're not under

98

arrest. This is a friendly conversation. From one person who knows the game to another."

"Friendly for now," Detective Martinez said. He was overplaying his part. Maya felt bad for Daisey. She was better than her partner.

"Look," Detective Daisey said. "We just need to know what happened. You know how this works: If you don't give us another suspect, all we've got is you."

"Do you want us to come after you?" Martinez said. He wore a dark suit with an ugly yellow tie. It looked like the sort of tie one of his kids might have picked out.

Daisey must have really pissed off her CO to get stuck with this idiot.

"You told the officer that you left, took a walk, came back, he was dead?" Daisey said. "So help us figure out who would go in there and kill him, so we don't *have* to dig into you."

Daisey was going to be tough. She wasn't bluffing: As soon as Maya walked out of here, they'd come at her with everything they had.

"I'd like to speak to my lawyer." Maya paused, delivering the next word as almost a dare. "Please."

The detectives had more stamina than Maya imagined. They spent another half hour asking questions about Rick and the reunion and the evening, even as her response never varied.

They went from friendly to threatening and back again, but she simply intoned the same sentence over and over again. There was something meditative about the routine. Maya felt like she was playing tennis, and all she had to do was get out of her head and let her body take over. Her muscles knew what to do. "I'd like to speak to my lawyer." Breath. "Please."

Eventually, they gave up and handed her a cordless telephone.

"Taryn," she said to her groggy, confused assistant after dialing the poor girl's cellphone. "I've been arrested. I'm at the Central Division station. I need you to call Craig. As many times as it takes. Wake him up, get him down here. Thank you." She said it like she was asking her assistant to order flowers.

Maya figured it was daylight by the time the door opened again and Detective Daisey led Craig Rogers inside.

He wore a light blue suit, perfectly tailored of course. He even looked well rested.

Without a word, Craig began examining Maya the way he'd once looked over her drafts back when she'd been his associate. He was dispassionate. Precise. Exacting.

She knew that he was looking for anything in her appearance—an unexplained bruise, a tear in her blouse—that could be of use later. There

100

wasn't much for him to work with. Maya was disappointingly presentable.

He turned to Detective Daisey. "Some privacy, if you wouldn't mind."

When Daisey left, Craig sat down across from Maya and put a hand on her arm.

"That was smart," he said. "Not letting them take the blood sample till you got here. The possibility of contamination . . . It'll be worthless."

Even under these conditions, the compliment from Craig still made her proud.

"Are they going to arrest me?"

"Not this morning," he said. "They need more, and what they really need is for you to do something stupid. So, my professional legal advice: Continue not doing anything stupid." He squeezed her forearm warmly. "Now. Shall we get the hell out of here?"

At noon, Maya woke up in her own bed to the chime of the doorbell. Her first, pleasant thought was to wonder what she was doing at home, asleep, in the middle of a Thursday. But as she threw on pants and hustled to the front door, the previous evening returned to her.

After they'd left the police station, Craig had told his driver to take her to her house in Silver Lake. He'd then told Maya to get a few hours' sleep. He was not going to interview a client who'd been awake for twenty-four hours, no matter who she was.

She opened the door to find Craig holding two white paper cups of boutique pour-over coffee. He handed one to her as she led him inside.

His eyes drifted across her kitchen. Beyond the floor-to-ceiling windows lay the Silver Lake Reservoir. There were joggers on the dirt path, their bright workout clothes shining like neon. "This is Silver Lake?" Craig asked.

"Yes."

He seemed satisfied. "It's a lot nicer these days."

He buried himself in his iPhone as she went to shower and dress. The hot water felt good, so long as she didn't close her eyes. The moment she did, all she could see was the dead body. Its broken angles, its crimson halo. She turned the knob all the way to cold. If she let herself process what had just happened, she'd fall apart.

When she felt—or at least looked—something like herself again, she returned to her living room to find Craig sitting calmly on the couch, working two iPhones simultaneously. They'd multiplied while she was showering.

He flicked off both screens, placed the phones facedown on the couch, and gave her his full attention.

She looked him right in the eye. "I didn't kill—"

"—I'm going to stop you right there." He opened a briefcase that he'd placed on her coffee table and handed her a sheet of paper and a pen. "First, I need you to hire me."

She instinctively scanned the retainer agreement. It was identical to the one she gave her own clients. She signed at the bottom.

"I went out walking," Maya said. "We can find a camera on the street that caught me, or someone in the lobby who saw me come back, we can—"

He raised a hand like he was directing traffic. "I know what you said to the officers, back at the hotel. We'll get footage from all the nearby businesses. But of course, you were still in shock when you gave the officers that story. Now, after some rest . . . Well, you know how this works. Let's be careful about what you say to me."

He didn't have to go on. Anything she told Craig now would limit his range of potential defenses if she was charged with Rick's murder. It would be unethical, per the California bar, for him to present a defense that he knew for a fact to be a lie. He needed flexibility to create a story that would adequately address whatever evidence the prosecution submitted.

"The way I explain it to my clients," she said, "is that if they tell me they were at Disneyland, I can't go into court and argue that they were on the moon."

Being innocent often made it *harder* to

construct a good defense. Innocent people always wanted to shout out what really happened from the rooftops—but sometimes the best defense, legally speaking, wasn't the truth.

Coming forward with a story too soon, she remembered, had been Bobby Nock's first mistake. When the LAPD first interviewed him, he didn't have a lawyer. He told the cops that he'd been in the public library at the time of Jessica's disappearance—but video evidence later proved that that wasn't true. He'd constructed his story before he knew what evidence the police had assembled, and his version of events was not a good fit for the facts.

Craig would not let Maya make the same mistake.

"Let's wait to look at everything the cops have," Craig said. "And then I'll tell you what your story is."

"What do they have so far?"

He leaned forward. "Your fellow former juror Mr. Leonard was killed in your hotel room. His body wasn't moved. You phoned 911 at 10:56 P.M. The producers of the docuseries have video footage of Mr. Leonard leaving the restaurant downstairs at 8:38 P.M. You left a few minutes earlier, at 8:32. You already told the cops you met, together, in your room?"

Maya was embarrassed on two counts of stupidity: inviting Rick to her room, and then telling the cops about it. "Yes."

104

Craig sighed. "Let's come back to that. But so: Rick was killed by blunt-force trauma to the skull. Wound is on the back of his head. A single blow, sharp and deep, it penetrated brain matter. And there was blood on the edge of the desk. The angle of the desk edge seems a decent fit to the depth of the wound."

"So he tripped," Maya said, forcing herself to analyze the scene clinically. "He fell and hit his head on the side of the desk."

Craig raised an eyebrow. "Or, much more likely, he was pushed."

Maya tried to work it out. "There was a fight? A scuffle? He fell back . . ."

"He would have died quickly."

If Craig was trying to reassure her, this last comment wasn't helping. She didn't want personal reassurance; she wanted professional detachment.

"So you think it could have been manslaughter?"

He nodded again. "There was no sign of forced entry."

Shit. "So whoever went in there—" She recalibrated in the face of his withering gaze. "So if someone else were to have gone into my room and killed him . . . Rick would have let them in."

"Indeed." He took a moment.

This was going to get worse.

"There is good news," he continued, "and there is bad news."

"I want the bad news, please."

"You would, wouldn't you?" He shook his head. "I'm going to give you the good news first, because we could use some. In 2010, Bobby Nock was convicted for disseminating child pornography. After eighteen months in Chino, he was paroled."

That wasn't news. "The child porn was a bullshit charge."

"How so?"

"The DA failed on murder, so he argued that he could separately prosecute Bobby Nock for the nude photos that Jessica Silver had texted him. She was underage. . . ."

"Dissemination?"

"He had a cellphone and a laptop. He sent the photos from one device to another."

"You need a second person for dissemination."

"The cellphone was technically registered to his mother."

Craig looked up at the ceiling, as if genuinely impressed by the prosecutorial gall. "You weren't kidding about the bullshit."

"The DA was hell-bent on putting Bobby Nock in jail for *something*. The judge allowed a bench trial, citing the publicity from the murder case—the gears of justice turned as efficiently as possible."

This was the kind of thing that really got Craig going. His disgust, nurtured over years of watching the justice system get away with wanton displays of power, was always close to the surface.

"Where does the good news come in?"

He nodded. "Bobby Nock has disappeared."

"What do you mean, 'disappeared'?"

"I mean that some months ago—let me be more precise . . ." He picked up one of his iPhones and scrolled to the relevant information. "*Five* months ago, Bobby Nock broke his parole. As a registered sex offender, he was required to check in weekly with his DOC officer. Five months ago, he didn't show up. Cops went around to his place—nothing. Vanished."

"How does someone like Bobby Nock just vanish?"

"I once represented a man—a middle school girls' soccer coach—who did his three years for . . . well, you can guess. . . . But the whole act of going around knocking on doors every time he moved, telling his neighbors he was a child rapist, he couldn't take it anymore. Left the state, got a new name—there isn't much of a mechanism to track these guys down. Sex offender registries are state-by-state."

"Bobby Nock is famous."

Craig shrugged. "Where does Robert Blake live?"

Maya frowned. "The actor who killed his wife? I don't know."

"Exactly. What about George Zimmerman? Amanda Knox?"

"She didn't do it."

"My point being, if you saw one of them on the street, new haircut, would you recognize them? Once the trial fades . . . People still talk about it, they still recognize the names." She couldn't tell if he was referring to her. "But the only people still digging are family members and conspiracy theorists and bloggers."

"And jurors, apparently," Maya added.

"And the occasional podcaster. Like, for example, your new friends at *Murder Town*. They were trying to find Bobby for the show. To no avail. Like I said: good news."

"You talked to them already?"

"Who?"

"The producers."

"Mike and Mike did." Craig currently had two associate attorneys named Mike. They were fresh out of UCLA and USC law schools, respectively, and were both beefy, blond, work-hard, play-hard types. One wore glasses, one wore contacts, but other than that it had been difficult, at first, to tell them apart. Rather than assigning them to separate tasks, Craig seemed to take a perverse pleasure in teaming them up. He'd seen to it that they were bound at the hip.

Maya was pretty sure that Mike and Mike loathed each other.

If Mike and Mike were already involved, then so were a half dozen others at the firm. Their investigators would be reinterviewing everyone the cops interviewed. The paralegals would be rummaging through transcripts. If Maya had tried to distance her professional life from the world of the Bobby Nock trial, well, so much for that. By now every one of her fellow jurors would have their own file in Craig's office. Soon, her co-workers would know things about these people that Maya never did. And they'd know about her too.

Craig seemed to read her thoughts. "Did you think I wasn't going to ask everyone to drop whatever else they were doing to focus on this?"

Maya knew that she should say thank you. But she was humiliated by the thought of so many people she worked with combing through her life.

Craig appeared to have more important things on his mind than her feelings. "Putting on layperson glasses, there were two people who might have wanted to kill Rick Leonard: the juror he'd spent months attacking in the press . . ."

"That would be me."

". . . and the convicted child pornographer and accused murderer of Jessica Silver who was terrified that Rick had found new evidence that could finally prove his guilt."

Maya grimaced. This theory was tenuous.

"You don't like it?" he said. "That was my good news."

"First of all," Maya said, "Bobby Nock isn't a murderer."

"Respectfully, you are the only person in America who thinks that."

"Second, you want to argue that Bobby Nock came out of hiding to sneak into our hotel—one of the few places in the world in which there were literally dozens of people sure to recognize him—in order to murder Rick before he could broadcast whatever evidence he had?"

Craig looked as if there was nothing implausible at all about this. "I don't need to prove it happened. I just need them to fail to prove that it didn't."

Maya ran her hands through her hair. If that was the best they had, then this was not going to go well.

Maybe "he tripped and fell" really was their best theory.

"You said there was also bad news?"

Craig folded his hands over his lap. "One of your fellow jurors has given the police a statement to the effect that you and the deceased engaged in a sexual relationship ten years ago."

Maya did her best not to react. "Who said that?"

"Mike and Mike are asking around."

The thought of Mike and Mike asking after

the details of her sex life was horrifying. She imagined the silent looks they'd give each other as they duly committed the rumors to the case file. She imagined the paralegals correcting any typos in the reports, the assistants scanning copies of every sordid page. It was mortifying.

But it was the least of her problems.

Craig continued, "The story that our team has put together is that you and Rick Leonard were romantically linked during the Bobby Nock trial. And that this was a secret you kept from everyone—family, friends, the other jurors. And certainly the court, which would have kicked you both off that trial in a heartbeat."

He spoke matter-of-factly, but his look was expectant. He clearly wanted as much detail as he could get. But how could she make him understand what it had been like?

"It's complicated," she said lamely.

Craig took this as an affirmation that the story was true. He accepted it without judgment. "This is bad news because, one, now the prosecution's theory won't be that Rick Leonard's former fellow *juror* killed him in a fit of revenge. Now it'll be that Rick Leonard's former *lover* killed him in a fit of passion." He paused. "Which will play better . . . to a jury." The irony was unavoidable.

Maya felt dumb repeating herself, but she didn't know what else to say: "I'm telling you. I—" She measured her words carefully. "Someone else must have come into my room after I left."

"I'm not yet convinced that that's our best version of events."

"What?"

"The former-lovers bit could work to our advantage."

"How?"

"If we argue self-defense."

Maya stared. "You want me to argue that I killed Rick Leonard in self-defense?"

"I'm not sure yet. But look at you—a woman your size—you've got an angry ex-boyfriend in your hotel room. Maybe you broke his heart all those years ago. He's never gotten over it. He's yelling, he's calling you foul names, he's banging his fists against the walls—maybe this ex-boyfriend has a history of domestic violence—so you're in fear for your life, no one comes running to the sound of your screams, you push this violent ex-boyfriend against the table. . . ." Craig looked like he was picturing himself describing this scene in a courtroom. Like he was listening for the way the words would sound to a jury.

He pursed his lips. "It's not bad."

She rubbed her palms together. To claim responsibility for killing someone she hadn't in order to avoid punishment for that very killing would be to reach a dizzying new height of crazy. But Rick wasn't the man that Craig had described.

"Rick Leonard does not have a history of domestic abuse," she said.

Craig sank back into the couch. "All right, let's talk about history."

CHAPTER 6

MAYA
FEBRUARY 1, 2009

Maya Seale moved from Brooklyn to L.A. on the first day of February, 2009, just two weeks after she'd frozen half to death in the ebullient crowd at the inauguration in Washington, DC. She'd flown across the country with her boyfriend, Hunter, whose new job at a Century City financial firm had spurred the move. They'd flown into San Francisco, bought an old Honda from Hunter's brother, who lived there, and then loaded their possessions into the trunk. They made jokes about manifest destiny as they drove down the coast.

Highway 1 wound its fractal curves along the edge of the endless ocean. About halfway down the coast, they hit a nasty crunch of traffic. Cars and trucks were backed up for nearly a mile. Maya joined the throngs who'd left their vehicles and were ambling down the road. No one seemed to know what had happened, but neither did anyone seem particularly surprised by the holdup.

Then she saw the helicopter. It had just lifted off from beyond a bend in the road ahead, and below it hung white straps leading to a medical stretcher. On the stretcher, a man's body lay prone on a long board. The body was wrapped in some kind of orange bandage.

One of the other motorists said that he heard that the man on the stretcher was a rock climber who'd fallen on the cliffs ahead and was being medevaced out. But there wasn't much chance of survival.

Maya hadn't even made it to L.A. yet and she'd already seen someone dying.

In those early months, she had felt as buoyant with promise as had the country around her. She and Hunter rented a California Craftsman bungalow in Los Feliz with a sloping hillside yard. Hunter's co-workers all said the house was "cozy," but to Maya it felt gargantuan. She'd been in New York for so long she'd forgotten that in other places, people her age could afford to live in such luxury. Every morning she'd juice a fresh grapefruit from the tree in the backyard. Then Hunter would head to work and Maya would stare at the blank screen that she could only hope, by the force of will, would fill with the novel she told her friends back in New York that she was writing.

Writing had only been the most recent of her unfulfilling pursuits. After college, she'd reasoned that since she liked to cook, she should take a job in a hotel kitchen. But she'd found

115

that she didn't like cooking on a line, and that she *really* didn't like being castigated for over-buttering someone's scrambled eggs at six-thirty in the morning. Next she'd ventured out to Argentina with a friend, to explore, hike, and drink too much. She found assorted translating jobs to pay for it all, but hadn't put much of a dent in her student loans. So after enough backpacking to last her a while, she'd gone to New York, where footloose people were supposed to find callings.

Maya hadn't. Instead, she'd found a series of underpaying jobs at bitchy websites and unproductive production companies and stifling Wall Street firms. Pushing around paperwork in the HR office at one of those firms, she'd met Hunter. He was an associate in the wealth management department. She would *never* have imagined herself with a banker—what a bland, interchangeable bunch—but Hunter had style. He was so sure of who he was, what he wanted, and how he was going to get it. When he got an offer to transfer to Los Angeles, she was ready for another change.

Hunter, for his part, had seemed thrilled about arriving in California with a girlfriend in tow. If they'd contemplated a coming engagement, it had probably been because that was what people in their position did. Hunter's career was on track. It was time for him to get his personal life locked down. And living in that new house, with an actual white picket fence—a term she'd heard before, without knowing what exactly it referred to until she had one—gave them both a chance to play at a life that felt splendidly natural.

She'd walk to nearby coffee shops with a laptop poking out of her canvas tote and strangers would smile at her on the street. People really did that in L.A. She made new friends at the dance studio in Atwater Village. She was even writing, or at least filling pages, with her impressions of what it was like to be young and buzzed on educated opinions that just maybe people might want to read.

When the jury summons arrived in the mail, Maya wasn't sure how they'd even found her so fast at her new address. She'd adamantly refused to change her voter registration from New Mexico, where she'd grown up, so as not to waste her vote in either New York or California. Beyond that, she didn't think much about the summons. Jury duty might be interesting—one of the many new and informative experiences to which she should keep herself open. It might even provide some fodder for her writing. Who knew what sorts of oddballs she'd meet in the jury pool?

She called the number as requested, and was informed by a recorded voice to appear at 8:45 A.M. on May 29 at the Clara Shortridge Foltz

Criminal Justice Center. She brought her laptop for what she believed would be a mini-adventure. She figured they'd have Wi-Fi.

That very first day, she sat down next to Rick Leonard.

Right away, jury service isolated her from Hunter. It was tricky to go home every night and keep silent about the case. What could she say to him? The trial itself had barely begun and, perversely, he had access to more information than she did. He could google everything about Bobby Nock and Jessica Silver, while Maya was under strict instructions to remain in the dark. Ironically, Hunter was the one largely keeping information from her.

Their dinner table conversations were reduced to the idle chatter of acquaintances. In New York, it had seemed like they had so much in common. But now she was having trouble remembering what those things had been. Hunter began to feel like more of a stranger than the other jurors. At least they laughed at her dumb stories about South America.

And then came the sequester. She'd never heard of a jury being sequestered in the middle of a trial before.

It was hard to describe the lonely crowding of the trial's next weeks. They spent more time in the jury room than in the courtroom, while the lawyers debated points of law to which the jurors weren't privy. It seemed as if more attention was paid to what they would not hear than to what they would.

More and more, Maya grew curious about those closed-door debates among the lawyers. What were those all-important matters that were being kept from her? She found herself clutching at every bit of legal jargon she'd hear before Bailiff Steve removed her from the courtroom. What exactly was the "catchall" exception to the ban on hearsay evidence? Why did California apparently treat it differently than other states? Why did that mean that they wouldn't be hearing testimony from Jessica Silver's family housekeeper?

Pamela Gibson, the defense attorney, seemed super bad-ass every time she'd interrupt the prosecutor's questioning. "Objection, Your Honor. Leading." Or "Objection, Your Honor. Facts not in evidence." Maya didn't understand all the legal reasoning, but she knew how to count: The judge sustained almost all of the defense's objections, and only about a third of the prosecutor's. Gibson projected a compelling air of hyper-competence.

Maya had never before been fascinated by the law. But she also realized that she hadn't been exposed to it before, not up close. As she sat there every day, staring at the face of Bobby Nock, trying to follow along as his fate hung on the ins and outs of impenetrable procedural detail, all she knew was that she needed to know so much more.

JUNE 18, 2009

"It's about one-way streets," Rick Leonard told her one morning over breakfast. They were in the hotel restaurant, at their own table. The others ate nearby in groups of three or four. It was amazing, Maya thought, how quickly they had divided themselves into factions. Fran, Yasmine, and Lila were at one table. Peter, Cal, Kellan, and Arnold were at another. Trisha, Carolina, and Jae sat together at a third. Kathy and Enrique stood by the buffet counter.

Only Wayne sipped his coffee at a table all his own.

The lines had formed first by gender and then by ethnicity. Maya hoped that this was not the work of some terrible, vestigial instinct and was instead simply coincidence.

"Your thesis?" she said.

"Yeah," Rick said. "The effect of one-way streets on poverty and segregation in American cities."

"Your doctoral thesis at USC is on one-way streets?"

"One-way streets are one of the most effective tools local governments use to preserve racial segregation."

120

"One-way streets are racist?" She raised an eyebrow.

"I'm being serious." But he laughed, so he wasn't being *that* serious. "The point isn't that one-way streets are racist. The point is that one-way streets can be a powerful force in urban planning. Which streets funnel traffic into which other streets defines the contours of neighborhoods. This is what I study. Historically, when cities like Chicago, Detroit, or L.A. have wanted to act like nothing racist is happening but still subtly encourage all the black people, or all the Latin people, or all the Japanese people, or what have you, to stay in the same space, they've turned two-way streets into one-way streets to do it."

"This is by far the longest conversation I've ever had about one-way streets."

He sighed with playful, exaggerated condescension.

It was fun to tease him. There seemed to be a part of him that enjoyed the back-and-forth of being teased.

"Chicago's Hyde Park," he continued, "is the classic example. Barack Obama's own University of Chicago is a lovely upper-class island planted right in the middle of a poorer, historically black neighborhood. So how has the city preserved the upscale enclave over a half a century? With a maze of one-way and dead-end streets between

Cottage Grove and Lake Shore Drive. Lake Shore is a major freeway."

"I thought only California had freeways."

"So highway, then."

"What's the difference between a freeway and a highway?"

Rick paused. "I think it has something to do with whether or not there are on- and off-ramps? This isn't really related to what I do."

"I thought you were supposed to be an expert."

"On one-way streets. Highways are two-way. My point is that Hyde Park's one-way streets make it really inconvenient to drive through the campus, if you're trying to get from the highway to the poorer neighborhoods on the west. It's not segregation through fiat—it's segregation through subtle inconvenience."

"The city draws the one-way streets . . ."

"And everyone travels in the same direction."

Rick's plate was still full of mushy scrambled eggs. He'd forgotten to eat. It was cool, the way he made her look at something as simple as one-way streets in an entirely new way.

"What about L.A.?" she asked.

"Well, downtown, just west of Skid Row . . ." he began. But then, abruptly, he stopped.

"What?"

"I guess I can't talk about L.A."

"Why?"

"Because one of the big forces behind L.A.'s

infrastructure planning is . . . well . . ." He whispered: "Lou Silver."

Maya nodded. Of course he was right to hush up. It would be against the rules to talk about Lou Silver. Talking about him would essentially mean talking about the case.

Maya respected the look she saw in Rick's eyes just then. It was the look of someone who wasn't going to skirt his commitment to justice by breaking a rule that was there for a reason.

"I understand," she said.

But still she was dying to know: What did Rick think of the case? What did he think about Bobby Nock? Or the line of conflicting DNA experts who'd been paraded through the witness box all week? She searched for a clue on his face. She wished so much that she could ask him. That they could just for a minute talk about the thing that consumed their days.

For her part, Maya was feeling more and more confident that Bobby Nock had been railroaded. How many times, in the United States, had murder charges been brought against a defendant when there wasn't even a body? The defense attorney had actually posed this question to one of the testifying detectives and then provided the answer: 480 times . . . *since 1800.*

Bobby, the defense attorney suggested, had a better chance of getting hit by lightning. And then getting hit by lightning again.

Unless, of course, there were other forces at play. Like, for instance, if the police simply needed to arrest *somebody* for the murder of a billionaire's daughter, and Bobby made a convenient scapegoat.

Was there any chance, Maya kept asking herself, that Bobby Nock would be on trial right now if he was white?

She didn't think so. And while she wouldn't dare say it out loud, she was sure Rick agreed with her. Not because he, like Bobby, was black. That would be reductive and essentialist and, frankly, offensive. No, no. Maya knew in her heart that Rick agreed with her because he was savvy and thoughtful and fair-minded. Because a man who was this well versed in the segregationist history of one-way streets must be considerably more attuned than she was to the systemic discrimination that had resulted in the tragic prosecution of Bobby Nock.

Silently, Maya looked into Rick's bright, dark eyes.

She could see it there, even though it remained unspoken between them.

They were on the same side.

JUNE 24, 2009

The jurors were all in the van, headed back to the hotel in silence. They'd heard six straight hours

124

of forensic testimony, and everybody seemed kind of fried. Follicles of hair that matched Jessica Silver's DNA had been found in the front passenger seat of Bobby Nock's car. Tiny drops of blood, also matching Jessica Silver's DNA, had been found *both* in the front passenger seat of Bobby's car . . . *and in his trunk.*

Maya reminded herself that the defense attorney hadn't begun her cross-examination yet. Up to this point, she'd presented quite a reasonable explanation for everything the prosecutor offered.

But this didn't look good.

As the van dropped them off, Lila leaned in and whispered in Maya's ear, "Kellan's room. Twenty minutes."

Twenty minutes later, Maya knocked on Kellan's door. Kellan had a long-hair, California surfer vibe about him. He was by far the most gregarious of them all; everyone liked him, though he seemed to spend most of his time with Peter. Maya had never been to Kellan's room before. She didn't think Lila had either. Six other jurors were inside. Soon all the rest arrived.

"So," Kellan said, taking charge. "Here's the deal. I have something that I think you're all going to want to see. It has nothing to do with Bobby Nock or Jessica Silver, or our ability to render a fair and impartial verdict. But technically I'm breaking the rules. So I guess what I want to say is this: I trust all of you. I hope you trust me too."

125

Maya was fascinated by the mystery of what Kellan might have.

"If you don't want any part in this, just leave now. No questions asked, no hard feelings." He turned to make eye contact with each of them, one by one.

They all stayed.

"Okay then." Kellan went into his bedroom and returned with a brown paper bag. He reached inside. Was it cocaine? Amphetamines?

Out of the bag came a DVD of the Will Ferrell movie *Step Brothers*.

Fran picked it up from the coffee table, gazing at the cover like it was a precious jewel. Next came *Harry Potter and the Order of the Phoenix*, *The Reader*, and *Yes Man*.

"Where did you get these?" Rick asked.

Kellan shook his head. "Sorry. The only way this works is if I keep my connect protected."

The jurors passed the DVDs around. Fran had never heard of *Yes Man*. Lila said it was pretty funny. Trisha asked if Kellan thought she'd like *Taken*.

That night, Maya, Rick, and Lila stayed up late watching *The Reader* in Lila's room. Rick made a joke about how it was the perfect "high-middle-brow" movie. Maya found his pretentious streak endearing. He still teared up toward the end.

When Lila feel asleep, Maya sensed Rick inching closer to her. But they did not so much as touch.

Maya had never cheated on someone in her life and she wasn't about to start now.

The first time she called Hunter at their assigned nightly hour and he didn't pick up, she was relieved. Then she felt guilty for having been relieved. She should want to talk to her boyfriend. That's what people did when they were apart. They spoke on the phone every day and they missed each other.

Still, finding thirty minutes' worth of stuff to say to him, when she couldn't talk about the thing she was doing all day, was impossible. It wasn't like he had much to say about his job either. The stilted pauses grew unbearable. She found herself watching the clock whenever they talked, wondering how long she'd have to stay on the line so as not to hurt his feelings.

After he missed that one call—a work dinner had gone late—she told him not to worry about it. She felt good about being able to forgive him. Theirs was not the kind of relationship in which either of them was the bad guy.

She began calling every other night.

Then every third.

JULY 6, 2009

Maya and Rick were watching *Michael Clayton* on his bed. And then, in an instant, they weren't.

127

They were completely sober. They knew what they were doing. The feeling of Rick's skin against hers was thrilling and scary and dizzying.

At six the next morning, she snuck back to her room, one floor below his. She showered, dressed, and made a much-needed coffee in the single-serving brewer. She realized that if she died that day, no one would know the previous night had ever happened.

On the phone with Hunter that evening, she was garrulous. She spoke at greater length about that morning's breakfast buffet than anyone, ever, had spoken about scrambled eggs.

Of course, she felt guilty. Brutally guilty. But the only person with whom she could discuss her sickening guilt was Rick. Cheating didn't feel the way she thought it would. Affairs were things that cowards chose when their relationships weren't giving them what they needed. Infidelity was the refuge of romantic weaklings. That was how affairs were talked about among Maya's friends, more than one of whom had found themselves in the role of the cheated on. But none of the betrayals for which she'd provided consolation, validation, and alcohol had sounded anything like this.

She spent the next night with Rick. Somehow the idea of going back to her room to be alone with her guilt seemed unbearable. The third night, Rick suggested they sleep in Maya's room. It came off, honestly, as gallantry.

Their mutual impropriety bonded them even further. What should she do about her boyfriend? What could she say to him, and when? They discussed this openly. Between them, there would be no secrets. Finally, there was someone from whom neither had to keep a thing.

In the private space of their two-person world, they could talk about the entire universe outside the trial. They could talk about everything that wasn't in front of them, which was most things. The novels they'd admired, the films they hadn't, why Rick had chosen graduate school, why Maya never had, and what love was supposed to be about, anyway.

They agreed that love should be, first and foremost, about total and complete truthfulness.

The clandestine nature of their relationship created a feedback loop: Their romantic secret could only be picked apart and philosophized about together. So they wanted only to spend more time with each other. Sex was both the cause of their closeness and its effect.

Their subterfuge became a routine: Some nights she would sneak up to his room via the back staircase, the alarm for which they'd learned wasn't actually hooked up to anything. Other nights, Rick would sneak down to hers. It wasn't hard to avoid the guards that late. The mornings were trickier. They'd have to tear themselves out of bed early to beat anyone else into the hallway so they wouldn't be spotted. Every other morning, when Maya crept from Rick's room, she experienced a single moment of terror as the membrane between their secret world and the one outside broke. And then the danger was gone and the world she'd left was a dream again.

There was one morning, about ten weeks into the trial, when Rick left Maya's room and then immediately returned.

"Wayne saw me," he said as he hurried back in.

"What do you mean, he saw you?"

"I went into the hall . . . Wayne was there."

"What did he say?"

"He didn't say anything."

"What did *you* say?"

"*I* didn't say anything."

"Did he see you coming out of my room?"

"I don't know. He saw me, walked by . . . gave me this look . . . and then he was gone."

"What sort of look?"

"Like . . . a look."

"A look like he knows?"

Oh, the hours that they spent discussing that look. Was a smile involved? At what pitch were his eyebrows? Did he really make no sound at all?

They never found out what Wayne knew, or who he told, if anyone. He obviously never ratted them out to the judge. If any of the other jurors ever found out, they never said a word.

And as the trial ground on, Maya and Rick remained steadfast to their one spoken commitment: They never discussed the case.

Breaking so many other rules was what made keeping that one sacrosanct. Of course they wanted to talk about Jessica Silver as they lay in bed, wrapped around each other like twine. But they were there to provide Bobby Nock a fair trial. If that didn't happen, then all the sacrifices they'd made in order to serve would have been for nothing.

Because they could not talk about the present, they talked about the future. On those late nights among the crisp hotel sheets, they planned.

Maya loved the way he talked about the future. Rick painted *such* scenes. They were varied, they were compelling, they were detailed:

When the trial was over, Maya would leave Hunter. Rick would move out of Gil's apartment. Together, they'd find a new place. Wouldn't Echo Park be fun? The future of Los Angeles was to the east. Rick would finish his doctorate. Maya would finish her book. Surely their time on this trial would provide great fodder for them both.

They would share each other with their families immediately. By then, they would have hatched a narrative in which their romance had not been consummated until the trial was over.

The relationship they invented for themselves was deeply romantic. Two like-minded

131

compatriots met, by blind luck, while performing a just act of civic service. What were the odds that out of all the Angelenos summoned to jury duty, these two would have been thrown together?

They joked about it being the sort of cheesy story that the *New York Times* wedding section would eat up.

Together, they invented a future in which they reinvented their past. Maya fell for the person Rick hoped he would eventually be. Rick seemed to fall for the person she genuinely thought she was on her way to becoming.

Lying beside Rick on those nights, Maya could hear the faint sounds of the city below. The low hum mingled in her ears with Rick's slow breathing as she felt herself on the precipice of something wonderful.

SEPTEMBER 28, 2009

Mere minutes after the trial was over, the jurors were led into their room to begin their deliberations. Maya could barely contain her excitement. Finally, after four months of principled silence, so much that had long gone unspoken among them could be discussed. She kept glancing at Rick, who was avoiding eye contact. He must have been just as overwhelmed with anticipation as she was.

But before the group fell into any conversation

about the case, their foreperson decided that they should start with a blind vote. The foreperson distributed index cards and black Sharpies. Everyone leaned over their papers as they scribbled.

Maya wasn't sure how all of the others would vote. Rick, of course, would be on her side, as would Lila, Trisha, probably Kathy.

The foreperson collected the cards and read them aloud:

"Guilty. Guilty. Guilty. Guilty. Guilty. Guilty. *Not guilty* . . . Guilty. Guilty. Guilty. Guilty. Guilty."

Maya went dizzy. How was this possible? She didn't know what to say as everyone searched one another's faces, trying to figure out who the holdout was.

"Maybe," Fran Goldenberg said, "we should go around the room one at a time and share our thoughts."

"Maybe," Rick said, "the person who voted 'not guilty' should go first."

Maya wasn't even aware of what she was doing as she slowly raised her hand.

CHAPTER 7

HOW MANY PEOPLE KNOW ALL THIS?
NOW

The midday sun revealed specks of dust on the surfaces of Maya's living room while she told Craig everything.

"You were the lone holdout for not guilty?" Craig asked.

"Yes." She leaned back in her chair and took a sip from the white paper cup of coffee. It had gone cold.

"And Rick was committed to his 'guilty' vote."

"Yes."

"That sounds . . . tense."

"By the time we got back to the hotel that night, my throat was sore. The idea of arguing more with Rick . . . Nobody said a word during dinner. The silence was awful, just twelve people chewing. After everyone else was asleep, Rick rang my doorbell. As usual. He came in, and . . ."

She took another sip of cold coffee. "We were both delirious by that point. I said I couldn't talk anymore. He said we didn't have to talk, we could just lie down and go to sleep. He said he just wanted to feel close to me. But there was no way . . . Our whole relationship had been built around avoiding the case. But now—how could

I lie there next to him and not talk about the fact that he wanted to send Bobby Nock to jail? It wasn't right to argue without the others. The court's rules were clear: No side conversations outside the jury room. It was even more important then than it had been before. I told him we had to pause."

"How did he take it?"

Maya knew where Craig was going. "Not well."

"He was angry?"

"He didn't understand. He kept saying, 'What about us? What about our life together? You just don't care?' But that was the whole problem. Rick was a man of certainties. He needed to be *certain* about Bobby Nock murdering Jessica Silver just like he needed to be *certain* that we were going to be together. He couldn't live with not knowing. And I—well, I didn't know. He kept asking, how could I be sure Bobby hadn't killed her? And I kept saying, 'I'm not sure! I don't think he did it, but he might have. . . .' And that just made Rick angrier. I get it. Wanting to know. Everybody wants to know. But maybe growing up means accepting that you're not always able to."

Maya took a long breath. "He was so disappointed in me. But he didn't understand that I was disappointed too. Finding out that we weren't good for each other, that this divide between us was too wide—I don't think I've ever been so disappointed about anything in my life."

"He left your room angry, that night?"

"He left my room sad," she insisted.

"And then . . . ?"

"That was it."

"You never slept together again?"

"No."

"And you never again spoke about your sexual relationship?"

She shrugged. What else could she say? Their connection had been based on a mutual misunderstanding. Once the illusion was shattered, their imagined future had evaporated.

Their grand romance turned out to be a fling.

Craig nodded. Either he understood or he never would. It didn't matter one way or another to Maya's defense.

She explained that the tension between her and Rick had only grown as the deliberations went on. She was able to pick the other jurors off one by one—while Rick seemed to argue only with her. He dug in harder. It was as if he'd thought that by convincing her of his argument, he could convince her to resume their relationship. It had finally gotten down to eleven to one against him. Still, he wouldn't give in. Maya knew how hard it was to argue against eleven people who were all aligned against you. Yet Rick had remained steadfast.

He had asked the judge to declare a hung jury.

136

The judge had refused. They'd made it this far, and they weren't allowed to throw it all away and leave the court to start again with a new bunch of jurors.

That had been the thing that finally turned Rick: the idea that if they didn't return a verdict, then Bobby's fate would be in the hands of another group of strangers. The justice that Jessica Silver deserved would have to be meted out by people who, for all Rick knew, wouldn't care as much as they had.

"If we don't do this," Rick had said, "then who will?"

If eleven out of the only twelve people who were qualified to decide this case were sure they had to vote "not guilty," then so be it.

When Rick conceded, it felt like he was giving up any hope that he could convince her, and at the same time, any hope that they could ever be together.

Maya had never told this story to anyone before. Not to her then-boyfriend Hunter—for obvious reasons—even when they broke up a few months after the trial. Not to her family, not to her friends, not to her co-workers. She certainly hadn't said a word to any of the other jurors.

Courtrooms were her campfires; she knew well how to spin a barn burner at the dark oak of the jury box. But her relationship with Rick had existed for so long only as memory that she fumbled in her attempt to wrangle it down into language. Turning those sensations of guilt, defiance, and exasperated loss into a narrative she could share, in her living room, on a Thursday afternoon, felt dishonest, even though she was telling the truth. Her words sounded tawdry, or they sounded naïvely nostalgic, or they came off as clinical.

How could she describe the events surrounding the most singular experience of her life to someone who hadn't been there? Speaking to Craig, she kept imagining Rick sitting beside her. He was the one person who could have helped explain what it had been like.

And now he never would. Had she hoped that one day they could have sat down and sorted out what had happened? Tried to make sense of it, together? Maybe that's what she had really wanted from him, last night. Proof that what she was forced to remember alone had once been real, and once been shared. Talking about him now, she wondered whether she'd loved him. Whether he'd loved her. They'd never used the word, then. Would he, now? Or would he have, yesterday, if only she'd asked, before someone came into her room and bashed in his skull?

For the first time in years, she found herself truly missing him. Not the Rick who'd gone on television and called her names; not the Rick whose shame over conceding had curdled into an unforgiving obsession; but the Rick who'd lain under her on a hotel bed, his hands stroking her hair as he talked about the cruelty of one-way streets, the injustice of roads on which there could be no turning back.

"How many people know all this?" Craig asked when she was finished.

"You're the first person I've ever told. But I have no idea who Rick talked to, after the trial. Family, maybe? Friends? Maybe no one."

"And Wayne Russel?"

Maya sighed. "I don't even know what he saw. Or thought he saw. Much less what he could have told anyone."

"Someone else knows at least some of this story. Because someone told the cops this morning."

She'd spent plenty of time wondering, over the years, whether anyone else knew her secret. "Wayne didn't come to the reunion."

"He lives in Colorado. The producers told Mike that they contacted him. He said two words and hung up."

"What two words?"

" 'Fuck no.' "

"That sounds like him."

"Maybe he told the cops. Or maybe he told the person who did. And then last night, you invited Rick back to your room."

"Yes."

"Did you have sex?"

"No."

Craig paused. "On this point, total honesty is to your advantage. We can get you examined. If you had sex—especially rough sex—we might be able to find minor vaginal tearing. We could use that. . . ."

"I get it," she said. "But I swear: We didn't have sex. We just . . . talked."

"About?"

"Our lives now? We had a drink. And then we talked about how surreal it was that we were having a drink. The cops will find Rick's DNA on one of the glasses. Then . . . we started arguing."

"About?"

Maya sighed. "The only thing we ever had to argue about."

Craig seemed sympathetic, if detached. Maya's and Rick's warring perspectives on a decade-old murder case seemed interesting to him exactly to the degree that it helped him keep her out of jail.

"Rick had some new evidence," Craig said, "or so he told the television producers."

"He wouldn't tell me what it was. Said he was planning a big reveal in front of the cameras."

"He gave the producers the impression that this evidence would be Bobby Nock's undoing."

"Which doesn't make any sense. Double jeopardy."

"There are exceptions."

"Federal charges? No prosecutor in the world would touch that, it's a Fifth Amendment nightmare."

"Let's say that he was hell-bent on trying. What would he need to get a U.S. attorney to bite?"

Maya tried gaming it out. "First thing would be a federal nexus. Murder is a state crime, so he'd need to bring a charge like . . . kidnapping across state lines?"

Craig looked at her encouragingly. He'd had the same thought. "A body across the Nevada border would do it. Or an item of the girl's clothing, anything that indicated she'd been transported across a state line before she died."

"But unless this evidence was airtight—I'm talking about Bobby Nock's prints on a knife covered in Jessica Silver's blood—Rick would still need to convince a U.S. attorney that the new trial would work out better than the last one."

"Such as by publicly revealing evidence of jury misconduct in the first trial?"

"You think Rick was going to go public with what happened between us?"

"I certainly hope not. Because that would give you a crystal-clear motivation for killing him."

She thought back on her conversation with Rick in the hotel restaurant. She realized how little she'd learned from it. What the hell had he been doing for the last ten years?

141

What hadn't he told her? Honestly, what *had* he?

"How about the other jurors?" Maya asked. "Did Mike and Mike get alibis for them?"

Craig flicked through messages on his iPhones. "Do you have reason to believe one of your fellow jurors would have wanted to kill Rick and frame you for it?"

It was hard to picture any of the others doing something like this. And yet, if Maya had internalized one truth from the doubt surrounding Jessica Silver's death, it was that no one was safe from their fellow citizens. Anyone could be killed; anyone could be suspected. Anyone could find themselves at the end of a long line of bad decisions and feel they had no other option but to do something terrible.

If Bobby Nock didn't kill Jessica Silver, people always asked Maya, *then who did?* She had to admit to harboring the most unsatisfying opinion of them all: She didn't know. But if anything, her ignorance only made her more fearful. Because it meant that Jessica's killer, like Rick's, was still out there. All these years, he or she had watched Bobby endure a trial, a conviction in the court of public opinion if not by the jury, and the systematic demolition of his entire life. What had the real killer made of it all? If Maya had been right, then there was a villain loose among the people of Los Angeles. It could have been anyone. It felt, some days, like it was everyone.

As if the city itself had swallowed Jessica up.

"Any of them might have," Maya said.

Craig looked surprised.

"Do you think I'm paranoid?" she asked.

"I think there's a reason I hired you in the first place."

Maya smiled. Only Craig would find value in her well-honed distrust.

"None of them," Craig said, "provided alibis to the cops. Few of them, as far as Mike and Mike can tell, even said a *word* to the cops. It would seem that whatever lessons you learned ten years ago about avoiding traps in the criminal justice system, they learned them as well."

Maya was impressed. She tried to imagine motherly Fran Goldenberg telling the officers to fuck off when they came to ask where she'd been at the time of the murder.

But of course, if none of them gave the cops anything, that would make it all the more difficult for Maya to figure out what had really happened to Rick. And to stay out of jail herself.

She was in a precarious position. "Are Mike and Mike at the office? I'd like to see whatever they have."

"I'll send you anything interesting," Craig said. "After I see it. But you are not going to the office. You're on leave."

It was as if he was reminding her of a conversation they'd already had.

"You're suspending me?"

"No, you volunteered to take some time off."

"I thought—you're my lawyer—"

"You get one or the other. Either I'm your boss, or I'm your lawyer. But as to the former, I can't have you doing business on the firm's other cases. Not until this is over."

He stood.

"So what am I supposed to do?" Maya said.

"I will commend again to you my first rule: Continue not doing anything stupid." He plucked his briefcase from the couch.

Maya couldn't imagine sitting in her suddenly foreign house, alone, waiting to be arrested. "There has to be something I can do to help."

"I'd like you to think back on the cases you've tried, and to ask yourself whether a single one of your clients has ever done anything productive to help in their defense."

She had to admit that he was right.

"I am presently leaning toward self-defense," he continued. "And until we make a firm decision, the only thing for you to do is literally nothing."

And then he was gone.

Maya spent the next few hours reassuring a growing number of people that she was just fine. Her parents and a smattering of friends had all left voicemails or sent texts after seeing reports of the murder. The articles hadn't listed her as a "person of interest" in the case, thankfully, but they did mention that Rick's body had been found in her room. The implications were clear. She could only imagine with horror the look on her dad's face when he'd performed his familiar breakfast ritual and sat at the kitchen table of her childhood home in Albuquerque, clicking through nytimes.com.

"Is it bad that I'm kind of glad he's dead?" her dad said as soon as she'd gotten him on the phone and convinced him that she wasn't in danger.

"Dad."

"Sorry. But after all the crap that man said about you in his book . . ."

She told him that she'd discovered the body. Then she lied about the rest, omitting the police interrogation and the need for Craig's involvement, to prevent him from jumping on the next plane to L.A. Once she started talking, she couldn't stop the image of Rick's corpse from flickering before her eyes. She thought about all the different ways she'd seen his body: as a clothed stranger, a naked lover, a fierce combatant, a lifeless corpse.

She had to get off the phone. "Please tell Mom that I'm okay."

The next call was to her colleague Crystal Liu, who did not believe for a second that Maya was anything close to okay.

"Those assholes from the jury are setting you up," Crystal said.

It hadn't been easy for Maya to make close friends since the trial. She'd too often find herself repeating trite, prepackaged answers to the inevitable questions. The worst part was that after these conversations, Maya would feel even more isolated.

Crystal, God bless her, had spent the first half of 2009 on a furious bender and the second half in rehab. She'd missed both the disappearance of Jessica Silver and the acquittal of Bobby Nock entirely. On the rare occasions that Maya's notoriety came up, Crystal talked about it the way one would the plot of an old soap opera: bizarre, unfathomable, laughably overcomplicated.

Now ten years sober, Crystal was an unflappable member of Cantwell & Myers's arbitration department. She took on all the most contentious and messy negotiations, as if she thrived on being the voice of calm at the center of those storms.

During Maya's first week at the firm, Crystal had taken her out to lunch. She hadn't asked about the trial even once.

"Which assholes from the jury?" Maya asked.

"All of them. Together."

Crystal must have gone directly to Mike and Mike, who apparently had been unable to fend off her probing questions.

"You think all eight of them—the ones who were there last night—hatched a plan *together* to kill Rick and then frame me for it?"

She could hear Crystal sigh on the other end of the line.

"I'm fine, by the way," Maya said.

"No, dude," Crystal said. "You're not. You want to know why? Because you trust too many people."

The therapist whom Maya had tried seeing after the trial had told her just the opposite. So had the therapist she'd tried after that. Maya disagreed with Crystal's analysis, but she appreciated her bluntness.

"There are camera crews outside the office," Crystal continued. "It's a zoo down there— they're taking shots of everyone coming in and out of the lobby. They're looking for you."

"Well, I'm home. My name isn't on the property records. They haven't found my address yet."

"They will. A story like this . . . 'One of the jurors on the Bobby Nock jury killed another juror'? I could sell a tape of this phone call to TMZ for fifty grand."

"You're saying this in an effort to gain my trust?"

"I already have your trust. I'm saying this so you'll get the fuck out of there."

Maya instinctively looked around. The photograph she'd taken in Argentina, of chickens

147

smoking on a street-corner grill, hung on the wall. This was her home. Its location was well hidden from the public. Not even the Internet service was in her name.

"Dude," Crystal said, "come stay at my place."

"Thanks. I'll think about it."

"I asked Craig if I could join your team."

"I haven't even been charged."

"How many other suspects do you think the police have? This much attention, they'll make a move. Soon."

"What did Craig say?"

"Ha ha ha."

"He laughed?"

"I asked him in an email. He wrote back 'ha ha ha.'" Crystal paused. "I'm going to read that as 'no.'"

Maya wasn't sure if Craig had left Crystal off the team deliberately, so that Maya could go to her off the record. Rarely did things happen by coincidence in Craig's professional life.

Maya gazed out the window. The sun was already on its downward curve toward the western Hollywood Hills. "You want to help?"

"Fuck yes."

"*Murder Town*—the TV adaptation, not the podcast—has a PA."

A long pause on the other end. "I would imagine they have several."

"Shannon. Early twenties, white, blond, kind

of distressingly earnest. She took me to my room yesterday."

"Okay."

"Find her."

"Why?"

"Rick wouldn't tell me what his mysterious 'new evidence' against Bobby Nock was. But someone at the TV show has to know."

"Gotcha. And you think this PA will give up whatever she has because . . . ?"

Maya couldn't believe she was about to say this. "I'm her hero."

Crystal's *are-you-fucking-kidding-me* look was a natural gift in negotiations. Maya imagined it now.

"Yeah, okay." Crystal sounded incredulous, but pleased to have been given a task. "What are you going to do?"

Maya pictured Detective Daisey, who would almost certainly be at the station right now, preparing the evidence to secure an indictment against her.

Suddenly, she was angry again. Angry at herself for inviting Rick to her room last night. For storming out. For breaking his heart and allowing him to break hers. She hadn't killed him—and yet if he'd never met her, he'd be alive today.

Then she was angry at Rick too. For reminding her of how much she'd cared about him just before he'd gone away forever. For not being here to comfort her through the pain of his loss. For

149

somehow, once again, turning her into the villain.

Leave it to Rick to go and die and have it seem like it was *her* fault.

"The other jurors won't talk to the cops," Maya said. "But maybe they'll talk to me."

One of the Mikes gave her phone numbers and home addresses for Lila Rosales, Jae Kim, Trisha Harold, Cal Barro, Fran Goldenberg, and Peter Wilkie. The others had apparently gone to greater lengths to protect their privacy.

Lila's house in South Los Angeles was a short drive away. Maya took side streets to avoid the traffic. She passed block after identical block of squat single-story homes. When people said that L.A. felt like one big suburb, this is what they meant: an endless expanse of homes, fenced and yarded, with no city in the distance. If having one's own piece of land had once been the American dream, then this part of L.A. served to mock it. There was land enough for everyone. But there wasn't much to do with it.

As she drove, Maya found herself counting the one-way streets.

She arrived at the house, unlatched the chain-link gate, and rang the bell. A sixty-something man in jeans and an old T-shirt answered. He was mostly bald, with a round potbelly. He recognized Maya immediately. "Lila doesn't want to talk to you."

"Are you her father?" Maya said. "I've heard a lot about you."

There was a long moment of silence as he stood guard at the door.

"Lila doesn't have to talk to me if she doesn't want to, but can she tell me that herself? You don't want to send me away without even asking her, do you? She'll be mad."

He looked at Maya as if she was yet another burden sent by a cruel God to test him.

She remembered that Lila had grown up here. She was raising her son in the same house in which her parents had raised her. Maya had gotten the impression at the reunion that the longest period of time Lila had spent unsheltered by these walls was during the trial.

Had Lila ever wanted to leave? Would she ever get the chance to?

With a weary sigh, Lila's father led Maya inside.

Lila was playing with her son, Aaron, in his bedroom. The moment Maya entered, she jumped up and embraced her. "I was so worried about you."

The room was small, the walls painted light blue. The floor was littered with multicolored plastic trucks. Aaron was methodically smashing them together in head-on collisions.

"You weren't kidding about the trucks," Maya said.

Lila looked around. "This used to be my room. The walls were pink, then."

Lila turned to her father, who watched them warily from the doorway. "*Papá! Dejarnos solos.*"

He left, but he didn't seem happy about it.

Lila's eyes had dark circles beneath them. She had the distracted, jittery look of someone who hadn't slept in a while. Maya guessed she probably looked about the same herself.

"Did you see anything last night?" Maya asked after explaining her situation. "Or hear anything?"

"I was with Aaron. We went up to our room around seven-thirty, eight o'clock."

Lila's hotel room was a floor above Maya's and down the hall; the chances of her having heard an altercation from so far away were nonexistent.

"You never left?"

Lila shook her head.

Maya wanted to ask Aaron whether his mommy really was in the hotel room with him all night—but then the idea of asking a five-year-old to corroborate an alibi made her feel like an asshole. Plus, anything she got from Aaron would be useless. Small children were not the most reliable witnesses.

"Did you have fun in the hotel last night?" Maya asked him.

Aaron went on smashing his trucks.

"Was it weird, sleeping in a strange bed?"

He didn't so much as look up at her.

"The cops woke us up," Lila said. "One A.M.? Two? I guess right after they took you away? They asked me a few questions about you—I didn't say anything—and then they cleared us out of the hotel. We came back here. He's having . . . a day."

Maya scanned Lila's face for any hint of a lie. Could she have snuck into Maya's room while Aaron was sleeping and killed Rick?

But then: Why? And what sort of sociopath brings their five-year-old along on a mission to murder?

"Did you see the others?" Maya asked. "After the cops woke you?"

Lila said that she'd seen Fran in the hallway, along with Cal and Trisha, but given the chaos, that's all she remembered. There were so many cops.

"Can I ask you one more question?"

"Yeah."

"Who do *you* think killed Rick?"

Lila turned away, as if the idea that any of them could be guilty of murder was a suggestion too dark for her to contemplate. "Are the cops sure it wasn't just an accident? When they came by here this morning, to question me again, they said probably Rick's head hit the table. So maybe he just tripped and fell?"

Maya remembered that Lila had been among the first to come to her side in the deliberations.

She'd always been suggestible. Or perhaps she'd just been the most eager to see the best in people.

Maya wondered if that was a trait that could be learned. She had always wanted to be a trusting person. But it just wasn't in her. Not anymore.

Maya called Trisha Harold next and learned that the cops had told her not to go back to Houston for a few days. Jae Kim had offered her a pull-out sofa. They were only ten minutes away.

The houses in Koreatown were tightly packed. The lawns were sparse, with fledgling sprouts of grass. Rick had once gone on a whole diatribe about how few plant species were actually native to this area. Not even palm trees came from Southern California, he'd said. Los Angeles had been built on a desert, just an afternoon's drive from Death Valley. So in the 1930s, the city had planted tens of thousands of the lush trees, all imported from Mexico. She couldn't remember, now, what his point had been. All she could remember was how animated he'd gotten, his nude body draped over the ugly hotel comforter while she gently stroked his back.

Maybe Rick had meant that nothing was supposed to thrive here. Los Angeles was either an inspiring tribute to civilization's ability to withstand an infertile soil, or the withering edifice of a generation's best-laid plans to grow something that should not live.

Jae met her at the door. She'd seen him only the day before but she was again struck by how much older he looked. He'd lost most of his short white hair, and his unshaven stubble was patchy. Yet even at his age—and she hated that this was her next thought—he was muscular enough to have bashed Rick's head into a table.

The Craftsman house was overstuffed with things: squat chairs and decorative bowls and, on every table, framed family photos. Jae hadn't seemed like the sentimental type, but he was clearly a keeper. A stack of newspapers was piled on one of the chairs.

Trisha was already setting out a third plate for dinner when they entered the dining room. She was dressed for her interview taping, Maya realized, in formal black pants and a white button-down shirt. She probably hadn't packed more than a few changes of clothes for what she thought would be a one-night trip. The effect made her seem like the most rested among them.

Maya couldn't remember when she'd last eaten. She was grateful for the steaming chunks of stewed pork ribs that Trisha ladled onto her plate.

"Just because you're under arrest for murder," Trisha said, "doesn't mean you should skip meals."

"I'm not under arrest," Maya said. "Yet."

"I didn't see anything funny last night," Jae offered. "If that's what you want to know."

"It is."

"I stayed at the restaurant late. I had a few too many." He sipped at his light beer. "It was stupid, getting drunk in front of everybody. I don't even remember going back to my room."

Claiming to have been too drunk to remember anything, Maya thought, was a great way not to get caught fudging details. There would be nothing to disprove.

"The cameras in the restaurant should show what time you left," she said.

He didn't look concerned as he chewed on a pork rib.

"I left right after you did," Trisha said. "Right after Rick."

"You went straight to your room?"

"Yeah."

"When did you fall asleep?" Maya asked.

"Hard to say."

"Did either of you see me again? After I left the restaurant?"

Trisha and Jae exchanged a look.

"When would we have seen you?" Trisha said.

Maya reasoned that telling the truth to Trisha and Jae wouldn't hurt her potential defense. Anything she said to them would be hearsay, no matter what theory of the crime Maya later chose to employ.

"Rick and I went back to my room to talk. We had another drink. And then I left. He was still in

156

the room when I went out walking. By the time I came back, he was dead."

"Sounds like your talk didn't go too well," Trisha said.

"If anyone saw me leave—or come back—it could help prove I wasn't there when Rick died."

Neither Trisha nor Jae said they'd seen her after she'd left the restaurant.

"I figured that you two wanted to spend some time together," Trisha said. "When you left and then he left right after. It wasn't subtle."

Jae seemed confused. "What was going on with you and Rick?"

Maya looked at her improbable hosts. If it hadn't been for the jury, she couldn't imagine these two ever crossing paths. And now Trisha was sleeping on Jae's couch and helping him serve stewed pork. Had they been close ten years ago? Someone, possibly one of them, had told the cops about Maya's relationship with Rick. She needed to know who.

She deployed a technique she'd learned from one of her firm's investigators.

"Trisha knows," Maya said, looking right at her. She said it in a friendly way. Like *We're both in on this little secret, aren't we?*

Trisha took a long breath. "Yeah." She turned to Jae. "Cal told me."

How did Cal *know?*

"You and Rick?" Jae said, putting it together.

"You were . . . during the trial?"

Maya turned to Trisha. "What did Cal tell you?"

"It was pretty obvious," Trisha said. "Honestly. You guys thought you were so slick. But Cal said it'd been going on for a while."

Maya nodded. "And you kept this to yourself?"

"You think I'm a snitch?"

"No," Maya said. "Clearly not. Neither was Cal."

"Rick didn't put any of that in his book," Jae said, probably still wondering how he could have missed an affair happening right under his nose.

"Maya," Trisha said, tapping her long purple nails on the table. "What happened last night?"

Trying to read their faces, Maya repeated the truth once again. Jae looked blown away by an incomprehensible mystery. Trisha looked like she didn't really buy Maya's story—but maybe she'd give her the benefit of the doubt.

"Whoever went into my room and killed Rick," Maya said, "had to know he'd be there."

"You're not thinking about it the other way?" Trisha asked.

"What other way?"

"That whoever went into your room and killed Rick . . . well, maybe they were looking for you."

The thought had occurred to her. But then, in this scenario, someone went to kill her, and when Rick opened the door to her room, he or she just

. . . killed whoever happened to be there instead?

"Do you think anyone would have wanted to kill me?"

"From experience," Trisha said, "yes. But it's been ten years, so I'm not up on who you've been pissing off lately."

Maya appreciated the honesty. "Who else did Cal tell about me and Rick? And how did Cal know in the first place?"

Trisha shook her head. "No idea. He told me at lunch one day, near the end. It was just the two of us. I was trying to figure out why you were being so difficult about the deliberation."

"Cal said that *that's* why I was being difficult about the deliberation?"

"He was defending you."

"Who told him?"

Trisha shook her head again. "You should ask him yourself."

An hour later, Maya was sitting in Cal Barro's living room. His lime-green bungalow was tucked behind a half-dozen avocado trees on a winding Silver Lake cul-de-sac, only two hills over from Maya's house.

"Are you sure you don't want one?" he asked, raising a cocktail glass. "This has been our experiment lately, me and Don. Substituting Lillet for vermouth."

Maya declined. Cal's skinny, wrinkled arms

were exposed by a classic white T-shirt. His skin had the permanent tan of someone who'd spent decades under the California sun. The idea that he could have been a physical threat to Rick, a man thirty-some years his junior, was hard to swallow. Though not impossible.

She ran through her questions. But sadly, even though his room had been down the hall from hers, Cal hadn't seen anything of interest the night before.

On to thornier subjects. "How did you know that Rick and I were sleeping together?"

"I don't . . ."

"You told Trisha. Ten years ago. How did *you* know?"

Cal took a sip of his drink, circling a finger on the rim of the glass. "Wayne told me. He saw Rick sneaking out of your room one morning."

"Who else did Wayne tell?"

"No one, I don't think. We were trying to protect the two of you."

"Who else did *you* tell?"

Cal paused before answering. "Kathy. She was getting suspicious. . . . We were trying to keep you from getting kicked out. Or worse."

Maya believed him. If he'd wanted her kicked off the jury, he could have seen to it easily.

"No one else?" she asked.

"No one else."

"Who killed Rick?" Once you got them talking

honestly, it was best to ride the wave fast and hard until it crashed.

Cal set down his glass. "I've been thinking a lot about this. It's tricky. But at the end of the day, the simplest explanation makes the most sense."

"Which is?"

"That you killed him."

Cal sounded apologetic, as if the thing that was hardest for him about voicing such a suggestion was the breach of decorum.

Maya didn't let herself react. "You really think I could have done it?"

He grimaced. "You think *I* could have. Don't you?"

She sighed. He was right. "I think it's unlikely."

They were both perfectly capable of imagining the worst of each other.

Suddenly she heard noises from the street—some barked exclamations and boots against pavement.

Cal got up and peered out from behind the blinds.

"Men with cameras," he said.

"Press," Maya said. "They found you."

"No. They found you."

She went to the window to see, but he put up a hand to stop her.

"What are they doing?" Maya said.

"Do you drive a white Lexus?"

"Yes."

Craig nodded. "They're taking video of your car. They must have located it, somehow. . . . It doesn't look like they know about this house. Me. They're just setting up around your car."

"How could they find my—damn it. The car is registered to my law firm. Someone there must have . . ." There were plenty of people at the firm who could have leaked her car registration info for money. Young associates, interns, support staff. With it, someone could probably hack the car's location apps.

"I've got to get out of here—I'll go home. They probably don't have my home address yet. But if I go out the front, they'll see me. Do you have a back door?"

She could imagine the debate playing out in Cal's mind: Was he really going to help sneak a potential murderer out of his house?

"Please," Maya said.

Cal sighed. "Down the hall. The door goes to a porch. You can hop the porch to the empty lot behind. One of those staircases is back there."

Silver Lake was etched with secret staircases between its hills. Hidden from view, they weren't on many maps, but they allowed for foot traffic up and down the hills without use of the wide streets and their inconsistent sidewalks.

"I am going to note," Cal said, following behind her to the back of the house, "that what I am doing does *not* make me an accessory to murder after the fact. I'm not obstructing justice. I don't *know* that you killed Rick, and the only people from whom I am hiding you are paparazzi."

"Agreed," Maya said, opening the back door. "Thank you."

"Maya," he said just before she shut the door behind her.

"Yeah?"

"I used to really like mystery stories."

She had no idea where he was going.

"Agatha Christie," he said. "All of them."

"I remember you reading those, when we were sequestered."

"I can't read them anymore."

"Okay."

"I think I figured out why." He took a breath. "In the stories, there's always an answer at the end. Resolution. The detective confronts the killer; the killer admits it. We know for sure. But out here—it's not like that. Out here, maybe somebody goes to jail. Maybe somebody doesn't. But we never know the truth. The real, whole, definite truth. It's impossible."

Maya didn't know what to say.

He gestured to the nighttime city behind her.

"You should go," he said. "And I really hope you didn't kill him."

Lined by tall bushes and lit only by infrequent streetlamps, the hidden staircase to the next hill provided decent cover. She could see a bigger, better-lit street up ahead, at the top.

She wasn't being followed. Whatever roaming camera crew had found her car, they could stake it out for weeks.

She nearly screamed when her phone vibrated in her pocket.

Jesus. Calm down.

It was Craig. "Where are you right now?"

"Why?"

"Because a traffic camera at the corner of Third and Alameda took a photo of a red Ford F-150 running a light at 1:08 A.M. last night. Colorado plates."

"Okay . . ."

"The plates were registered to one Wayne Russel."

Maya froze. "Wayne? But I told you, he didn't come to the reunion."

"Are you sure about that?"

"He wasn't there. The producers told us he'd declined. I even talked about it with Fran and Trisha. Nobody had heard from him in years."

"So why was his truck in L.A. last night?"

Instinctively, Maya looked over her shoulder. Nothing.

"He's not answering his home phone in Colorado," Craig said. "Which tracks, since he's here. We can't find a cell number for him. I don't believe the cops have either."

"Why would Wayne tell everyone he wasn't coming, and then . . . secretly pop up in L.A.?" She wasn't sure if she was asking Craig or herself. But the answer to this question could be the key to her exoneration.

She remembered the time that Wayne and Rick had nearly come to blows in the jury room. Wayne had loomed over Rick, slamming his fist on the table. They had been on the same side for most of the deliberations—which, paradoxically, had strengthened their antipathies.

Craig spoke quickly. "You said that sneaking into that hotel would have been an insane move for Bobby Nock. He'd have been recognized. And maybe you're right. But what about someone who'd lived there for five months and knew its every nook and cranny?"

Maya imagined herself sneaking into the Omni Hotel unnoticed. Could she? Probably.

"I want you to go home," Craig said, "and I want you to pack a bag."

"Why?"

"Because Wayne Russel told everyone that he wasn't coming to the reunion, only to be caught secretly in the vicinity at the moment of Rick's death . . . and now nobody has a clue where he is."

CHAPTER 8

CAL
JULY 9, 2009

Cal Barro would have thought it'd be pretty hard to make an LAPD detective blush. But even the bald head of Detective Ted Kandero—a thirty-one-year veteran of the force—turned pink as he read aloud the text messages between Jessica Silver and Bobby Nock.

" 'Can't wait to feel your tight wet pussy,' " Detective Kandero recited on the witness stand. He tried desperately to avoid eye contact with Morningstar.

"Did Jessica respond to that message?" Morningstar asked.

"Yes." Detective Kandero took a deep breath. " 'Thinking all day long about your hard cock.' "

Cal stifled a laugh. The incongruity of this tight-assed LAPD guy having to say "hard cock" in a court of law was something else.

"That was when?"

"That message was sent from Jessica's phone at 2:08 P.M., on January eleventh of this year."

"And then?"

Detective Kandero gave the prosecutor a pleading look. "Mr. Nock responded one minute later."

"Saying?"

He read again from a plastic-wrapped printout. " 'You wore that dress in class today just to tease me.' " Kandero looked up. " 'To' is the number 2." As if that cleared up a point that had previously been unclear.

"And then?"

"One minute later, Jessica wrote, 'I wasn't wearing any underwear.' " He paused. "There are some misspellings in there. . . . Should I say those out loud?"

Cal looked over at Elaine Silver, Jessica's mom, who sat, as she had every day for the past three months, in the gallery's front row. As usual, she was dressed all in black. Like she was attending a funeral. She gave no visible reaction to the testimony. She held her head high. She had the look of someone who would not be bowed by this horror, or by any other. Cal could not imagine having to sit here, in her position, listening to all of this. If Jessica's death—or, he should correct himself as the defense lawyer surely would, "Jessica's disappearance"—wasn't sad enough, watching this poor woman stoically endure the trial was nearly unbearable.

Lou Silver had never appeared by her side. Maybe it was just too much for him to take. Cal could hardly blame him.

Detective Kandero's lurid testimony took the rest of the morning. He was made to recite each of the two dozen indecent texts between Bobby and Jessica. He was made to describe both of the photos that Jessica had sent as well, though since they depicted a nude minor, both lawyers had agreed not to show them in open court.

The descriptions, thank goodness, would suffice.

Cal spent the lunch hour eating take-out falafel as he read his paperback Agatha Christie. He'd been thinking a lot about the decision to murder. He could imagine wishing that someone else was dead. But the idea of wanting to be the one to kill them? To perform the physical act of raising a blade and bringing it down into the body of another human being? That seemed hard to fathom.

The thing that made Agatha Christie mysteries his favorites was that they always had a limited number of suspects. With Sherlock Holmes, practically half of London could have committed the crime. But with Agatha, there were only a handful of suspects, laid out plainly at the start. And even though they could be hard to keep track of as the story sped along—who was the Lord of Whatever, again?—you could be sure that one of them had done it. Agatha played fair—there wasn't some new character lurking at the end who you'd never heard about. Each of her books had its own ingenious twist. In *Murder on the Orient Express*, the twist was that all twelve of them did it. In Cal's favorite, *The Murder of Roger Ackroyd*, the twist was that the narrator did it. In *Curtain*, which was the saddest one, the twist was that the detective did it. Say what you will about the old girl, but every possible permutation of who might have done it? Agatha did it.

Why did Agatha's characters murder each other? It was usually for money. Sometimes for revenge. Very rarely, someone killed for love.

Cal observed the fourteen others in the jury room, who were variously eating, reading, chatting, or doing puzzles. Could any of them become killers?

What a strange cast of characters these people were. In a way, the Clara Shortridge Foltz Criminal Justice Center had proven a more exotic locale than the Orient Express. This place wasn't more than four miles from Cal's house, right on the Silver Lake–Los Feliz border. He could walk here from nearly all the properties he owned or managed. Eastside real estate—or at least property management—had been Cal's business for twenty-five years. The rents had risen steadily as this area went from arid, palmless dust bowl to peak eighties leather boystown to hipster-café-and-Pilates cornucopia. His partner, Don, had been around here as long as he had. And yet the Los Angelenos he'd found at the courthouse were entirely foreign to him. Geographically, they were his neighbors. Officially, they were his peers. So how was it that they seemed to have teleported in from another planet?

There was something kind of grand about the idea that only in this courtroom could these randoms assemble. All it took for people in Los Angeles to speak to their neighbors was for one of them to kill another.

At the end of the lunch break, Cal found himself at the men's room urinals, standing next to Peter Wilkie, who took it upon himself to break the silence:

"Those text messages, right?"

"Quite the scene."

"You ever get text messages like that?" Peter asked. "Like, from a guy?"

Cal shrugged.

"Some of the stuff I've gotten from girls, I mean, you would not believe. A Pulitzer Prize in nastiness. I bet for gay guys . . ."

Cal smiled politely. There was a species of straight men that got this funny envy in their voices when they talked about what they imagined was the carefree sexual abandon of gay life. It was like they were jealous.

"I just got a cellphone last year," Cal said, heading over to the sinks. "My nephew tried to show me how to do the texting thing, but I mean, why wouldn't you just call somebody?"

After lunch, Gibson, the defense attorney, had her turn with Detective Kandero.

"Officer," she said, meandering toward the witness stand like she had all the time in the world. "You must have been pretty shocked when you saw those text messages between Bobby and Jessica."

"Yes, ma'am."

"Scandalized, even?"

"If you say so."

"A lot of provocative language for a girl that age."

Kandero smiled slightly. "Well, I have a girl that age. You'd be amazed."

Cal had to agree with the cop. The things kids saw online these days.

Gibson nodded in a friendly way. "And her teacher, no less."

The judge glanced at Morningstar, like he was looking for an objection. But the prosecutor stayed quiet. He'd been objecting a lot lately, so maybe he was saving his ammunition.

"Sure," said Kandero.

"What conclusions did you draw from these text messages?"

"Pardon?"

"What did those text messages make you think had occurred?"

"Had occurred?" He thought for a moment. "I

mean, they were between the defendant and the victim."

"Just so we're clear, though, at this point, when you learned of these texts, Bobby Nock was not the defendant, and Jessica Silver had not been declared a victim?"

"Sure. Right. Yes."

"But you assumed that these messages meant that they were engaged in an inappropriate sexual relationship?"

"Yes, I did. Which would give him motive for killing her."

"Ah," Gibson said. "Right."

She stood there for a moment, like she was lost in thought. And then she looked back to the witness box, like something had occurred to her for the very first time.

"Oh, one question," she said. "Why did you think that?"

Cal wasn't sure where she was going with this, but she certainly had his attention.

"Well," the detective said, "if Bobby Nock needed to conceal from the school—from the Silver family—that he and Jessica were having sex—if he needed to make sure that she wouldn't tell anyone what they were up to—that would be a pretty good motive for this crime."

"No, I'm sorry, let me rephrase that. Why did you think that Bobby Nock and Jessica Silver were having sex?"

Detective Kandero just stared, dumbfounded. "The text messages were . . . pretty explicit."

"They were graphic."

"Yes, ma'am."

"But did they ever, at any point, indicate that Bobby and Jessica had already *had* sex?"

Cal could hear people shifting around the room. "Ma'am?"

"Well," Gibson said, "take the first message you read for us, this morning."

"I don't have it in front of me."

She read from her notes. " 'Can't wait to feel your tight wet pussy.' Was that it?"

"I believe so."

" 'Can't wait . . .' " she said again slowly. "If you said, right now, 'I can't wait to eat a turkey sandwich . . .' Well, would anyone take that statement to mean that you'd already had lunch?"

The detective looked flustered, to say the least.

Cal was beginning to see where Gibson was heading.

Damn, she was good.

"Objection." Morningstar stood. "This is a ludicrous hypothetical."

"On what grounds?" the judge asked.

Morningstar paused. "Beyond the scope."

Gibson turned to the judge. "He put the detective on the stand to testify about these text messages. He asked the detective to draw inferences from the language in these messages.

173

If we've expanded the scope of the witness's testimony, the state is the one who expanded it."

The judge took a moment to think. "Overruled," he said.

Cal would not claim to know a thing about the legal technicalities involved, but even he could tell that the defense attorney had done something super smart.

"Detective?" she said.

"I . . ." the detective said. "I . . . I don't think the defendant here was talking about a turkey sandwich."

There was laughter from the gallery. Cal looked at Elaine Silver. That poor woman.

Gibson smiled. "Fair enough. How about the next message? Shall I read that one back for you as well?" She checked her notes. " 'You wore that dress in class today just to tease me.' "

"I think," Detective Kandero said, "that that one means that the defendant liked the victim's dress."

She hit him with a stern look. "Alleged victim."

"Alleged victim," he corrected himself.

"Thank you," she said. "So, I'm seeing these references to things that Bobby 'can't wait' to do, or things he's 'thinking about.' But—and look, I can't claim to know for sure—but I don't see anywhere where these messages reference something they actually have done?"

Detective Kandero picked up his plastic-wrapped sheets of printouts. He flipped through them faster and faster as he scanned over the pages.

"I know, right?" Gibson said. Her tone was breezy. Like she was just some dumb teenager herself, in over her head, not quite sure what she was doing here in this big formal courtroom.

Cal was impressed by the ease with which she went back and forth between predator and prey.

"Objection, Your Honor." Morningstar stood again, maybe sensing a change in the headwinds. But if his move was to get out in front of it, he failed. Because Cal could hear the stress in the man's voice as he said, "Not in the form of a question."

"I'll rephrase, Your Honor," Gibson said calmly. "Detective, while these text messages and photographs—all sent on the same day, by the way—indicate a shockingly inappropriate teacher-student relationship, has your investigation produced any concrete evidence— of any kind—that proves that Bobby Nock and Jessica Silver actually had sexual intercourse?"

Detective Kandero was still flipping through the papers. The text message that he hoped for was not to be found. Finally, he set the sheets back down.

"No, ma'am," he said. "It has not."

Cal heard another murmuring from the gallery. It was loud enough that the judge had to bang on his gavel to keep everyone quiet.

"If Bobby and Jessica were not actually having sex," Gibson said, "then where does that leave the prosecution's theory of Bobby's motive for this crime?"

Detective Kandero failed to hide his frustration. "Just because they might not have been having sex doesn't mean he didn't kill her."

"Of course, Detective. Of course. But . . ." She gestured to Morningstar. "My friend across the aisle has suggested that Bobby Nock murdered Jessica Silver to hide a clandestine sexual relationship. And so I'm asking you, in your professional opinion, whether the prosecution's case makes nearly as much sense if the relationship wasn't precisely sexual?"

Morningstar was on his feet in an instant with an objection. This time he won. The witness did not have to answer that question.

Cal could feel a tremor of doubt begin to form.

CHAPTER 9

HE DIDN'T DO THIS ALONE
NOW

It was nearly eleven by the time Maya made it up the hill to her house.

The bright glow of Lou Silver's new downtown backlit the Silver Lake hills. The only nearby light came from her neighbors' windows, a distant warmth tucked behind their curtains.

The street in front of her house was empty. She allowed herself to relax a little, seeing that she was, for the moment, right: No one had yet discovered her home address.

Then she saw something moving across her front lawn.

For a second she was sure she was imagining things. Her stomach twisted up with fear.

A human shape revealed itself in the gloom. It was the outline of a person against her own lit windows. Someone was walking quietly between the palm trees in her front yard.

Maya crouched below a neighbor's wooden gate. She could feel her pounding heart.

Whoever it was slipped through the dark to the edge of her lawn. If this was a paparazzo, the only shot that would be worth any money would be of Maya. His best bet would be to wait across the street for her to appear. But this guy was creeping around her lawn.

Wayne.

Maya knew that she should run fast as she could back down the block and call 911. But by the time the police got there, Wayne would likely be gone. The prosecution would find a way to use that call against her. If she was in their position, she'd do the same thing.

Maya pulled out her cellphone, holding it against her chest to cover the bright light of the screen. She turned on the video camera.

She jumped up from behind the gate and sprinted toward her lawn. She held out the phone and thumbed on the flashlight.

"Shit."

A woman's voice. A familiar one. She held her arm in front of her face, startled by the light.

"I'm calling the cops," Maya said.

"Wait, it's me."

Shannon, the young PA from *Murder Town*, lowered her arm.

"What are you doing here?" Maya said.

"Your friend Crystal gave me your address. . . . I'm trying to help."

"How is this helping?"

Shannon raised a large manila envelope above her head. She looked like she was surrendering to an armed SWAT team, rather than an attorney with a cellphone.

"I don't believe you'd kill anyone," Shannon said.

"Thanks."

"Rick gave the show access to all of his files. Everything he'd learned about Jessica Silver's disappearance."

"What did he find?"

"I don't know." Shannon held out the manila envelope. "But this might tell us."

Shannon waited while Maya quickly threw some clothes into an overnight bag and stuffed a laptop and a random assortment of chargers into her briefcase.

"We'll take your car," she said to Shannon.

"Where are we going?"

"Somewhere safe."

There wasn't any traffic as Shannon drove Maya west in her brand-new black BMW.

"Nice car," Maya said over the hum of the engine. She wondered how a PA could afford a BMW.

"My parents," Shannon offered, without having been asked.

Crystal Liu's house in Santa Monica was shielded from the street by a row of manicured bamboo.

Just before midnight, she answered the door in sweatpants and an old T-shirt.

"Big date tonight?" Maya said.

Crystal ignored her and turned to Shannon. "Did you really tell her she's your hero?"

"What?" Shannon said unapologetically.

In Crystal's tastefully minimalist living room, Shannon opened the manila envelope. It contained a packet of information for new *Murder Town* employees: instructions on parking, payroll services, sick day policies, and how to log in to the show's cloud storage systems.

Using Crystal's laptop, Shannon logged on. "Everything Rick gave to the show should be stored online."

"Can anyone track this?" Maya asked.

"Sure. You're using my log-in, but from Crystal's IP address."

"Explain."

Shannon rolled her eyes. Maya had not felt this old and useless since the last time she'd seen her.

"Crystal's laptop has a unique IP address. If anyone from the show searches for the physical location of the log-ins, they'll see that this one happened from her computer. But why search? No one has broken into their system. I'm sure they've given the cops access already. There are probably a bunch of new IP addresses logging on to the system already tonight."

Maya turned to Crystal, who nodded. "Do it."

Shannon downloaded a huge cache of files marked "Presentation from Rick Leonard."

"If they check," Maya asked, "they'll see that we used your info and they'll fire you."

Shannon shrugged. "Can I be honest with you?"

"You haven't been?"

On Crystal's laptop, Shannon clicked open the cache. "This job kind of sucks."

Later, Maya learned that Shannon wasn't even getting paid. She was interning, and seemed to have descended from some manner of Connecticut money, the exact nature of which Maya never explored.

The three took their positions on separate couches. While Shannon worked on Crystal's laptop, Crystal made use of her iPad. Maya powered up her own computer.

Crystal took the lead on the files about the Silver family. Shannon took the science. Maya assumed responsibility for the bulk of the documents: the ones concerning Bobby Nock.

Rick's ten-year investigation into Jessica Silver's disappearance had been exhaustive. Maya had expected no less, and yet still the extent of his obsession was breathtaking. There were detailed files on every element of the case: the chemistry of DNA, complete with transcripts of a dozen interviews with forensic experts; the physics of cellphone triangulation, complete with a twenty-page explanation of the radio-wave technology on which wireless networks operated; the history of Lou Silver's real estate empire, with not just financial data but quotes from former employees; a genealogy of Elaine Silver's family, showing the hardscrabble upbringing from which she'd risen before marrying the soon-to-be-billionaire Lou; Jessica Silver's report cards, going all the way back to kindergarten; and, of course, countless pages on the life and misdeeds of Bobby Nock.

Maya thought of her own folder on the case, the one that Rick had seen in her hotel room. Had he imagined that he'd find an obsession there to rival his own? How paltry and thin her little folder must have seemed.

Had he looked through it, alone in her room, before someone had murdered him?

Had his last thought of her, before he died, been disappointment?

Maya went to make coffee after 1:00 A.M., which she hadn't done since law school.

She was struggling with Crystal's sleek Norwegian coffee machine when Shannon appeared at her side. In a few seconds, Shannon got the machine to work.

"Do you think it was Wayne?" Shannon asked.

Maya admitted she didn't know. Wayne's lie—and simultaneous disappearance—made clear that he was certainly hiding *something*. But it also gave credence to Crystal's theory that multiple jurors were involved—that there was some kind of conspiracy at work.

"Wayne might be a killer," Maya said as she poured coffee. "But he's not a planner. He's a blunt-force asshole. If he did this, I don't think he did it alone."

"Thank you," Crystal called from the other room, vindicated.

Shannon had the look of someone who'd been transported into a scene from her favorite TV show: exhilarated, nervous, and strangely incredulous that this could all actually be happening to her.

Maya was stunned by the number of people Rick had talked to. She found interviews he'd conducted with teachers at the school, college classmates, childhood friends. There were notes on everyone, audio recordings of many of them.

"When did Rick have time for all of this?" Maya asked.

"He's had ten years," Crystal answered.

"Is this *all* he's been doing for ten years?" Maya wondered aloud.

"Yes," Shannon said.

Maya turned to face her. "What do you mean?"

"We started putting together tape on Rick. A few weeks ago. I mean, I didn't, they never let me, like, *do* anything. But he provided some background on where he'd been."

"Where?"

"Here," Shannon said. "L.A. He dropped out of his PhD program six months after the verdict. There was tension with the other grad students, some of the professors, something like that? It was hard to follow. Like he'd become a lightning rod at the school. But not in a good way."

"There's good controversial and bad controversial," Maya said, "and Rick was the wrong kind?"

"Yeah."

"So he just stayed in L.A. and . . . ?"

Shannon shrugged. "Obsessed."

"He published that book," Crystal said. "The one about how terrible you are."

Maya gave Crystal a look.

"But after that?" Maya asked Shannon. "What did Rick do for money?"

"It sounded like the book had covered him for a while. He saved a lot. Invested okay, I think. I don't really know about that stuff."

Shannon was *definitely* from East Coast money.

"You're telling me," Maya said, "that the only thing Rick was doing since the trial was investigating the disappearance of Jessica Silver?"

"That's what he said. I think he was pretty alone. The whole thing was tough on his family.

184

His parents split up, after the verdict. They both still live in . . . where was it . . . ?"

"North Carolina," Maya said. She remembered hearing about Rick's parents. During the trial, their respective families had been one of the safer topics of conversation. She was almost offended that Shannon now knew more about his family than she did.

Rick hadn't wanted to tell Maya any of this. *Why?*

"I cannot believe," Crystal said, "that he couldn't let the trial go."

Maya understood perfectly.

"None of us let it go," Maya said. "Even if we pretended to."

Crystal, for once, had nothing to say.

Only yesterday, Maya had told Rick so confidently that she was over it. That she'd stopped wondering who killed Jessica, stopped caring.

What self-serving crap.

Maya was a third of the way through her digital stack of files when she pulled up something curious.

"Rick went to visit Bobby Nock," she said. If Rick's investigation had been this thorough, of course he would have found a way to interrogate the suspect himself. But she couldn't believe that Rick and Bobby had actually met and she hadn't been there to see it.

"When?" Crystal asked.

Maya read the brief account. "Bobby was living in some little town a few hours north of here. Rick went to visit on April fifth. But that's all the file says. He spoke to him—but there's no transcript, no recording, nothing."

Shannon frowned. "That seems . . . weird, right?"

Maya nodded. "There are *pages* here on Elaine Silver's poor cousins in Florida. The trailer park she grew up in, before moving to L.A. and meeting Lou. But there is no transcript of Rick's one conversation with the man he spent ten years trying to put in jail?"

"Who has now," Crystal noted from the couch, "disappeared."

Maya frowned. "He disappeared five months ago. That's what Craig told me. . . ." She looked at the date of Rick's visit again. "When *exactly* did Bobby's P.O. report him for violating his parole?"

Crystal and Shannon looked at each other: Was that information in here somewhere?

Maya texted both Mikes.

One responded in twenty seconds, the other fifteen seconds later.

"Bobby violated parole on April ninth," Maya read from her phone. "And no one has seen him since."

Crystal looked up at her. "Bobby Nock disappeared four days after Rick's visit."

"So whatever Rick found," Shannon said, "was scarier to Bobby than breaking parole."

An hour later, Maya finally pushed the laptop away from her in frustration.

"There's nothing else here," she said. It was after 3 A.M. and Santa Monica was eerily quiet. Maya was startled by the volume of her own voice. "Rick found another scientist who supported the prosecution's argument that Jessica's blood was in Bobby Nock's trunk? Big deal."

"That's not a big deal?" Crystal said.

"It's not *new*. I have skimmed through hundreds of pages of this stuff, and there's nothing here that wasn't debated to death ten years ago. Okay: There's some new forensic technology? It doesn't prove anything definitely. The sworn statement of a guy at a key-duplicating place near Bobby's apartment who saw a girl he *thinks* looked like Jessica walking past on the day she disappeared? Again: big deal."

Shannon looked down at her own screen. "Same here. I mean . . . everything here is basically stuff I already knew."

"I didn't know *any* of this," Crystal said. "But nothing in what I've read makes me think, if I'm Bobby, 'Oh yeah, I definitely have to disappear now.' "

Maya stood. "Whatever Rick found, he didn't put it in here."

Shannon seemed perplexed. "But this is everything he gave us." She stood, stretching her back. "He was supposed to take us through it the next day. The day after he . . . well, today. Jesus, is that still today?"

Crystal looked at the clock on her screen. "Yesterday, technically."

"No one from the show looked through this stuff?" Maya asked.

"Not really. We were waiting for him. And who knows if anyone will, now. With the cops and everything."

"The cops won't go through all of this," Maya said. She thought about Detective Daisey, who was off compiling a case against her. "The cops have their sights on me, and they'll gloss over everything that doesn't help put me away."

Crystal swiped across the screen of her iPad. "Huh. Well. Looks like there's at least *something* in here they'll be interested in."

"What do you mean?" Maya said.

"There's a file here," Crystal said. "At the bottom. It's labeled 'Maya Seale.' "

"What's in it?" Maya sat down beside Crystal.

Crystal clicked. On the screen appeared photos of Maya. Some from the trial. Some from before. And some were from . . . *Some were of her in other courtrooms. On other cases. Long after the trial.*

"Dude," Crystal said.

Shannon joined them on the couch. "Look, there's another folder of court records. Are these for all of the cases you've tried?"

Maya felt cold. A shiver rippled across her skin.

"Your law school transcripts are in here," Crystal said. "Jesus . . . You got an A in torts?"

Maya felt a familiar knot in her stomach. "Why did Rick spend all this time researching . . . me?"

Crystal clicked into another folder. This one was marked "Jae Kim."

Photos of Jae filled the screen. There were pictures of younger men who resembled him; Maya assumed they must be his sons. There were employment records for all of them.

"It wasn't just you," Shannon whispered.

Maya reached out to the keyboard. She closed the Jae Kim file and moved the cursor to the next one. There was a dossier on every single one of them: Lila Rosales. Fran Goldenberg. Kathy Wing. Peter Wilkie. Carolina Cancio. Wayne Russel. Yasmine Sarraf. Trisha Harold. Cal Barro.

"Rick didn't spend ten years just investigating the case," Maya said, the knot in her stomach tightening. "He was investigating us."

CHAPTER 10

PETER
JULY 10, 2009

Peter Wilkie still smiled whenever he remembered the first night he'd snuck into a girl's hotel room while she was asleep. He'd been crazy nervous. He'd been sweating so much that his palms dampened the keycard she'd left for him at the front desk.

It had felt like the longest elevator ride in the world. *What if the keycard didn't work? What if the woman freaked out when she saw him and decided she'd made a huge mistake?* Man, he'd been such a spaz.

He'd arrived at the fifth floor of the Long Beach Hyatt, room 521. He still remembered the room number. Sure enough, the keycard had worked. He'd tiptoed through the darkness, across the carpeted floor. There she was in bed, sound asleep. Her hair had covered up her face.

He'd hoped she looked like the photos she'd sent the day before.

He'd taken off all his clothes—underwear too—and slid under the covers. She'd stirred a little, but hadn't woken up.

He'd lain there for a minute. He'd been scared,

sure, but also exhilarated to lie next to a sleeping stranger. He'd thought: *Who* am *I?*

He'd coughed, like a stage cough.

She'd rolled toward him and opened her eyes. She had a brief moment of panic. Like, *Who is this person and what is going on?*

Then she'd grabbed the back of his head and pulled him toward her and without so much as a word they'd fucked all night.

Just like she'd requested in her email.

That was two years ago. It had probably been the hottest thing he'd ever done up to that point. Nuts, wasn't it, that it had taken him that long to learn how much wildness you could get up to on Craigslist.

Thank God for the Internet.

The idea had come from a buddy of a buddy. Drunk off his ass in one of those divey strip clubs on Sunset, the dude had told Peter that the problem most guys had was that they weren't honest about their intentions. Guys always had to mess around with all this innuendo: "Would you like to have a drink sometime?" "Why don't I drive you home—no funny stuff, I promise!"

What was the point of all that crap? It wasn't actually fooling anyone.

So the guy had shown Peter the post he'd put online: "Hi. I'm a well-educated, athletic, healthy, sexually adventurous, STD-free man in his 40s. Looking for one-night only, anonymous sex. You're in charge. Is there anything you've always wanted to do, but your boyfriend/husband/girlfriend isn't interested? Tell me your deepest fantasy and I'll be your man. No names, no conversation, no contact after."

And then the guy had shown Peter the responses he'd gotten. . . . They were unreal. Three or four times a week, some girl would email with some super-specific fantasy. "I want to have sex in Runyon Canyon where everybody can see us. . . ." Or, "I want to tickle you till you can't take it anymore, and then get on top, and hold you down while I keep tickling and we . . ."

The following day, Peter had put up his first post. "Hi. I am an educated, single, straight, white male, 30s, in search of your deepest unfulfilled fantasy. . . ." He'd gotten a response within hours. "I've always wanted to wake up next to a stranger in a hotel room, somebody I've literally never said a word to. . . ." And then, sure enough, that weekend he'd found himself slipping into a room at the Long Beach Hyatt. His second post, though, got no responses. So he'd started experimenting with the language.

The trick, he'd found, was to be unsensational. The more straightforward and plainspoken, the better. Be clear, be direct, be succinct. Let them know that whatever they were most afraid of, you were not.

Then he found that scientific-sounding language helped too. "Sex is good for you!" his posts would start. "Studies have shown that having a fulfilling sex life decreases blood pressure and increases life expectancy by 5–8 years." That was bullshit, but anytime you said "studies have shown," people believed whatever you put after. The less porny his posts were, and the more science-y, the more responses he'd get.

One girl wanted to blast music super loud. She said her husband wouldn't let her put on any music at all, everything had to be perfectly quiet. When Peter had met her, she'd brought a big iPod speaker and put on Beethoven. Or Brahms? It was classical, definitely.

Then he messaged with a girl who asked for something more aggressive. "I want you to break into my apartment—not actually break in, I'll leave the door unlocked. But I want you to come in like you're a robber, wear a mask. . . ." At first, Peter didn't think he could do it. He felt ridiculous putting on the ski mask. But when he pushed open her door, found her in the shower . . . the rush was killer. The thrill was better than the fucking.

It had been weird, after that, to go back to gentler fantasies. Putting on a fireman's uniform or dripping warm honey or whatever. It didn't have that same burst of *fuck-yeah-this-is-happening* adrenaline. He found one woman who asked to be grabbed in the staircase outside her apartment, while her key was still in the lock. It was amazing. He found another who—no joke— wanted him to break in through her kitchen window. He'd tried to smash the window with his elbow, like they did in the movies.

The glass hadn't budged, and for a week after his arm hurt like hell.

The last time he'd posted was just a few days before jury selection. The girl had responded almost immediately:

"Dear Mr. Healthy Sex Life—I never thought I'd be someone who did things like this. I just want you to know that I'm not this kind of person AT. ALL. But my Husband"—they always made some excuse for their husbands—"can't do much Physical anymore"—some extenuating circumstances or whatever—"and you sound totally trustworthy. AND SAFE. Being SAFE is Important to both of us."

She'd been one of those random capitalization people. (Husband? Physical? Important? What was the train of thought that had led her to capitalize those words?)

She'd wanted it to happen in her tiny West Hollywood pool house. So that night he'd gone over, found the gate open, per instructions, and then slipped through the glass doors to find a woman waiting for him in bed. He had been told to wear latex gloves, like the kind doctors

194

used. They sort of smelled like the condoms.

Another satisfied customer.

Peter would think, sometimes, about all those desperate nights when he was young and had to beg or cajole girlfriends into sex. How had he lived like that? This was so much more honest. So much more real.

Only now, just look at him: Walking down the hallway of the Omni Hotel. Headed back to his room after another long day in court. Nothing to do but jack off in the shower and watch some stupid movie Kellan had smuggled in. When was the last time Peter had even had sex? Like, any kind of sex, not even crazytown Internet sex. He was starting to go out of his mind.

The good folks at the courthouse had confiscated his BlackBerry as soon as the sequester had started. Peter was horny as a dog, more bored than he'd ever been in his life, and there was no end in sight.

He passed his electronic key over the lock on his door just as Lila Rosales was leaving her room. He couldn't believe she wore jeans that tight in court. But it's not like he was complaining. She was the hottest of the jurors, by far. It wasn't even close.

"Hey," Lila said.

Peter's hand gripped the doorknob.

"Hey."

He could smell something floral and sweet in

the recycled hotel air as she walked by. He kept watching until she finally disappeared into the elevator.

Then he went into his room and slammed the door.

Man, he was really starting to lose it.

That afternoon, Gibson, the defense lawyer, had on that black skirt, the one that went just above her knee, and that white top that was thin enough that Peter could sort of see the outline of her bra underneath. He'd seen this outfit before. It was a fave.

That's how bad things had gotten: Peter was getting this turned on by the outline of a bra.

She had this way of striding across the floor when she was tearing into one of the prosecution's witnesses. Some guys were turned off by that sort of confidence, but not Peter. He wasn't some kind of misogynist. He was into girls who knew what they wanted and knew how to get it.

That day was all about Jessica Silver's DNA. Gibson had an easy explanation for why Jessica's hair and blood had been found on Bobby's passenger seat: Bobby hadn't denied that he spent time with Jessica after school. Sometimes he'd given her rides. Her hair could easily have gotten onto the seat that way. Likewise, she suffered from frequent nosebleeds, any one of

196

which might have left behind a tiny drop or two of blood against the dark cloth seat.

Peter, and probably everybody else, had been willing to buy that. But how did her blood get in his *trunk?* It didn't take a genius to figure that if you've got somebody's blood in the trunk of your car, something pretty bad had gone down.

One of the police's forensics experts, a Chinese woman wearing a pantsuit, had been going on about something for a while when Peter realized he should try to pay more attention. He hadn't been sleeping well since the trial started. He was finding it harder to stay focused through day after endless day of testimony. He wasn't getting much exercise. He wasn't doing anything physical, sexual or otherwise.

"Both samples," the expert said, "were delivered to my desk by the clerk."

"He put them on your desk?" Gibson said.

"There's a table that I use. We set the samples on it, before I put them through the polymerase chain reaction machine. That's the machine I described earlier."

He started thinking about the best messages he'd gotten from girls online. He thought about the first one, of course, just the thrill of sneaking into that hotel room. . . .

There were a few scattered gasps from around the courtroom. Peter snapped back to attention.

"And so putting both samples beside each other

on the table like that," Gibson said, "was in clear violation of departmental protocol?"

"Technically," the expert said.

"That sounds to me like a 'yes,'" Gibson responded. "And am I correct that something could have happened to those two samples while they were sitting next to each other on the table?"

"It's extremely unlikely."

"Isn't it correct that if any part of the sample from the passenger seat touched the sample from the trunk, then trace amounts of Jessica's DNA—just as you found—would be in the trunk sample?"

"It's highly unlikely."

"I'm sorry, could you answer the question please?"

Peter enjoyed the brief staring contest that unfolded between the two women.

"Yes," the expert said, "*if* there was contamination while they were both sitting on the table—"

"The same table, which, against departmental protocol, you'd allowed them both to occupy?"

"*If* such a contamination occurred, which would be highly unlikely, then yes, to answer your question, that could produce the test result I found. But again, it's highly unlikely."

"'Unlikely,'" Gibson repeated. She turned to face the jury. "'Unlikely' sounds to me like someone has doubts."

• • •

The judge dismissed them early that day. Peter rode in the van with the others back to the hotel. He couldn't stop from staring at Lila, who was in the row in front of him. How old was she? Nineteen?

There was no way she was still a virgin.

By the time he'd made it into his room, he was hard. His plan was to run straight to the bathroom to take care of business. He wasn't excited about it, like it was something fun to do. He was twitchy about it. Anxious, even. Like horniness was a medical condition and he just needed to take his pills.

He pushed open the door to his bathroom.

There was the maid, bent over the sink, scrubbing at something hard to reach. Her uniform fit snugly against her full body. She looked so good, bent over like that.

The water was running full blast. She hadn't heard him come in, had she?

He wasn't quite sure what he was doing— or what he was planning to do—as he stepped closer. It felt like something was happening but whatever it was, he wasn't the one doing it.

It was just . . . instinct.

He was inches away when she heard him. She started to turn toward him, shocked, but he put his hands on her shoulders. Hard. Taking control, the way he was used to.

"Sir!" she said. "Oh! Sir?"

She was confused. He pressed himself against her, making things clear.

"Sir, please," she said. "No."

But the way she said it, it sounded just like those girls who'd emailed him. The ones who'd liked to protest. Who'd gotten off on pretending to say no.

He put a hand over her mouth.

She was scared, just like all the others were scared. It made him harder.

He pushed her against the sink.

She wants this, Peter thought, confidently, definitively, as he ripped off her uniform top and a single worn button clattered against the cold floor.

CHAPTER 11

MIRACLE
NOW

Maya had long ago shaken off the illusion that there were people free of incriminating secrets. She'd put enough witnesses on the stand to know there would always be some past transgression with which a person's testimony could be impugned. So reading through the dossiers Rick had prepared on their fellow jurors, she was not surprised. She was impressed, however, by the skill with which Rick had teased out their sins.

She began with her own. Sure enough, here were details of the affair: "I, Rick Leonard, had a three-month affair with Maya Seale that began on the night of . . ."

Finally, here was Rick's account of what had gone on between them. She realized how desperate she was to hear his narrative of their relationship: Would he describe it the same way she had? What had he really felt about her? What had he thought she really felt about him?

But she found no answers here. His written account was brief, his language dry, his tone legalistic. Rick was an unsensational, unsentimental witness to their misconduct. His inner thoughts had never before been so painfully remote.

The dossier on Maya went on to include lists of her clients, along with their alleged crimes. She found arguments that she'd used against the police. She found transcripts of the testy courtroom interrogations to which she'd submitted forensics experts. She found exhaustive descriptions of every professional interaction she'd had with law enforcement, not all of which had been cordial. She even found a mention of Detective Daisey, whose policework Maya had questioned on the Belen Vasquez case. (No wonder Daisey was so set on putting Maya in jail.)

It was easy enough to see what Rick was after. He was working to demonstrate anti-police bias. *Maya Seale could never have fairly judged the case against Bobby Nock because she would never have believed the police, no matter what the evidence said.*

The case he put together, by sheer strength of implication, wasn't half bad.

Maya said nothing to Crystal and Shannon while they too read her dossier. She watched their faces as they came upon her affair. Shannon kept frowning and looking up at Maya, as if to confirm that what she was reading was true.

Crystal looked into Maya's eyes only once as she read, a sly smile on her face. "It's always the ones you least suspect."

• • •

The dossiers were devoted only to biases, lies, and illegality. Moments of kindness, truthfulness, and uprightness had been omitted. Anyone would look like a villain in a catalogue of only their worst decisions.

Jae Kim had apparently lied on his juror questionnaire, which was a felony. He'd once done construction work for Lou Silver. Had he disclosed this information, he would never have been allowed to serve. Why had he lied? What had he been hiding? What, exactly, was his financial relationship with Silver?

Wayne Russel had suffered a violent and debilitating accident only a year before the trial. He'd experienced severe PTSD, in the form of claustrophobia leading to aggressive outbursts. One incident had even led to a run-in with the police. Had he been too emotionally unstable to have dispassionately rendered a verdict?

Lila Rosales had dated a boy when she was in high school who was later jailed for armed robbery. She didn't disclose this on her questionnaire. Why? Similarly, she hadn't put the identity of Aaron's father on his birth certificate. Why? And what *had* happened to Aaron's father, who seemingly played no role in her or Aaron's lives? Was Aaron's father, perhaps, also in jail? If so, that might indicate bias against law enforcement.

Cal Barro had been arrested for public lewdness outside a gay bar in 1974. He'd pled guilty and paid a fine—but he'd failed to disclose this to either the court or any of his subsequent employers or business partners. There were two ways, Maya realized, that Rick could spin this. Either Cal was an unrepentant sexual predator who would be prone to forgive Bobby's misdeeds, or else—more plausibly—Cal was one of the many gay Californians busted by undercover cops in stings back when even "not wearing clothes associated with your gender" was a crime. In which case, Cal might not be a huge fan of the police.

On and on the dossiers went, full of suspicions large and small. Reading about an unproven accusation that Fran Goldenberg had covered up for her son after he'd embezzled money from their synagogue's after-school program, Maya found herself feeling too disgusted to keep going. Some of this stuff was slander; some of it was innocuous; but any of it, if exposed to the public in the right context, could be used to tarnish a life.

Even just asking questions about these things, publicly, could be ruinous. *"Guilty or not, why didn't you tell anyone? . . . So were you lying then, or are you lying now?"*

Armed with these dossiers, Rick could have made mincemeat of them all.

"He was trying to prove jury interference," Shannon said. "Is that what it's called? He was going to use this stuff to get the verdict tossed out."

"No," Crystal said. "Acquittals can't be vacated. It's a basic Fifth Amendment principle. Any lawyer Rick consulted would have told him that there's no way to re-try Bobby Nock."

"Not in California," Maya said, remembering what Craig had suggested. "And not for murder. But federally . . . He could use these dossiers to demonstrate to the U.S. attorney's office that even though the first trial had failed, a new one might succeed. Or, never mind the law. He could have simply used these to put public pressure on them to do something. Do *anything*."

"He gave these files to the show," Shannon said. "So he was definitely willing to go public with all of your worst secrets."

Maya glanced at the list of names on the screen.

Eleven jurors. Eleven reasons to have wanted to stop these dossiers from getting out.

Just before 4:00 A.M., Shannon turned to Maya: "Who is Margarita Delfina?"

Maya struggled, at first, to place the name. "Margarita . . . Umm, I think she was one of the maids. At the hotel. She was there the entire time we were sequestered."

Shannon gestured to the dossier on Peter Wilkie.

205

Rick had collected a signed statement from a man named Steven Prince. It took Maya a second to realize that this was "Bailiff Steve." Now retired from the California courts.

"On July 11, 2009," Bailiff Steve had written, "Margarita Delfina reported to me that she had been sexually assaulted by the juror Peter Wilkie. According to Margarita, she had been in Peter's room when he came from behind and attacked her. After a struggle, she was able to push him off of her, and then to escape into the hallway."

Maya remembered her own concerns that one of the maids might find sex-soiled sheets in her room. In light of what she was reading, those concerns seemed ridiculous.

Bailiff Steve's account went on: "I confronted Peter with the allegations, but he denied them. Margarita could provide no corroborating evidence, so I declined to bring this incident to the attention of the court. Or the police. In hindsight, this was an inexcusable lapse in judgment for which I take full responsibility."

Maya was appalled that Bailiff Steve hadn't reported this. But she understood why Margarita hadn't pursued things any further; the woman hadn't been eager to publicize an allegation that she couldn't hope to prove.

Crystal shook her head. "So this asshole just got away with it?"

Bailiff Steve went on, in his statement,

to say that at the time he hadn't wanted to jeopardize the trial over what might have been a "misunderstanding." Only now, retired and with the benefit of ten years' reflection, had he been willing to go on the record to Rick about it.

Crystal sighed as she finished reading. "Do you ever wish you weren't a defense attorney?"

Maya took in the tasteful and effortlessly expensive décor in Crystal's living room. She could not have afforded such luxury on the fees of saints.

"Yeah," Maya admitted. "I do. But then I remember what the alternative would be. . . . I don't think I could be a prosecutor."

Shannon was scanning through the files. "There's no statement here from the woman. Did Rick ever contact her? It doesn't say."

"There's no way Rick wouldn't have reached out to Margarita."

"Maybe he couldn't find her?" Shannon said.

"He found everybody else," Crystal said.

Maya grabbed the phone from her jacket pocket. With a few taps of her thumb, she got the number.

"Omni Hotel Los Angeles," came the voice on the other end of the line. "This is Greg."

"Greg," Maya said, "I'm calling to speak to a member of your housekeeping staff. Margarita Delfina. Has her shift started yet today?"

It was a shot in the dark.

"Margarita Delfina . . ." Maya could hear

Greg tap-tap-ing on his keyboard. "She doesn't start until six today. Can I put you in touch with someone else from housekeeping?"

Maya hung up.

"Maybe," Maya said, "she was working the night of the reunion."

There was a quiet moment in Crystal's living room. It seemed as if they were all playing out the various awful scenarios in their heads.

"What do you think happened that night?" Shannon said, finally.

"I don't know," Maya said. "But now we know that Margarita, Peter, and Rick—one of the few people who knew he'd attacked her—were likely all in that hotel at the same time."

Boyle Heights was a flat slab of urban sprawl. Driving past the darkened strip malls and chain burger stands, Maya felt like she could be in any midsize city, anywhere in America. She struggled to remember the last time she'd slept. The past few days streaked together in an adrenal blur.

It was just after 5:00 A.M. when Maya found the address that had been mentioned in the dossier, a squat, wooden, two-story set close to the quiet street.

She got out of the car. There were lights on inside the house. She opened the squeaky gate, walked across the slim yard, and knocked on the front door.

The middle-aged woman who answered wore the bland gray work uniform of the Omni Hotel. Her long, dark hair was post-shower wet. She seemed so small. Maya tried to picture how hard she must have fought to repel an attacker of Peter's size.

"Are you Margarita Delfina?" Maya dimly recalled the woman in front of her from ten years ago. Maya hadn't interacted with her much. She'd been, she realized with shame, otherwise occupied.

Margarita nodded.

"Do you know who I am?"

Margarita stared for a moment. *"No hablo inglés."*

"Entonces hablaremos en español," Maya said. "But"—she went back to English—"I don't think it matters what language we speak."

Margarita's eyes went hard. "What do you want?"

"Ten years ago, Peter Wilkie attacked you. Two nights ago, you saw him again at the hotel. I need to know what happened."

Margarita didn't blink.

"I don't want any trouble," she said.

"I'm on your side. No one is in any trouble. Except for Peter."

Margarita gazed down at her stockinged feet.

"What happened?" Maya said. "What happened two nights ago? And what happened ten years ago?"

Margarita appeared to make a decision. "The other night, I didn't see Peter at the hotel. I saw Rick Leonard."

She looked past Maya at the street that was just starting to turn orange in the dawn.

"You want to come in?"

They sat in the kitchen. Upstairs, Maya could hear the sounds of children. Faucets being flipped on and off, doors opening and closing, an unceasing patter of sibling bickering. Two boys, it sounded like.

"My husband is asleep," Margarita said. "Upstairs." As if to let Maya know she had protection in her own home. Maya hated the idea that she and Margarita had been positioned to be wary of one another.

"When did you see Rick Leonard in the hotel?" Maya asked.

"In the afternoon. When the TV people were taking him to his room. I was scared."

"Why?"

Upstairs, one of the boys yelled something in Spanish at the other. The tone of brothers fighting was identical in every language.

"He came to me. Right here." She gestured around the cluttered kitchen. "Maybe one year ago? He came and said that he knew what happened. He wanted me to make a statement. I said no way."

"Why?"

Margarita shook her head angrily. "What would happen? Who cares?"

Her phrasing stung. "I would care. A lot of people would care. Whatever Peter did . . ."

"I'm not talking about that," Margarita said defiantly.

"You don't have to. Not right now."

"You remember those DVDs?"

Maya was momentarily confused. "What DVDs?"

"Your other friend snuck them into the hotel. Way back then."

"You knew about that?"

"I was how he got them in. In my cart, with the cleaning supplies. He paid me. It was illegal."

Maya was furious. Margarita had felt she had to keep quiet about a horrible assault because she'd been guilty of a minor legal infraction. But Maya also understood. Violating the terms of the sequester could be a felony; she would certainly have been fired.

"I told your friend Rick to go away," Margarita said. "He was angry. He said he needed me. What he was doing, some big plan, I don't know. I don't care. I told him no. He went away. Then a year goes by. . . . Then I saw him at the hotel, the day before yesterday. They took him to his room. I still clean that floor. . . . It was the afternoon. He found me in the hall. He said he still needed me to talk. I said no. He said he was going to tell everybody what happened. My husband too. Everybody. I said no! He said that terrible man— Peter—that terrible, terrible—he was coming. I told the manager I was sick and went home early. And then, the next day . . . I saw on the news Rick was dead."

Maya could see the cracks of pain, long ago paved over, appear on Margarita's face. Maya would bet her life that Margarita was telling the truth.

"Okay," Maya said. "Rick knew what Peter did to you. If Peter knew that Rick knew . . . then that's an awfully good reason for Peter to have killed Rick."

"I don't know what happened to your friend. I don't want anything to do with this. Do you understand? My husband. My kids. My job. I don't want anybody knowing."

"Okay."

"You promise me."

Maya looked her in the eye. That was the very least she could do for this woman. "I promise."

Margarita nodded.

"I think I can help you." Maya felt the itch of an idea forming.

"I can take care of myself."

"I know," Maya said. "But you could also use a lawyer."

Maya spent the next day trying, but she couldn't get Bailiff Steve on the phone. Crystal was able to do some quick digging at the courthouse. It turned out that the Bobby Nock trial was the last one Steve worked before he retired. Now he lived near Sacramento. He didn't pick up at the number Crystal called.

So Maya took her only other option: She called Peter.

He accepted her invitation to meet more easily than she had expected. He offered up his house. She didn't think she could coax him to come to Crystal's, since he didn't know her, so she had no choice but to agree. Given the publicity surrounding their lives, anywhere public was out.

He said he had work obligations he couldn't reschedule, so the earliest he was able to meet was nine that night. This gave Maya a few hours to squeeze in at least some moments of rest, but as she lay on Crystal's bed, forcing her eyes to close, she found sleep impossible.

Perhaps her eyes had been closed for long enough already.

Peter Wilkie lived in the kind of mansion that he would never call a "mansion." He'd probably call it a "Spanish colonial home." Maya figured that anybody who lived in an airy four-bedroom in Venice these days would be too modest to use the "M" word.

The house was right off busy Venice Boulevard. She could hear the sounds of peak drinking hours on the main drag nearby as she eased Crystal's car into the driveway. She buzzed from a keypad and the steel gate opened. It smoothly shut behind her and the noise of the city suddenly fell away.

Peter's house was even bigger up close. Two stories, and seemingly composed of limitless recesses that were hidden from the outside world.

Peter greeted her at the frosted-glass door. He wore a cardigan, white T-shirt, jeans, no shoes. "Good to see you're roaming free," he said.

"Cops are patient," she said. "They like to wait for just the right moment to strike."

Inside, his house was surprisingly tasteful, if coldly bland. "My designer is the shit," he said after she'd complimented him on the fashionably worn leather chairs.

She hated having to play this polite game with him, but she was here for a reason.

They sat on white canvas couches in a darkened sunroom. The walls were decorated, sparsely, with huge black-and-white nature photographs. Maya didn't think she saw a single personal item—a family photo, an old keepsake—anywhere.

He opened a metal case on the glass coffee table. It was filled with vape pens.

"You want some?" he offered. "We make them. Not the weed, the electronics. The real money is in the ancillary businesses." Peter went on about the purity of vaporizer technology, but his eyes kept returning to Maya's purse, which she held on her lap.

Crystal had forced her to bring an old canister of pepper spray, which Maya thought was ridiculous. She'd interviewed plenty of rapists before, and she wasn't worried about Peter attacking her. But Crystal had reminded her that if Peter had killed Rick to keep what he'd done to Margarita quiet, they had no idea what he was capable of when cornered. Now, in Peter's dark sunroom, Maya was happy to have it.

"You okay?" Peter said.

"Just tired."

"You want a hit of CBD oil? We make that too. You won't get high or anything but it's good for . . . tension."

"No, thanks."

Peter tucked the vape pen into the pocket of his cardigan. "Remember all those DVDs we used to watch? The ones Kellan snuck in?"

"Yeah."

Peter grinned. "Amazing how much shit we got away with."

She couldn't tell if he was testing her—or just bragging.

Fuck this guy.

"Margarita Delfina," she said, "has not yet signed a statement saying that you sexually assaulted her in your room at the Omni in July of 2009." She watched Peter freeze. "But I have

215

sworn statements from another, contemporary witness. So my question to you is, what should we do about this?"

If you want to get someone to confess, don't ask them about whether or not they committed the crime. Treat their guilt as a foregone conclusion; as if the pressing issue is what's to be done about it.

Peter frowned. "Who said I assaulted someone?"

"I can't tell you, but that's not the point. The point is, I'm not the only one who has a statement about this. Rick did too. And Rick is dead."

If you bring up more serious allegations, admitting to potentially lesser ones will seem easier.

"You think I had something to do with Rick getting killed?"

"You had the best motive of all of us."

He stood. Instinctively, she did too.

He walked over by the windows and opened a wooden cabinet.

Oh God, was Crystal right?

Maya reached into her bag and gripped the mace. Her fingers fumbled as she tried to find the button.

From the cabinet, Peter removed a bottle of whiskey and a single glass. Then turned to face her. Her hand was buried inside her bag.

"Do you really think I'm going to hurt you?" he said.

"I'm not taking any chances."

Resigned, Peter lowered himself back down on the couch.

"I made a stupid mistake," he said.

"I don't think that quite covers it."

He told her his story, presuming she knew it in more detail than she really did. He told her about the messages he used to put online, the responses he used to get from unknown women, the unexpected addiction he'd developed to the danger and thrill of the sanctioned violence. The withdrawal. He'd been confused in his hotel room that day. The conditioning, Maya had to understand, was what had done it. He was in treatment now, where he'd learned that his sense of normal sexual response had gotten all fucked up and so at the time he really hadn't thought he was doing anything wrong. He knew better now, of course. He'd never done anything so fucked up since, and he never would again. He was so sorry.

Maya wasn't sure she believed him. But it didn't matter.

"Is that what you told Rick?" She wasn't exactly overcome with sympathy.

"I never talked to Rick about this. I didn't even know that Rick knew. That anyone—" She could see him putting it together. "*Fuck.* Bailiff Steve. He was the only other person who knew. He asked me about it, back then. I lied, said nothing happened. He let it go."

"Bailiff Steve sure had your back."

He settled into the couch. "I'm really fucking sorry about what happened. But there's nothing you can do to me now. I looked it up. I mean, with the reunion and everything, I thought about it. . . . Statute of limitations is ten years." He checked his watch as if it had a dial that measured decades. "It's up."

Maya couldn't argue with that. She reached back into her purse and pulled out her phone.

She turned it so Peter could see the screen: The voice recorder was on.

She hit the red button.

"You are absolutely correct," she said, "that there is nothing I can do to you legally. California no longer has a statute of limitations on rape, but it did then, and then it was ten years."

She reached into her bag again and removed a folded set of papers. "A civil suit, on the other hand . . ."

She tossed the papers down on the coffee table.

Peter leaned over them, reading quickly. "You're suing me?"

"My client, Margarita Delfina, is deciding whether to sue you. She hasn't made up her mind yet. But the thing of it is, you sell pot for a living. Legally. And to do that you need a license. Any criminal convictions, the state board can revoke your license. My guess is that even without a criminal conviction, given the evidence we have

218

and the severity of this charge, the civil suit alone will probably . . . If my client decides to file this, I can get someone on the board to revoke your license in five minutes."

She gestured toward the rest of the house. "Nice place. It'd be a shame if you had to sell it."

Neither of them moved. She wondered if he was going to come at her. She didn't think he was dumb enough to try to kill her.

He had to know that the recording backed up automatically to the cloud; trashing her phone would be pointless. And might constitute a fresh criminal charge.

"What do you want from me, Maya?"

She put the phone back in her purse, then walked to the door. He followed behind like a wounded puppy.

"When my client makes a decision, I'll be sure to let you know."

She stepped out into the night air. She could feel the mist from the ocean. It was energizing.

He stayed in the doorway, helpless, as she got into Crystal's car.

"I didn't kill Rick!" he shouted after her. "I swear! I didn't kill Rick!"

As she drove away, she worried that he might be telling the truth.

"So much for doing what I told you," Craig said later that night, after hearing everything she'd done in the last twenty-four hours. "Which was, if I recall, *absolutely nothing.*" She was on her cell, back in Crystal's house.

"Peter Wilkie had a motive to kill Rick," she said, "and I can prove he assaulted a woman in the past. Wayne Russel's motive is unclear, but his lie about not attending the reunion is certainly suspect."

"You take any twelve people off the street, you'll find twelve different criminals. You've done good work here. But . . . I remain undeterred from my initial strategy."

"You still want me to argue self-defense? I didn't kill him!"

"What was that?" Craig said. "You're breaking up. I didn't hear that."

"Sorry."

"The LAPD will test Rick's clothes," Craig went on. "The glasses you and he used. Anything you two might have touched."

"DNA?"

"Hopefully, they'll find someone else's DNA in there—Peter's, Wayne's, I don't know, *anyone's.* But if they don't . . ."

"They'll charge me."

There was an ominous silence on the line.

"Testing takes . . . forty-eight hours?" she reasoned. "Seventy-two?"

"I don't need to remind you," Craig said sweetly, "that being charged with murder is not the end of our work. It's the beginning."

This was Craig's version of a pep talk.

"What you have on the other jurors," he continued, "is solid. But is it more incriminating than Rick's dead body in your room, with your DNA on him, and his blood on your hands?"

He let the question hang.

"At this stage," he said, "there's no point in trying to stop the indictment. So I wouldn't go telling them everything we have on the other jurors just yet, especially, as with this Peter Wilkie atrocity, things they might find for themselves. There isn't much we know that they don't, so I would suggest holding on to what little we have until we know just how we want to use it. I would be focused on planning for our defense. And our defense, unless anything changes in the next forty-eight hours, should be self-defense."

She took a deep breath.

"You still there?" he said.

She tried to imagine swearing on a bible that Rick Leonard had attacked her. The thought was too offensive to contemplate. How could her best legal option be the scenario furthest from the truth?

She had to find another way out.

"There has to be something missing from Rick's files," she said, ignoring Craig's point. "Something that was so terrifying to Bobby that as soon as Rick confronted him with it, he ran. So what is it?"

"Well . . . Rick wouldn't tell you. He wouldn't tell the TV producers. He wouldn't tell *anyone*. And now he's dead. So how do you intend to find out?"

Maya thought through it. The answer she arrived at was so obvious it was embarrassing. "There is exactly one person who has to know what Rick's evidence was. I'd better find him."

Miracle, California, was about as small as towns got. It was situated near the coast, ninety minutes north of Santa Barbara, surrounded by miles of agricultural fields. Roses to the south, berries to the west, lettuce, in long thin rows of green leaves against the pitch-black dirt, to the east and north. Its population numbered only 207. Unlike most small towns, all of its inhabitants were men. Every single one of those men had been convicted of a sex crime.

Miracle was the last known address of Bobby Nock.

Maya had heard talk of this place from one of her former clients. An unassuming guy who was unfailingly polite when he came to her office, the client had had to register as a sex offender—which was fair, given his compulsion for masturbating in public places—though she'd been able to spare him jail time. But one of the problems with being a registered sex offender, Maya had learned, was that it was hard to find a place to live.

The restrictions on the housing options available to sex offenders, especially after release from prison, were as varied as they were draconian: The men had to stay a half mile away from schools, from public parks, from daycare centers, from religious institutions that provided early childhood education, sometimes from swimming pools and all-ages halfway houses. Even if they were legally permitted to live someplace, they found that not many landlords were comfortable renting apartments to admitted sexual predators. And then, even if they were able to get a lease, their mandated walks through their new neighborhoods to knock on every door and confess their crimes weren't just humiliating; they would typically prompt a quick response from the neighbors. Leases were broken without explanation, windows were egged, graffiti was sprayed. "Pervert" was the usual epithet of choice. Sometimes it was worse.

No politician ever lost an election by being too tough on child rapists. So more crimes were added to the list of those which required registration in the database. First it was making banned pornography, then it was merely consuming it—even if the consumer was unaware that the subjects of the pornography were genuinely underage. Verbal harassment became as punishable as physical contact.

More and more men had been cast out of society

and needed a place to live in peace. A grim real estate market was born. It produced towns like Miracle. Whether society needed protection from these men or they needed protection from society depended on one's business model.

Maya left L.A. just after midnight. She borrowed Crystal's blue Tesla and drove north up the 101, hoping to reach Miracle by dawn, when the men who had jobs in the nearby lettuce fields would be getting up. She didn't think that getting any of these men to talk to her would be easy, so she wanted as many bites at the apple as she could get.

Then she reminded herself that she probably shouldn't use any metaphors about forbidden fruit around hundreds of rapists, flashers, and child molesters.

A few hours later, Maya watched a candy-colored California dawn break over a field of blooming roses. She turned off the 101 and onto a dirt road, plumes of dust kicking up behind her car. She arrived, in the first moments of a new day, at the most desolate place she'd ever seen.

Miracle was really just a single intersection, no stoplight, surrounded by a few dozen trailers. Between them was mostly soil, pocked with deflated tires, weather-worn husks of old furniture, and, most cruelly, a few empty kiddie pools. She pulled her car over to the side of the road and got out.

She waited.

It didn't take long for men to start emerging from the trailers, dressed almost identically in old jeans and sweat-stained T-shirts. They spotted Maya instantly, which was to be expected, as was their next move, which was to hide their faces as if they were still perps outside a courthouse. Maya lifted her hands into the air, showing them that she didn't have a camera.

"I just want to ask a few questions!" she called out. None of them seemed to care. She was an out-of-towner driving a Tesla, so anything she wanted from them was suspect. And since she was a woman, everything about her foretold danger.

The next few hours were spent approaching sex offenders one at a time as they left their trailers. But none would say a word to her. It was after nine before she even got someone to acknowledge her. The working crowd had gone for the day, so there hadn't been much movement until a hulking man in flannel pajama pants opened his front door. He was white, with curly blond hair and an easy 250 pounds of unwashed bulk. His stubble decorated a face that had once probably been handsome. He froze when he saw her. But instead of ducking back into his trailer, he looked around, like he thought he was being pranked on a hidden-camera show.

"Are you Delia?" he said.

"My name is Maya. I was wondering if I could ask you a few questions about someone who used to live here."

The man huffed, disappointed. "You don't know Delia?"

"No." She approached his trailer. He didn't stop her.

"Five months ago," she said, "a man named Bobby Nock lived here. African American. He would have been about thirty-five."

The man stared off into the distance, as if trying to figure out how this information could be used against him.

"I'm trying to find Bobby Nock," Maya said. She reached into her pocket and removed a hundred-dollar bill. She held it up to make sure the man could see it flap in the wind. "Can you help me?"

The man looked at the money. Then gazed out at the emptiness surrounding them. He nodded. "Come in."

He opened the trailer's screen door and went back inside. She had no idea what was waiting for her in there.

Not another soul was in sight. There was a single bar of reception on her phone.

She was both terrified and ashamed of herself for being terrified. She didn't know anything about this man: what he'd done, when he'd done it, or how he'd ended up here. Like any of her clients, he deserved the benefit of her doubts. And yet going alone into a trailer with someone who'd been convicted of some kind of heinous crime seemed *obviously* stupid.

Maya reminded herself why she'd come. She'd already seen one dead body that week. She'd already been alone with one confirmed sexual predator. And the person who killed Rick was not inside that trailer. Which meant that however dangerous it might be in there, something much more dangerous was waiting for her out here.

Inside, the trailer was cleaner than she'd expected. If the man didn't take much care of himself, he did take care of his home. There were even decorations on the wall—thrift-store oil paintings of boats.

He stood at the sink, filling two glasses with water.

He handed her one. "I don't have a Brita or anything."

"That's okay," she said. "Thank you."

He sat on a corduroy loveseat. The air was warm and stuffy.

"Who's Delia?" Maya asked.

"My buddy's daughter. She was supposed to come visit him. So he said."

"Must be nice to get a visitor." She felt like an idiot.

He shrugged. "I dunno."

"What's your name?"

He thought for a moment. "Hank."

She smiled. "That's not your real name, is it?"

He shrugged again. "Does it matter?"

Maya held up the hundred-dollar bill. "How long have you lived here?"

Hank gestured to the bill. "Lemme see that."

She handed him the bill. He held it in one hand while touching it, softly, with the fingertips of the other.

Maya inched away from him. "How long have you lived here?"

"Eight years." A pause. "Maybe a little more."

"Did you know Bobby Nock?"

"Guy who murdered that girl?"

"Do you think he murdered that girl?"

"He told me he did."

Maya gave him a long, hard look. "Bobby Nock told you—*Hank*—that he murdered Jessica Silver?"

Hank set the bill on the nearby counter. "Do you want me to say that he told me he murdered her?"

Maya sighed. Out of relief, frustration, or just need of momentary release, she wasn't sure.

"I only want you to tell me the truth," she said.

Hank gave a half shrug. "It's your hundred."

"Did you know him?"

"I knew him."

"Do you know where he went?"

Hank shook his head. "One day he was here. Then he wasn't. It took a while for anyone to notice."

"Why?"

"Guy was quiet. Kept to himself. Didn't have a job."

"What'd he do for money?"

"Fuck if I know. Family? A lot of us, we just have family. They won't visit, they won't even call. But they'll send a check."

Maya pulled up a photo of Rick Leonard on her phone.

"Do you know this man?"

Hank squinted. He seemed to be processing that this young black man, Rick, was different from the young black man, Bobby, who'd lived here. Which was a good sign, in regards to his memory. Though Bobby and Rick didn't really look much alike.

"Bring it here," Hank said.

Maya stepped forward, holding the phone out in front of her like a lantern.

"Closer. Give it."

Maya stood above him and placed her cellphone in his outstretched hand.

"This is a different guy," Hank said.

"Yes."

"Is his name Rick?"

Maya tried not to react. "How do you know that? Was he here?"

"Yeah. Couple months ago. He was looking for Bobby too. Came by a couple times. He was persistent."

"Was he here before Bobby left? After?"

Hank looked at the ceiling, like he was struggling to remember. "I only saw him after. He said that he'd talked to Bobby before; they were friends or something? I didn't really buy it. But then Bobby'd up and vanished and he needed to find him."

"What'd you tell him?"

"What I told you."

"Did anyone else tell him something that you didn't tell me?"

"How would I know what someone else told him?"

"Because you guys all talk and you're not a fucking idiot."

For the first time, Hank smiled. "I appreciate that." He stood, his large frame filling the compact trailer. "But I don't think your man would have found much of anything here. He gave some of the guys a number to call, if anything came up. But, I mean . . . what's gonna come up?"

"Did he give you the number?"

He went into the back bedroom area of the trailer. She could hear him scrounging around. Instinctively, she inched closer to the screen door. She found Crystal's pepper spray still in her purse and gripped the trigger. If he came out of there with a knife, she might be able to outrun him or fend him off. If he came out with a gun, she was dead.

Instead, he emerged with a slip of paper.

He handed it to her. The phone number had an area code of 310—Los Angeles.

Maya didn't get any more from Hank, or whatever his real name was, and she didn't stay long.

Outside, she gobbled up the fresh air. The sun was relentless. She took shade inside the car and gathered herself for another go-round with the citizens of Miracle.

But first, she took out her cell and dialed the number that Hank had provided. She braced for Rick's voice on the outgoing message. How awful that would feel, hearing him engaged in the mundane tasks of his life.

A woman's voice answered after only one ring.

"Good morning," came the voice on the other end of the line. "Lou Silver's office."

There was a long pause. It was deathly silent inside Maya's car, parked on the outskirts of a desert town whose every inhabitant was the perpetrator of a terrible crime.

"How may I direct your call?"

CHAPTER 12

JAE
SEPTEMBER 27, 2009

A lot of folks loved talking smack about rich people, but Jae Kim was not one of them. Some folks thought there was something noble about being poor. Jae figured that was because they didn't know much about real poverty. He had spent nights, as a kid, without a roof over his head. Without food. If he had a choice between poor and rich, he'd choose rich every day of the week. The only people who didn't want to be rich, he was sure, were people brainwashed into thinking that they never could be.

The guys at the construction site where Jae worked would see pictures of rich people in the newspapers or magazines and act like those men in dark suits or those women in flashy underwear—somehow half the rich women you saw in magazines were in their underwear—must all be a bunch of crooks just because they'd had to make some hard choices to get where they were. Maybe they were all crooks, every single one. But Jae had known plenty of poor folks who were crooks too. At least those men in the newspapers and the magazines—guys like Bill

Gates, Steve Jobs, Warren Buffett—they'd built companies. Those women—Oprah and Jennifer Aniston and Angelina Jolie and Donna Karan—they'd built themselves into brands. Being rich was a mind-set. There was no better sign that a person *didn't* have money and was *never gonna* have money than if he thought it was a big joke to make fun of a person who did.

That was the real motherfucker about being poor. It pickled your brain. It made you think your situation was everybody's fault but your own. And everyone around you thought the same way. Some poor folks stewed in those thoughts, marinated in them for a lifetime and then passed them on, generation to generation.

Now, Jae thought, if you took a look at the kids of rich people, why did they always end up *even richer* than their parents? It was because from day one they'd been grown into the right mind-set.

If Jae had one wish for his own kids—three girls and a boy, four through fourteen—it was that they would learn to think like the people they wanted to be. Jae believed with the fervor of prophecy that his children could become like the people he read about. He'd heard people say stuff like "Oh, there are no more heroes anymore," but that was all part of that defeatist mind-set. If you thought you didn't need to look up to a hero, then good for you; you must not need to go *up*

233

anywhere. Jae didn't think like that and neither would his kids.

When was the last time that Jae had seen a movie where the hero was a businessman? Where the guy who built something from nothing wasn't a criminal poisoning the groundwater, but dredging wells in a once-arid stretch of desert? How come Hollywood never made *those* movies?

He was pretty sure he knew why. Because the Hollywood liberals, up on those hidden cliffs above Beverly Hills, felt so ashamed about the poor people nearby that they locked themselves away in their mansions and made movies that glorified the very victimhood that they couldn't stand to be near.

Which was all to say that Jae was pretty psyched to hear from an honest-to-God billionaire on the day that Lou Silver was set to take the stand.

Jae's first impression of Lou Silver was disappointment. *This* was the titan of industries, maker of markets, the Midas from Minneapolis, as a magazine had once proclaimed him? Lou's shoulders hunched forward. His face sagged, like his skin had lost the muscle to hold itself in place. Jae had read about how billionaires had magnetic presences—you were supposed to be able to feel it when they walked into a room. Not Lou. His suit seemed too big in some places and too small in others; at first Jae charitably thought that maybe Lou knew about some new European style trend. But no, Jae realized as he watched Lou settle himself onto the wooden chair, he was just wearing a suit that didn't fit.

Maybe no amount of money could protect a person from letting himself go after his only child was murdered.

It was curious to Jae that this was Lou's first appearance in court. His wife, Elaine, had been in the front row every day, always dressed in black. Like she was an avenging angel come to pass judgment on the affairs of men.

If someone had killed one of Jae's kids, you better believe he'd have been just like Elaine: sitting front row in that courtroom morning to night, 24/7, 365.

Lou was the prosecution's last witness. Over the past months, Morningstar had assembled his case piece by piece: bloodstains and DNA and sexting and, finally, the strange call from Jessica's phone. She'd called her house line—or, as the defense attorney kept reminding everyone, *her phone* had called the Silver house line—after she'd left school on the afternoon of her disappearance. The answering machine had picked up. No message had been left. When the call was made, Jessica's phone had been downtown—or, as the defense attorney kept reminding everyone, it had been within a twenty-five-acre area that encompassed much of downtown as well as four major highways.

Morningstar had suggested that, most likely, the location of the phone meant that Jessica was on her way to or from Bobby's apartment. Morningstar had painted a vivid picture: Bobby had taken Jessica into his car that afternoon, driven her to his place. Either on the way to his apartment to have sex, or on the way back after having sex, they'd gotten into a dispute. Maybe she wanted to end their scandalous affair, or maybe she just wanted to tell her parents about it. Bobby had become enraged, and then killed her right there in the car. Her blood was everywhere. Then, realizing what he'd done, he'd stuffed her body in the trunk—hence the blood found there—and buried her somewhere way out in the desert.

All in all, Jae was feeling that the case was solid. If Bobby Nock *hadn't* killed Jessica, then he'd made a really bad choice of students to molest.

Lou had come, presumably, to provide the last link in the case.

His voice was quiet. "My name is Lou Silver. I was born in Minneapolis, Minnesota, and now I live in the city of Los Angeles." Jae leaned forward to hear better. He noticed that his fellow jurors were doing the same thing. "I'm a businessman."

There was a kind of power, Jae realized, in getting fifteen people to lean in when you spoke.

Morningstar asked Lou to describe the nature of his businesses.

Gibson, the defense lawyer, objected. She said something about "relevance," and then they debated back and forth. This had been pretty normal for the trial—a few questions, some lawyerly argument, another question, some more lawyer back-and-forth, and so on. If the arguing got too involved, the judge would send the jury away.

"I am the founder and CEO of Silver Properties," Lou answered finally. "I am a founder and board member of SunRay Insurance. I am the majority shareholder in Allied Metalwork, Allied Concrete, Allied Glassworks, and Allied Renovations. Which are, contrary to their names, less allied than you might think." It sounded like a joke that he'd made before. It got a few smiles. "I am also the founder and CEO of Silver Ventures. And I work for my wife when it comes to the Silver Foundation."

There were a few more smiles around the room. But Jae was frozen solid. The name Allied Concrete had smacked him just like . . . well . . .

Jae hadn't just done work for Allied Concrete— he'd been subcontracting for them three and a half months ago. He'd been taking paychecks from them right up until the moment he'd been called away to jury duty.

He wanted to punch himself in the head, like

a cartoon idiot. He'd known that Lou Silver owned some "Allied" companies—how could he not have realized that the concrete company was among them?

Lou went on about his new construction downtown, while Jae remembered that he'd sworn, under oath, that he had no personal or financial connection to Lou Silver.

Oh God, he realized, he'd actually met Lou before! Or at least they'd been in the same circle of managers outside a construction site in Century City. Lou had been one of the many anonymous white guys in suits who wandered down to visit that day. But Jae definitely hadn't spoken to him—of that he was 95 percent sure.

Maybe 90 percent.

Jae suddenly felt warm. He shifted in his chair. Fran Goldenberg sat next to him every day, and she glanced over. She mouthed, "Are you okay?" Then she offered a sip from her water bottle.

Jae waved her off and turned back to Lou. He couldn't let Fran know. Or anyone else. The other jurors weren't really his friends, and they'd rat him out the first second they had to. But then, what person in L.A., Jae figured, didn't have some kind of connection to Lou Silver? If Jae hadn't even noticed his, any of them could have made the same mistake.

Jae did his best to focus on the testimony. The

prosecutor was asking Lou to describe his last conversation with his daughter, the morning of her death.

There was a quick objection from the defense.

"We've talked about this before, Your Honor," said Gibson wearily. "Jessica Silver's 'death' has not been introduced into evidence."

"Sustained," the judge said, rolling his eyes at Morningstar. "Let's not do this again."

Morningstar nodded apologetically. "What was your final conversation with Jessica about?" he said to Lou. "The day of her *disappearance?*"

Lou shook his head sadly. "You know what the worst part is? I can't even remember."

Lou described his daughter as trusting, softhearted, kind, goofy, and increasingly able to keep dark secrets from him. He said that he'd had no idea about what was going on between Jessica and Bobby. He blamed himself. Had he been too consumed with his work? Unforgivably inattentive toward his family? Or was there an age at which one's children become strangers in one's own home? These foreign creatures with their own tribal customs and codes?

Jae thought that Lou sounded kind of impersonal when he spoke about his daughter. In a way, it made the guy seem sadder. Like he didn't know how to talk about the terrible thing that happened to him, so he did his best only to talk about terrible things in general. Morningstar asked Lou a bunch of factual questions—what time did she usually get home from school, when did he start to worry about her absence, was it usual for her to go unaccounted for that long— but Lou responded mostly by pleading his own inability to have known much of anything, when it came to Jessica.

Morningstar kept turning to the jury after every answer, paying special attention to Jae, to Carolina, to Fran, to Kathy, and to Enrique. Jae realized that they were the jurors who had kids. For the first time, he felt like the prosecutor was trying to manipulate them. Sure, what Lou Silver was living through was every parent's nightmare. It was certainly Jae's. If *Lou Silver* of all people could not keep his daughter safe, then what chance did anyone else have?

Still, for Morningstar to keep harping on what kids did when their parents weren't around— it didn't feel right. If Morningstar thought he needed to bully the jurors like this in order to win, what did that say about his case?

The mood in the room was grim when Gibson stood slowly, as if waiting for something in the air to clear.

"I'm so sorry, Mr. Silver," she said. "This must be awful for you."

Before Lou could speak, Morningstar objected. "I don't think I heard a question, Your Honor."

The judge gave him a look like the guy was

being a stickler, but he wasn't wrong. He turned to Gibson. "You can get right to your questions, Counselor."

She nodded. "Yes, Your Honor. I'll try to keep this brief, for Mr. Silver's sake."

Gibson addressed the witness box. "How many different businesses do you own?"

Morningstar objected. "Relevance."

Gibson shook her head. "I'm having déjà vu."

"Overruled," the judge said to Morningstar. "You opened the door."

Gibson walked to the center of the courtroom, addressing the jury as much as—if not more than—her witness. "Have any of your business interests ever stirred up any controversy?"

Lou took a deep breath. "As much as any business of its size."

"I'm sorry, was that a 'yes'?"

"Yes."

"Anybody ever threaten to kill you?" She was looking straight at Jae.

Did this have something to do with his connection to Lou? But how could she know?

"Of course they have," Lou said.

She spun around on her high heels. "Of course?"

"My developments have displaced tenants. Angered community organizations. People have sent letters. It's awful, the things people will say when they're angry. But it's all talk."

"Did anyone ever write you a letter saying that they were going to hurt your family?"

"I'd imagine."

"Did anyone ever write you a letter saying that they were going to rape and murder your teenage daughter before burying her body in the desert?"

The specificity of the comment startled everyone in the room.

"I don't remember," Lou said.

If someone wrote a letter like that to me, thought Jae, *I'd remember it.*

"Then allow me to refresh your memory." Gibson took a paper from her desk and showed it first to Morningstar. Whatever this was, he'd seen it before. She brought it up to the judge, who dutifully catalogued it as "defense exhibit 101."

"Permission to approach the witness?" she said. The judge nodded.

She approached the witness box and handed the paper to Lou Silver.

"Will you read that for me, Mr. Silver?"

He looked to the judge, like a child asking permission. The judge nodded.

" 'Dear "Jew" Silver,' " Lou began. " 'You are destroying this city. You deserve to watch your cunt daughter raped and murdered, and then have her body buried in the "dessert" so you can never find it. Maybe I will do that. Maybe. If you are lucky.' " He looked up. "It is unsigned."

242

Gibson didn't appear in the mood for levity. "Buried in the desert?"

"It says 'dessert.' "

"Do you remember receiving this letter?"

"I don't."

"It came to your home address."

"So the police told me. After Bobby Nock was arrested for murdering Jessica."

"It didn't strike you as noteworthy?"

"Of course it struck me as noteworthy."

"Not noteworthy enough to make you think the letter writer might have been serious?"

"It was Bobby Nock who murdered my daughter."

Jae was almost sure he could see Gibson smile.

"You must have been shocked," she said, "when you saw the defendant's text messages with your daughter."

"I didn't see them until after he murdered her."

Jae had gotten enough of the hang of the rhythm of the trial to expect Gibson to jump on that—but to Jae's surprise she let it go. She just looked to the jury for sympathy. As if to say that they were all doing their best to handle the understandable outbursts of a grieving father.

"What did you think when you saw those messages?"

"That I couldn't believe it."

"That your daughter was communicating in that way with her teacher?"

"That *he* was sending those messages to *her.*"

Gibson appeared curious. "You were more surprised by his behavior than hers?"

"He broke the law. He took advantage of her."

"With respect, Mr. Silver, the content of those messages indicates that she was a willing partner."

What a rotten thing for that lawyer to say. To the girl's father! It wasn't right.

Morningstar hadn't made a good impression on Jae. But Gibson was even worse.

"How dare you," Lou said.

"Pardon," she said. "I didn't mean to offend you."

"She was fifteen years old," Lou said. "A child."

"I'm so sorry that you had to read such sexually explicit messages between your daughter and my client."

Lou remained silent. He seemed to stew in his anger.

"Had Jessica ever mentioned Bobby to you?"

"I don't think so."

"You don't think so?"

"I don't remember."

"Not even as her teacher?"

Lou shook his head.

Gibson looked to the judge for help.

"Mr. Silver," the judge said, "I'm afraid this court can only record verbal answers to the attorneys' questions."

Lou turned to the judge, now angry at him too. Lou didn't seem like someone who was used to being told what to do.

Jae figured that if he had a billion dollars, he wouldn't like people telling him what to say and when to say it either.

"No," Lou said.

"Mr. Silver?" Gibson said.

"The answer to your question. *No.* I don't remember Jessica ever mentioning that man."

"Did she usually tell you about her boyfriends?"

Lou looked sick to his stomach. "Pardon me?"

"Girls can be secretive about these things, especially with their fathers. It's perfectly normal. I was just trying to get a sense of whether she'd told you about previous boyfriends, before Bobby?"

"That man was not her boyfriend."

Gibson shrugged. "I'm sorry, what word do you think Jessica would have used?"

"He was her *teacher.*"

"When you read what your daughter wrote to Bobby, you must have really hated him."

"Yes, I did."

"Did you want to see him punished for talking to your daughter like that?"

"I wanted that black devil to get what was coming to him."

There were gasps throughout the courtroom, like there was a competition to see who could suck in more oxygen. Jae was pretty sure he heard someone actually say "Oh damn," but he had no idea who it was. Even the judge was frozen.

For her part, Gibson barely blinked. She gave the slightest sigh, as if she was weary of a world so virulently prejudiced against her client.

"No further questions," she said.

The judge called a brief recess. In the jury room, there was much eye contact but no conversation. They knew that if one of them said a word, they'd all be in trouble. But how do you stay silent after you've heard something like that?

Jae tried to silently communicate with Rick. Trying to tell him, *Like, hey, man. I know what those white people are up to.* But by the look on Rick's face, he wasn't having it. Or maybe Jae was not the guy he wanted to commiserate with.

Jae had sometimes found that black people would acknowledge to him just how racist white people were, but then feel this need to make it clear that they got the worst of it. Like Jae hadn't heard white people mimicking an accent that he didn't have, or talking about how he must be good at math or some shit. It annoyed the hell out of Jae when black people pretended they were the sole victims of the crap white people handed out.

He went up to Trisha, who he'd spent more time with anyway. She had this dry, quick humor that could be a riot when you caught her sarcasm. All he said to her was, "Damn." He felt like that got his point across.

Trisha just shook her head. "Well put."

Fran Goldenberg looked mortified. Was she embarrassed that Lou Silver, a fellow Jew, had been the one to say something so racist? As if it would make her look bad by association?

The mood was tense when Bailiff Steve delivered them back into the courtroom.

The judge called on Morningstar, who stood.

"The prosecution rests," he said.

The judge turned to Gibson. "Is the defense ready to put forth its first witness? Or would you prefer to adjourn for the day and put on a witness in the morning?"

Jae watched as Gibson paused. She whispered something in Bobby Nock's ear. For some moments, they whispered back and forth. Bobby finally nodded, and returned to staring at the desk in front of him.

Gibson stood.

"Ladies and gentlemen of the jury," she said. "The defense rests."

CHAPTER 13

I MIGHT BE THE BEST FRIEND YOU'RE GOING TO GET NOW

"I'd like to speak to Mr. Silver, please," Maya said into the phone. On the other end, the woman—whoever she was—didn't respond. After an uncertain silence, Maya added, "My name is Maya Seale."

"One moment," came the woman's voice. And then Maya waited through endless hold music while she gazed across the desolate expanse of Miracle.

What had Rick and Lou been doing together? Had Lou been helping Rick with his investigation, financially or otherwise? And why hadn't Rick told anyone about it?

Another man made an appearance on the front steps of his trailer. He stared at Maya's borrowed Tesla, trying to figure out what it—and she— were doing in such forsaken terrain.

"Miss Seale?" came the voice, returning to the line. "Mr. Silver suggests that you come by the office at nine tomorrow morning. Would that be all right?"

Maya said that it would.

She spent the next few hours trying to interview registered sex offenders, but none of the others would speak to her.

She had the afternoon to take the scenic route back down the coast. The winding road had been etched into the cliffs, perilously high above the beaches below. Just beyond the shoreline, waves crashed against rock outcroppings in beautiful white sprays. She wanted the time to think through everything she'd learned. And to relish what might be her last views of the ocean before she went to jail.

This was the first time she'd driven this stretch of Highway 1 since she'd moved to L.A. Staring out at the radiant water, she remembered the conversations she'd had with Hunter on their trip from San Francisco. On the rare occasions that she thought of Hunter, it amazed her how infrequently she did.

They'd broken up not long after the trial. But not because of her affair. What had happened with Rick had been a tragic mistake she'd already regretted. The person who stood between them, according to Hunter, was Bobby Nock.

"Could we talk about literally anything else for once?" Hunter had fumed two weeks after she'd returned home. "Hasn't that asshole ruined enough lives? Now he has to ruin ours too?"

They'd gone out to dinner, but someone had

recognized Maya at the restaurant. A woman in dark leggings and chunky jewelry had walked up to their table and said, "You were on the jury, right? I hope you're happy." Then the woman's embarrassed friend had grabbed her wrist and pulled her away.

Date night had disintegrated from there: a tense silence, some insultingly insignificant comment about random bullshit, another tense silence, a waiter's refilling of the water glasses, the crack of the ice cubes as they melted.

"I just want to have a good time tonight," he'd said.

What had he wanted to talk about instead? To this day, she wasn't sure. She'd asked him then, but he'd deflected, put it on her: "Anything else."

"I'm not your cruise director," she'd said in one of those fights, she couldn't remember which. They all blurred together in her memory. "It's not my job to keep you entertained."

"You're *obsessed,*" he'd said. That was definitely from a later fight, after she'd told him she wanted to go to law school. Maya thought it ironic that while her lack of "direction" in life had previously been a subtle source of tension in their relationship, her decision to go to law school seemed only to upset him more.

"What," he'd said, "you're going to become a lawyer so you can get Bobby Nock off the hook for murder? News flash: You already did."

250

"No," she'd tried to explain, "I'm going to become a lawyer because people like Bobby Nock and Jessica Silver both deserve a fair shot at justice."

Every day in this city, someone murdered. Every hour someone raped. Every minute someone stole. The police were arresting people left and right and some of them were innocent and some of them were not, but what did Hunter want her to do, sit on the sidelines? Finish some stupid novel that no one cared about anyway? Or write a memoir about how badly the justice system had treated *her?*

No way. She was not a helpless victim of a heartless system. She was not an innocent bystander.

Hunter could never understand that becoming a lawyer wasn't about endlessly reliving the trial. It was about embracing the most difficult and traumatic events of her life and owning them.

She'd left the old Maya behind in that courthouse. She was someone else now. And this new person, Ms. Seale, had been born in those rooms. She was at home there.

Hunter was married now. He lived in Portland. According to his Facebook photos, he cared passionately about the brewing of craft IPAs.

She made good time on the road until she hit rush-hour traffic around Malibu. The sun had just gone down, and the glow of a new downtown owned almost entirely by one man loomed in the distance.

Maya had encountered Lou Silver exactly once since the trial. A few years ago, she'd been in the Palisades at a climate-change fund-raiser sponsored by a beauty company. She was Crystal Liu's plus-one, and she was enjoying the rare anonymity. "I'm Maya, I work down the hall from Crystal," she'd said to the other attendees. That was all she was for the evening: another lawyer sampling oil-flecked crudités and the next season's fragrances.

Until she saw Elaine Silver across the room. For a second, their eyes met. Instinctively, Maya turned away. She couldn't be sure that Elaine Silver had actually seen her, or whether it had even been Elaine. She tried to convince herself that the elegant, sixty-something woman at the other end of the room was a different billionaire philanthropist and high-society maven. Then Maya wouldn't have to keep looking over her shoulder.

The feigned ignorance worked until the end of the evening. Maya was standing beside Crystal at the valet line and felt someone jostling behind her, a little too closely.

There was Lou Silver, ushering his wife toward the town car that was waiting for them.

"Miss Seale," he whispered as he passed.

252

And that was it. The Silvers got into the car without another glance in Maya's direction.

"So," Crystal said a few minutes later as they sped off into the night. "Meet anybody interesting?"

Lou Silver's various companies occupied adjacent floors in his Century City complex's southern tower. Each block of floors represented a different area of his interests: real estate, insurance, private equity, "innovation," whatever that meant. The Elaine and Lou Silver Foundation had half a floor among the finance people. His personal offices were at the top.

Lou looked older than Maya had imagined he would. People described old age as a gradual descent, but with Lou it seemed to have been a steep cliff. Ten years ago, at fifty, he'd looked middle-aged. Now he no longer parted his hair to hide the balding, and the dark liver spots on his hands were prominent. When he walked across his corner office to greet her, she noticed the deliberation in every step.

His face had the same weary expression.

"You'd think," he said, "that we'd have done this before now. Hi. I'm Lou."

She accepted his handshake. "I didn't think we'd ever do this."

"Why?"

"Because you told *The New York Times* that my

mother must have dropped me on the head a lot as a baby."

He took in her candor and reciprocated it. "Well. You set free the man who killed my Jessica."

"This is going well."

He smiled. "Better than I thought it would, honestly. Will you sit?"

He gestured to a pair of couches. From one wall of windows, Maya could see to the ocean. From another, the Hollywood Hills. From a third, the skyscrapers of downtown, and even the Inland Empire beyond.

"So," Lou said. "You called me."

"Why did Rick Leonard give your phone number to a sexual predator who lives in a town called Miracle?"

Lou didn't miss a beat. "Oh, okay, good. I was wondering where you'd gotten that private number. Rick gave it out because it was the line to my investigative services."

"You have investigative services?"

"He didn't tell you?"

"No."

"Hmm." Clearly, this was not the response he'd expected. "Well, for the last few years, Rick Leonard has essentially *been* my investigative services."

"He worked for you?"

"Two years ago, thereabouts, Rick came

here to see me. He told me all about his own investigations into Bobby Nock. He was convinced that he could prove Bobby's guilt, but he'd need time, manpower, resources. He was practically broke. I'd read his book—I knew he was on the right side. I gave him everything he asked for."

Maya was surprised by Lou's forthrightness.

He looked at her. "Were you expecting me to try and hide these things from you?"

"I don't know."

"Why should I?"

His point was confoundingly reasonable.

"You've heard about Rick's death," she said.

"Just evil."

"Rick was?"

"Bobby."

"I'm sorry?"

"Bobby Nock murdered Rick." He made it sound as if it was the most obvious thing in the world.

Maya didn't think it was even plausible. "You're convinced of that?"

Lou seemed offended. "Bobby Nock killed my daughter. After you, in your infinite wisdom, set him free, he has spent a decade hiding from the justice owed him. Rick Leonard, bless his soul and with the blessing of my help, had been digging into Bobby. Rick discovered evidence against him. So Bobby killed him for it."

"Do you realize what you'd have to believe in order to argue that Bobby Nock killed Rick?"

"Do tell me what I believe."

"Bobby would have had to know, first, *that* the reunion was taking place. Then he'd have had to know exactly *where* the reunion was taking place. Then he'd have had to find a way in to the hotel without being seen—by any of us: dozens of people who'd recognize him in an instant. And *then* he'd have had to know that Rick was going to be in my room, *and* when, *and* that I wouldn't be there."

"Perhaps one of the essential differences between me and you is that I don't put anything past Bobby Nock."

In fairness, Maya thought, this was probably an accurate description of their situation. "You know the cops think I did it?"

"I do."

"But you don't?"

"No." He paused. "The thing that's going to be hardest for you to accept right now is that I am likely the only person who believes you're innocent. Which means that even though I'm sure that you're the most gullible, pigheaded person in the entire Golden State, I might be the best friend you're going to get."

She couldn't believe what she was hearing.

"I know," he said. "Strange bedfellows." He sat back on the couch, spreading his arms out like the wings of an angel.

Lou's hatred of Bobby obscured everything else in his field of vision. There was no implausibility too far-fetched to believe, so long as it implicated Bobby.

"So what did Rick find?" she asked. "With all of your muscle behind him?"

Lou's face clouded with disappointment.

"Not good," he said. "Not good."

"What?"

"I was hoping you knew."

"He didn't tell you?"

Lou sighed. "Rick was very clever, and highly motivated. There's nothing like apostasy, you know, to spur a man to greatness. I wanted justice because of what Bobby did to my daughter. But Rick wanted justice because of what Bobby had made him do to himself." Lou leaned in toward her. "At least Rick admitted his mistakes. Unlike some of us."

Maya stopped herself from taking the bait. She reminded herself that the last thing she needed was to get into a debate about who'd killed Jessica Silver. Especially not with the girl's father. What she needed—the only thing she needed—was information that served her defense.

"Are you really still so sure?" he asked, as if annoyed by her composure. "All these years later? After everything that's happened? One almost has to admire the consistency. *Almost.*"

"If Rick was working for you, you must have access to his notes. His files on Bobby."

Lou clucked his tongue. "I do. They're not hidden—he gave them to the TV producers as well."

"I've seen what they have."

"So you understand. There is no big revelation in those files. He didn't tell me, either. Oh, I asked him. Many times. I can show you a hundred emails. He just kept saying that he had something good, *really* good, *tremendously* good, but that the timing had to be perfect. We fought about it."

Everything about this sounded insane. "Why would Rick find something incontrovertible, then hide it from you? Of all people?"

Lou tapped a single finger against his lips. The gesture seemed vaguely scholarly. "It's nice, isn't it? That you and I are finally asking the same questions."

Lou took in the skyline beyond his windows. "Jessica always liked the water."

Maya followed his gaze—all she could see was miles of cityscape. "Okay."

"Ever since she was little. Most babies hate bathtime? Not Jessica. Loved it. When she was older, swimming lessons. Then swim team. Every weekend she'd go to the beach with her friends. I'd be here. Right in this office. I worked too much. I still do, but now, what else, you know? I would see her at night, her long hair was still wet.

I could smell the salt water. I'd say, 'Jessica, you have swim team all week and then on the weekend you just swim in the salt water?' She said it was meditative. That's the kind of girl my daughter was. She would say a thing was 'meditative.' "

Maya didn't know what to make of this. Or what to say in response.

"I wish I could have met her," was the best she could come up with.

Lou shook his head. What she had to say was irrelevant. "You know what Elaine keeps telling me? 'Punishing Bobby Nock won't bring Jessica back.' "

"You disagree."

"I keep telling Elaine, let's try. And then we'll see what happens." He placed his hands on his lap. "That's why I'm going to help you."

"How?"

"I know where Bobby Nock is."

Maya didn't believe him.

"Rick figured it out a month ago," Lou explained. "And *that* information, thankfully, he shared with me. I'll share it with you."

"Why?"

Lou smiled. "Because if I tell you where Bobby is, you'll go and talk to him. To exonerate yourself, you need to figure out what Rick had on Bobby. He might have an inkling."

"Why not go yourself?"

Lou shrugged. "What am I going to do?" His

frame shook as he rose. "And more importantly, what are the chances that Bobby talks to me? Or my people?"

"Not high."

"But what are the chances that he'll speak to *you?* His misbegotten savior?"

The cold logic by which Lou was able to calculate everyone's respective interests, and to employ only those that aligned with his, was impressive. After years of negotiating with opposing counsels, she'd learned to identify a manipulative personality when she saw one. But Lou was a different breed. It was as if he knew the secrets to crafting a Rube Goldberg machine made only of base human desires.

Perhaps, Maya thought, this was how he'd become a billionaire. Not by exerting his will on others, but by organizing others into exerting their wills on one another. Everyone was working for Lou Silver, whether they knew it or not.

"Okay," she said. "I'll bite. Where's Bobby Nock?"

"Before I tell you where he is, there's something I want from you."

"What?"

"I want you to tell me the truth."

Maya was confused. "When have I lied to you?"

"You avoided my question earlier. Now I want to know. Are you really—*really*—still so sure that you were right ten years ago?"

After all the people who'd tiptoed around this question over the years, she appreciated that Lou had the temerity to ask it outright. If he almost respected her consistency, then maybe she almost respected his candor.

"Or maybe," he said, "just maybe . . . could Bobby have killed my Jessica?"

Lou's face seemed gaunt with craving.

She knew why he cared about her answer. She understood what it was like to have argued for so long that the result of the argument no longer mattered—the only thing that provided any relief was not *being* right, but showing that from the very beginning you *had been* right. That's what Lou really wanted. It was too late for justice. He'd never find peace. So the only satisfaction he could hope for was to hear her admit that she'd been wrong.

Maya wanted to tell Lou that the thing he craved was going to torture him for the rest of his life. The fate they would all have to live with was the hardest one to accept—that they would never know for sure. Their punishment for being people who demanded answers was that they would be forced to go on in perpetuity with their doubts.

In courtrooms all across this city, Maya had seen people get verdicts they'd wanted, and she'd seen just as many get ones they didn't. But the verdicts had nothing to do with truth. No verdict ever changed a person's opinion. Juries weren't gods. The people who went into those courtrooms looking for divine revelation came out bearing the fruits of bureaucratic negotiation.

Maya wanted to tell Lou that this need for vindication had become the mire of their whole petty country. Every day, they woke up fervently hoping for the headline that would prove, definitively, that their guys were the virtuous ones and the other guys were the absolute worst. But news of that certainty would forever elude them. Every new revelation that seemed to damn the people with whom they disagreed would be followed by a new rationalization. For every failed prediction, there would come a mitigating circumstance. They would double down on their most weakly held convictions because the alternative felt unbearable, and the bums across the aisle would follow suit. She wanted to say that the only thing worse than being wrong was having a bottomless need to prove that you never were.

But she didn't tell Lou any of that.

Instead, Maya told Lou what he wanted to hear. She did it because she was the last person on earth who should be instructing Lou Silver on how to live out his days. And she did it because he'd asked her an honest question, and he deserved to hear from her an honest answer.

"Mr. Silver," she said, running her fingers through her hair, "I'm not sure of much of anything anymore."

CHAPTER 14

KATHY
SEPTEMBER 28, 2009

"What are *you* going to do?" Kathy Wing's husband, Albert, said on the other end of the phone. She could hear the TV in the background. "You're going to crack the case?"

Kathy hated to picture Bailiff Steve at his station listening to this call. She wanted to remind Albert that they weren't the only people on the line, but in her experience, "reminding" Albert of things he already knew tended to go badly.

So instead she said, "Tomorrow is closing arguments. And then we deliberate. I'll be home soon."

"*Four months,* Kath," Albert said. "Who's been looking after Sarabeth for four months?"

Sarabeth, their daughter, hadn't even finished her college essays yet, that's how good a job Albert had done at looking after her. But there was no point in fighting about that now.

"I know how much you've been doing without me. I promise I'll make it up to you when I'm back. The trial is almost over."

"What are you even doing there? Administering justice? You're not a lawyer, you're not a judge,

263

you don't know the first thing about any of that stuff. You are one capital-I Idiot if you think you're going to make some kind of a difference."

She sighed. Albert could be tough, that was for sure, but he was right. What *did* she think she was going to do?

The thing, though, was that she'd made a promise. She'd told the State of California that she'd serve. Yes, they were asking more of her than was fair, but if she walked out on her responsibilities, on her word . . . well, what kind of example was that for Sarabeth?

Kathy had seen the victim's mom, Elaine Silver, in the gallery. She'd watched that woman hold her head up high, every day, with Bobby Nock barely twenty feet away. Even yesterday, when her husband, Lou, had said that awful thing. Kathy was not going to blame a woman for the terrible stuff her husband said. If the courtroom ever heard half the stuff *Albert* said . . .

Kathy only hoped she could be as strong as she'd seen Elaine be if anything—God forbid—ever happened to Sarabeth. She felt like she hadn't only promised California that she'd serve—she'd promised Elaine too. And that meant something.

But just try explaining any of that to Albert.

She had a pretty good idea of what he'd say if she tried to talk about her duty to some billionaire's wife.

"Maybe," she said instead, "they'll pick me to be an alternate. Wouldn't that be good? Then I'd be home . . . well, it could be tomorrow."

The judge had told them that at the end of the trial, three alternates would be randomly chosen. The alternate jurors would be dismissed instantly. That meant that Kathy had a one-in-five chance of being home for dinner tomorrow.

"A capital-I Idiot!" Albert said. "They are taking advantage of you, and you don't even have the sense to see it."

It was best to let him blow off steam when he got in one of these moods.

"You tell them you need to be an alternate," he said.

"The judge said that it's random. I don't think—"

"You tell them. You are coming home tomorrow and that is that."

Kathy imagined Sarabeth in her room right then, not finishing her college essays. Maybe it would be best for Kathy to go straight home. Being an alternate wouldn't mean shirking her duties, would it? Three of them would have to be alternates. One of them might as well be her. "Okay."

"Okay?" Albert sounded suspicious.

"I'll tell them."

"They don't need *you* to get to the bottom of all this," Albert went on as if she hadn't already agreed. "Finding the one piece of key evidence that'd been missing the whole time? That's not you, okay? The criminal justice system will not collapse if you come home to your family."

Kathy hoped that Bailiff Steve had nodded off by now. But she doubted it. "I said I'll tell them."

"Just imagine." Albert laughed to himself. *"Chief Inspector goddamned Kathy."*

The next morning in court, Morningstar went through his closing argument pretty quickly. Kathy would have thought that he'd try to put some more heart into it—what poor Jessica must have suffered, what Elaine and her husband had endured—but maybe after yesterday's flaming pile of you-know-what he felt the need to take the temperature down.

He focused their attention on the three pillars of his case: text messages, bloodstains, lies to the police about where Bobby had been at the time of the murder. "When my friend across the aisle there does her best to confuse you," he said, "I'll ask you to hold on to these three basic, fundamental truths. *Texts. Bloodstains. Lies.* She'll say that maybe the defendant was a misunderstood young man. Maybe he was. But . . . *Texts. Bloodstains. Lies.* She'll say that maybe the police rushed to suspect him. Maybe they did. But . . . *Texts. Bloodstains. Lies.*"

He concluded by holding up a nearly life-

266

size photograph of Jessica. It had been taken by a security camera as she left school on the day of her disappearance. It was the last photo ever taken of her.

Kathy had seen this image a dozen times over the course of the trial. Morningstar kept returning to it. Now, he balanced it delicately on a stand. If the trial was a song, the photo was the chorus. The repetition was the whole point.

Kathy could never forget this image, not even if she wanted to. Jessica wore her school uniform. Navy skirt, just below the knee, dark leggings, white button-down shirt. Her blond hair tucked back. Seeing the photo this big, Kathy could even make out the detail on the locket clinging to Jessica's clavicle.

The locket had been a gift from her father, they'd learned. A commemoration of a trip they'd taken years before. The silver locket made Jessica look even younger than she was. It was oddly childlike, Kathy thought, on the neck of a girl diving headfirst into an adulthood for which she was not prepared.

Kathy tried to imagine getting Sarabeth to wear a locket that her father had given her. *Good luck with that.*

Morningstar finished his closing argument and left the image standing there. As if the shot of Jessica in her school clothes and child's locket was what he most wanted them to remember.

Gibson's tactic was just the opposite of the prosecution's. Wherever he'd been certain, she suggested wishy-washiness. Wherever he'd been clear, she sprayed ink into the water. The numbers related to the forensic science took many forms—micropercentages, parts per million, margins of error—and Gibson tossed them around with a dizzying speed.

On the subject of Lou Silver, she took the high road. She never even mentioned what he'd said the day before. Instead, she created a vague cloud of suspicion surrounding his enemies. There were people who wanted to do him and his family harm. It was not *her* legal responsibility to show that they had abducted Jessica. It was the prosecution's responsibility to prove that these people had not.

Gibson always used the word "abducted" in reference to Jessica. Kathy had never once heard her say "killed."

Gibson never explained why she hadn't put on a defense. Not a word about why Bobby Nock hadn't taken the stand.

She was acting like she'd already won the case. Like the prosecution had failed to prove a single thing, and so she had nothing to rebut.

After Gibson thanked the jurors for their time and service, the judge announced that they'd reached the end of the trial.

"I will now reveal which members of the jury have been randomly selected as alternates," he said. "If I call your number, please stand and accompany the bailiff back to my chambers. The State of California thanks you for your service. As do I."

Kathy could feel everyone around her getting tense. She was sure that she was the only one who wanted to be an alternate. Trisha had said the other day that she couldn't imagine sitting through months of this only to get sent home without delivering a verdict. "Too much of a tease for me," Trisha had said.

Kathy would have felt the same way, but Albert had made a good point. If she had to deliver a verdict on the guilt or innocence of Bobby Nock, which way would she vote? "Guilty," maybe? She wasn't the best person to deliver a judgment. Now, Maya—there was somebody itching to get into the jury room and vote. Same with her "friend" Rick. Trisha had said that Maya and Rick were sleeping together, but Kathy didn't think it was any of her business. Or any of Trisha's, for that matter.

Then there was Wayne. He should definitely be an alternate too. He'd been getting jitterier, staring out the window for long silent spells. Last week he'd needed twenty-five minutes to "soak up some sun," as he'd put it, before he'd get on the bus to court. Bailiff Steve had had to call the judge and tell him they were running late. She didn't know how much more Wayne could take. Or how much more they could take of him.

The judge read the names.

"Juror number 906," he said.

Arnold Dean stood. He looked like he was hyperventilating.

"Juror number 552," the judge said.

Kathy nearly got whiplash turning to see Enrique Navarro stand. Enrique took the news without much reaction.

That left only one spot between her and Wayne.

"Juror number 873."

Kellan Bragg stood.

All three of them followed Bailiff Steve to the door.

Kathy was stunned. It had all happened so fast. She hadn't gotten a chance to say anything, to explain her situation. There was no good reason to send those three home instead of her.

Before she thought about it, she raised her hand.

Everyone stared.

"Juror number 690?" the judge said. "If you'd like to speak to me about something, we can do so in my chambers."

Kathy lowered her hand sheepishly. *What an idiot.*

"Before your deliberations begin," the judge told the now-twelve jurors, "we will randomly select one of you to serve as foreperson. All communications to this court—that is, to me— must be delivered by handwritten notes, on slips we'll provide for you, from your assigned foreperson. Your foreperson will be charged with managing the conversation you'll have in the jury room, and running the process by which you deliberate. The only ground rules assigned by this court are as follows: One. All deliberations must be conducted inside the jury room, with all twelve jurors present. That is to say, no side conversations, and no conversations at night, back at the hotel. You will deliberate in that room, all together, until you reach a verdict. Is that clear?"

Kathy nodded.

"Two," the judge said, "there is only one charge against the defendant. Murder in the first degree. You may find him guilty of this charge, or you may find him not guilty. But any decision you make must be unanimous. If you have any questions about the definitions of the charge, or about any of your instructions, you can request further explanations by way of the handwritten cards, sent by your foreperson, as discussed. Is *that* clear?"

Kathy nodded again. She just wanted to get through these instructions so she could go back to the judge's chambers and clear up this mistake.

The judge opened a manila folder and tore open

a sealed envelope inside. "Your jury foreperson will be . . ."

He removed a single sheet of paper from the envelope. "Juror number 690."

"I can't stay here," Kathy said to the judge in his chambers a few minutes later. "I need to be home with my family."

The judge leaned back in his creaky chair. He'd taken off his robe already, revealing a dark suit underneath. Kathy had never seen him without the robe before. He seemed strangely naked, despite having a suit on.

"If you have childcare responsibilities that would prevent you from serving, you should have mentioned them earlier."

Kathy didn't want to lie to a judge. "It's not that."

"What is it?"

How was she supposed to make him understand? "Most of the jurors want to stay. Why can't the ones who want to stay, stay, and the ones who want to go, go?"

The judge scratched at his balding scalp. "The long answer is, because that would make the pool of jurors self-selecting, which would prejudice the results. The short answer is, because I said so."

Kathy listened to her own frustrated sigh, and realized that this must be what Sarabeth experienced in the face of Kathy's own pronouncements.

"It's normal to feel nervous," the judge said gently. "You have a big responsibility in front of you."

"That's just it. I don't know about all this stuff. My husband said—well, this is too big a decision to put on me."

"Did you ever think that it's precisely *because* you 'don't know about this stuff' that the decision has to be yours?"

What was wrong with this guy? *Talk about a capital-I Idiot.*

"I've already dismissed the alternates," the judge went on. "So if you leave before a verdict is reached, I will have to declare a mistrial. And if you don't have a binding reason to leave, I can hold you in contempt of court."

When Kathy finally got to the jury room, the others were all standing around.

Why weren't any of them sitting?

"Do we have assigned seats?" Fran asked.

They were all looking at Kathy for an answer. "I don't know."

"Maybe we should sit in order of our numbers," Fran said.

"I don't think it matters," Rick said.

"In court we sit according to our numbers," Trisha said.

273

"Guys," Wayne said, "it's our room. We can make our own rules."

They looked at Kathy again. She felt panicked. For the last fifteen years she'd been a pharmacist, which meant that she'd become experienced at calming people whose prescriptions for anti-anxiety meds had run out. But the only people she'd ever organized or led were her daughter's annoying friends.

"Let me read the judge's instructions again," Kathy said.

"Oh, for fuck's sake," Wayne barked. He walked to the door and, to everyone's shock, opened it. "Bailiff Steve?" he called into the hallway.

Bailiff Steve appeared. "What's wrong?"

"Does it matter where we sit?"

Bailiff Steve looked like he was amused by the question. "I'm not allowed to answer any legal questions. But . . . the room is yours. You run things in the room however you like. As long as you obey the judge's instructions."

"Thanks," Wayne said. And then Bailiff Steve shut the door.

"Everybody take a seat," Wayne said. He kept his chair by the window.

They sat in a random order. Fran looked grumpy about it, and Kathy didn't know what she could do to make Fran feel better. Instinctively, she wanted to. But then all eyes were on her again—everybody was waiting for instructions.

"Maybe," Rick suggested, "we should take a vote."

Kathy distributed index cards from a pile that had been left for them on the table. She experienced a satisfying release in tearing open the plastic wrapping on the pens. Passing them around, she felt for a brief, calming moment like she was back handing out after-school crafts to Sarabeth's old playgroup.

"Okay," Kathy said. "Okay. We'll do a blind vote. Everybody write yours down. Pass them here."

Nobody moved. Kathy wasn't sure what they were waiting for.

She looked around for guidance.

"Everyone write either 'guilty' or 'not guilty,' " Rick said, gently. He was helping. "And then Kathy can read the results, and we'll see where we are."

Kathy turned to her own paper. She had no idea what to write. Who was she to say who'd killed Jessica Silver? How had she even gotten herself into this mess?

She peeked over at Trisha's paper. Trisha sat in the adjacent seat, her index card covered by her forearm. When Kathy craned her neck, she could see it.

She wrote down the same verdict Trisha had.

At least Trisha seemed like she knew what she was doing.

275

. . .

A minute later, Maya raised her hand. "It was me."

Kathy could not believe it. The rest of them were all in agreement.

What in the world was Maya thinking?

Rick looked devastated. As if Maya had betrayed him personally. Which, since they had their own thing going, maybe she had.

"No way," Jae said.

"It's really just me?" Maya said. "I figured some of you would think he was guilty. But . . . all of you?"

Yes. All of us. Once Maya realized how unpopular her position was, she'd have to change her vote. How crazy would she have to be to argue with all eleven of them?

"Trisha," Maya said, "you don't have any doubts about this?"

Trisha looked incredulous. "A doubt or two? Sure. But, I mean . . . come on."

Maya turned to Rick, who looked away. "I would have imagined that the jurors of color would be more alarmed about what we saw in court yesterday."

"What the hell does that mean?" Trisha said.

Kathy thought she might just die.

Maya seemed hurt. "I'm on your side."

"Because I'm black," Trisha said, "and Bobby Nock is black, and Lou Silver is a racist, I should vote 'not guilty'?"

"No," Maya said. She looked to Rick again for help. She didn't find any.

"Maybe," Kathy said, trying to do *something* to take the temperature down, "Maya can explain why she thinks Bobby Nock is innocent. And we can answer her points."

She felt like she was defusing an argument between Sarabeth and her cousins. Albert was no good when the kids got upset, he'd always get to yelling himself. So at least this was something Kathy knew how to do.

Maya shook her head. "Other way around."

"What?" Fran said.

"The burden of proof is on the prosecution," Maya said. "You tell me why you're so sure he did it. And then we can debate those points."

There was a chorus of annoyed sighs from around the table.

"Are you telling me," Jae said, "that you can stare at that guy in the courtroom, and say to yourself, 'This guy looks innocent'?" At the word "look," a few people shifted uncomfortably in their seats.

Kathy instinctively turned to Rick and Trisha—did they take that as a racial slur? Kathy couldn't tell. But if the jury's two black members didn't think that Jae's comment about the black defendant's "look" was racist, then it wasn't.

"What about his 'look'?" Maya said. "What do you mean by that?"

If the awkwardness had been just bearable before, it wasn't anymore. What gave Maya the right to do this? They were supposed to be having a civilized conversation.

Jae made a *can-you-believe-this-lady* face in Trisha's direction.

"The road to hell," Trisha said sadly, "is paved by white people trying to help."

The tension was thick. Kathy realized that she was about to cry, and squeezed her hands into tight fists to try to keep her tears at bay.

"When I look at Bobby Nock," Maya said, "all I see is an innocent man."

CHAPTER 15

EAST JESUS
NOW

East Jesus, so Lou Silver informed her, was some kind of unincorporated hippie art enclave on the other side of the Salton Sea. Situated in the middle of the desert, it lacked legal status, much less an official police force. Maya wondered who would even have the authority to arrest someone there, were anyone patrolling it for parole breakers, which no one was. Lou gave her the GPS coordinates and remarked that it was a very good place for a very bad man to get himself lost.

After a seven-hour drive, Maya turned off the highway onto a single-lane road, and then off that onto a barely marked dirt path. The sun was just setting as she drove slowly through the darkening plumes of dust. The Tesla sedan wasn't exactly built for off-roading. The electric car felt unsteady on the rocky desert ground.

She flicked on her brights as the last daylight disappeared. Only a few feet of barren landscape was visible before her. For someone born and raised in New Mexico, Maya found herself surprisingly unnerved by this stretch of nighttime desert. She reminded herself that this week alone,

279

she'd already been on the wrong side of a police interrogation room and inside a colony of sex offenders. She could probably handle an artists' commune.

East Jesus's nearest "town," of sorts, was Slab City, but its inviting pack of mobile trailers was well behind her. The lights in her rearview mirror disappeared as she explored ahead into the darkness.

And then she saw what seemed to be a glowing sprawl of Christmas lights ahead. They blinked red, green, blue, and yellow from atop some kind of construction. Driving closer, she began to make out a few structures closer to the ground. Some were shaped like tin sheds. Others looked like gigantic piles of trash. The vague contours of the tallest one came into view. It couldn't be, she thought, what it looked like. . . .

Maya stopped the car.

It was a pile of doll heads about four stories high. They were illuminated only by the holiday-colored flickering lights at the top.

And bizarrely, there was a doorway at the bottom. The door was open.

She got out of the car.

"Steady now," came a man's gravelly voice from behind her. "Turn around. Real slow."

Maya spun to find a red-bearded man dressed in a stained gray jumpsuit. He wore a headlamp with an LED light, which blazed into Maya's eyes. It was hard to see the man's face, but there was no way she could miss the shotgun he was pointing directly at her.

She raised her hands.

"I don't want to shoot you," he said.

"That's reassuring," Maya said. "I don't want to get shot."

He smiled. A smart-ass always recognized another of its kind.

"What's that?" he growled.

Maya realized she was still holding her car key. "Car key. I'm going to drop it. So don't, I don't know, freak out when it hits the ground."

"I'll do my best."

She dropped the key. She flinched at the sound when it smacked against the hard desert.

The man used his headlamp to illuminate the ground at her feet.

Thankfully, he pointed the gun away from her. "Are you a cop?"

She used one foot to tilt the car key toward him so he could see the Tesla logo. "No."

"You don't look like you're here to rob us."

"Do you guys have something out here worth robbing?"

He appeared to think this one through. "Doesn't everybody?"

"I'm looking for someone."

The man gestured to the encampment behind

him. "We have rules. Nobody in or out after dark."

"I'm sorry. I didn't know."

"It's on the website."

"I didn't know you had a website."

He made an irritated face. "Instagram. Snapchat. Facebook. We got 'em all."

"No Twitter?"

He shook his head. "Fuck Twitter."

"I had a feeling that you and I would get along."

He took a long look at her clothes, her car, her comfortable leather flats. "Who are you?"

"My name is Maya Seale."

He didn't recognize her name, which was a good sign. Wired for Internet though this place clearly was, it didn't seem like this guy—or the folks around here—would be keeping up on the news out of L.A.

"What do I call you?" she asked.

He considered his answer carefully, and then smiled. " 'Call me Ishmael.' "

"Okay 'Ishmael,' " she said. "I'm looking for a man named Bobby Nock."

"It's from *Moby-Dick*."

"I know."

"There's no Bobby Nock here."

"He might be using a different name."

"Then it sounds like he might not want to talk to you."

"He does," she said. "He just doesn't know it yet."

Ishmael's light flashed across Maya's eyes every time he moved his head. The effect was disorienting.

"How do you know this Bobby guy?" he said.

Maya thought for a moment. "I got him out of jail once."

It wasn't a lie. Not exactly. Ishmael seemed satisfied by her explanation.

"Come on," he said. "I'll take you into the camp."

He released his grip on the gun, retracting it safely across his chest, then walked past her car toward the flickering Christmas lights.

Maya followed the spilled light from his headlamp. "What *is* that?" she said, gesturing up ahead.

"That," he said, "is East Jesus."

East Jesus, Maya learned, was an unregulated collection of large-scale art projects inhabited by their artists and their artists' drinking buddies. Had she seen *the doll house?* The man who'd made that apparently lived in it, with a few helpers. Some folks lived in tents beside their projects, especially if they helped out in the camp's central structure, which was almost like a real building. It had walls made of drywall, and a roof, and a makeshift stage with a grand piano for the musicians who drifted through. They had a decent lighting rig, Ishmael assured her, for the people who came by to shoot music videos.

"People shoot music videos here?" she asked.

"Sure." He took her past a wall composed entirely of broken old televisions, spray-painted with single-word messages. "GOVERNMENT." "TRUST." "FASHION." "KILL."

"I mean," he continued, "this place is pretty fucking weird."

He sounded proud.

Behind the broken-TV wall there was a firepit. About two dozen people were milling around the fire, drinking, smoking pot, or just lying on the ground, staring rapt at the flames. Some of them had the wide-eyed looks of people tripping on hallucinogens. Others were calmly discussing dinner.

The volume of drugs on offer explained the security concerns. It wasn't clear whether most of the inhabitants were dealers taking sabbaticals to make art, or artists taking sabbaticals to deal drugs. The lines, around here, were blurry.

"This is Maya," Ishmael said to the group by the fire.

"No visitors after dark!" barked a woman. She was white, had a shaved head, and was wearing something like a toga. Or maybe it was just a bedsheet.

"It's cool," Ishmael said. "*She's* cool." He was still casually carrying the shotgun. No one seemed to give it a second look.

"I'm looking for an old friend," Maya said.

284

"He used to go by 'Bobby.' Black, mid-thirties. Glasses. Real skinny . . . at least he used to be. It's been a while."

The woman exchanged a glance with Ishmael.

"Can you take me to him?" Maya asked.

Ishmael and the woman seemed to silently negotiate whether doing this would be in violation of some equally unspoken code.

But after a moment, they both froze. Ishmael's eyes locked onto something over Maya's shoulder.

From the other side of the fire, a man in dark jeans and a red-checked button-down came toward them carrying a bucket, the liquid sloshing over the lip as he walked. He was even skinnier than Maya remembered.

As soon as he saw Maya, he stopped and stared. The light from the fire danced beside him.

Maya realized they'd never actually spoken to each other.

"Hi, Bobby," she said.

"Hi."

"Can we talk?"

Slowly he set the bucket down. "Maya Seale," he said. "I just can't imagine what we'd have to talk about."

Ishmael led her and Bobby to some kind of tepee. When he pulled back the flap and she saw what was inside, she wondered whether she was

285

on hallucinogens too. The tent was filled with teddy bears arranged into dioramas of violent acts. Some of the bears held tiny toy guns, some held knives; one of them even had a bow and arrow. They were lit by a few spotlights pointed upward from the wood floor. Garish shadows of murderous animals loomed across the tepee walls.

Could you get a contact high from acid?

"How did you find me?" Bobby said after Ishmael left. His voice was hushed, as if he was afraid that even here, someone was listening.

"Rick Leonard."

"He told you where I was?"

Maya tried to figure out how to read this response. "He told Lou Silver."

Bobby nodded. Like this is what he'd expected. Or feared. "So you're working for Lou now too?"

Maya thought for a moment. "I honestly can't tell."

He took that as affirmation. "All of you—Lou, Rick, everyone—you're all just going to hunt me to the ends of the earth, forever? Like I'm Frankenstein's monster?"

"He fled to the arctic," Maya said. "At least you ended up somewhere warmer."

He almost managed a smile. But not quite. "I used to teach that book."

"To Jessica?"

"At the school."

"Rick isn't hunting you anymore."

She examined his expression carefully—did he really not know what had happened over the past three days? "Rick is dead."

Either his instantaneous flash of surprise was genuine, or else he was quite the actor.

"When?"

"Three days ago."

Bobby didn't seem overcome with sadness at the death of the man who'd tried to put him back in jail. But he did look concerned. His brow furrowed. Lit from below, he looked like he was listening to a ghost story at a campfire. "How?"

"There was a reunion. All the jurors met at the Omni Hotel for the trial's tenth anniversary. Someone killed Rick at the reunion."

He crossed his arms in front of him and began pacing the tent. He struck her as someone who'd learned to be careful about what he said, and that he shouldn't give her anything unless he knew exactly what she already had. Maya couldn't blame him for not trusting her.

"You think," he said, "that I killed Rick Leonard?"

"No. But Lou Silver does."

"That sounds about right. What do the cops think?"

"The cops think *I* did it."

He peered at her as if suddenly she had become the most fascinating person in the world. *"You?"*

"Yeah."

His mouth formed a strange and bitter smile. He seemed almost tickled by how utterly the tables had turned. "In the future," he said, "everyone will be charged with someone else's murder for fifteen minutes."

"Any tips?"

"Yeah." He toed his boot against the floorboards. "Make sure you get a good jury."

Maya figured that was a compliment. "I need your help."

"How could I help?"

"I need to know what Rick told you when he found you in Miracle."

"You know I broke parole. You know what'll happen if anyone finds out I'm here."

"I do."

"So why should I help you?"

"Because you owe me one."

The lights carved sharp shadows into Bobby's face. This close, she could see the lines that had formed there. Traces of prison, traces of persecution, traces of having been hunted. There was a scar on his jawline that hadn't been there before.

This guy had gone to hell and back. Who knew what that could do to someone?

Ten years ago, she'd thought he was a decent young guy who'd made a couple of really bad decisions. But whatever he might have been then, she realized that she had no idea who he was now.

"I'm genuinely impressed that you have the fucking gall to say that to me," he told her.

"You read Rick's book, didn't you? You know that I convinced eleven people to set you free."

He didn't try to deny it. "Do you remember the day Lou Silver testified? In my trial?"

"Yes."

"And how after he said that 'black devil' thing, it was my lawyer's turn to put up our defense? But she didn't?"

"Yes. I remember all of that."

"It was because of you."

Maya thought she must have misheard him. "What?"

He smiled strangely, like he was recalling a dream in which the laws of physics had been broken. The kind of nightmare that only made sense to the dreamer. "We had a whole defense prepared. Character witnesses, people who could say they were sure I hadn't touched Jessica. Old friends. My brothers. Even another teacher. We even had an alternate theory of the crime. But my lawyer and I, we kept debating what to do."

Maya could imagine what those witnesses would have said in court, because after the trial she'd heard all of them speak on television. It had been shocking to learn so much more about Bobby after she'd already rendered a verdict.

Not until she was at home had she heard Bobby's parents talk about his childhood in Virginia. Not until then had she seen his UVA roommate talk about the pop band they'd been in; Bobby had played piano. At last, Maya had learned why Bobby had moved to L.A. in the first place: An older friend from UVA was teaching at Jessica's school and put him up for a job as a music teacher. He accepted, only on arrival there was some mix-up with the school and the position disappeared so he'd become a part-time English teacher instead. He'd only taught one class, four days a week. He'd tutored piano freelance on the weekends for extra cash.

"If you'd put up all those witnesses," she said, "we'd have expected you to testify yourself. It looks bad, to a jury, to send a bunch of friends and family to defend your good name but not to do so yourself."

"That's exactly what my lawyer said."

"But if you'd testified yourself, you'd have opened yourself up to the prosecution's evidence of prior bad acts."

"You heard about those?"

"After the trial. You beat up a kid when you were in high school. Felony assault, but you were a juvenile, you got community service."

" 'Felony assault'? Two older kids tried to take my wallet. We fought, and somehow I won. I still don't know how that was possible. But they both said I'd started it, so I was the one who got arrested."

"Because you didn't testify, any mention of your previous conviction was inadmissible. That was a smart move on your lawyer's part."

"The whole time, we weren't sure what we were going to do. On the one hand, we wanted to tell everyone who I really was. And what I think happened to Jessica. On the other hand, putting me up there would open the door to the 'assault' conviction, which seemed like it might go badly, and I mean, really badly. Up until that day, we still weren't sure what the best move was. But then Lou Silver spouted that racist bullshit . . . and Gibson saw how you reacted."

"The jury?"

"You."

Maya didn't understand what he was trying to say.

"Gibson leaned in and whispered in my ear, 'All we need is one. And I think Maya Seale is our one.' "

Maya tried to imagine what the expression on her face had been. She tried to remember if she'd shifted in her chair; if she'd gasped, as so many of the others had. She didn't know. She realized that she'd been so focused on Lou in that moment that it had never occurred to her that Bobby's lawyer could have been just as focused on her.

"I don't . . ." Maya stammered. It never

291

occurred to her that even before the deliberations, she was already affecting the trial's outcome.

"You know how to play Hearts?" Bobby said. "Actually, I still have no idea how to play Hearts. Gibson does. Did. She said we were going to 'shoot the moon.' I guess it's a risky move that either works very, very well—or you lose in a second?" He snapped his fingers. "I figured that given the stakes . . . fuck it."

It seemed that Bobby Nock's lawyer had a better eye for people like Maya than Maya did. It didn't feel good, to be so thoroughly known by someone who'd only seen her face across a courtroom. It was no comfort to learn that she was an identifiable type: the idealist. The crusader.

The rube.

"Why are you telling me this?" she said.

"Because if I agree to help you, it won't be because I owe you shit. You didn't stick your neck out for me—you did exactly what you were supposed to do. What you were *picked* to do. Believe it or not, there are people in my life for whom I'm honest-to-God grateful. But you are not one of them."

Maya did not need a pat on the back from him. What she needed was information. "So if you won't help me out of gratitude, why will you?"

"Because I didn't kill Jessica."

It took Maya a moment to understand that this wasn't merely a statement. It was a pact.

"I didn't kill Rick," she offered in return. And without another word, they reached an agreement.

"What happened when Rick found you?" she asked. "Why did you run, after?"

Then he did something she hadn't seen him do in all of the hundreds of hours that they'd spent together, silently, in a courtroom.

He laughed. The sound was higher than his speaking voice, like a child's. His laugh sounded like it came from a part of his lungs that didn't get much use. "Let's take a walk."

The first thing Bobby did was to show her evidence supporting his alibi for the night of Rick's death. As they strolled across the encampment, he told her that he'd been right here in East Jesus. One of the photographers in the camp had been taking photos all week. Rick took Maya by the photographer's tent and showed her the digitally time-stamped photos. Bobby's face was visible in the shots.

Provided the time stamps were accurate, the only way that Bobby could have killed Rick was if he'd been able to make the five- to seven-hour drive to L.A., commit a murder, and then make the five- to seven-hour drive back in the span of seventy minutes.

Bobby's own tent was near the tower of dolls' heads. The tent was just big enough for a sleeping bag, a box of water, a flashlight, and a few decorative touches.

"I'd offer you a seat," he said, gesturing to the lack of the chairs. "But . . ."

Hung on the tent's wall, beside the sleeping bag, Maya saw a crayon drawing of an alligator. The alligator was bright red, with orange teeth. Its incongruity with the surroundings couldn't help but catch her eye. For a second she thought Bobby might have taken up crayon art, but then realized that it must be the work of a child. He had two younger brothers, she remembered. Did either of them have kids? It was as if Bobby had preserved only this one remnant of what could have been a normal familial life.

She had seen Bobby's family in the courtroom. His parents attended every day, sitting on the opposite side from Elaine Silver. They'd been more visibly distraught than Elaine, or maybe they just hadn't been hiding their grief. Maya had tried to fathom the depth of their suffering. Lou and Elaine Silver's daughter had vanished from them in an instant. Jerry and Alana Nock's son was slowly taken away from them before their eyes, day by day, over months. Maya didn't know which was worse.

"Rick Leonard didn't have anything on me," he said, finally answering her question. "He showed up at my trailer in Miracle one day, all ready to interrogate me. To finally get me to confess, or something. I told him to go away."

Maya had trouble believing this. "So then why did you run?"

"Because he was going to keep coming. Him and everyone else. He said with the ten-year anniversary coming up, there were going to be specials. More press. I wasn't hard to find. It was all going to start all over again. So . . . I just couldn't take it. Not again. One of the guys in Miracle told me about this place." Bobby shook his head. "Pause a moment to think about how shitty my life has become: I'm taking real estate recommendations from pedophiles."

Maya searched his face: Could this really be the truth?

Rick hadn't even told Bobby what he'd found?

"You could have gone home."

"Home?"

"Your parents. Your brothers."

"I think they've been through enough."

"It seems like you've been through more than enough yourself."

"Have I?" Bobby kicked the toe of his boot into the hard dirt. "I can think of someone who went through a lot worse." He looked up. "Jessica."

And then, as if it was the most normal thing in the world to do, Maya asked Bobby a question that she'd wondered about—hypothesized about, strategized about—for ten years.

"Bobby," she said, "who do *you* think killed Jessica?"

He smiled grimly. "It's been so long since anybody's asked me that."

He looked over at the child's alligator drawing on the wall. Like something in it was melting something inside him.

"Her dad used to hit her," Bobby said.

Maya could feel the breath catching in her throat. "What are you talking about?"

"She showed me the bruises. He hit Elaine too, she said. It had been going on forever. Anything could set him off. If Jessica left the lights on at night. Or turned the wrong lights off. Or was late for dinner. Anything. I think I was the first person Jessica told. She was terrified of him. Shit, I've never even *met* the guy and I'm terrified of him. You grow up in a house like that—he is the gaseous exploding star, and everyone else, her included, is a barren rock planet. That was her metaphor, actually. I remember her saying it, right after she showed me the cigarette burns on . . ."

He stopped. As if he wanted to protect Maya from knowing the worst.

"She said her mom got it as bad as she did. But Elaine fucking Silver wasn't going to do anything about it. She was in deep, taking that shit for decades."

Maya's mind was spinning. She'd often wondered whether Lou was hiding anything. When something happened to a teenage girl, everyone's thoughts went to the father.

Statistically it made sense. But in all this time there hadn't been so much as a word about any abuse.

She tried to picture frail, sunken Lou Silver committing such horrible acts of violence. He didn't seem capable of it. But then, how many abusers looked the part?

"Why didn't you say this at the trial?"

"I had no evidence other than my word. And if I took the stand and swore that Lou Silver physically abused his daughter . . . well, what was it you were just saying?"

Maya understood. He'd have opened up the door to his previous conviction. Testifying about the abuse Jessica suffered might have been accurate, but it would have been bad legal strategy.

Sometimes the truth was an especially poor defense.

"You know what the worst part is?" Bobby continued. "That's how it all started, between us. Jessica needed to tell someone what was going on at home. She was scared, she was confused, she didn't trust *anybody*. . . . But for some reason she trusted me." He squeezed his hand tightly, like he was trying to break his own bones. "And look what I did."

"That's when you started spending time together . . . alone?"

Bobby nodded. "Here was this poor girl living

through hell and you know what I thought? I thought I could help."

He shook his head ruefully. "You ever think about all the fucked-up shit we end up doing because we tell ourselves that we're *helping?*"

Maya wished she thought about this less. "Yeah."

"I told myself I was *helping* when I took her for coffee after school. I was so sure I was *helping* when I told her to go to the counselors, talk to the principal, hell, talk to the cops. . . . But she kept saying no. She made me promise I wouldn't tell a soul. She said, 'Who is anyone going to believe, you or my dad? What could anyone do?' I don't know if she was wrong. You think somebody like Lou Silver gets arrested? You think somebody like Lou Silver goes to jail? No way. Worst thing that could've happened to him is that Elaine would finally bolt with Jessica. Which I also advised. 'Tell your mom that if you both stay there,' I said, 'one of you is going to get killed. Take your mom, get in a car—hire a private plane, you can afford it—and go.' But she wouldn't leave without her mom. And her mom wouldn't leave. Her mom said it would be okay. Her mom said she was handling it, Lou would stop. No one would get killed. . . ."

He let that last word reverberate through the gloom.

"So what did I do? I promised not to tell. To

keep her talking. I tried to get her to go to the counselors. We kept meeting. I was new to L.A. I didn't know a lot of people. I was lonely. Coffees happened more and more. I mean, what else was I doing after school? She talked about what she wanted from her life—a little town somewhere. Quiet, away from the city. A farm, maybe. She was going to have kids and they'd have a nice dad, a good dad, the opposite dad from the one she'd had. And it wasn't all heavy. Did you know she was funny? People see her photo on TV, or they hear all these facts about her life—they don't know that she was actually just really funny. She hated the water. Strangest thing about her— terrified of getting eaten by sharks or something. I guess she used to be on the swim team but then she stopped, on account of the cuts and bruises— she couldn't put on a bathing suit—but she lied and told her parents she was still swimming. I'd see her on the weekends and before I'd drop her off at home she'd dunk her hair in the sink so it was wet. She'd tell her dad she was at the beach all day. Why the beach? I never knew.

"Then we were texting. It was playful, joking around. I knew I shouldn't be texting with a student, but I got off on the attention. How pathetic is that? I needed the attention of an abused fifteen-year-old to feel good about myself. Maybe she was the first person who looked up to me. And I said, 'No one is getting hurt here. I haven't done anything wrong.' So I kept spending time with her. The dirty texts, the dirty photos—they were a joke. She took my phone one day. *She* sent all those sexual messages back and forth between our phones. When I finally figured out she had mine, and I found her after school and she showed me what she'd done—she was laughing so hard. 'You're so fucked if anyone sees these.' She thought it was hysterical. What a practical joke. I deleted the whole chain from my phone, but I guess she left them on hers. And then, later, once the cops got hold of them . . ."

Maya remembered a detail from the trial: All the really explicit texts between Bobby and Jessica had been sent on the same day. His explanation was oddly plausible. Even if he was only offering it now.

"Can you imagine," he said, "if I had offered that story in my defense? Would anyone have believed me? Would *you*? It was better to act like I actually had sent those messages. But that was the whole problem with my defense: Our relationship *was* inappropriate. I admit that. It was just so much stranger than we could explain.

"Like the car stuff! That was the most ironic part, the stains from her nosebleeds, the hair in the front seat. Do you have any idea how much fucking time we spent in my car? Just driving around? It was so much more than the prosecutor even thought. L.A. is thirty percent roads. Did

300

you know that? Jessica told me, said her dad talked about it all the time. So we'd drive. And text. I still don't even know how those tiny drops of blood got in the trunk. I guess my lawyer was right and the evidence lab really did screw up. But we spent so much time in that car, I'm sure her DNA was everywhere. What happened between us was wrong. It was my fault. And then one day . . . she was gone."

Maya was damned if she didn't believe him. She always had, hadn't she? He'd failed Jessica terribly. He knew it. But then, everyone else had too. Jessica's parents, Jessica's teachers, and even Maya, who, if Bobby's story was true, was currently working with Jessica's abuser.

"Did Lou Silver kill his daughter?" Maya whispered.

"That was the defense we would have put up. An 'affirmative defense'? Maybe Lou found out about Jessica and me. Maybe she told Lou that she'd told me about him. They never found her body, right? Well, who has the resources to make a body disappear? *Really* disappear?"

There had never been any physical evidence—not a stitch—that implicated Lou. But then, that was Bobby's argument, wasn't it? To believe that Bobby killed Jessica, one would have to believe that he'd done a poor job of it, leaving blood in his own car. To believe that Lou killed Jessica, one would have to believe that he'd done such a good job of it that no one had even suspected him in ten long years.

Maya knew that she could believe Bobby's story about the abuse without believing his accusation that Lou was the killer. It was the same line of thinking that she'd applied to Bobby—he'd done something terrible, but that did not *necessarily* make him a killer.

Going back and forth between Lou and Bobby, Maya felt trapped in some horrible, endless spiral. Lou and Bobby were the two most important men in Jessica's life, and neither had protected her.

"You never said any of that, because . . ." This was the part that somehow made Maya even more sick to her stomach. "Because of me."

He laughed with a bitterness that had fermented over the years. "You know what gets me sometimes? The justice system worked. I did something inappropriate with a teenager and I went to jail for it. People like you talked about what an injustice it all was, but when you think about it, really . . . what was the injustice?"

Maya looked at their surroundings. This strange place did not look like any kind of justice that she understood.

"You have to tell people this."

Bobby looked at her like she was an idiot. "Who? Why?"

Maya felt confounded. This accusation was too explosive to keep to themselves. And yet . . . Bobby wasn't wrong. There was a reason he hadn't gone public. They could tell the police, but what would the police do? The only crime here was an old and unprovable one. They could talk to the press and attempt to shame Lou Silver publicly, but again, they had no evidence save the testimony of a man who most people believed had murdered Lou's daughter.

Lou and Bobby could go on accusing each other of atrocities for the rest of their lives and it wouldn't make any difference. Nothing would ever bring back what they'd lost.

"So what are you going to do?" she asked him. "Run forever?" What he'd done was wrong. But that didn't mean he deserved to be persecuted endlessly for it. Not while there were people out there whose crimes, even against Jessica herself, had been even worse than his. "There are people who care about you."

"*Who?*"

"I watched your family in the courtroom. I stared at your mom for hundreds of hours, trying to imagine how anyone could be as strong as she was to sit there every day. You can't tell me she ever stopped believing in you, or that your father ever stopped trusting you. Don't you think they miss you? Don't you think they want you close?"

Bobby gave her a withering sigh. "You have no idea . . . You think you know me so well but you don't. You have no idea who I am."

She looked away, her eyes falling on the crayon alligator drawing. The long red body. The orange teeth bared and ready. The childlike attempt at terror seemed such a sad contrast to the drugged-out horror show of their surroundings.

She gestured to the drawing. "I know you like alligators."

Bobby managed a laugh. He wasn't going to discuss the drawing with her. Not with someone whom, even after ten years, he barely knew.

"I thought about writing to you," he said instead. "After the trial."

"To say what?"

"That I was sorry I'd ruined your life too."

"What I did . . . it wasn't for you."

" 'You didn't ruin my life' would have been a nice thing to say just then."

"I did it for a principle."

He raised an eyebrow. "How's that working out?"

There was no one, Maya thought, to whom she'd less like to defend the high priority of principle. The man hunched in a small tent in the middle of the desert was either the victim of a horrific injustice or the perpetrator of one.

Or both.

And yet somehow, he'd found a sense of calm about the justice of it all. Or maybe that wasn't quite right. Maybe Bobby had just moved on from worrying about "justice" at all.

"I thought about writing to you too," she said.

"To say what?"

Maya shrugged regretfully. "That's why I never wrote."

Bobby sighed as if he was lost in the grim memories of his former life. "Was everyone there? At the hotel?"

"Everyone?"

"The jury."

She nodded.

"How are they?"

She realized that he didn't know any of them. They were all just faces he'd stared at for hour after hour, day after day, month after month. He'd probably learned their names on television.

"What must you have thought of us?" she said.

He frowned. "I hoped you were trying to do your best."

A sadness washed over her. Despite Bobby's understandable bitterness, this was the most generous thing he could have said.

And it broke her heart.

The moment was interrupted by the rising sound of commotion outside the tent.

Opening the canvas flap, they found chaos. Across the campsite, people were running in every direction at once. Bobby led her into the fray, and together they saw what was freaking everybody out: five black SUVs, headlights

305

blaring, racing toward the camp like an invading army.

Headlights sliced across the dark. As the SUVs got closer, people put their hands over their eyes, shielding themselves from the painful lights.

Ishmael appeared beside her. He held his shotgun at his waist.

Then the SUVs were upon them.

A few of the artists fled back to the tents. Two others had drawn guns.

The SUVs turned, forming a horizontal wall. It was only then that she saw the BuzzFeed News logos on their sides.

Ishmael raised his shotgun.

"No!" Maya yelled. "No guns!"

"Fuck that," he said. The SUVs came to a stop. Dirt burst into the night sky.

"Please!" Maya placed her fingers gently on the barrel of his shotgun. "They're not cops. They're reporters. They're not here for you."

"They came here for *you?*"

Cameramen poured out of the SUVs.

Maya glanced at Bobby, who was frozen in the lights.

He directed his terrified, bitter glare at Maya.

And then he ran.

He was quickly enveloped in the panicked crowd.

She needed to chase after him—but she also needed the confrontation between the stoned-out-of-their-mind desert people and overzealous reporters to end peaceably. The camera lights beamed across the shotguns to Maya's left and right. She shouted a plea for calm. No one was listening. Given the commotion, they wouldn't be able to hear her even if they were.

There was only one option. She raised her hands and stepped into the no-man's-land between the press and the guardians of East Jesus.

One step at a time, she felt her way across the dirt.

Five cameras trained on her.

"Everybody!" she screamed, turning back to the artists. "Let's take a deep breath. No one wants to hurt anyone. No one needs to get hurt."

She addressed Ishmael: "They're reporters. They're here for me."

He didn't seem convinced.

"Is Bobby Nock with you?" one of the reporters shouted.

"Bobby Nock is in there," Maya yelled. "But if you barge in after him, my friends here will feel threatened, and they will be within their legal rights to protect themselves. Some of them are armed."

She addressed the artists: "Friends. I really think it would be smart to lower your guns. These people aren't here for you. If someone gets hurt, we're all in a ton of trouble."

Finally, Ishmael lowered his shotgun.

Seeing what he'd done, his compatriots followed suit.

"Motherfuckers can't come in here," Ishmael yelled.

She shouted to the reporters: "This camp is private property. You go in—they have a legal right, California state law being what it is, to shoot you." This was total bullshit, but she figured the reporters wouldn't know.

The reporter answered: "Can we talk to Bobby Nock?"

"You going in there is a nonstarter. I'll go in, find Bobby, see if he'll talk to you. I can deliver a message."

No objection from the press. She addressed the camp: "That okay with you?"

"Only you come in," Ishmael said.

"Only me."

"Ask Bobby why he ran," came the reporter's voice.

"Okay," Maya said. She refrained from pointing out that the answer would assuredly be, *You.*

"And," the reporter said, "ask him if he killed Jessica Silver."

"Asked and answered," Maya said reflexively. "But I'll do my best."

"You don't spook too easy," Ishmael said as Maya walked past him toward the camp.

"It's been a long week."

• • •

Ishmael stayed on the front lines while she maneuvered through the commotion in the camp. Without too much searching, she was able to find her way to Bobby's tent. She found him throwing all his worldly possessions—what few there were—into a duffel bag.

"You led them to me," he said, as if she were just one in a very long line of people who'd sold him out.

"Maybe," she said. "Or maybe I wasn't the only person Lou told about where you were."

Bobby shook his head. Why should he care about her rationalizations?

"You can't keep running," she said.

"The fuck else am I supposed to do?"

If the cops caught him, he'd go back to jail for breaking parole. That would mean another six months in Chino, maybe twelve, and then back to Miracle. Then the cops would find some other way to violate him back to prison. This would be the ebb and flow of the rest of his life: prison, a colony of sex offenders, prison again.

Bobby Nock was only thirty-four years old, she realized as she watched him stuff boxers into his bag. His face looked thin; his whole body looked wired to the point of breaking. His life was far from over. But no sliver of hope or even possibility of freedom remained. This was his lot; there was nothing she or anyone else could do about it.

Running was his only move now. This is what it had come to, for this man whose life she'd once believed she'd saved.

"I'm on your side." Maya knew this was a pretty lame response. But it was true.

"I know." He said it like he was speaking to a child.

He grabbed the alligator drawing from the wall. "You want to help me, Maya Seale?"

"Yes."

He held up the alligator drawing. "Then you remember this."

She looked at the alligator. The orange teeth, bared for a fight, were too big for the animal's frame. In even this silly picture, there was a tinge of violence.

"I don't have much of anything that's mine anymore," he said. "That reminds me that even though I've made mistakes—that even though I've done wrong things—I'm not the person they all think I am. So whatever happens, whatever they say about me next . . . you remember that I was, once, an actual human being."

He folded the drawing and put it in his bag. Then he pushed past her and out of the tent.

She didn't chase after him. She followed slowly, watching him run, the duffel bag bouncing on a shoulder that didn't seem built for the weight.

He disappeared into the darkness.

CHAPTER 16

TRISHA
OCTOBER 4, 2009

Trisha Harold watched the news cameras that arrived, as if on cue, at 5:00 A.M. each morning. She felt, not for the first time, like an accidental performer, thrust onstage in a play she'd never agreed to star in. The roles had been cast. The audience had assembled. The reviewers were ready with pen and paper. She felt as if the curtain were about to rise on a bloody Jacobean drama of revenge and deceit—only she hadn't learned her lines. She felt like she was in *The Revenger's Tragedy* by way of Christopher Durang.

She turned away from her hotel room windows to the short bench at the foot of the bed, on which she'd set her clothes, neatly folded in advance of the coming day: Laying her clothes out the night before was a habit she'd picked up as a teenager—a way to start the new day off efficiently, given the inevitable late nights of theater rehearsals. She'd thought she wanted to be an actress then. Musicals were her first love. She'd taken more quickly to the melodies than to the choreography.

Between eighth and ninth grades, she'd spent

311

the best summer of her life at a Michigan arts camp. She'd gotten to do Fantine, Roxie Hart, and a few side characters from *Into the Woods*, all in the span of two months. She still listened to the Broadway cast recordings of those shows. Most days at City Hall, where Trisha set up (and repaired, and re-repaired) IT systems, she could put her headphones on and imagine herself on a faraway stage. But she'd never felt like she was acting a part as much as she had during this trial.

Four wearying months had passed, and not once in that time had anyone mentioned that Trisha was one of only two black people on the jury. That she was the sole black woman. She'd tried making jokes about it a few times—to Jae, to Fran—but they'd ignored her, pretending not to hear.

Some days all she wanted was for one of the other jurors to just hand her the script they'd written for her in their heads: the angry black woman fighting the tyrannies of the LAPD.

Maya was the worst, Trisha thought as she dressed. Once Maya had set off on her insane mission to save Bobby Nock, she had expected support from Trisha that Trisha was not inclined to give. Maya seemed offended that Trisha could possibly have arrived at a different conclusion. She seemed offended precisely because Trisha wasn't playing the role in which she'd been cast.

Maya kept saying that there was no way the prosecution would have gone forward with a

312

murder trial without a body if the defendant had been white. Trisha kept saying that while that might be true, maybe the reason they'd gone forward was that Bobby had *clearly and obviously done it.*

The guy had had sex with his teenage student, for Christ's sake. For Maya to pretend that racism was the only reason he was in trouble only demeaned the genuine problems inculcated by American racism. If everything was racist, Trisha had tried to say, then nothing was. Was Bobby Nock really the guy who most needed defending against the systematic injustices of law enforcement?

Over the past week of deliberations, Trisha had watched Maya win a few converts to her side. Lila had been easily swayed by a commanding voice. Carolina had been confused by the endless claims and counterclaims of the evidence. Cal had enjoyed playing detective; Maya had sent him off digging through the information they'd been given to find some evidence of who the *real* killer might have been.

Trisha steeled herself for another day of wearying debate.

She left her room and trotted into an open elevator. She found Rick Leonard inside.

"Hey," Rick said.

"Hey." Trisha stood beside him in silence as the elevator doors closed.

He'd spent most of their sequester with Maya. Trisha had watched them drift away from the others during meals. She'd seen them disappear behind hotel room doors to watch the smuggled movies. Trisha had been unsurprised when Fran had told her that Wayne had spied Rick sneaking out of Maya's room early one morning. If they thought they were fooling anybody, well, they were not.

Rick had seemed genuinely shocked, on the first day of deliberations, to find himself on the opposite side of the case from Maya. Trisha had watched a cold front settle in between them. The two of them had hardly spoken to each other since.

"How are you today?" Rick asked, breaking the ice.

What could she say in the space of an elevator ride that would accurately answer this question? "Tired."

He nodded empathetically. "Hopefully, we can go home soon."

"How do you figure that'll happen?"

"Maya will back down."

Trisha had witnessed the way Rick had directed all his arguments in the jury room toward Maya. She'd noticed the way he kept looking at her. That boy was smitten. And he was acting the way lovesick boys always did when they were ignored: obsessed, angry, oblivious to everybody else.

Meanwhile, Maya was making progress. She'd won Jae to her side just yesterday. The more Rick focused on her, the more she focused on everyone else.

"No," Trisha said as the elevator doors opened on the lobby. "She won't. Not before you will."

She exited in the direction of the restaurant, ready for coffee and another long day of not allowing herself to be bullied by people too deluded to see what was right in front of them.

They started each day's deliberations with a fresh vote. It was supposed to be Kathy's job to lead them through it, but starting on day two Maya had snatched control of the process. Honestly, Kathy had seemed relieved. Lately, though, as everyone else wore each other down, Kathy had been gaining energy. She had reserves that Trisha hadn't predicted. She was speaking out more. It was as if, for the first time in her life, Kathy found herself listened to. And she discovered that she enjoyed being heard.

That morning, Kathy seemed to take pride in passing out index cards and Sharpies and then leading them in the ritual reading of their twelve verdicts. They stood at nine to three in favor of conviction.

"Why don't we go through the text messages again?" Kathy suggested.

Fran grimaced. Reading the texts out loud was

clearly not her favorite jury-room activity. Trisha doubted that it was anyone's.

The messages had become the paramount battleground in their arguments because they provided their only window into the defendant's state of mind. The prosecutor had put a single charge before them: murder in the first degree. As defined by California Penal Code, section 187, which the judge had read aloud now many times, first-degree murder was "the unlawful killing of a human being, or fetus, with malice aforethought." (The "fetus" bit came with paragraphs of clarification, but since it had no bearing on this case the judge had skipped over it.) The final phrase was the one that had provided Maya with a hole through which to puff the translucent smoke of her doubts. "Malice aforethought" took many paragraphs to explain, in the California Penal Code, but the gist was this: In order for them to vote "guilty," they'd need to believe that Bobby had not only killed Jessica, but that he'd planned the murder ahead of time.

That's how Maya had won Jae to her side. In his opinion, Bobby had probably murdered Jessica in a spur-of-the-moment kind of situation. Maybe she was going to tell someone what they'd been up to; maybe she didn't want to keep doing it anymore; whatever. Maya had said that if Jae believed that, he had to vote "not guilty." And in this way they realized that a jury's votes were like Tolstoy's families: All "guilty" votes had to be alike in reasoning. But all "not guilty" votes could be for different reasons and still reach the same result.

"The point you're going to emphasize," Rick said, "is that we can't say for certain that Bobby and Jessica were having sex."

"That's right." Maya had to stand and lean over to reach the stack of printed text messages that was among the evidence left for them on the table. " 'I'm not wearing any underwear.' If they'd just had sex, Bobby would already know that."

Fran sighed loudly. This whole thing was murder on *her,* wasn't it?

"I think," Cal said, "that dirty messages might not lend themselves to being read so literally."

"What's the point of this?" Fran interjected suddenly. "Whether they were involved like that, whether they weren't . . . aren't these messages bad enough?"

"To get him fired from his job?" Maya said. "Yes. To get him convicted for murder? I don't think so."

"But fear of losing his job," Rick said, "was the motive. The texts are plenty of evidence for that."

"You think Bobby would kill Jessica—this young woman whom he clearly cared about—just to hang on to his job?"

" 'Young woman'?" Trisha said. Her tone, she realized, was probably harsher than she'd intended.

"She was fifteen," Maya said. "You'd prefer 'girl'?"

"She was fifteen," Trisha said. "I'd prefer 'child.' "

"My daughter is seventeen," Kathy said, "and there is no way she is old enough for this type of stuff."

"I'm not saying it's right," Maya said. "I'm saying that whatever happened between Bobby and Jessica was maybe more complicated than we can know."

Maya quickly glanced at Rick. That was all Trisha needed to figure out what was really going on here.

Maya was projecting, wasn't she? She was living with her boyfriend, back in the real world. She was practically married. Her thing with Rick broke more rules than just those of the court. Trisha was pretty sure she knew where Maya's insistent live-and-let-live morality was coming from.

"We're all sinners?" Trisha said sarcastically. "Who but God can weigh our private sins?"

Maya flinched. As if she was being called out for a secret that Trisha could not possibly know. "I'm saying that it's hard to take a look at someone and claim to know who they really are."

Trisha had always been uncomfortable with anger, but honestly she could not take another minute of Maya's sanctimonious bullshit.

"Don't *you* think you know *me?*" Trisha said.

"Okay," Kathy said. "Maybe we should take a break."

"No," Trisha said. "I can't keep listening to this. To all these implications. Maya, do you want to just say what you really mean?"

"I . . . I don't . . . What I mean?"

"You think I *have* to identify with Bobby Nock in all this. That our blackness is the most defining feature about us. It's okay, Maya. It doesn't make you a racist. This is the craziest thing about good, well-intentioned white people, isn't it? What lengths you'll go to not to come off as in any way racist. Heavens! So instead of saying, 'Bobby is a man and Trisha is a woman, so they don't have much in common,' you're saying, 'Bobby is black and Trisha is black, so *that* must be what they have in common.' What's the salient feature? The defining part of an object?"

She didn't even totally know what she was saying anymore. She was just so frustrated.

"Jae," Trisha went on, caution to the fucking wind. "You're Korean."

"Yeah," he replied uncertainly.

"Is being Korean the most interesting thing about you?"

Jae frowned.

Rick turned to Trisha. "Let's keep this chill, okay?"

She refused to acknowledge him. "Jae, I bet you have a thousand things going on in your life more interesting than being Korean. But that's what we're talking about right now, because somehow that one word, 'Korean,' becomes a wall. A mural! A painting of a person, blocking someone else's view of you, Jae, a real live person."

This was pouring out of her now. Words overflowing, coming from some deep and weary place.

"Rick, you're black. So tell me: How much do we have in common?"

"Right now," Rick said, "we both think Bobby Nock is guilty."

Trisha nodded. "Well, that gives us something to talk about."

"I don't know how anyone can look at this case," Maya said, "or how anyone can look at *anything* . . . except through the lens of their own experience. That's all I mean. That nobody is impartial here. Nobody can just look at the facts. Because we're not arguing about what the facts mean—we're arguing about what the facts *are*. You say the text messages are one fact. I say they're not; not the same way. You say the bloodstains are facts. I say I don't know if they are."

"Please, you guys."

It was Lila's voice. When Trisha turned, she saw that Lila was on the verge of tears.

"It's okay, sweetheart," Fran said. "Maybe we should take a break."

"Everyone in this room is a good person," Lila said.

It was such a kind and generous statement that instantly Trisha felt embarrassed. By the looks on the faces around the table, Trisha didn't think she was the only guilty party.

Why was she escalating her fight with Maya? What was she trying to prove? What did she even want from all this? If Bobby Nock went to jail for the rest of his life—if he lived out his remaining years in torment—what good would that do?

Maybe at the end of the day it was all performance. If she voted "not guilty," she was performing the defiant-black-lady role they'd all anticipated. If she voted "guilty," she was performing a rebellion against that same role. There was no way out, was there? Either she was who they wanted her to be, or she wasn't, but either identity existed only in the shadow of their expectations.

The best part of being a teenage musical theater prodigy had been the lives she was able to inhabit. The centuries-dead English noblewoman, the prairie-dwelling American girl. She could be one person one day and another the next; she was locked into nothing except the moment itself. If she'd thought that being on this jury would allow her to be similarly freed of preconception, then she was as naïve as Maya. As easily manipulated as the poor dead girl whose face shone from every photograph on the table.

Had Bobby Nock killed Jessica Silver? Trisha didn't *know.* Not for sure. Not beyond a reasonable doubt. Maybe it had been an accident, like Jae thought. Maybe Jessica had actually attacked Bobby for some reason and he'd defended himself in a bloody fight to the death, as Wayne had inexplicably suggested. Maybe it had been spontaneous fucking combustion.

After four months in a courtroom, could she honestly say that she knew the first thing for sure about any of these people? Bobby or Jessica or Lou or Elaine or any of these strange characters beside her? They were actors in costume, sweating under the hot lights. They took the stage for only a few brief, evocative scenes, before retreating back into the wings.

But no one had the script, and no one knew their lines, and the longer this show went on, the more lives would be churned up by its fictions.

So to hell with returning for the third act. To hell with what it would do to all of them. Better a "guilty" man went free, whatever that even meant anymore, than that Trisha pretend for a moment longer to be someone who could see the truth.

She sat up in her chair. She placed her hands on the table, holding her spine straight.

"All right," Trisha said. "All right."

She looked Maya dead in the eye as she gave her what she wanted.

"Not guilty."

CHAPTER 17

SURRENDER
NOW

The reporters' vans were already speeding into the distance by the time Maya made it through the dwindling chaos to the edge of the camp. The glow of their taillights receded behind the murky cloud of dust left in their wake.

Ishmael was there, shotgun lowered at his side.

"Why are they leaving?" she asked him.

"A car took off," he said. "Other side of the camp. I think they think it's your buddy."

"His name is Bobby."

"Yeah . . . so he killed a girl?"

Where would she even start?

"I don't think so," she said.

She found her car and began the long drive back to L.A. She'd been around too many loaded guns in the last day to be tired. Going over the looming black mountains dotted with sunken half-towns of the Inland Empire, Maya imagined what the first settlers to come to this land had thought when they peered down from these same ridges. They couldn't have known that the ocean awaited them. Had they allowed themselves to dream that they would emerge to find something so beautiful?

An hour later, Maya crested the overpass above the train tracks west of Monterey Park, where acres of shipping crates announced the approach to the city. They signified that L.A. was a crossroads. A place from which people and things traveled all over the world.

Bobby had told her that L.A. was 30 percent roads. Was that even true?

Somewhere around Boyle Heights, her phone rang. It was Craig.

How could she possibly describe what she'd experienced in East Jesus?

"Hey," she said into the phone.

"I'm not the young man I once was," Craig said.

"Okay . . ."

"My memory deserts me from time to time. But I have this distinct recollection of giving you one cardinal rule. Do you recall that rule?"

"Don't do anything stupid."

"And yet . . ."

There were so many things she'd done over the past few days of which he wouldn't approve.

"What did I do?" she said.

"There is video of you, on the Internet, in a place that is improbably called East Jesus. You are standing in front of some gun-toting hillbilly meth dealer, claiming to be able to broker a deal with Bobby Nock."

Christ, Maya thought. *It's online already.*

"That was fast."

"That was stupid."

"I found Bobby."

"Clearly."

"He didn't kill Rick."

"You don't know that." She could hear the annoyance in his voice.

She told Craig about her meeting with Bobby, about the photographs and the time stamps that provided his alibi for Rick's murder.

"So all you've done," he said when she'd finished, "is to *eliminate* a possible suspect?"

She had to admit that this was, technically, true.

"The DNA analysis came back," he said. "I only just heard."

She awaited the result she most feared.

"Yours was the only DNA found on or around Rick Leonard."

There it was. The final nail in her coffin.

She knew what he'd say to be encouraging: Absence of evidence is not evidence of absence. This didn't prove that only she could have killed him; it just meant that whoever had killed him hadn't left any hairs or saliva or other bodily fluids behind.

She didn't want to hear his pep talk.

"So what happens next?" she asked, though she knew the answer.

"The LAPD is going to arrest you for murder."

• • •

Thirty minutes later, Maya arrived at Crystal's house to find Craig already there. Given that it was just after 1:00 A.M., Crystal was in sweatpants. She didn't seem self-conscious about wearing them around her boss. It was, Maya supposed, her house.

Crystal wrapped Maya in a strong hug. "You're not fucking in jail yet," Crystal whispered softly into Maya's ear. Craig was less demonstrative about his concern, greeting her with a simple, silent nod.

She was grateful for them both.

Crystal made ginger tea that none of them drank as they went over their options.

Option one was to argue that either Peter Wilkie or Wayne Russel had killed Rick. Peter had motive but little means; Wayne had means but little motive. "Pick your poison," as Craig put it.

Option two was to pick *both* poisons, and to down a few others for good measure. "Maya didn't do it but here's a laundry list of people who could have." To make this argument most effective, they'd want to expand the list of suspects as much as possible. Now that Maya had unhelpfully removed Bobby Nock from such a list, they'd want to fill it out with all the other jurors. Jae Kim's dossier said he'd lied about a connection to Lou Silver, right? He'd had a few too many drinks, hadn't he, on the night of the murder? Per the dossiers, Cal Barro had had an undisclosed run-in with the law as well. Maya had to point out the suggestion that eighty-year-old Cal had physically overcome thirty-eight-year-old Rick was . . . weak. But then, as Craig noted, the point of option two was not to make a slam-dunk case against anyone in particular. It was only to crowd the field with suspects.

And then there was option three.

"Here's what I like about self-defense," Craig said. "It takes all their evidence and spins it on its head. They say only your DNA was on the body? Great. We agree. That's because Rick only attacked you. They say you concealed a sexual relationship with Rick, lying to your friends and family and even the court, for years? We say, 'Of course she did!' Rick was an abusive shithead and you couldn't get out of it, you were ashamed, etc. Even the nature of Rick's wounds: a single blow to the back of his head from the table? That sure looks to me like a physical altercation that got a little out of hand. We can explain *everything*."

"Except," Maya said, "for the identity of Rick's actual killer."

Craig looked at her like she was a child. "My job is not to find Rick's actual killer. My job is to prevent the State of California from convicting you of murder."

Maya looked to Crystal for support. She didn't get any.

"I spoke to Ben Gao an hour ago," Craig said, referring to the head deputy district attorney. "He wants to schedule a surrender for 10 A.M. tomorrow."

Maya felt numb. She'd been in court with Ben Gao, though she'd never gone up against him head-to-head. She wasn't senior enough at the firm for that.

A lot of the head deputies could be assholes, but not him. Mostly she remembered him as being polite, soft-spoken, and consummately thorough.

She didn't need Craig to tell her that the only way a self-defense argument would work would be for her to get on the stand and tell a terrible, untrue story. She'd have to lie under oath that Rick had attacked her and she'd fought back. She'd have to commit one crime to avoid punishment for another crime that she hadn't. She'd have to say Rick was "violent." "Prone to fits of anger." Could she really make herself testify to a story that was both untrue and cruel to the memory of a man she had once cared for? Not to mention infused with racial and gender subtext that was horrific to contemplate?

She'd be turning herself into that contemptible white woman from *To Kill a Mockingbird*, the one who falsely claimed that a black man had raped her just to save her own skin.

"As a black man in Los Angeles," she said to

Craig, "don't you think my claiming that Rick attacked me is . . . well . . ."

"Racist?" Craig asked.

"At the very least, taking advantage of the racial biases of the court?"

Craig made a face like he was ruing the God who'd put him in this position. "As a black man in Los Angeles, I have argued forty-one criminal cases at trial. I have negotiated hundreds of plea bargains. I have sued the LAPD over police brutality six times. And won, five times. As a black man in Los Angeles, I am arguably the best criminal defense attorney in this city—but who would argue? As a black man in Los Angeles, I do not want anyone—especially my employee and, yes, my friend—to go to jail for a crime she did not commit." He sighed. "As a black man in Los Angeles, you know what I want most of all? Justice. I fail to see the justice in your spending the rest of your life behind bars."

Crystal shot Maya a castigating look: *See what happens when you try to argue with the boss?*

"I don't know if I can do it," Maya said weakly.

She watched as they exchanged a glance. Clearly, they'd already discussed this behind her back.

"You don't have to decide tonight," Crystal said calmly. "Get some sleep. Talk to your family. If you surrender yourself tomorrow morning, you won't have to register a plea until the arraignment."

After I've already been in jail for a day.

Crystal must have been betting that a day or so in jail would soften Maya up to a self-defense plea. All her most enlightened principles would be reduced to the bare necessities of survival. How quickly would she break?

Maya realized that she was being handled.

She'd wasted so much time doing exactly this with her own clients. The plainly guilty career criminals were a breeze. They were professional and transactional and she always knew where she stood with them. It was the innocent people, or the civilians who'd made one tentative step into a life of crime and found they weren't cut out for it, who were a pain. Their feelings required constant maintenance. Comforting smiles were essential. Hands needed holding, sometimes literally.

Craig checked his watch. "Well, I'm going to get some sleep myself. I suggest you do the same. Talk to whoever you need to talk to. And I'll be back here by eight A.M. to pick you up."

"You'll take me in?"

Craig came over to her and squeezed her hand. "Maya. Of course."

After Craig left and Crystal went to bed, Maya didn't know what to do with herself.

What does one do before one goes to jail?

She called her father. It would be one hour later in Albuquerque. He'd be sound asleep, probably

331

on the couch, as late-night MSNBC blared from the TV.

She'd had practice at the fine art of not worrying her parents. The trial had been hard on her dad, arguably worse on her mom, for whom preserving a patina of normalcy had seemed both vital and impossible. Maya hadn't been allowed to talk to them about the trial, of course, and any other conversational topic would be overheard by Bailiff Steve. Her parents had filled the silences by giving her updates on their lives: Her mom was completing the Master Gardener program at New Mexico State University; the Tomato Fiesta was coming up soon; the new rock wall in the wash behind the house was coming along nicely.

They had tried to keep her on the line for every minute they could.

They'd had to reconcile themselves to getting more information from cable news than they did from her. Maya learned later that they'd taken to watching hours of CNN every day. They were grateful for its immediacy. For whatever tenuous sense of closeness to her that all those cameras and all those talking heads were able to provide.

But then came the verdict. In a flash, the news cycle turned against her. The volume of public excoriation was overwhelming for a tax advisor and a homemaker with no preparation for the public eye.

"Dad?" she said now when he picked up. "Don't freak out."

This was a horrendous start.

"What's wrong, honey?" he said, groggy. "Let me turn down the . . ."

She could hear him fiddling with the remote. "It's going to be okay," she said. "Trust me. My lawyer and I are taking care of it." A brutal pause. "But I'm about to be arrested for murder."

All in all, the conversation that followed could have been a lot worse.

After, she closed her eyes for a while as she lay, fully clothed, atop Crystal's guest room bed. She knew she wasn't going to sleep. She couldn't stop thinking about the point at which everyone would abandon her. Her parents, her friends, her colleagues . . . how soon would they cut her loose?

She pictured Bobby Nock, running forever across the barren desert. Alone.

He'd done an awful thing. How bad did someone's crime have to be before everyone else was allowed to abandon all sympathy? What was the line past which no one could be expected to follow?

Maya's abandonment had been only partial when, in most people's eyes, she'd set a guilty man free. Would it become complete now that, in the eyes of the State of California, she'd become credibly accused herself?

• • •

Crystal made protein smoothies for breakfast.

"You want to talk about it?" she said as she handed Maya an oversized glass.

"Nope." Maya took a sip. *Bananas, orange juice, strawberries.* She tried to savor a taste that she might not experience again for a very long time.

"Okay then." Crystal picked up her phone, and that was that.

Craig arrived promptly, as usual. They were silent for most of the ride. The stop-and-start of L.A. at rush hour was worse than usual. Occasionally he spoke up to recite details that she already knew about the detectives who'd take her in, about the prison where she'd stay, about the mundane procedures of prisoner intake.

She'd given similar speeches herself. Defendants never paid any attention.

She and Craig arrived dutifully at the Central Division station. Detective Daisey and her partner, Detective Martinez, were waiting for them in the alley off Sixth Street. Four plainclothes officers provided halfhearted muscle. No one was expecting this to turn into a scene.

Maya recognized Head Deputy DA Ben Gao, watching with the cops and quietly, patiently supervising.

Craig got out of the car first and then opened the door for Maya.

"The next time I see you," he said softly, "will be at your arraignment. So please think about how you'd like to plead."

Maya didn't imagine she'd be able to think about much else.

"If you want to come inside," Detective Daisey said, "we can always talk before we take you to the jail."

Craig actually laughed. Not a fake laugh but a real, honest one from his gut.

"Please, Detective," he responded.

Daisey smiled. It had been worth a shot. She removed a pair of plastic wrist restraints from her pocket.

Maya handed her cellphone, wallet, and keys to Craig. Better to have him hold on to them than the Department of Corrections.

Without a word, she turned her back to Daisey and extended her arms behind her.

"You can keep your arms in front," Daisey said. "If it's more comfortable."

Never had the line between the two tiers of American justice been more apparent to Maya than when a cop asked her how she'd like to be arrested.

She faced Daisey, holding her hands in front of her body. Daisey gingerly slid the restraints over her hands, then tugged. She was bound.

"Maya Seale," Detective Daisey said, "you're under arrest for the murder of Rick Leonard."

CHAPTER 18

Yasmine Sarraf listened to Rick and Maya's truly top-notch, grade-A bickering. It was really something: the subtle condescension, their bad-faith "just to be clear" disclaimers, the mercilessness with which they jumped on every poorly chosen word to catch the other in an accidental inconsistency. The thing that Yasmine kept thinking?

These two are perfect *for each other.*

Just the other day, Fran had told her that Rick and Maya were doing it. But Fran didn't know if they were a "couple," or if they wanted to be, or *what* the deal was. Would they make a good match? Maybe Yasmine was just a hopeless romantic—that's what her husband, David, had always said—but as she observed the viciousness of their debates, she felt positive that she was witnessing the kind of love that lasts.

You had to really care about someone to fight with them this hard. You had to deeply care about someone's opinion to be this offended by how totally wrong they were.

Yasmine came from a long line of arguers.

Her parents were straight up the best she'd ever seen. Persian Jews, they'd hightailed it out of Tehran after the revolution. When she was little, she knew that the game was on when her parents switched over to Farsi. English was for grocery lists and doctor's appointments. All the good arguing happened in Farsi. Her mom usually started with a quick barb—"So you like this, living in filth?"—before crescendoing with character assassination—"You just don't respect anyone but yourself!" Her dad liked to lob a cruel laugh—"Ha! That's what you think?"—before trotting out his woe-is-me material—"Maybe I should stay at the shop, where at least they like having me around!"

After storming off to separate rooms, they would then spend multiple days speaking to each other only via their kids. Yasmine and her brother Dariush would dutifully deliver the messages.

"Yasmine," her mom would say, "please tell your dad that if he's going to smoke on the porch he has to shut the windows."

"Dari," her dad would say, "tell your mom that she leaves the clothes in the dryer too long."

Every few weeks, Yasmine would hear her parents tearily forgive each other behind the closed doors of their bedroom. She could hear their emotional apologies, followed by a passionate round of—well, she tried not to think about that part.

Bickering was a hobby they shared, and it had kept them together for thirty-five years.

In contrast, Yasmine's husband, David—Upper West Side family, divorced parents who hadn't spoken in twenty years, a mama's boy but a total sweetheart—had spent half his life in therapy. So when they got into an argument and her voice rose half a decibel, he would say something like "Yasmine, you've just never had a model of a healthy adult relationship."

The slightest disagreement sent David into days of sulking. If she so much as snipped at him, he'd ask to schedule a "family meeting." David's "coping strategies" were about as romantic as an interoffice email.

And *that* was supposed to be healthy?

Yasmine thought about the way the lawyers in court fought. "The adversarial system," that's what it was called. The attorneys on each side did their best to win, no-holds-barred—and whatever emerged from the mess of broken limbs was called justice.

That made sense to Yasmine. It seemed as if it made sense to Rick and Maya too.

It was sweet, how much they had in common.

Today's battleground was the state of Peter's vote. He'd expressed some ambivalence about the text messages. ("I mean," Peter had said, "we've all sent a girl a text or whatever that we shouldn't have, right? I'm not gonna send a guy to jail over that.") Maya had sensed that his vote might be up for grabs, and she'd gone right for it. ("If the text messages don't matter, and I agree they don't, then what does the prosecution even have?") But of course, Rick wasn't going to let Maya take Peter so easily. ("What else, besides cellphone logs, Bobby's own lies, and a bunch of DNA?")

That last point about the DNA in Bobby's car had seemed most important to Peter. ("Just, for me, there's nothing more important than the science.") Which meant that they were all, somehow, for the thousandth time, going back over the bloodstains.

"So then how," Rick said loudly, "did Jessica's blood get into Bobby's *trunk?*"

Maya looked annoyed. "They can't prove it was Jessica's blood. Remember the lab technician?"

"She said it was Jessica's blood!"

"She said that her sample tested positive for Jessica's DNA. But she confirmed that the forensics person who first went over the car failed to follow proper procedure."

" 'Proper procedure.' That's so weaselly—if you jaywalk, you're not following procedure. If you sign your rent check with a red pen, you're not following procedure. There are so many procedures that someone is always not following one of them."

"I sure hope," Maya said, "that if somebody ever kills you, the forensics people standing over your bloody corpse remember to follow procedure."

Rick's voice dripped with sarcasm: "I appreciate that."

"Now, you two," Cal said. "Let's take a breath."

Peter spoke up. "The forensic technician . . . she said she was confident that the blood in the trunk was Jessica's."

"That's right," Carolina added. " 'Confident.' "

"But," Trisha countered, "she also said she couldn't be one hundred percent sure."

Yasmine was amazed that Trisha was arguing for the "not guilty" side now. At least she wasn't trying to say that Bobby was definitely innocent; Trisha's cutting comments were all in favor of doubt.

"Only," Wayne said, "after the defense lawyer nattered at her for a while." Wayne had spent all morning sitting catatonically in his usual window seat, eyes closed. When asked if he was awake, he'd only nodded. These were his first words of the day, and they took everyone by surprise. "She can't say it a hundred percent. But she's an expert and she believes the blood was Jessica's. I just don't know how, in good conscience, you can get around that."

There was a moment of silence as everyone took in Wayne's sudden entry into the conversation.

"It's not about what she believes," Trisha said. "It's about what she can prove."

"Well," Wayne said, "she sure seemed like she knew what she was talking about. If she believes it, I believe her."

"Why?" Maya said, quieter.

"Because she looks honest."

Yasmine recognized the quick flash of a smile on Maya's face. Yasmine's mom made the same face when she had her dad right where she wanted him.

Maya repeated Wayne's words back to him. " 'Because she looks honest.' "

"That's what I said."

"What about the forensics technician 'looks honest' to you, Wayne?"

"Maya," Rick interrupted, "the woman is a scientist."

Yasmine looked at Peter. He was physically leaning away from Wayne, as if he was trying not to fall into the hole that had just opened between them.

"Let Wayne answer," Maya said.

"I don't see what you're getting at," Wayne said.

"You think," Maya said to Wayne, "that the forensics technician is more believable, more honest, than Bobby Nock. And maybe she is. But that's what this all comes down to, in the end, isn't it? Who do we believe?"

341

"There are lots of reasons," Peter said, "to believe or not believe any of these people." He was trying to steer them clear of these waters, but it wasn't going to work.

"You're right," Maya said. "We can sit here for another year talking about bloodstains. Talking about how many DNA particulates were in which sample, how many hours this vial or that vial sat unattended on a laboratory desk, all of that bullshit. But it doesn't really matter. Not to any of us. This isn't about 'facts.' This is about people. This is about *one person*. Do we believe Bobby Nock? Or do we think he's lying?"

"I think," Wayne said, "that that boy seems like a guaranteed fucking liar."

Yasmine could feel the way the word "boy" landed in the room. She couldn't believe Wayne had gotten riled enough to say something that fucked up.

Trisha sucked in air, like she'd been hit in the stomach.

Peter closed his eyes, as if mortified to be on the same side as Wayne.

Rick jumped in. He knew that his supposed teammate's ugly slip made him look bad too. "The *reason* Bobby isn't trustworthy," he insisted, "is that he's lied before. To the cops, to the school, and to everyone who might have found out about his utterly inappropriate relationship with one of his students." Rick turned to Wayne, agreeing

342

with and castigating him at the same time. "We have good, solid reasons not to believe Bobby."

Wayne either wasn't getting it or he wasn't having it. "I dunno," he said. "I think the boy is just a no-good piece of shit."

Yasmine could see Rick's frustration. Wayne had let their team down. The damage was done.

Maya went straight for the weak spot. She gestured to Wayne while speaking to Peter. "This is your argument. This is what your side really boils down to. You can dress it up however you want. But is this really what you want this jury to say with our verdict?"

Rick objected: "Don't turn Peter into Wayne."

That certainly got Wayne's attention. "Pardon me?"

"Peter and I," Rick said, "aren't making the same point you are."

"You think? Maybe I'm just saying what you know but don't want to say out loud." Wayne leaned forward, resting his elbows on the table. Yasmine could feel the table move from the bulk of his body. His right heel tapped rapidly at the floor, even faster than it did most days. Yasmine was worried that he was going to explode, maybe today, maybe tomorrow, definitely sometime soon.

"Don't tell me that you know what's in my head," Rick said.

"Don't call me a racist."

The "R" word certainly woke *everybody* up.

Peter's face froze. A white guy like him, living in California, would be deathly afraid of being on the side of the bigots, accidentally or not. Yasmine could see the calculation going on in his head: *Was it racist to vote the same way as Wayne, even if I did it for different reasons?*

"Nobody called you a racist," Jae said to Wayne.

But Wayne was on one of his tears. He was sure he'd been insulted, and he was going to fight back.

"Rick was thinking it," Wayne said, leaning farther across the table toward Rick. "Weren't you?"

"What is it about the word 'racist' that gets everybody so upset?" Rick wasn't backing down either. "You'd think it was the most offensive word in the whole English language. Which is funny, because I guarantee I can think of one that's worse."

Thank God he spared them the N-bomb.

Rick continued. "It's not a toggle. It's not a binary construct. 'This person is racist.' 'This other person isn't.' A one or a zero. It's a structure. A framework."

"Okay, man," Wayne scoffed.

"Think of sexism. Fuck, think of sexual orientation. Think of the concept. Racism is about racial orientation. To say you made judgments about Bobby Nock because he's black isn't saying you're some irredeemable redneck son of a bitch, dragging around a rope and a hood. We think of 'racists' as these other people—this subset of subhuman assholes. The villains in all those ridiculous movies with beatific white saviors. When the villains are so clear, we can tuck ourselves into bed at night knowing that we're nothing like them. But what if it's not so clear? What if it's more complicated than *here's some heroic non-racist white people* and *here's some villainous racist white people?* What if, for me, the most pressing questions are not about how 'racist' you think you are or can prove that you aren't. I don't give a shit whether you think you're a one or a ten on some kind of racism Kinsey scale. I care about what you're going to do about it."

Wayne looked like this whole speech was strangely amusing. "I don't know what you're talking about. But you're the one who brought up 'racist.'"

Yasmine could see that Peter had been turned. She had seen Maya do it to Carolina, and then Lila, and then Trisha, and now she'd done it to Peter. Yasmine watched the younger woman sink back into her chair with a look of satisfaction on her face.

Maya had figured out that Wayne and Rick believed the same thing, but for conflicting reasons. She'd cleaved their union in two and sent Peter fleeing. It'd be safer for him to vote with Maya than to be tarnished by remaining on their side. Instead of debating with Maya, now Wayne and Rick would debate with each other. One of them was sure to piss the other one off so much that he'd end up on Maya's side too.

Who'd killed Jessica Silver? Yasmine did not have a clue.

It didn't matter anymore. Getting in Maya's way would be pointless. She was going to take them each down, one by one, until finally even Rick had fallen.

CHAPTER 19

I'M SO SORRY
NOW

All in all, jail wasn't so bad. There was too much press surrounding the case for Head Deputy DA Gao to risk keeping Maya with other prisoners. If she was released with so much as a scratch on her, Craig would deluge the state with civil suits. So she was treated well. Which, in the L.A. County lockup, meant that she was largely left alone.

She was taken to a holding cell of her own and a few hours later informed that her arraignment wouldn't happen until the next morning. Craig had prepped her for this, though she'd have predicted it herself. In case the judge granted her bail, Head Deputy DA Gao would want to be able to say she'd spent at least a night behind bars. He could get two news cycles out of it: her arrest today, her arraignment tomorrow.

She lay back on the hard metal bench that, unless one counted the lidless toilet, constituted the only real furniture in the cell. She had a lot of time to think, as afternoon drifted into evening and evening evaporated into night. This was the worst part of her brief time in jail. She was privy

347

to no one's thoughts save her own. And it was her own that she most wanted to get away from.

After a breakfast of powdered eggs and fried potatoes, she was transferred by the Department of Corrections to the courthouse. Responsibility passed from one department to another, from city to state. If she was shivved in the court's hallway, it would be a crisis for a different set of lawyers.

After a brief trip in the police van, she was taken to the Clara Shortridge Foltz Criminal Justice Center, where she was then ushered, in restraints, down the hallway where she and Rick had once done crossword puzzles. She was taken past the back door to the courtroom where she'd acquitted Bobby Nock. She could hear her own footsteps against the tiled floor behind a courtroom where a few years before she'd won an acquittal for a teenage girl who'd killed her abusive uncle. Maya thought about all the different roles she'd played in this building. No matter what turns her life took, she felt as if this place was her fated destination.

Once again she was delivered to a holding cell where, once again, she was the sole inhabitant. The court and the prison were treating her like a hothouse flower. She'd wondered whether this experience would reveal the guts of the criminal justice system from the perspective of an accused person. She was disappointed when she discovered it would not. She was special, protected by an unspoken privilege, even here.

If only all defendants were treated with such care. If only Bobby Nock had been.

Her hearing would be Judge Anita Fontaine's first of the day.

Maya's parents were in the gallery. She would have had trouble recognizing her mother had she not been seated next to her dad, a still rock in a blue blazer. Her mom was typically an enthusiastic person, full of color and festooned with bright chunky jewelry. She befriended every waiter she met, and somehow elicited the life story of every local shopkeeper from whom she bought a scarf. But this morning, her hair was unkempt. Her eyes were bloodshot from crying, her face sunken.

Her dad raised a hand as she entered.

She did her best to smile at them. To silently reassure them that this process was just routine.

In the pew across the aisle were two people she assumed were Rick's parents. They looked in even worse shape than Maya's parents. They had divorced years ago, Maya remembered, but still they sat together. A woman who Maya guessed was Rick's dad's new wife sat on his other side.

Had they arranged a funeral for Rick over the last few days? She didn't even know. She'd been too busy trying to make sure she wouldn't end up exactly where she was right now.

Rick's parents glared at her. It was a cold, hard look, but it also held something back, as if they didn't want to let Maya see the depth of their sorrow. No matter what the court said, Maya was sure that they would hate her for the rest of their lives.

The gallery was half-filled with press and a few associate attorneys Maya recognized from her firm.

Craig was waiting for her alone at the defense table. Across from him, Head Deputy DA Gao sat with two junior lawyers from his office.

Maya sat beside Craig. She was so numb that she barely noticed as the bailiff removed her restraints.

"Are you all right?" Craig whispered.

She stretched her wrists. "Yeah."

"Will the defendant please rise," Judge Fontaine said. "Maya Louise Seale. You've been charged with murder in the first degree. Murder in the second degree. Assault in the first degree. And kidnapping. How do you plead?"

Bobby Nock's prosecutors had tried for an all-or-nothing murder-one shot. It had been a risky move, Maya knew now, a rare one born of overconfidence, and they'd lost. Gao would not make the same mistake. He was going with a buckshot approach: Fire a bunch of pellets at her and see what strikes an artery. He would argue, in effect, multiple theories of the crime simultaneously. If the jury believed she'd planned to murder Rick ahead of time, they could convict on murder one. If they came to believe that it was a spur-of-the-moment thing, they could go with murder two. If they believed that Maya hadn't intended to kill Rick, but only hit him recklessly, and his death was only a preventable accident, they had assault one.

Kidnapping was some bullshit. If the jury believed that Maya had *detained* Rick, against his will, in her room, by threat of force, for even one second, this would legally constitute kidnapping. There was no chance that anyone believed that Maya had "kidnapped" Rick, but the charge allowed the jurors some leeway. If there was one holdout on the jury who wanted to acquit—someone like, say, her—kidnapping could provide the group with a compromise.

"How do you plead?" Judge Fontaine asked again.

Craig leaned in and whispered, "So what'll it be: chicken or fish?"

Maya was grateful for the attempt at casualness. For Craig, the decision before them wasn't about morality or conscience. It was purely a question of strategy.

If Craig were unprincipled, it would have been easier for Maya to choose. But he was just the opposite: His principle was to do his goddamned job. There could be no stronger commitment to making the justice system work than his. His resolution was the Platonic ideal of a concept from a first-year law school lecture for which she'd been half-awake: In an adversarial system, it is the solemn duty of both adversaries to do their very best to win. Let the system worry about producing truth.

Still, in a room full of lawyers, the last thing she thought anyone was going to get was truth. No one was here for justice.

Maya touched Craig's hand. "I can't go up there and lie."

Craig placed his other hand on top of hers. "You know you're a lawyer, right?"

She saw genuine worry in his eyes. "I'm really sorry."

Judge Fontaine spoke: "Counselor, I'll need a plea. Now."

"Yes, Your Honor." Craig squeezed Maya's fingers, then whispered, "In my professional opinion, you are making a terrible mistake. I implore you to reconsider. Whatever I say today will get reported in the press and begin to color the opinions of prospective jurors. No changing our mind later. We pick one story, right now, and we do not waver, not ever, until you are cleared. Please let me make that story self-defense."

Maya squeezed back. "Thank you. You are absolutely right. But I didn't kill Rick Leonard."

Craig cringed. Now that she'd said those words

to him, he was legally forbidden from arguing self-defense. "Goddamn it, Maya."

In an instantaneous flash, he was facing the judge. "Your Honor, as I know—as the whole world knows—my client is innocent. She pleads not guilty to all charges."

Maya heard the murmurs from all around the courtroom. She looked over at DA Gao, who remained stone-faced.

"A plea of 'not guilty' is so recorded," Judge Fontaine said. "As to bail, what does the state recommend?"

"The state does not recommend granting the defendant bail, Your Honor," Gao said. More murmurs throughout the room. Maya was pretty sure she heard her mother crying.

Gao continued: "The defendant has means and resources and is plainly a flight risk. She is a known associate of Robert Nock, another convicted criminal who fled justice. We believe strongly that if this court grants bail to Ms. Seale, no matter the amount, that will be the last this court ever sees of her."

Judge Fontaine took this in. "And you, Mr. Rogers?"

Craig responded by turning to Gao. "How *dare* you. Your Honor, I'm not even going to bother pointing out that my client has been an upstanding citizen, respected in her community, for a decade. I'm not going to waste your time by discussing her stature in the legal community as an ABA-certified member of the California bar, who has sworn a duty not only to her own clients, but to this very court. I thankfully need not address her record of previous criminal offenses, because she has none. Instead, what I will say is this: Ten years ago, my client supported our community by serving on a jury. In this building, my client did exactly what we ask of all our citizens. And now she's here, in that chair. Her notoriety, due to her service, makes her imprisonment dangerous. It was the state's malfeasance, let me remind you, that first compromised her privacy. If anything were to happen to my client while under the custody of the state that once betrayed her, not only would the state's negligence in sending such a well-known citizen into a disreputable population constitute ample grounds for a lawsuit, but it would discourage exactly the sort of civic participation that is the very lifeblood of this court. There is a whole class of jurors, defendants, and, yes, even prosecutors, who would suffer irreparable harm as a result of such a decision. The greatest burden would not be borne by my client—but by a justice system that would be rendered unable to function as a result of a single, disastrous ruling."

A long moment of silence followed.

Gao probably should have said something, if only to appear to have been anything other than bowled over. He didn't say a word.

Judge Fontaine spoke. "Bail is hereby set at one million dollars."

"Very well, Your Honor." Craig looked at the bailiff. "I have a check ready. Whenever you are."

The judge banged her gavel, trying to silence the chatter from the gallery.

Craig sat down and leaned in to whisper in Maya's ear. "You're the boss."

Maya was released less than an hour later. Craig collected her from holding and led her to a town car, double-parked on Hill Street. He helped her into the back, where her parents were waiting.

This was definitely the hardest part. Her mom was weeping, and when she put her arms around Maya, her dad seemed to be unable to hold himself back. They both held her wordlessly. Craig sat inches away, politely flipping through emails on his phone.

"Mom," Maya said. "Dad. Really. I'm fine. It's going to be fine."

Did she really believe it? She'd have to try.

"Okay," was all her dad was able to say. "Okay."

"I'll pay you back for the bail money. My mortgage . . ." The thought of her parents having to come up with a cashier's check for 10 percent of the one-million-dollar bond this morning was awful. Maya found herself ashamed that after everything she'd accomplished in her life, her parents still had to bail her out of prison.

"Let's take you home," her dad said.

"I wouldn't recommend going back there," Craig suggested. "Press will get the address eventually, if they haven't already. I'd prefer that the three of you stay somewhere private."

"Okay, yes, that's smart," Maya's dad said.

"Why don't you take my Malibu house for the week?" Craig said. "My husband is in New York. No one will be there."

"Malibu," Maya's dad said, as if wrapping his brain around the idea.

Maya nodded at Craig. "Thank you."

"Malibu will be good," Craig said. "I'm just sorry about the traffic."

Craig's house was three compact stories just off the main drag of Malibu Road. The design was homier than Maya might have imagined: more wood, less glass, more framed personal mementos on the walls than grand pieces of abstract art. But as she stood on the first-floor patio, she could see nothing but ocean.

"Is Craig always like that, in court?" Maya's dad said as he stood beside her at the railing. Craig had stayed in L.A.; he'd gone to his weekday home in Hancock Park.

"I've never actually seen him in court. He runs the firm. He hired me out of law school."

"He seems like a good one."

Maya remembered when, in high school, she'd borrowed her dad's car and then her friend had left the roach of a joint sitting on the dashboard. She'd been in so much trouble with her parents . . . until, two weeks later, someone at school narced on her for having weed in her locker. When it was searched, they found a few stray crumbled leaves. The principal called in her dad and her dad took her side entirely, threatening to sue the school if they pursued punishment without any meaningful evidence. He even lifted her curfew from the earlier infraction. He could be stern, but as soon as he felt that she was under threat from someone else, all he wanted to do was protect her.

She wasn't sure how to say the thing she needed to, now. She thought her dad would be offended, but at the same time, if she didn't speak, would a part of him always wonder about the answer to a question he'd never have the courage to ask?

"Dad . . ." she began hesitantly. "Look, just so you know . . ."

"What?"

The black waves slid with a hush onto the sand. "I didn't do it."

He gave a start, like he'd been spooked. "Sweetheart . . . I . . . Oh, sweetheart . . ."

"You would never think that. I know. But I'm just telling you. Flat out. I didn't kill anyone."

357

He slowly rocked back and forth on his heels, his hands gripping the metal rails. "You know that even if you did, I'd still love you."

Was she offended or touched? She couldn't be sure. "I know."

"You'll see, when you have kids. It doesn't matter what they're guilty of. You protect them."

"Dad . . . I'm saying, I didn't do it."

He took a breath, and let go of the railing. "Well, in that case, we're really in a pile of shit, aren't we?"

That night was surreally domestic. The three of them made dinner together. Maya's mom went grocery shopping and led them in salting a fresh branzino; her dad managed the cleanup efforts. Maya poured gin cocktails from Craig's well-appointed stash. They watched a movie on the huge wall-mounted television. It was like a Thanksgiving weekend, or one of the drifting days post-Christmas when she was home for a spell.

They didn't say another word about the murder.

The next morning, Maya woke to find her dad already in front of the television, finishing the movie that he'd fallen asleep halfway through the night before. There was, so Maya remembered, quite a twist at the end. Her dad didn't want to miss it.

She was puzzling over Craig's coffeemaker when she heard a phone ring. It took her a moment to realize that it was the house's landline. She hadn't realized there even was one.

Five rings later, she found it by the breakfast nook.

"Hello?" she said. "This is . . . Craig Rogers's house."

"It's Craig. Turn on the TV."

She could hear the sounds of the movie from the next room. "My dad is watching—"

"The news, please."

Maya took the phone into the next room and grabbed the remote from her dad's side.

He was about to object, but then saw the expression on her face. "Honey?"

"Which news channel?" Maya said into the phone.

"They're all showing the same thing."

Maya flipped to CNN. A banner took up the entire lower third of the screen: BOBBY NOCK DEAD OF APPARENT SUICIDE.

Her dad gasped.

"What the hell is going on?" Maya said.

"Police found his body in a motel in Texas," Craig said. "Fox and CNN are saying there was a note; MSNBC can't confirm. Also . . ."

The screen filled with a hastily shot photo of a dingy motel room. There was an old bed with a faded floral-print blanket and a wooden coffee table. On the coffee table was a blurry white piece of paper and a silver locket.

Even in this poor photo, Jessica Silver's locket shone bright.

Maya recognized it instantly. Struggling to process what it meant, she tried not to scream.

"Is that . . ." Maya's mom said. "Is that Jessica Silver's locket?"

Maya would know the locket anywhere. She'd stared for so many hours at that final, enigmatic picture of Jessica taken by her school's security cameras. Maya knew exactly what Jessica had been wearing just hours before her death. The navy school uniform. The white sneakers. The bright locket, made of real silver.

The text of the note filled the screen:

I'm so sorry, handwritten in blue pen.

Maya went dizzy.

"But he didn't do it," Maya said to Craig, weakly. "He told me . . . in the desert. . . . He was telling the truth. . . ."

Maya had been so sure.

"On this point, you have been remarkably consistent. It doesn't look as if the cops have had time to test the locket for Jessica Silver's DNA."

"It's her locket," Maya admitted.

She remembered the duffel bag that she'd seen Bobby take with him. She thought of the few mementos he'd stuffed inside. Could the locket have been among them?

She struggled to fit this revelation into her view of the world. Nothing was making sense.

"Let's hope," Craig said, "that it's not Jessica's locket. Because if it is, and the DA can prove that Rick Leonard knew about it . . . your motive for killing him just became crystal clear."

CHAPTER 20

Fran Goldenberg was getting ready for bed when she heard a strange sound from the direction of the bathroom. She had become familiar with the nighttime noises of the Omni Hotel. This one was new.

It was a kind of dull, irregular heaving. A human sound.

She pressed her ear against the bathroom wall. Wayne's bathroom was next door. She could hear him showering sometimes in the morning. She hated to think that he could hear her do the same.

It sounded like he was throwing up.

"Wayne?" She knocked her knuckles against the wall. "Are you okay?"

No response. Just heaving.

"Wayne?"

Still no response.

She was worried. She put on her slippers and stepped out into the hallway. The twelfth floor, at this hour, was eerily quiet.

She tiptoed to Wayne's door and knocked again.

Where was Glen, the night guard who was

362

posted, 24/7, by the elevator? She went down the hall to find a strange guard, not one she recognized, in Glen's chair. The substitute guard was sound asleep.

Should she wake him up? And say what—that she'd heard weird noises from Wayne's room? She'd sound crazy, or nosy, or paranoid, or all of the above. What if *she* got in trouble for being out of her room at this hour?

In hindsight, Fran might have admitted that she was more than a little stressed when she snatched the guard's keycard from the folding table next to his chair. She wasn't a rule breaker by nature. Wayne and Maya—those were rule breakers. Maybe being trapped in here with them was rubbing off on her.

She went back to Wayne's room, slipped the card through the lock, and pushed the door open.

"Wayne?"

All the lights were on inside. The bathroom door was open.

She heard the heaving sound again.

She approached the bathroom.

Wayne was lying on the floor in the fetal position. Vomit and spit were all over his face, his chin, and the cold tiles.

Fran knelt down beside him. He heaved in a violent spasm. Not much liquid came up. Just a thin stream of bile.

"Wayne," Fran said. "Wayne."

His eyes were open, thank God.

"Fran?" he mumbled.

"What happened? Are you okay?"

It was then that she saw the empty pill bottle on the floor below the sink. With one hand she held Wayne's head and with the other she reached for the bottle.

She didn't recognize the name on the label. Were these sleeping pills?

"Fran?" His voice was weak. But at least he was talking.

"Yes, honey," she said. "I'm here."

Fran hadn't been there when her oldest son, Josh, had died. He'd been halfway around the world. By that point she hadn't even had a phone number for him in months. He'd been in Thailand, she found out eventually. He'd gone there to drink, to do drugs, to do whatever else would blot him out. She'd learned there was even a name for people like the person Josh had become: a *death-pat.* He'd traveled to a cheap country with a good exchange rate to obliterate himself until, eventually, his heart stopped.

Had the hotel room the Thai police found him in looked like this? Had Josh died on such a cold tile floor?

Her youngest, Ethan, had gone to get the body back.

"Wayne, honey . . . did you take all these pills?"

He nodded. He seemed embarrassed. "It was a

mistake." He was whispering. "I tried to get it all out."

"Throwing up is good," she said. "Getting the pills out of your stomach. You're going to be okay." She was trying to believe it herself.

He was crying. Maybe tears were all he had left to expel.

She tried to stand, setting his head back on the floor.

"No," he begged her. "Please."

"I need to make sure you're safe."

"Don't tell anyone."

She took a breath. "Wayne, I have to get a doctor."

"Please. Please. Please."

He was nearly twice her size. But curled up on the floor, she couldn't believe how small he seemed.

"I got it all out," he pleaded. "All gone."

She'd had enough first-aid training from her sons' school camping trips to figure that all a hospital would do was pump Wayne's stomach. And there was nothing left in there to pump.

She filled a glass with water from the sink and again knelt down beside him.

"We'll make a little deal," she said. "You're going to drink this water. And then we're going to make sure you throw it all up. And then we're going to do it again. And again. Until we make sure there is nothing left in your stomach. Then you're going to drink a bunch *more* water. Then we're going to stay up. All night. Until I'm sure you're well." She fed him his first sips of water. "And then, in the morning, we can talk about next steps."

He looked up at her, making eye contact for the first time.

"I gotta get out of here," he whispered in between sips.

"The bathroom?"

"No . . . *here* . . . I don't think I can take it anymore."

Fran held him tight. She held him the way she'd never gotten to hold Josh. She set Wayne's head on her lap and ran her hands through his stringy blond hair. When was the last time Josh had put his head in her lap like this? Had he ever let her stroke his hair? Whenever she'd told him how much she loved him, he'd turned away. The simplest, most basic and direct displays of affection were too much for a boy—and then a man—who didn't believe he deserved them.

She leaned back against the tiles and closed her eyes. She wasn't going to go to sleep; she wasn't going to check out for even a moment.

"We gotta get out of here," he mumbled again.

Yeah, Fran thought. *We do.*

The next morning, Fran took her index card and her pen and for the first time she wrote the words "not guilty."

There were ten votes for not guilty and two votes for guilty. Only Jae and Rick remained in the latter camp.

"What happened?" Rick asked Fran and Wayne. Only yesterday, they'd been on his side.

Wayne just shrugged. "It's my vote."

Fran fished for the photograph of Jessica Silver. The last one taken, of her at school, wearing her uniform and sparkling silver locket.

Fran held it up for all to see. "We can debate this or that all day. We have, for many days. But the point is, we don't know. We just don't know about Bobby. We don't know about Jessica. We don't know what was really going on in her head, in his head, what she'd been hiding from her parents or everybody else. . . . And that's the point."

Fran touched the edge of the photo with her thumb as if she were caressing the girl's face. "Jessica Silver deserves our best. She deserves to have the world know for sure who killed her. If we convict Bobby Nock, the investigation is over. The cops walk away. All the cameras outside every morning, the press, they'll go hunting for the next victim, the next big mystery. . . . But Jessica deserves better than that. This light of a girl, she deserves better than for this to end here, in this room, with the twelve of us tired people and our best guess. I can't speak for Wayne. But I'm voting 'not guilty' because we don't know, and all I can hope for is that one day, maybe, we all will."

CHAPTER 21

THE WEEK'S FRESHEST ROTTEN NEWS
NOW

Maya and her parents flipped through cable news channels and smartphone screens for the latest updates. They took turns reciting fresh reports from Twitter, Facebook, every pop-up-ad-laden website with "news" in its address. Each update muddled or outright contradicted the one before. What to believe? Maya's dad breathlessly read aloud anything from Twitter that opened with the word "verified." Her mom read the established, old media outlets—*The New York Times*, *The Washington Post*, CNN, her local *Albuquerque Journal*. But these sites only updated every half hour.

Someone on Maya's mom's Facebook feed posted photos of the motel where Bobby was found. Twenty minutes later, a journalist on Maya's dad's Twitter feed posted the same photo stamped with the word "debunked." Apparently it was a photo of a similarly named motel where someone else had committed suicide four years earlier.

The UK's *Daily Mail*—with astonishing

efficiency, given its distance from the scene—published quotes from an eyewitness at the motel. The eyewitness said that before Bobby Nock hanged himself, he'd murdered another guest who'd recognized him. This news was even harder for Maya to believe, but when it was confirmed by an Associated Press affiliate on Twitter, she began to give it weight. But none of the cable channels had mentioned it.

An excruciating ninety minutes later, the Associated Press acknowledged that their confirmation of the *Daily Mail*'s story had been based on the same eyewitness account. Thirty-five minutes after that, *The Dallas Morning News* identified this "eyewitness" as a known hoaxer. Within the hour, the *Daily Mail* story disappeared from the Internet, as if it had never existed. Links landed on error pages. Tweets were expunged. Screenshots were all that remained of a story that had circulated among millions of people across the world. The AP added a confounding "editor's note" to the end of their story, saying that the entire article had been retracted, but they were leaving the page up in the spirit of transparency. Or, Maya figured, in the spirit of capturing the last handful of clicks on a known falsehood.

The hours drifted on. Information arrived ("Bobby Nock Wrote 45-Page Suicide Manifesto"). Information was contradicted ("Update—Bobby Nock Did Not Write a Suicide Manifesto").

Political implications were extracted from the scant facts like drops dredged from the bottom of a long-dry well ("Bobby Nock's 'Black Lives Matter' Suicide Note Proves Fallacy of Identity Politics"). After five hours no one—not Maya, not her parents, not anyone else—could reasonably claim to be better informed than if they'd just taken a nap.

Toward the end of the afternoon, the local sheriff in Broward, Texas, held a press conference and laid out what most anybody following the story already knew.

Bobby Nock had been tracked to the motel by representatives of an Australian tabloid. When banging on his door produced no response, the reporters had been able to convince the motel clerk to open the room, where they found Bobby hanging from a ceiling fan. A suicide note was found by the police on a coffee table, just inches from his feet. The handwriting matched the form that Bobby had filled out at the front desk, when he'd checked in under the name Chris Rummel.

The suicide note did indeed say, simply, "I'm so sorry."

Beside the body, the sheriff of Broward confirmed, was a silver necklace. Photos of the necklace, he noted, had already been leaked to the press.

The sheriff had one new piece of information to add: long, blond hairs had been recovered from the locket's clasp. A DNA test was under way. But to his eye, he said, the color of the hair matched that of Jessica Silver.

Jessica. Rick. Bobby.

Maya watched the sun set on the far side of the ocean while the three deaths twisted around and around in her head. The murder of Jessica Silver had set into motion a chain of events that had resulted in the murder of Rick Leonard. The murder of Rick Leonard had led to the suicide of Bobby Nock. Maya had fought for some manner of justice, or truth, but it had resulted only in the laying to waste of more lives. Soon this cycle of death and destruction would come for her too.

Maya still couldn't believe that Bobby had killed Jessica. She could, however, imagine him so hopeless and alone that he'd killed himself. Over and over, she searched for any other explanation for his death. Over and over she kept coming back to Lou Silver.

If Lou had killed Jessica, as Bobby had suspected, and then taken the locket from her dead body . . . kept it for ten years . . . and only now planted it on Bobby . . . after murdering him and somehow making it look like suicide . . .

But here the logic broke down. Why would Lou have saved the locket? Even if he had, for some inexplicable reason, taken his daughter's locket after murdering her, why not plant it on Bobby a decade ago? Wouldn't the locket have been most incriminating when Bobby was first under investigation? If Lou—or anyone else—was trying to frame Bobby for murder, they'd done a spectacularly bad—and untimely—job of it.

Maya tried to conjure up some kind of grand conspiracy theory that would explain the frustrating illogic. But every scenario in which the "real killer" was framing Bobby strained credulity.

In the days following Bobby's death, she called Craig frequently, trying out her increasingly baroque theories on him. He was a patient audience, especially since he didn't have any stake at all in who'd killed Jessica Silver.

"What about Rick's mysterious new evidence against Bobby?" she asked him. "We still don't know what it was."

"Unless," Craig offered, "the evidence was the locket. If Rick found out, somehow, that Bobby still had it, and then confronted him about it in Miracle, or tried to steal it, and that's why Bobby ran . . ."

"So why wouldn't Rick just tell me that? Why all the secrecy?"

"I have no idea. Maybe Rick had some plan up his sleeve?"

"None of this," she pleaded, "explains what happened to Rick in my hotel room."

"Unless," Craig countered gently, "you killed

him in a struggle. Because that theory explains everything."

But I know I didn't kill him, she wanted to scream. She elected to spare Craig any further protesting of her innocence.

Maya thought about the gun-toting dealers she'd met in East Jesus. And the sex offenders she'd met in Miracle. Would any of them have been willing to kill Rick on Bobby's behalf? Certainly any of them could have done what Bobby couldn't: sneak into the Omni Hotel undetected. But how on earth was Maya supposed to prove that in court?

Maya had hired a psychologist once to evaluate a client. The psychologist had been great on the stand. She'd gone on and on about the "cycles of violence" in which Maya's client had been both victim and perpetrator. The woman made them sound like ocean tides: as inescapable as the gravitational pull of the full moon.

To Maya, "cycles" sounded too much like just deserts. She did not believe in karma. To her, violence was a sickness, a contagion. Everyone who came into contact with it became a carrier. Its survivors, its bystanders, all served to bring more violence into the world.

Maya felt like a fool. She could blame the wickedness of the world all she liked. But if the week's freshest rotten news held true, then she would eventually have to admit to herself, and to everyone else, that these most recent disasters—the murder of Rick Leonard, the suicide of Bobby Nock, her own upcoming prosecution—were happening because ten years ago, she'd been wrong.

Maya remained in Malibu under the watchful eyes of her anxious parents. They spent most of the time sitting on either the living room sofas or around the kitchen table, trying not to obsess over the constant stream of news and rumors. They took turns informing each other of things they'd learned ten seconds before.

Bobby Nock's family's lives became a hell once again. His parents were hounded for their reactions to their son's suicide. They were treated like criminals. Bobby's dad even apologized to Lou Silver. On camera, he said that while he'd always believed his son before, now the truth was unavoidable. He was so sorry that his boy had taken the life of someone else's child.

Maya called Lou Silver the morning after the suicide. The same woman answered his line and said that Lou would call her back. He never did. Maya called again, the next day and the day after, but the woman only repeated that Lou would return Maya's call as soon as he could.

Maya had to accept that she'd served her purpose. Had Lou told the reporters to follow her to East Jesus? Probably. But even if he hadn't, he knew that sending her to Bobby was sure to provoke some sort of reaction—from Maya, from Bobby, or from prying eyes. Lou wanted Bobby punished, one way or another, and using Maya as the catalyst had been yet another way to inflict pain. Lou's plan had worked even better than he'd hoped: Bobby was dead. Lou wouldn't have any future use for her.

Had Lou abused Jessica, as Bobby had claimed? Even if Bobby had killed her, he could have been telling the truth about that. Maybe Lou had abused Jessica and then Bobby had killed her. Or maybe Bobby had conducted an inappropriate relationship with her and then Lou had killed her. As far as Maya was concerned, they could both go to hell.

Lou gave a press conference two days after the suicide. Maya and her parents watched from Craig's living room. They could hear the gentle thrum of the ocean from the open windows.

Lou stood beside Ted Morningstar, now retired, on a dais that had been constructed on the front steps of the courthouse. They took turns congratulating each other on their vindication.

Lou appeared taller on television. Almost handsome. Or perhaps she just wasn't used to seeing him smile.

Maya had seen Morningstar on TV a few times since the trial. He gave legal commentary sometimes, detailing all the ways in which clever defense attorneys used "the race card" to garner sympathy for their clients. He'd written a mystery novel at some point, Maya remembered—a loosely fictionalized version of the Jessica Silver murder in which he was the hero. He'd cast himself as a Dirty Harry type, an honest straight-talker done in by all the "race hustlers." There was something perverse, Maya had thought at the time, about the way that a girl's death had allowed so many of them to live out their own heroic fantasies. Morningstar had always wanted to be Clint Eastwood. Gibson had probably wanted to be Johnnie Cochran. Maya had thought she was Henry Fonda from *12 Angry Men*. The one juror brave enough to tell the truth to her blind and callous peers.

Maya picked out an alert face among the row of civil servants standing in the background: Head Deputy DA Ben Gao appeared ready and able to continue cleaning up this awful mess. His presence at the conference suggested that even though Bobby Nock had, by some stroke of luck, escaped full justice for his crimes, Maya would not be so fortunate. If she thought they'd hounded Bobby to the ends of the earth, just wait till Ben Gao was done with her.

Lou Silver was joined on the dais by his wife, Elaine. She appeared as blankly unreadable as her husband was ebullient. Maya leaned in closer to the screen. If Bobby had told the truth about the abuse, then Elaine had both suffered and concealed terrible behavior. What was going on behind the impassive lines of her carefully arranged face?

There was something macabre about Lou's evident thrill at being able to comment on the confession. "I am relieved," he said to the cameras, "to be able to say that justice has been served."

And yet who could blame him? For a decade all he'd sought was the justice that people like Maya had said could not be delivered. Despite the doubters, despite the wearying passage of time, he had persevered.

A reporter asked Lou to comment on the jury that had acquitted Bobby. In the background, Ben Gao flinched.

Lou gathered himself before responding. "I don't blame the jury. They were taken in by Bobby Nock, as so many others were. They made a mistake. But I believe they made an honest one."

"Do you believe," a reporter asked, "that Maya Seale murdered Rick Leonard?"

Photos of her own face filled the TV screen.

"I think it's up to a new jury to make that determination." Lou shook his head, as if he was ruing the capriciousness of destiny. "I do wish that they could have admitted their mistake. Maya Seale . . . well, you can see what happens when somebody digs in their heels and can't acknowledge they were wrong."

The reporters threw more questions at him, but Lou wouldn't comment further on what he said was "a criminal investigation with which I'm less familiar."

They showed the footage of Maya taken in East Jesus. She looked like Bobby's accomplice. The way the camera lights hit her eyes in the dark desert night, she seemed possessed. "How long has she known where he was?" the anchor asked when they cut back to the studio. "How long has she been protecting him?"

"Goddamn it," her dad said from beside her on the couch. Her mom placed a comforting hand on his knee.

"Dad," Maya said. "It's okay."

"They can't say this stuff about you!"

She knew better than to turn off the TV. Nothing would be served by hiding this from him. He'd be binge-watching repeats all night no matter what.

"Who cares what they say about me?" she said.

He looked at her like she really was the lunatic they made her out to be. "I do."

And it nearly broke her heart again.

Maya discovered that being a pariah was easier the second time.

She'd had lots of practice at letting the

comments go, along with all their nasty implications. A late-night comedian made a joke about Bobby Nock's "power over white girls," for which he then had to publicly apologize. The public hadn't learned of Maya's relationship with Rick, so far, which at least spared her that indignity. But most of the TV commentators did think she'd killed him. "Did Bobby Nock Train Juror to Kill for Him?" was the most outlandish of the mainstream headlines. Without consulting the record, everyone patted themselves on the back for having been right about Bobby before. It gave them solid backing for their conviction that Maya was guilty now. The predictability of the arguments lessened their sting.

This time around, Maya knew better than to feel gratitude toward her occasional defenders. Even those who claimed to be on her side now— those intrepid reporters and eager legal beagles— would throw her under the bus the first time they found an opportunity to be somehow bipartisan in their opinions. The plum microphones were reserved for those who broke with their own "sides" just enough to seem fair-minded, like a Republican who was in favor of gun control, or a Democrat who wanted to eliminate the estate tax. Some targets were so easy to hit that everyone had to take their shot. "Surely we can *all* agree . . ." And sure enough, what they could all agree on was that Maya had circumvented justice at every turn.

She found herself fondly remembering all the public accusations Rick had leveled against her, ten years ago. They'd cut so deeply, then. And now? How quaint they seemed. How reasonable and measured, compared to this current frenzy. She realized that what she most wanted to say to Rick, were he here to listen, was simply: "I forgive you."

Would he care? She'd never know. But it was the truth.

She would make it through this, armed with the practical callousness of experience. She knew what people were saying about her, and why. She had more pressing concerns. She had to keep herself out of jail.

On the fourth day following Bobby's death, just as the news cycle began to shift, Maya made the drive back to L.A.

She returned to the offices of her law firm as a client.

Everyone was painfully polite about it. The receptionist gave her a hug. Crystal was sent for. Maya had to be "brought back" now. She was not free to roam wild through the halls.

"This is so weird," Crystal said as they embraced.

"You're telling me."

Did Maya still technically work here? She could only wonder as she followed Crystal to Craig's office. They were interrupted frequently by colleagues with hugs and words of encouragement. She was currently on leave, but soon, as the weeks wore on, she'd need to have a frank talk with HR. Her cases, at least the ones with upcoming court dates, had been reassigned. The longer-term ones could wait to see how long Maya's absence would last.

Craig was waiting for her, leaning back against the front edge of his wooden desk.

"Hi," he said.

"Hi," Maya said.

Crystal looked back and forth between them. "Just make sure she doesn't go to prison, okay?"

Then she left, closing the door behind her.

"So we're arguing that you're innocent," Craig said as Maya took a seat, "against my better judgment. Which means we have a lot to do. Most pressingly: Who killed Rick Leonard?"

Maya knew this was coming. "I want to play the field."

"So we argue that it was Peter Wilkie? And/or Wayne Russel? And/or the rest? I got the dossiers you sent. They're . . . Jesus."

"I know." Among the craziest of the moment's ironies was that Rick had provided them with the best trove of evidence with which to acquit Maya of his murder.

"Plus," Maya added, "any one of Bobby Nock's friends from either Miracle or East Jesus. I'm sure Mike and Mike can find a few of them with assault convictions and flimsy alibis."

Craig seemed pleased. "I'll put them on that right away."

"Do we have anything new on Wayne?" Maya said.

"Nothing yet." Craig shrugged. "It's only been a week."

Maya thought about the dirt on Wayne contained in his dossier. The accusations within it weren't laudatory, but they hardly seemed bad enough to kill over.

Still, even if Rick's file on him was thin, Wayne's deception about his whereabouts on the night of the murder made him a promising suspect. "He stayed in touch with Fran Goldenberg, after the trial. She told me, at the hotel that night."

Craig wasn't impressed.

"Maybe she knows something about where he is now," Maya added.

Craig considered this. "I'll send Mike."

"I'll go myself."

"Fran is both a potential witness against you and a potential alternate suspect. I do not want you talking to her."

Maya raised an eyebrow. "Did Mike— or Mike—talk to her earlier? Right after the murder?"

"Yes."

"What did Fran tell them?"

"Nothing."

Maya let Craig's answer stand as confirmation of her point.

Craig folded his arms across his chest. "Okay, fine."

Maya turned to leave.

"Please don't make my job any harder than you've already made it."

Maya smiled. "I thought you were the best criminal defense attorney in L.A."

She was already shutting the door behind her when she heard him yell, "And don't you dare forget it!"

Fran Goldenberg still lived in Los Feliz, in a single-story house on Tracy Street, a quiet road that sprouted at an irregular angle from one large avenue and then vanished, half a mile later, into another. Tucked away up a few redbrick steps, the house was dark when Maya rang the bell in the early afternoon. No one answered the door.

Waiting in her car, Maya thought through her major reservation about the theory that Wayne had killed Rick: *Why?*

Did it have anything to do with the evidence Rick had found on Bobby? But why would Wayne care? He hadn't commented on the case publicly in years. Hadn't he gone to Colorado to get away from the whole thing?

Or had Wayne entered Maya's room that night in the hope of killing her, but then found Rick instead? After everything Maya had put Wayne through, she could imagine him wanting to kill her. But actually attempting it? And then why, when the door to her room opened and Rick was there, would Wayne kill Rick instead?

After spending over an hour with these circuitous thoughts, Maya finally spotted the woman who might know at least some of the answers. Fran Goldenberg was walking along Tracy Street. Her short hair was tucked behind one ear, and she wore stylishly thick black glasses. If her hair hadn't been naturally white, Maya might have mistaken her for a schoolboy. Her arms were full of unwieldy flower boxes.

Maya stepped out of her car.

"Hi," she said. "What're those?"

Fran gave a start. "Succulents."

"You need a hand?"

Fran shifted the plants in her arms. "What are you doing here?"

"You've seen the news?"

"There's a lot on the news these days. Every day, these days."

"Can we go inside?"

Fran handed one of the flower boxes to Maya and led the way up the steps. There were fresh-cut flowers liberally placed throughout the Spanish-style home, Maya noticed, as Fran brought her into a kitchen at the side of the house. The white tiles on the countertops had been trendy decades ago, fallen out of fashion, and were now trendy again.

"I didn't know you had such a green thumb," Maya said.

"Retirement."

"I've always meant to take up gardening. My mom loves it."

"What stopped you?"

"Time, I guess?"

Fran poured herself a glass of water. She didn't offer one to Maya. "There's a lot more of that than you might think."

There was a loud creak of floorboards from upstairs. "You have houseguests?"

"My son," Fran said. "He came into town after . . . what happened last week."

"My parents are here too. They're kind of driving me crazy."

"How are you holding up?"

Were she inclined to answer honestly, Maya would have to say that she was scared shitless about potentially spending the rest of her life in prison.

"Did you hear that Wayne is missing?" she asked instead.

Fran picked up a stray petal that had fallen from one of the flowers.

"And that he was in L.A. the night of the

murder? Do you have any idea where he is? Or why he was in L.A. that night after telling everyone he wasn't coming?"

Fran threw the dead petal in the trash. "We didn't stay in touch, really."

"You two seemed pretty close, by the end."

"Of the trial?" Fran seemed dubious. "He was having a hard time. We all were. . . . When I'm having a hard time, I like to help. My sons told me once that it was a compulsion. Helping."

Maya understood the feeling.

The floorboards creaked again. Fran looked irritated. "Will you excuse me? I should make sure he doesn't need anything."

She left and Maya could hear her footsteps up the house's central staircase. And then, only silence.

Maya gazed out the windows to a small rose garden in the back. The driveway curled around, behind the house, leading to what had probably once been a garage but now was likely a toolshed. Parked in front of the shed was a huge red truck.

A Ford F-150.

Quickly, she drew her phone and pulled up the license plate of Wayne Russel's red Ford F-150. They were the same.

Wayne Russel was here.

Maya sped from the kitchen into the living room.

"Maya?" Fran was descending the central staircase. "Is something the matter?"

Maya looked past Fran up the stairs—she was terrified of the unstable liar on the second floor.

Her first thought was to run—but then Fran would put it together. She'd tell Wayne, and by the time Maya called the cops and they arrived, he'd be gone. Maya would have no evidence that he'd ever been here.

"No, no," she said to Fran, and gestured to a vase of freshly cut roses in the living room. "I was just admiring the flowers."

Fran clearly took pride in them. "It's hard to make things grow here. The soil."

"Someone once told me that no life was ever supposed to be here. Something about the desert." Maya knew she should get the hell out of there. But if she did, she might be running right into a life sentence. If she could get back into the kitchen, she could snap a photo of the truck. That would at least give her something to use.

"Rick told me that," she added.

Fran took the last step off the staircase. "It must be so hard. To have everyone think you killed him."

"Do *you* think I killed him?"

"Of course not." As if the suggestion were insane. As if it were not an opinion held by half the city.

There was another creak from upstairs.

"Everything okay up there?" Maya said. "With your son?"

Fran's eyes went to the ceiling. "One second."

The second Fran was out of view, Maya hurried to the kitchen. She took out her phone, pointed the camera through the window, and snapped a photo of the truck. She checked the image: The license plate was readable. This was good. Time to go.

She spun around.

Wayne Russel was standing in the doorway.

He wore blue jeans, a black T-shirt, and heavy boots. His shirt was loose but she could still see the contours of his muscles. She had forgotten how big he was.

She felt the back of her legs pressing against a cabinet.

"Maya," Wayne said, "I'm not gonna hurt you."

She could see Fran behind him in the doorway, looking petrified. "He won't. Really."

With two taps of Maya's thumb against her phone, she hit the last number dialed.

Somewhere, Crystal's phone was ringing.

She could hear the sound from her phone. *Pick up.*

"By the time this call connects," Maya said, "they'll be able to place the GPS of my phone right in this kitchen. They'll know exactly where the call come from. Cell technology is a lot better than it was ten years ago. If you do to me what you did to Rick, there's no way you'll get away with it."

This was not exactly true, but Maya did not think Wayne or Fran would know that.

She still heard only ringing on the other end of the line.

"I didn't kill Rick," Wayne said.

"Join the fucking club."

He stepped into the room. He was still feet away but seemed to loom over her. "You gotta put down the phone. I don't want the cops to . . ."

Fran placed a hand on his shoulder. "You don't want the cops to do what?" Fran was talking to Wayne, not to Maya. "Maybe it's time you talked to the cops."

"They'll get me. For what happened to Rick."

Maya heard Crystal's voicemail pick up. "This is Crys, leave a message . . ."

Fran said: "If you don't talk, what are they going to do to *her?*"

Maya had her phone to her ear. "This is Maya. I am at the home of Fran Goldenberg and . . ."

There was fear in Wayne's eyes. But there was also genuine concern. "Are they really going to put you in jail?"

Maya nodded. "They already did. I'm out on bail."

"Put down the phone," Fran said, "and we'll tell you everything we know."

Maya looked back and forth between them. Somehow, Wayne seemed more scared for Maya than for himself.

She could not believe what she was about to do.

"I'll call you back," Maya said into the phone. And hung up.

She was trusting these people with her life. "Okay. So. Who the fuck killed Rick Leonard?"

Wayne leaned against the doorway. Fran exhaled.

"The thing that gets me," Fran said, "is that we don't even know."

A few minutes later, they were all in the living room. The vase of roses provided a sweet scent as Fran told her everything.

Wayne had changed his mind at the eleventh hour about attending the reunion. The thought of all of them meeting without him had been harder to handle than the thought of having to face them all again. So he'd gotten in his truck, filled up the tank, and hit the road. Only by the time he arrived in downtown L.A., it was late. Real late. And as he pulled up outside the Omni . . .

The cops were everywhere. Something bad had gone down.

"I saw you," Wayne said, addressing Maya. "I saw the cops take you away."

"That's when I saw him," Fran said. "After they arrested you."

Fran explained that the cops had woken everyone up and sent them all home. She'd seen Wayne in his truck, just sitting there in the driver's seat.

"If the cops saw him," Fran said, "he'd look deceitful."

"He *was* deceitful," Maya said.

Wayne shrugged.

"So I brought him back here," Fran said. "At first the plan was just to figure out what had happened. But no one was talking to the cops, and the cops weren't saying anything to us—how Rick had died, if someone killed him. We didn't even find out about the traffic camera for two more days."

"Two more days in which they suspected me of his murder."

"Well," Fran said, "think about it from our perspective."

"I'm trying."

"From our perspective, maybe you'd killed him."

Maya turned to Wayne. *Anybody could kill anybody, right?*

"I saw you and Rick," Wayne said. "Back then. Rick was coming out of your room one morning."

"I know."

"So I figured . . . I dunno."

"Understand," Fran said, "Wayne didn't do anything wrong. He's a good person."

Maya would have laughed if the whole thing weren't so brutal. The number of times in her life in which horrific behavior had been justified because someone was "a good person"! The

391

volume of atrocities she'd been privy to that had been committed by people "just doing their best." She'd heard it from defiant clients and their indignant families. She'd heard it from overzealous prosecutors whose "hands were tied" as they followed the law's most draconian interpretations. She'd heard it from her fellow jurors. Even worse, she'd turned on the TV to hear people say it about her.

Maya had no more sympathy for supposedly "good" people whose decisions had led, time and time again, to the misery of others.

"You're both telling me," she said, "that you had nothing to do with Rick's death, and you have absolutely no idea who did?"

Neither of them said a word. They sat firmly, solidly, like stones prepared to sink together.

Fran truly believed that Wayne was blameless, and so her deceit on his behalf—a lie purely of omission—had been, she'd thought, justified. They both had genuinely believed that they were doing the right thing.

Maya was furious. She was just like Fran, wasn't she? She'd covered up for a killer that she—and only she—had believed. Now she knew better.

"Do you want me to go to the police?" Wayne said. "I will. If it'll help you."

The horrible irony was that it wouldn't. Wayne's story was loosely exculpatory—for him. Leaving him missing was a lot more incriminating, and thus a lot more useful to her defense. In some deeply depressing way, his disappearance, all this time, had been far better for her case.

"You want to help me?" she asked. "Help me find Rick's killer."

They agreed to re-canvass. They would talk to all the jurors again, to see what new information could be teased out given the events of the previous week. Maya told Wayne and Fran what she had on Peter. Fran was shocked. Wayne volunteered to beat the living shit out of him, personally. Maya would have let him do it if it wouldn't have potentially complicated her lawsuit on behalf of Margarita.

When she'd visited Jae, Trisha had been there. Now that Trisha was, presumably, back in Houston, Wayne would try Jae again.

Fran would talk to Yasmine and Kathy, neither of whom Maya had gotten an opportunity to interrogate. Fran would undoubtedly have better luck.

Maya would return to the places she'd already been in the hopes that somehow something would break.

Lila Rosales had red eyes when she answered her front door. She was trying, poorly, to hide the fact that she'd just been crying. "Maya, hey . . . Sorry, it's not a good time."

"I tried calling," Maya said, embarrassed. "But then I realized I was nearby, so . . . I can come back."

"God, no, what's wrong with me?" Lila concealed a wipe of her eyes by pretended to scratch an itch on her nose. "I'm so glad you're not in jail. You must be going through . . . I can't imagine. Come in."

She led Maya into the living room, where her father stood with his arms crossed. He glared at Maya for interrupting the argument that they'd obviously just been having. The last week must not have been easy on them either. Lila exchanged a few quick, tense sentences in Spanish with her father, the result of which was that he left to go run an errand.

After he was gone, Lila turned to Maya. "I really gotta get my own place."

"Every time I talk to *my* dad, I feel like he's going back and forth between wanting to save me and wanting to strangle me."

"Yeah."

From the back of the house came what sounded like Aaron crying.

Lila sighed wearily. "Wait here a minute?"

While Lila tended to Aaron, Maya wandered the front half of the small house. The kitchen was spotless. Empty beer bottles rested in a box by the sink, awaiting their turn in the recycling bin. Sippy cups and rubber-tipped spoons were drying on the rack. It occurred to Maya that she should have brought some of Fran's flowers as a gift.

Was it polite to bring flowers to someone's home when you were investigating a murder?

The refrigerator was adorned with Aaron's drawings. In crayon and marker and finger paints. Animals of all kinds. A big yellow lion. A bear that, for some reason, was bright purple. Even an angry, red alligator . . .

Maya felt a familiar sensation of cold. She must be exhausted. The alligator looked *exactly* like the one in Bobby Nock's tent. The big, chomping teeth, the red scales, the pinpoint eyes . . .

This was insane. How could Bobby have a drawing made by Lila's son?

She heard Lila enter the kitchen.

Maya pointed to the fridge. "Why did Bobby Nock have a drawing that your son made?"

Lila stopped moving.

"Maya," Lila said. "I need you not to do anything crazy right now, okay?"

CHAPTER 22

LILA
OCTOBER 19, 2009

Lila Rosales couldn't take her eyes off Bobby Nock. He sat at the defendant's table, staring off into the same unfathomable distance that he had every day for the past five months. She sat in the second row of the jury box—the same spot from which she'd viewed the entire trial—peeking over Fran's shoulder. She had spent countless hours just like this, imagining what was going on in his head. What he must have thought of these lawyers, the judge, this whole proceeding . . .

She knew so much about him. And yet what did he know about her?

Her name had been on the news, but was he allowed to watch the news? After all this time, he might not even know her name.

"Has the jury reached a verdict?" the judge asked.

Kathy stood. Lila craned her neck to better see Bobby's face.

"We have, Your Honor," Kathy said.

"Please hand your verdict to the bailiff."

Kathy handed the paper to Bailiff Steve. They'd filled it out and folded it up back in the jury room. Each one of them had signed their name to the bottom of the page.

Bailiff Steve carried the paper to the judge. Lila mostly kept her eyes on Bobby, who, even now, didn't react in any way she could see. The judge's expression didn't change either. The ability to keep a good poker face was probably in his job description.

Bobby's mom and dad weren't even trying to hold themselves together. They made sense to Lila. They seemed like the only ones who were behaving like real people. His mom was crying. His dad had his arm around her. They were totally focused on Bobby, though he didn't seem to pay them any notice at all.

Well, Lila thought, she couldn't blame Elaine Silver for the blank look on her face. That woman had lost a child, and after a tragedy like that she was entitled to wear any face she chose.

Lou Silver was sitting next to his wife. Lila hadn't seen Lou since the moment he'd personally sunk the prosecution's case. Bad as that was, she still felt so sorry for him, for everything he'd been through.

The judge silently read the verdict, folded the paper again, and passed it back to the bailiff, who delivered it to Kathy.

"Would the foreperson read the verdict aloud?" the judge said.

Kathy's hands were shaking as she unfolded

the paper. She looked left and then right, as if confirming with the others, one last time, that they were united. "On the charge of murder in the first degree," Kathy said, "we the jury find Robert Nock not guilty."

The courtroom was creepy-quiet. The prosecutor didn't budge. Bobby looked stunned. Finally, he gave a start when his lawyer placed a hand on his shoulder. Gibson leaned in and whispered something. Lila wished she could hear what it was.

Then Elaine Silver shrieked. A single shriek of pain. It was the only sound Lila heard.

Lou Silver did the strangest thing. He smiled. It was bitter, vengeful, and resigned. As if he'd been prepared for the worst and the verdict had given him just that.

Lila wanted to tell the Silvers that she was so sorry this had happened but that this verdict was for the best. None of this felt the way she'd imagined. She'd known that there wouldn't be applause, like at the end of a movie. But she'd figured there'd be some kind of outward sign of a job well done. When you did well at school, the teacher gave you an A. But here? After everything that she and the others had given—after all the hard work they'd done to win Bobby's freedom— this was it? A tear, a shriek, a few coughs. Even more left unsaid than there had been before.

Lila wanted to scream too. Why didn't this feel like a victory?

"This concludes the case of *The People versus Robert Nock*," the judge said. "Ladies and gentlemen of the jury, your service is over. The bailiff will take you back to your room to tend to a few final items of paperwork. And then you will be released."

The way he said "released" sounded like they were caged animals about to be thrown into the jungle after getting soft and fat in captivity.

"This court thanks you for performing a service above and beyond what is asked of any citizen. We know how much you've given to the justice system. And we are grateful."

The judge didn't sound grateful. He sounded pissed.

Before Lila realized it, the other jurors were on their feet. A bottleneck formed beside her as the group began exiting the box. Wayne loomed above her, looking down expectantly. *Time to go.*

Lila felt silly. Of course the *courtroom* wasn't the place for joyful outbursts. Of course she'd have to wait till she got home. Her dad and mom would be really proud of her, for saving a man's life. So would her sister. Maybe her cousins would even come over, with the babies who by now—*Jesus*—were probably toddlers!

She'd have the ending she was due when she got home. She would return a hero.

A pair of LAPD officers drove her back to South Los Angeles to the home she'd lived in for her entire life. But a few blocks away, they hit a patch of bad traffic. She didn't remember these streets ever having been this packed. When the cop car turned onto Lila's block, she saw what was causing it: The pack of press outside her parents' house was almost as big as the one she'd seen outside the court. The cops hit their lights, dispersing the crowd, then pulled into the driveway behind her dad's old Ford.

Her dad opened the front door and a million cameras flashed. He was dressed up, like this was a special occasion. When he saw her face, he looked like he was about to cry. Lila reached for a door handle, then remembered that cop car doors didn't open from the inside.

The officers got out and did the honors for her.

She was still in shock as her dad wrapped his arms around her.

"*Te amo*," he said. "*Querida*."

The press kept their distance as he led her back into the house, his strong arms around her.

Inside, her mom, her sister, the cousins, and the two babies were waiting. They hugged her all at once. Lila realized that she was crying.

Finally, she was home.

Lila couldn't remember when she'd ever felt like her parents were proud of her before. She'd never been on one of the teams at high school, like her brother. She'd never run track like some of her cousins. She knew that her parents loved her, knew they'd do anything for her, but she'd never felt like she'd done anything to make them proud.

Until now.

"*¿Qué has hecho?*"

What have you done?

It was her mom.

Lila was confused. Her mom sounded just like she had when Lila had stayed out past curfew and got caught trying to slip back into the house. Her mom had been half relieved that she was safe and half furious at Lila for scaring her. Lila realized that something was wrong as she took in the expressions of her family through her tears. That wasn't pride on their faces—it was worry.

"It's okay," her dad said, trying to calm her family. "Let her be."

His strong hands held on to her shoulders. "*Querida*, it's all going to be okay."

Her dad sounded like he was trying to reassure himself as much as her.

He'd always been a bad liar.

She was kicked out of beauty school.

Only a few reporters had shown up there, harassing her classmates about what kind of student she was, whether she'd had any extracurricular contact with her own teachers, and other nonsense questions. But the administrator still said her presence was a distraction. "We have to consider all our students," the woman told her.

Lila was furious. She hadn't broken any rules, she hadn't done anything wrong. How was it fair to punish her like this? What was she supposed to do?

Finding a job was a joke. Her name was common enough that it didn't set off any alarm bells right away, but her potential employers all figured out who she was soon enough. The first few applications, she was dumb enough to put "State of California Court System" as her previous employer. (They had paid her $1,436 for her five months of jury service. Her dad used it to pay down the debt on his Mastercard.) But even when she left that information out, she had to explain why she'd dropped out of school—and once she said "jury service," all it took was a few quick Googles for the interviewer to put it together. Payless, Trader Joe's . . . She was even rejected for a shift management job at Cold Stone. She'd worked the scoop at Cold Stone when she was in high school. And now, at nineteen, she couldn't get the job she'd had when she was fifteen.

She started sleeping later and later every morning. She tried to make herself helpful around the house, but it seemed like every time she put the serving bowls away in one drawer, her mom would tell her that they belonged in another. Nothing she did was right. She was more tired than she'd ever been before. She wished she could just curl up under her childhood sheets and sleep forever beneath the pastel butterflies.

Lila had been home for two weeks when some asshole chucked a rock through the living room window. Lila wasn't scared, but her mom was. The next week, it was toilet paper flung over the roof. This one had to be some kids from the neighborhood. But her mom acted like they were being invaded. Hadn't her brother's stupid friends done the same thing when they were younger?

Her dad was drinking more, Lila noticed. On the rare occasions when she took out the trash, she could hear the loud rattle of empty Corona bottles at the bottom of the bags. He was piling the rest of the family garbage on top again. A few beers wasn't a worry, but hiding the bottles was another thing altogether.

Her dad was dead sober, though, when he explained why the verdict was such a shock to everybody on the outside. He told her about Bobby's previous assault conviction. Apparently it had been all over the news for months but the jury hadn't been told. Or, Lila thought, it was all over the news *because* the jury hadn't been told. Who cared, anyway? Why did everyone act like just because Bobby had gotten into one fight in high school he must have murdered a teenage girl? They had taken that one little fact and blown it up. They acted like they knew him.

She was the one who'd spent all those months in a courtroom with him, getting inside his head. She knew he was a good person.

She watched his old friends on TV talking about his upstanding character. She saw his former students talk about how kind he'd been, how understanding. She felt vindicated. Hearing what all these people had to say, she felt like more information had been kept from her, during the trial, than had been disclosed.

She saw Rick on the TV too. She watched him apologize for the decision they'd all made, together. She watched him say terrible things about the other jurors—and she watched him save his worst insults for poor Maya.

Jae's interviews weren't as cutting, even though he'd switched perspectives just as quickly as Rick had. Trisha only said a few things publicly, but what she did say seemed to put her on Rick's side.

Seeing the other jurors on TV gave her a strangely homesick feeling. No one out here in the real world understood what she'd been through. Only those eleven other people did, however much they might have hated each other.

She called Yasmine. Finally, she'd be able to talk to somebody who was going through the same thing she was. Lila wanted to meet somewhere quiet, but somehow each time Yasmine rescheduled their plans for the dead of night. Like all Yasmine wanted was to get out of the house and go dancing. They dressed up. They sipped cranberry cocktails in loud places with dance floors. They got drunk and then as soon as guys started flirting with them, they'd disappear. At least with Yasmine around, they never ended up paying for their own drinks.

Yasmine was done talking about Bobby Nock. Lila felt like she'd never gotten the chance to start.

Their nights out grew more infrequent. What Lila wanted, more than anything, was someone who'd been there. Someone who she could reminisce with about Bailiff Steve without having to explain who he was, or how weird it had been that they'd spent so much time with him, even though he wasn't one of them.

Fran Goldenberg met her for coffee, once. But Fran didn't understand what Lila had lost when she'd gotten kicked out of beauty school. Lila tried to explain how she missed doing hair, missed getting to work with the different women, hearing their stories, but Fran nodded the same way her cousins did. Like she was just being polite.

"Well, dear," she said, "have you thought about what you might like to do instead? You're so young. You can go anywhere, do anything you want. What's something you've always dreamed of doing, but never got the chance?"

Where else was Lila going to go? Everyone she knew was here.

She didn't call Fran again.

She had trouble sleeping. She'd stay up all night and then sleep all morning. She barely had enough energy to pull herself into the TV room anymore. What was wrong with her?

She'd seen a show once about a guy who had a stomach parasite and slept all the time. She googled "parasite." But none of the other symptoms seemed to fit.

Of course, she thought about Bobby Nock. The news provided constant updates about what he was up to. The cops, she learned, were bringing charges against him for distribution of child pornography. Even the people on TV who hated Bobby thought this was a stretch.

When she was feeling sorry for herself, she reminded herself that Bobby had it worse. He'd been falsely accused of a terrible crime. Imprisoned for almost a year. And now, hounded still.

She wanted to reach out to him. And then it came to her: Why not write Bobby a letter? Why not tell him that she could only guess about what he was going through, but that she supported him all the way?

She knew that if she were in his position, she'd appreciate a letter of support.

"Dear Bobby Nock," she wrote. "My name is

Lila Rosales and I was one of the jurors in your trial. Number 429. No matter what anyone says, I know we made the right decision." She went on to tell him a little bit more about herself. About her life before the trial; about her life now; about how much she'd missed her family before but now they only made her feel more alone.

Before she knew it, she'd written him five single-spaced pages. She realized that this was probably the longest thing she'd written since high school!

She addressed the letter to his defense attorney. Just sending it made her feel better. She'd been able to get all that stuff off her chest, and even if he never got the letter, which he probably wouldn't, she was proud of herself for writing it.

She hadn't expected to get a letter back.

"Dear Lila," Bobby wrote to her three weeks later. "You have no idea how much it moved me to receive your letter. For all those months in the courtroom I wondered what you, and all the others, must have been thinking. I could never figure out what you must have made of me. Thank you for believing me, then. And thank you for still believing me now. I can only imagine how hard it's been for you, sticking up for me out there. Whatever I deserve for what I've done, I know that you don't deserve any of this.

"Thank you, too, for sharing so much of your life with me. You seem like a deeply decent person. I only wish I could have known you under different circumstances.

"Yours, Bobby Nock."

And below his name, an email address.

Finally, Lila thought as she read the letter for the third time. *Someone who understands.*

She emailed him back that night.

CHAPTER 23

A SECOND VERDICT
NOW

"Bobby Nock is the father of your son."

"*Shhh.* You have to be really quiet, okay?" Lila's body was frozen still. "You can't let Aaron hear us."

The grim details of two crimes a decade part interlocked in Maya's mind. "That's what Rick found out about Bobby. That's why he wouldn't tell me or Lou Silver or anyone else. He didn't find the locket. He didn't find out something about Bobby and *Jessica.* He found out something about Bobby and *you.*"

"Rick lied! He never found out *anything* that proved Bobby was a killer."

"Rick found out that after the trial you and Bobby had a relationship. That you had a son. That you kept it secret."

"My dad made us. When I told him I was pregnant—that I'd been seeing Bobby—he was so mad. He wanted Aaron to be able to grow up normal. In peace. Without anybody hounding him his entire life about his father the killer. Without anybody treating him the way everybody treated Bobby."

"But Rick was going to . . ." Finally, Rick's ingenious, all-or-nothing plan became clear. *"Fuck.* Rick was trying to use this information to blackmail Bobby into confessing to Jessica's murder, wasn't he?"

"Rick went to Bobby in that horrible town full of monsters. He threatened Bobby. He said to Bobby that he'd tell everyone what happened between us. He would ruin Aaron's life. Unless Bobby confessed to something he didn't do."

Maya was incredulous. "You're still convinced that Bobby was innocent?"

"Bobby was good," Lila said. "We both know that. He was good. Whatever happened with Jessica . . . Whatever he said he was sorry for in that note . . ."

"He had her locket."

"He was complicated."

Only days before, Lila had also learned that the father of her child, the man she'd loved, was a killer himself. "Complicated" didn't come close.

Lila refused to believe it. Maya had convinced her only too well, ten years ago.

"We were wrong," Maya said. "I didn't want to believe it either. I still don't. I keep hunting for some other explanation, but . . . I was wrong about him. The whole time. It was my fault. Bobby killed Jessica."

She'd never said those words before. They tasted like bile on her tongue.

"No," Lila whispered. "He didn't." She was struggling to hold herself together.

"You two still had some way of communicating," Maya said, "without anyone knowing. He told you Rick had threatened him."

Lila nodded. "Bobby had two choices. Confess, or watch Rick destroy Aaron's life. So Bobby did the only thing he could—the only honest thing. He ran. Disappeared. That's the kind of person Bobby was. He didn't want to cause any more hurt—to me, to Aaron, to anyone. He didn't even tell me where he was going. I was so scared . . . I wrote him a letter. But where was I supposed to send it?" Her fingers were shaking as she brushed her long black hair away from her face.

Bobby had lied to Maya, in East Jesus, about what Rick had said. Bobby had lied for the benefit of the son he was never allowed to see, the child whose alligator drawing was his one remaining connection to the life he could no longer have.

The sequence of events that led to Rick's death began to fall into place.

Rick had been fuming in Maya's room. He'd heard a knock on the door. He'd assumed, naturally, that it was Maya, returning to continue their fight. But he'd opened the door to find Lila standing in the hallway.

"Rick would have let you in," Maya said.

"I went to *your* room. Not his. I was looking for *you*."

411

"Me?"

"To tell you what was going on. Because I needed your help. Because I trusted you."

Lila's shaking hands clenched into tight fists.

"It doesn't seem that way."

"I thought that if anyone could help me, it would be you. That's why I brought Aaron to the hotel. So you could see him. So you'd understand."

"But you found Rick instead."

"It was an accident!" Lila pleaded, on the verge of tears. "At first, seeing him in your room, I was scared. Maybe he'd done something to you! But then he said I should come in. I kept looking around—where were you? What happened to *you?* He told me you didn't know anything. He hadn't told anyone what he knew— and he wouldn't, if Bobby told the 'truth.' Time was almost up; he was going on camera in the morning. I begged him. Maya, I *begged* him. 'Don't ruin the life of my son. Aaron never hurt anyone. Aaron deserves to have a life.' But he said no. He said, 'Ruin Aaron's life? Like Bobby ruined ours?' I've never seen anyone hate someone as much as he hated Bobby. . . . It was like Rick hated the obsessed creep he'd turned into, and he blamed Bobby for making him that way. We started arguing. He was yelling, I pushed him, he pushed me back, I pushed him again and he fell. . . . Oh God, it was an accident, Maya. You have to believe me. It was an accident."

412

Maya deeply wished that Lila was lying. She wanted to have gotten to the bottom of what happened and found the devil himself. But all she'd found was a terrified young woman who was desperate to protect her child.

"You left him there," Maya said. "You left him there for me to find."

"I never thought they would arrest you. I didn't know about you two—what was going on between you, back then. I only found out this week. When Rick was dead—he died in a second, I didn't know that one hit to the head, you can just die like that—I thought that . . . I don't know what I thought. If I stayed, the cops would find out about Aaron. If I left, I thought they'd think it was what it really was: an accident." She stepped closer. "I thought you could handle it. That's what I remembered most about you. All these years. No matter what happened—you could handle it."

If only, Maya thought.

Lila began to cry. She had tried to hold back these tears, but the struggle to keep herself together was too much.

Whether from instinct, protectiveness, or simple human decency, Maya put her arms around Lila and held her close.

Maya could feel the young woman giving up, placing herself in Maya's hands. She really believed that Maya could handle anything, and so she would have to.

413

Maya heard soft footsteps. Aaron tiptoed into the kitchen. He must have heard his mother crying. Seeing their embrace, he joined them. He wrapped one tiny arm around Lila's leg and another around Maya's. And there they stood— Maya, who had been trying to solve this crime; Lila, who had committed it; and Aaron, who would suffer the most in its aftermath.

Some time later, Maya and Lila sat at the small breakfast table. Lila nervously picked the fading polish from her nails. Aaron was back in his room, having been reassured that his mom was fine.

"What are you going to do?" Lila said.

Maya thought about her own former self. That innocent girl who'd first walked into the courthouse with an H-O-P-E pin on her backpack. That idiot who believed that anything was possible, who met eleven strangers in the jury room and thought that any of them could get out alive.

"What happened to us?" Maya asked. Then she realized what an impossibly odd thing that was to say.

But Lila seemed to understand what she meant.

"This place," Lila said.

Maya looked around. They were two women who were never meant to be in a room together; who never would have been. And yet here they were, with an impossible decision to be made from inside this cramped kitchen. Inside this forgotten neighborhood. Inside this booming city. Inside a great world that would never care about them for anything besides a lurid flash of infamy.

"What do we do about Aaron?" Lila said.

It was all such a mess. Maya could tell the cops that Lila had killed Rick—but Lila would deny it. Lila didn't want Maya to go to prison, sure, but if she was forced to choose between Maya and her own son . . . Maya would be hard-pressed to blame her for making that choice.

What evidence did Maya really have? Two crayon drawings of alligators? She didn't even know if Bobby's alligator had been found in his motel room. If Maya could get a court to mandate a DNA test—a big if—she could prove that Aaron was Bobby's child. But what bearing would that have on the criminal indictment against Maya?

If professional Ms. Seale were to look over the case, she would have to acknowledge that her current defensive strategy was actually stronger than arguing the truth. If she argued the field—"any one of these people could have done it"—she could use the dossiers, Peter's assault, Wayne's discrepancies, and who knew how much else. There was so much more potential evidence to be employed. The truth, as ever, was neither defense nor salvation. The truth didn't help anyone.

415

A thought entered Maya's head that was so perverse that she almost laughed. But the more she thought about it, it was the only thing that felt right.

If they wanted justice, or fairness, or any sort of reasoned moral outcome at the end of this trail of death . . . they would have to make it themselves.

"I have an idea," Maya said. "But it's fucking insane."

It only took eight phone calls to contact the other surviving members of their jury. She told them simply that Rick's killer had been identified, and that she hoped they would come together one more time to decide what to do about it.

Maya expected some pushback. Why would Wayne trust Maya not to throw him under the bus? Why would Trisha—who was already back in Houston—want to get herself involved again in any of this?

"Wayne will do whatever is best for everybody," Fran assured Maya. "So will I."

Trisha said she'd come because if she didn't, Maya would get to bully everyone into a decision without her.

Jae said that he was going to need to hear the evidence for himself.

Cal sounded impressed with Maya for having gotten to the bottom of it.

Kathy said that if Fran was going, then so would she.

Yasmine said that if they were *all* going, she wasn't going to be the only one left out.

Peter said he'd do whatever the fuck Maya wanted him to do.

Two days later, they assembled in Cal's living room. Cal's was selected for both its spaciousness and its neutrality: This was as level a playing field as they would find, given the secrecy they required.

Fran and Wayne sat beside Yasmine on a plush sofa.

Trisha, Cal, and Jae pressed up against each other on a smaller one.

Lila and Kathy pulled in chairs from the dining room. Lila looked like she hadn't slept in weeks.

Peter sat alone on a rocking chair that Cal had brought in from his bedroom. As Peter's foot tapped nervously against the floor, the chair rocked back and forth.

Maya stood and addressed the approximate circle as if she were in a courtroom.

"We are all here," she began, "because I know how Rick died. If you don't want to know, then this is your last chance to leave. But if you stay, I'm asking you to make a promise: You stay until the end. You stay until, as a group, we come to an agreement about the killer's punishment. Ten years ago, we made a decision together. Maybe we were wrong, but we were united. We have another decision to make today. And I don't think it's right for any one of us to make it alone. So if you're not ready to commit to this, please go. Nothing that happens in this room today need ever concern you again."

Maya looked at each of them, one by one.

Nobody moved an inch.

"Lila," Maya said, "would you like to tell everyone what happened?"

It didn't take long for them all to see where this was going. Lila's story was largely identical to the one she'd told Maya. She didn't sugarcoat it, or minimize her role in pushing Rick to his death.

While the group absorbed this, Maya addressed them again. She gave them the rest of the information they would need in order to make a decision. She told them about Wayne's surprise appearance outside the hotel that night, and she told them that Fran had lied on his behalf.

Then she told them about Peter.

Peter looked like he wanted to disappear into his seat as she described what she knew of his assault against Margarita.

Unlike Lila, he made an effort to defend himself. "You have to understand," he begged, "my mind wasn't right. . . . We were all losing it, you remember, and then I'd been getting into these experiences online with—"

"Shut the fuck up," Maya said. He did.

"The question for us is what should happen now. As far as I can tell, there are only two options."

Option one, she explained, was for her to go public with the truth. The whole truth, of course. They would roll the dice, and the result would be in the hands of the unpredictable police, the unprincipled media, and the unreliable courts. The most likely outcome was that Aaron would spend his life as the child of a famous murderer and his disciple, and potentially grow up an orphan; Lila would be accused of a crime that she would deny, with some degree of credibility; Peter would face no criminal charges and could likely defeat a civil suit from Margarita, whose name would also likely get dragged into the press; and, last but not least, Maya might still go to prison for a crime she hadn't committed.

Maya didn't have to work hard to conjure for them an image of the twelve people just like them—or perhaps nothing like them—whom the court would assemble to figure this all out. She well knew what those newly minted jurors would be like, filled with the best of intentions to ascertain the truth. They might even think they would find it.

Hopefully, Maya thought, none of them would end up killing each other. Given her experience, she couldn't be sure.

Or there was option two. This was trickier, and

it would require the participation of everyone present. "In option two," Maya suggested, "we decide to skip the truth. And go right for justice. Or the closest thing to justice we can manage."

"Justice for who?" Fran asked. "Rick? You? Lila's kid?"

"That's exactly the thing we can decide," Maya answered. "In option two, a few of you give me an alibi for the night of the murder. Doesn't matter who; we come up with a story just good enough to make the prosecution drop the case."

"We make sure you don't go to jail," Cal said, "but neither does Lila. Or anyone else."

"How?" Yasmine asked.

She could see Cal's mind at work already, constructing something baroque and vaguely plausible. "Maybe Maya was with Jae and Trisha when the murder happened, only they didn't tell the cops because they were still angry with Maya about the original verdict."

Trisha said, "Would anyone believe that?"

"It's like in *Witness for the Prosecution*," Cal said. "Where the wife's alibi is more believable because she only gave it begrudgingly." Seeing their blank faces, he elaborated: "Agatha Christie? There have been a couple of movies."

No one responded.

Cal continued: "Look, I'm just brainstorming."

"The point is," Fran said, "that we can work out something."

Maya said, "Next, Peter. The unavoidable truth is that there is no way to put you in jail. So we'll settle for the amends we can get. I've discussed this with Margarita, and what she wants, more than anything, is anonymity—she's seen what the lack of it does to people like us—and to get the hell out of that hotel. So, Peter, in option two, you will give Margarita a lot of money. And by that I mean a *lot* of money. Enough for her to retire from her long employ at the Omni Hotel and for her small children to go to private school."

Peter attempted an objection. "I don't know how much money you think I have, but my weed investments are kind of illiquid—"

"I don't give a shit," Maya said. "You'll figure it out. And then you'll figure out how to do the same for Aaron. Lila will raise her son and he will want for nothing."

She could see them all thinking it through. In option two, they would be judge, jury, executioner, and anything else that justice required of them.

"If we do something like this," Yasmine said, "then Rick's death will never be solved."

"As far as the public is concerned, yes. And of course, any decision we make will need to be unanimous. Because if any one of us breaks, we are all in a lot of trouble."

"It's a crime," Jae said. "Aiding and abetting." He paused. "That's what they call it, right?"

421

"Accessory after the fact," Maya said. "And, yes."

"So you're saying that we should all commit a crime to save Lila?" Trisha said.

"I'm not telling anyone what we should do," Maya said. "It's your choice. I'm asking what you think should happen now."

Cal said, "If Lila goes to prison—well, her poor boy."

"Bobby Nock's boy," Fran said.

"It ain't the kid's fault," Wayne said, speaking for the first time that day, "who his daddy is."

It was hard for anyone to argue with that.

Lila hesitated, but seemed to decide against defending the good name of her child's father. This wasn't the time or place.

Instead she said, "There's no one else who can decide. It has to be us." She stood. "Well, you."

She wouldn't be getting a vote, she explained. She'd leave them to decide what should happen to her.

Maya understood what she meant. So, it seemed, did the others. After all they had been through, separately and collectively, they knew they could not put her fate into the hands of the system. Into the hands of strangers. Into the hands of people like them.

After Lila left, Kathy got up. As if it was officially time for her to take charge. The crippling self-doubt that she'd shed inside the jury room ten years before had apparently never returned.

"Cal," Kathy said, "do you have any paper, pens, office supplies?"

He directed her to a kitchen drawer and she returned with a set of index cards and a box of Sharpies.

"A preliminary vote," Kathy said. "So we know where we stand."

No one objected.

She passed out the cards.

And then, for the first time in ten years, they took a vote.

CHAPTER 24

For thirty years, Carolina Cancio's sister Alana had owned, operated, and lived behind the House of Tarot, a small fortune-teller's shop on Sunset. Alana's long-dead husband had painted the outside all black. That worthless man had been so drunk that the white letters he'd put up above the doorway had come out crooked. All this time later, fifteen years after the night he'd gotten so wasted that he fell off the Shakespeare Bridge and died, the letters still hadn't been fixed. Which tells you something, really, about Alana.

Another thing about Alana: She didn't really believe all the superstitious nonsense she sold in her shop. She and Carolina were Catholic. Born and raised in Durango, they'd come to Los Angeles when they were still young enough to pick up English pretty quickly. Alana had prayed to the Virgin Mary, right beside Carolina. Alana had thrown half-pesos into the fountain near the basilica. She was not a godless woman. She was not like all the white kids who stumbled into the House of Tarot late at night, giggling like it was all a joke but really wanting nothing more than to believe that their futures could be read. Everyone had to believe in something, Carolina knew that. So maybe her sister wasn't taking advantage of the white kids, not exactly, when they'd knock on her door, ten, eleven o'clock at night, and pay forty-five dollars cash for a candlelit card reading. The customers always got what they'd come for.

"You've already met the love of your life," Alana would say. "You just don't know it."

That gave them something to tee-hee about.

Or Alana would say, "You worry too much about money." And they'd nod, like that was some kind of revelation, before handing over the cash.

The annoying part was that after they left, Alana would keep up the act. Did she really believe in the Fool, the King of Swords, and Death, which she always said really meant new life? She *had* to know better. Because Jesus had never said a word about the tarot, and Saint Paul had not once, to Carolina's knowledge, messed around with the dried bones of a dead cat. Heaven forgive Carolina for saying it, but her sister was full of *mierda*.

And now, if you could believe it, Alana wanted her daughter Sonya, Carolina's niece, to take over the House of Tarot and talk the same nonsense to more stoned white people.

Sonya was already grown, already the office manager of the tax preparation place nearby. She already had her own kids, husband, life—what did she need with the House of Tarot?

But when Carolina had explained all that, what had Alana said? She'd asked why Carolina was getting so involved in somebody else's business. Maybe, Alana had said, it was because Carolina's two sons were grown, gone, tending to families of their own in Riverside and San Luis Obispo. They never came back, they didn't care about their nosy old mama, and so she had to tell everybody else how to live their life. Because sticking her nose where it didn't belong was the only thing she'd ever known how to do.

When the jury summons arrived, Carolina left it out on the kitchen table for all to see. For two weeks, anyone who passed through her kitchen took notice of the seal of the State of California on the envelope. And when anyone—a neighbor, a friend, Alana, Sonya—expressed sympathy for her rotten luck at having to serve, Carolina got indignant. She was not being forced, at gunpoint, to go to jury duty. She was doing what any and every American must, performing a rite as important as the oath of citizenship she'd taken in 1964. This was nothing to moan about. This was a privilege rightfully earned through forty-five years of paying taxes and obeying laws and loving the country in which she'd married, raised two sons, become a young widow, and grown older and healthier than either of her own parents ever had. If her sister wanted to hold on to her embarrassing, immoral scams, then she was welcome to that life. But Carolina, at eighty-two years of age, could still show Sonya that there was a big world out there, and that when the State of California says that they need you to help determine the guilt or innocence of another citizen on a criminal matter, you go.

And then Carolina's dumb sister had the gall to say that Carolina was only doing it because she liked to judge people.

Carolina was the first juror selected. So on day one, she sat and did her puzzles while each of the others trickled in.

Right at the top was Juror 158. He seemed like he might be a bit of a bookworm. He was dressed up nicely, which Carolina appreciated.

The first words out of his mouth were, "Are you a fortune-teller?"

How did he know what she was thinking about? She felt like a fool when she looked down and noticed that she was carrying a House of Tarot bag. Funny that today, of all days, she'd borrowed one of her sister's bags to carry her puzzle books. Because that was the whole point: Carolina's sister claimed to be a fortune-teller, and the entire reason Carolina had ended up here was to prove her sister wrong.

"I don't believe in fortunes," she said to 158.

427

● ● ●

What a group they were! The sensible Jewish lady, who seemed not to brook much nonsense but cleaned up after them like they were all her kids. The funny old white man, reading a novel, who must be gay. (At his age!) The younger white guy who made a big show of slapping the other guys on the back. The Chinese lady who asked the bailiff three times what time the court usually finished up.

Carolina took stock of all of them before they could take stock of each other. And the main thing she kept thinking was, *What sort of lunatic God would put these people in a room together?*

It wasn't that any one of them made Carolina nervous. It was that once you combined them all . . . well, somehow it felt like these people were going to collide against each other like marbles. They were going to send each other in directions none of them saw coming.

They all seemed like decent folks. Like they were going to do their best to get justice for a girl who'd died before any of them could meet her. All they wanted to do was help. Carolina gazed across the jury room and saw fourteen people with nothing but good intentions.

So why couldn't she shake the feeling that the best intentions of *this* bunch of strangers were only going to make things worse?

"I don't believe in fortunes," she'd said to 158.

But she was starting to see why people did.

CHAPTER 25

GUILTY PARTIES
NOW

Jae Kim voted to save a boy from the lifelong punishment of public notoriety.

Cal Barro voted to keep a sensitive situation out of the rough hands of the police.

Yasmine Sarraf voted not to drag anybody else into this mess.

Wayne Russel voted to do what was best for the whole group.

Trisha Harold voted not to let a group of strangers tell them who they were.

Fran Goldenberg voted to put Aaron's interests first.

Peter Wilkie voted to save his own ass.

Maya Seale voted to right her initial wrong.

For eight different reasons, all eight former members of the jury in *The People v. Robert Nock* voted to lie in service of a brighter future.

The story they concocted was baroque. Once the difficult decision to dissemble had been made, the creative act of coming up with a narrative was a pleasant relief. Who would be the villain? Who would be their voice of heroism?

In this version of the truth, Maya had been with Trisha at the time of Rick's murder, arguing about what had really happened to Jessica Silver. But after Rick was killed, thanks to their previous experiences with the law, neither of them had wanted to say a word to the police. Trisha had confided the truth of Maya's alibi to Fran that morning. And then it would be Fran who would first tell this to the authorities now. Trisha would then admit to having kept quiet. Her lack of candor about Maya had not been illegal, and in fact, one reason for her silence had been that because she knew Maya was innocent, she'd trusted the justice system not to condemn an innocent woman.

This was the cleverest bit of bullshit they came up with. It was Cal's idea. Rather than express an earned distrust of the justice system, Trisha and Fran both proclaimed that it was their very faith in its efficacy that had provoked their silence. *We trust you to get it right,* they were saying, in effect. *But you didn't, so now we're coming clean in order to bail you out.*

They knew this story would become public, so they all needed to testify to this version of the truth to the police—and to everyone else—forever.

As always, they were most together when they were disobeying the rules.

• • •

When Lila returned and heard their decision, she cried. She went around the circle hugging each and every one of them. In a way, she told them, Aaron was all of theirs now. They were all giving him the life that his real father had nearly denied him.

At least one new life was created in between the litany of deaths. At least, Maya thought, there was one person in all of this who was genuinely, truly, to the very core of his soul, *innocent*.

Maya met Craig in his office the morning after the deliberation to tell him what had "really happened." She explained that not only would Trisha testify that she'd been with Maya at the time of Rick's death, but Fran would testify to Trisha having confirmed this to her at the time. No one else would contradict their story.

When she'd finished, the first thing he said was, "You're sure that they'll both testify to this?"

"They're calling the police this morning to do just that."

"And Trisha, Fran—not to mention *you*—understand the legal implications of this . . . admission?"

"We do."

Craig raised an eyebrow.

She continued, "Do you think they'll drop the charges?"

431

Craig considered it. "Not for a week or two. They'll want to put you through the ringer. Your compatriots as well. See if they can shake something loose. You know, in case any of you are lying about this—and of course I know you're not—they'll try to see if they can get one of you to crack. Or one of the others. Any discrepancy will do."

Maya didn't even blink. "Okay."

"With your permission, let's wait until they give their story to the police? When they have, the DA will call me—he will undoubtedly accuse *me* of all manner of deceit—and of course I will say that at no point have I ever done anything but take my client at her word." He paused for effect. "Then I'll go in with you. You'll tell them what you just told me. And not a single syllable more."

"Craig . . . thank you."

Somehow, the mutual understanding that she was lying to him and they both knew it did not inspire either of them to an emotional display. "You're welcome."

Two weeks later, the State of California dropped all charges against Maya Seale. The DA had already leaked the jurors' story to the press, who dissected it with all the fervor of a scandal among the English royal family.

The investigation into Rick's death was

reopened. But the detectives were not hopeful of further progress.

Maya's parents had stayed in L.A. for the whole month. When the charges were dropped, Maya's mother took a long walk, alone, just to keep herself together. Maya's dad no longer seemed embarrassed to cry in front of her. They weren't idiots. They must have known that the story that absolved their daughter was a lie. But never, not even once, did they ask her about it. There was a quantity of lies between child and parent that was acceptable—that had been in some way mutually agreed upon in the contract between them—and this, blessed miracle that it was, fit safely onto the pile.

A week after that, Maya prepared for her return to work. Now she could boast of having been a defendant as well as a juror. Her particular expertise would be in even higher demand. Craig elected to raise her hourly rate.

The night before she was due back in the office, she went out for a long dinner with Crystal. Over an icy plate of oysters, Maya attempted to address the issue of her alibi head-on. She didn't want Crystal to be angry with her, but nor could she tell Crystal the truth.

"Look," Maya said, "I'm sure this story about me and Trisha, the night of the murder, came as a big surprise. . . ."

"Oh, that bullshit?" Crystal interrupted with a laugh. "Here's the deal, okay? We're here. You're not in jail. So you tell me whatever you need to. And as long as you stay out of trouble, I promise I'm never going to ask."

Maya took a deep breath and then raised her glass of prosecco. Crystal gave it a clink with her glass of sparkling water.

The next morning, Maya finally entered her own office again. Mike and Mike were there to greet her. They seemed happy to see her back.

She still could not remember which of them was which.

A week later, she composed a letter to Rick. She sat on her back patio and wrote down the farewell she never got a chance to speak. She forgave Rick for everything: his public excoriation of her, his hounding of Bobby, his attempted blackmail of Lila. And she apologized for covering up the circumstances of his death. She hoped that if anyone could understand, it would be him. She felt that if another one of the jurors had threatened Lila's son, that Rick would have voted the same way. For once, she hoped, they might have agreed on something.

She said that she wished she'd told him that she loved him when she'd had the chance. She thought that maybe he'd once loved her too. If Jessica's death hadn't come between them, maybe they could have loved each other still. But then, if Jessica hadn't died, they never would have met.

Maya folded her letter up and lit it on fire. She watched as the ash flew into the air, carried away by the autumn wind.

The very next day, Lou Silver finally returned Maya's call. Or rather, one of his assistants did. The woman asked if she would come speak with Lou in person. "Mr. Silver," the woman said, "would like to put all of this unpleasantness behind us."

It was late on a Friday afternoon when she made her way to Century City. The sun was setting from every single one of the floor-to-ceiling windows as an assistant led Maya into his corner office. In all directions, Los Angeles was infused with a crimson glow. And there, sitting at his desk behind a few papers and a row of framed photographs, was Lou.

Had Bobby told her the truth about Lou's abuse of his daughter? Had, for that matter, Jessica told the truth to Bobby? Or had Bobby made it all up in order to keep Maya on his side? Maya had to accept that she would never know. At this point, maybe she didn't even want to.

"So." Lou ushered her into a leather seat by a large coffee table, then sat down beside her. "Are you going to say it?"

She would have laughed had not people so close to them both been killed.

"You were right." Maya looked him in the eye. "I was wrong."

Lou gave only the smallest nod. And then he frowned. It was as if he was disappointed but hadn't figured out why.

"Does it help?" Maya asked. "Knowing that you were right?"

He tilted his head. "I'm not sure just yet."

"You used me."

"I did?"

"You sent me to find Bobby in East Jesus. Then you sent those reporters after me. So that they wouldn't just find him—they'd find him with me."

"Oh. Yes. I did." There was no shame in his admission. The discovery of Bobby would be a bigger story if he was found in the company of one of his former jurors. More press would hunt him. Lou's only goal had been to torment Bobby in whatever way he could. Maya had just appeared in his doorway and presented herself as a useful tool.

"I'm angry about it," Maya said.

"At me?"

"Yes."

"You don't seem angry," he said.

What was she supposed to do? Yell at him for manipulating her in pursuit of the justice that she herself had long denied his murdered daughter? "I guess you'll have to take my word for it."

"I wasn't right about everything either."

"No?"

"Bobby Nock didn't kill Rick Leonard."

For Lou, on the subject of Bobby, this sounded like high praise. There was at least *one* sin of which Bobby was innocent.

"The police found the photographs," Lou went on. "The ones taken by Bobby Nock's . . . I don't know, 'associates' or whatnot. The photographer in the desert."

"They showed you the time stamps."

"They did. So I was wrong about that."

"Well," Maya said. "At least you were right that I didn't do it."

"It does make one wonder." He leaned in close. "Who *did* kill Rick?"

Now she understood why he was granting her even this small, indirect apology. He didn't know the truth about Rick's death. But he knew her story was bullshit.

Lou didn't care about Rick's life one way or another. Bobby hadn't killed him, so Lou's curiosity about who had was purely idle.

"Do you think we'll ever know?" she asked.

He remained perfectly still. "It's cruel. As soon as we proved, conclusively, who killed my daughter . . . we lost any clue about who killed your boyfriend."

If there was mockery or condescension in his referring to Rick as her "boyfriend," she couldn't hear it. But still the reference stung. "Maybe I'll have to find a way to make peace with never knowing. I've had a lot of practice at that."

"Or maybe the police will figure it out."

"I hope so."

"I hope that Rick's killer gets an excellent jury."

They were interrupted by the ringing phone. Lou answered it gruffly, then said to whoever was on the other end that he'd be right down.

He turned to Maya. "Will you excuse me for a moment? The Innovation partners . . . they're having some late-Friday crisis with their innovations."

He made a "one minute" gesture with an outstretched forefinger, and then he left her alone in his office.

She looked out at the sunset. It was a spectacular sight from this height. The eastern edge of the city was already dark, and to the west the last inches of the sun were about to vanish beneath the ocean. The sunsets in Los Angeles came on so gradually, and then they were over in an instant.

She circled Lou's desk to the western windows, chasing down the final flickers of daytime.

Idly, she took in the folders, magazines, and framed photographs on the desktop.

All the photographs were of Jessica.

Each was from a different stage of her short life. A baby picture, where the girl, eyes closed, was wrapped in a hospital blanket, lying snug in Elaine's arms. A preschool photo, where she bounced on a trampoline, yellow-blond hair flying in every direction. An elementary school photo, where she tried to crawl inside a dollhouse too big for her frame. A high school photo, where the teenager fake-smiled for picture day in her navy school uniform.

Maya realized how much she knew about the final months of Jessica's life but how little she knew of the fifteen years before. She'd never experienced the Jessica that Lou and Elaine had. In a way, Maya had only known the brief side of Jessica that they had not.

Maya imagined what it must be like for Lou to see these photographs every morning. Whatever had gone on between them behind closed doors, he wasn't trying to hide or forget, like so many people would. Keeping these photographs right here seemed bold. Proud. This had been his daughter.

Maya's eyes caught on one of the photos she'd never seen before—a shot of Jessica with her smiling family. There were Lou, Elaine, and Jessica—maybe she was ten or twelve—on some kind of beach vacation. Lou wore a silly Hawaiian shirt. Jessica and Elaine looked like they were the same person at different stages of life. They wore matching blue bathing suits. Matching white hats. And, around their necks, matching silver lockets.

Maya picked up the frame. The taste of brass—bitter and metallic—was in her mouth.

This was the locket that Jessica wore on the day she died. The one that Maya had seen in photos a million times during the trial. The locket that once made the cover of *Time* magazine.

Elaine had an identical one.

How was it possible that Maya had never, in all this time, heard a word about the existence of a second locket? There was probably no person left alive—save maybe only Lou—who knew more about the death of Jessica Silver than Maya. And yet she didn't know that this key piece of evidence—the very piece of physical evidence that finally proved, after a decade, that Bobby had been the killer—had a duplicate?

If Jessica and her mother had owned identical necklaces, then . . .

Maya looked up at the sound of the opening door.

She opened her mouth to interrogate Lou about what she'd found. But it wasn't Lou Silver who entered the office.

It was Elaine.

She wore a pure white pantsuit that matched her elegantly short white hair. Her heels clacked to a stop on the wood floor.

"Ms. Seale!" Elaine said with surprise. "I didn't know you were here."

Elaine started to smile at Maya, then saw the expression on her face. "Is something the matter?"

Maya angled the photograph so Elaine could see. "You and Jessica had matching lockets."

Elaine's mouth twitched slightly. "Perhaps I should fetch my husband."

"Where's your locket?"

"I'm sure I don't know."

"Ten years, and you never told anyone there were two lockets?"

"My husband must have just popped out, I'll find him."

"If Jessica had so much as touched your locket, it would easily have had her DNA on it. Maybe even a few of her hairs. It'd be nothing to plant a hair on it if you had to."

Elaine clasped her hands. "I don't appreciate this tone. I'm going to ask you to leave."

Maya's hand was shaking. "You know exactly where your locket is . . . because your husband planted it on Bobby's body. After he had Bobby killed."

Cold silence settled over the room. Outside, the wind had risen and Maya could hear it whipping the windows behind her.

"Let's take a deep breath before we say anything we can't take back."

"You know exactly what your husband has done. Stop lying for him. Stop helping him cover up his crimes."

"Crimes?"

"Lou's investigators had been following Bobby since Rick found him. They were following me too, weren't they? When I drove out there?"

"I have no idea what you're talking about."

"They were following Bobby when he got to that motel in Texas. . . . That's why Lou couldn't just send the press to East Jesus without sending me first. He needed another layer of protection. I found Bobby, the press found me, Bobby ran away again, and Lou's people followed him. They got to him in the motel. They made him write the suicide note. Only Lou would have composed such a perfect note: 'I'm so sorry.' Lou's people hanged Bobby and planted the second locket. You'd been keeping it for *years,* hadn't you? Did you know what Lou was going to do with it? Why did he wait so long? Why not plant it on Bobby ten years ago? Why wait till Rick was murdered?"

Lou hadn't killed Rick. So when someone had—not that Lou even knew who—he'd found a way to spin the whole, horrible situation to get what he'd always wanted: punishment for the crime Lou was still convinced Bobby had committed.

Unless . . . unless Bobby wasn't Lou's only victim.

"Bobby told me about the abuse," Maya said. "What Lou did to Jessica. What Lou did to you. Does he still?"

Elaine's face went as white as her suit.

"Please," Maya implored. "Only you know the truth about your husband. You can go public. I can help you."

"I don't know what you think is going on here," Elaine said quietly. "But whatever it is that you mistakenly suspect—I wouldn't make too much noise about it, not in your position. You don't have a stitch of evidence."

She was right. The mere existence of a second locket would raise questions, but it wouldn't come close to proving Lou was guilty of Bobby's murder. Or Jessica's. It wouldn't even prove that *Bobby* hadn't killed Jessica—a crime for which he had, legally speaking, already been acquitted.

"And of course even if you *could* prove something," Elaine continued, "any new questions about one death will undoubtedly raise questions about another."

The taste of brass in Maya's mouth was nauseating. Elaine was delicate, refined—and for the first time, terrifying.

Elaine wasn't a fool. Like her husband, she knew that Maya was hiding something. Elaine was betting that if Maya forced her husband's

443

hand, then they could force Maya to expose whatever it was that she so desperately needed to keep secret. Elaine didn't need to know whom Maya was protecting. She knew that Maya had something valuable to protect—and that whatever it was would be all the leverage she'd need.

Maya understood the terms of Elaine's threat. Maya would stay quiet about what Lou had done, or else they would discover and reveal whatever Maya had been party to. Justice for Bobby would be exchanged for justice for Aaron. The only way for that boy to have a life was for Lou to get away with murdering his father.

Maya felt sick. She wanted to get far away from these horrible people who were capable of such monstrous things . . . some of which she, apparently, was capable of as well. Did she hate that Elaine had helped cover up the crimes of her husband? Or did she hate that she herself was no better than they were?

"You don't have to do this," Maya said. "You don't have to cover up what your husband has done. You can be free of all this."

Elaine stepped toward Maya. "I'm sorry. You have to understand . . . I'm only doing this for Jessica."

"Jessica's dead. And all you're doing is stopping the truth of what happened to her from ever coming out."

Elaine tilted her head, as if she was trying to

444

solve a different puzzle altogether. "Oh. I thought you'd figured that out already."

Maya had no idea what Elaine was talking about.

Elaine spoke to her like she was addressing a child:

"Jessica is still alive."

"That's impossible."

Elaine carefully shut the door to her husband's office, then locked it.

"Open up your purse." Her voice was quick, direct, and so quiet as to be nearly inaudible.

Before Maya could process this, Elaine yanked the bag from Maya's shoulder and pulled out her cellphone. Elaine verified that she was not being recorded.

"My husband has made terrible mistakes," she whispered. "I'm not going to make excuses for him. He hurt our daughter. He hurt me. But I have lived at his side for too long to just give up and walk away. What would I do? Go back to Florida with whatever scraps I have left after his lawyers finish with me? No. I'm not going back to where I came from. And I can control my husband." She took a breath. "But I had to protect my daughter."

"Where is she?"

Elaine shook her head. "What would you have done, in my position? Married to this man who was capable of such kindness, in addition to his moments of . . . behaving otherwise. Jessica told me she was spending time with her teacher—with Bobby—well, that's when I knew things were going to go badly. She'd tell Bobby about the abuse, he'd tell the school, we'd lose *everything*."

"She'd already told him."

Elaine's eyes went wide. For the first time, Maya knew something that Elaine didn't—and it seemed to support her position. "Then it's a good thing I acted when I did."

"Your family fucking name was more important to you than your daughter's life?"

"Have you seen what happens to these men, accused of terrible things? Have you seen what happens to their *wives?*" Elaine shook her head, as if picturing the grim fate of those miserable, wealthy women. "We were not going to end up like them. No. Jessica, thankfully, had a plan. It wasn't even my idea. It was hers."

"Jessica wanted to . . . leave?"

Elaine nodded, encouraged by Maya's understanding. "She wanted to go far away and start again. As someone else."

A long-ignored piece of evidence from the trial emerged from the recesses of Maya's memory. "The call from Jessica's phone. The afternoon she disappeared . . ." Maya remembered the interminable days they'd spent forensically dissecting where the phone was when that call was made. But they'd utterly missed the point: *why* Jessica would have called home in the middle of being murdered—and then not left a message. "She was calling *you*."

Elaine seemed pleased. "That was the signal. So I'd know that our plan was in motion. I couldn't keep her safe, here. I couldn't protect Jessica from her father. But I could build a new life for J—" She stopped. "Oh, but I'm not going to tell you her name."

Maya wanted to scream. She felt helpless. She *was* helpless. "You sent her away to start a new life . . . and you framed Bobby for her murder?"

"No!" Elaine was defiant. "Without a body, we figured it would end up as just another unsolved disappearance. But then Bobby lied to the police about where he'd been! Why did he lie? He was scared, I suppose. Being interrogated by the LAPD. Trying to hide his relationship with Jessica. At every turn, he just kept nailing his own coffin shut tighter. It was painful to watch. Once the police found the text messages, discovered a black teacher having this relationship with his white student . . ." Elaine shook her head, as if the one who'd gotten a raw deal in all of this was her.

"Lou doesn't know," Maya said, realizing. "He really thought Bobby had killed Jessica. And you never told him otherwise."

Maya remembered her own elaborate theorizing about Bobby's death. She'd thought about whether Jessica's killer could have framed Bobby with the locket, and decided that the suggestion was unbelievable. And she'd been right: Bobby had been framed. Just not by Jessica's killer.

That, Maya realized, was why Lou hadn't planted the locket on Bobby before his initial arrest: because then, at the time of the initial trial, Lou wasn't trying to frame anyone. He genuinely wanted to get to the truth of what had happened to his daughter. He probably hadn't even thought, yet, about the second locket.

Elaine shrugged. "My husband has lied, sometimes, about some things. But his rage at Bobby—that was entirely genuine."

"So you watched as Bobby was arrested. You watched him—every day—at the trial."

Elaine nodded. "And then I watched you set him free. Ms. Seale—*Maya*—that's the real irony here." She placed a soft hand on Maya's shoulder. "I hope it gives you some comfort: You were right all along."

Maya felt a churning in her stomach.

She remembered the wail she'd heard Elaine Silver make when the verdict was read aloud in court. It hadn't been a cry of sorrow, had it? It had been scream of release. Justice, thank God, had been served.

"You helped your husband murder Bobby."

For the first time, Elaine looked guilty. "I didn't know he was going to do it. Weeks ago he took the locket from my closet—I'd kept it, as you said—but I didn't know what he was going to . . . I should have known. But there's nothing I can do about that now, is there?"

Elaine made it sound like the life of Bobby Nock was nothing more than milk spilled on her kitchen floor.

"Where is Jessica?" Maya asked.

Elaine held up a hand, like a crossing guard. "She lives on a farm, far away from here. She has horses. A partner. They have a daughter. My granddaughter. Who, like her mom, is safe from all of this."

Elaine looked swollen with pride. "She's happy. And that's all you're ever going to know."

The doorknob rattled.

Then a knock came from the hall outside.

"Hello?" boomed Lou's voice. "Maya? Are you in there?"

Elaine turned to Maya and whispered: "If you make any attempt to find my daughter, I will find out what really happened to Rick Leonard. If you tell any of this to anyone . . . there will be the same result. You're going to help me keep this secret because you were right, a minute ago—oh, the sheer number of things you've been so right about—we can help each other. We're on the same side. And the best thing for everyone involved—everyone who's still alive—is silence."

In a flash, Elaine grabbed the photograph from Maya's hand. She placed it gently back

449

on her husband's desk. And then, before Maya could even figure out what she might say, Elaine opened the door.

"Oh! I didn't know you'd—" Lou stopped when he saw Maya behind his wife. And took in Maya's expression. "What's the matter?"

"Nothing, my dear," Elaine said.

Lou could tell that something had gone on between these two women while he was downstairs. But perhaps he'd been married long enough to know that if his wife told him that an unruly situation was under control, he should take her word for it.

He searched Maya's disgusted face, trying to figure out how much she knew.

She, in turn, looked over at Elaine, who raised an eyebrow. *Well, Maya,* she seemed to be saying. *What's it going to be?*

It would take so little to expose Elaine Silver's crimes to Lou, and force Lou's crimes out into the open . . . which would expose Jessica and Aaron to unknowable harm.

The lives in Maya's hands—the lives that would be protected by her silence and complicity—had multiplied. And the strangest thing was that all of this, from the very beginning, had happened because first Lou, and then the police, and then Maya, and then Rick, and then Maya again, could not stop themselves from trying to solve mysteries that should just have been left covered in fog.

"Maya?" Lou said. "Are you all right?"

"Ms. Seale?" Elaine said.

Maya turned to the windows. The sky beyond was now black. The last vestiges of the sun had disappeared. She could make out only a few dim figures on the sidewalk below.

Maya found herself picturing the face of Jessica Silver. She would be twenty-five years old now. What would she look like? If Maya glimpsed her one day on the street, would she even recognize her? Probably not.

Maya imagined Jessica's daughter and Bobby's son among the shapes on the sidewalk. Twenty years from now, they could be adults passing each other on a street just like this one. They wouldn't give each other a second glance. They would go about their lives unaware of what crimes had once been committed on their behalf. Just two innocent strangers in a guilty crowd.

ACKNOWLEDGMENTS

Many collaborators provided invaluable support, both artistic and professional, throughout the creation of this novel. And yet one person's contribution stands alone—that of my editor, Susan Kamil.

Susan was this book's most fervent advocate and its most unsparing critic. To say that it wouldn't exist without her—and I don't mean "wouldn't exist in this form," I mean "wouldn't exist at all"—is not hyperbole. This is true for many reasons, among them that if I had ever dared send the previous sentence to Susan she would have plucked up her pen and mercilessly gored my awkward double negative. If you've appreciated even a single passage in this book, please know that there once existed an early draft of that passage in the margin of which Susan scribbled "BORING" in big block letters. I have spent more time on the phone arguing with Susan than with any other person in my life, because that's how much she cared. Her love of fiction has been both infectious and relentless, a gale force wind directed at only one thing: making writing better.

Susan Kamil passed away in September 2019, mere weeks after this book was finished and mere months before its publication. That we were given the chance to finish our work together is a blessing for which I'll always be grateful. That she never got the chance to watch this book enter the wide world is a tragedy for which I'll always mourn.

So as I use this page to give thanks, let me start here: Susan, thank you. I miss you. And of all the legacies you've left in so many lives, I can only hope that the most lasting one you've left in mine is that every day I will sit at my desk and endeavor to be just a little less boring.

Of course, creating this book required the contributions of many others. Let me give my further thanks to:

Jennifer Joel, my literary agent and friend for over a decade.

Priscila Garcia-Jacquier, Keya Vakil, and Matthew Rusthoeven, my research assistants and compatriots.

Dennis Ambrose, Benjamin Dreyer, Deb Dwyer, and Clio Seraphim, the terrifically professional team at Random House who did truly amazing work under the most difficult of circumstances.

Caitlin Decker, Ben Epstein, Suzanne Joskow, Johnathan McClain, and Scoop Wasserstein, who read early drafts and then told me how to make them better.

Neil Cohen and Anthony O'Rourke, who provided expert guidance and frequent corrections on matters of criminal law. Any errors remaining in this novel are my responsibility alone.

And a special thanks to Sam Wasson, who has never read a word I've written and never will.

ABOUT THE AUTHOR

GRAHAM MOORE is the *New York Times* bestselling author of *The Holdout, The Last Days of Night*, and *The Sherlockian* and the Academy Award–winning screenwriter of *The Imitation Game*, which also won a Writers Guild of America Award for best adapted screenplay and was nominated for a BAFTA and a Golden Globe. Moore was born in Chicago, received a BA in religious history from Columbia University in 2003, and now lives in Los Angeles.
MrGrahamMoore.com
Facebook.com/GrahamMooreWriter
Twitter: @MrGrahamMoore

Books are
produced in the
United States
using U.S.-based
materials

Books are printed
using a revolutionary
new process called
THINKtech™ that
lowers energy usage
by 70% and increases
overall quality

Books are
durable and
flexible
because of
Smyth-sewing

Paper is
sourced using
environmentally
responsible
foresting methods
and the
paper is acid-free

Center Point Large Print
600 Brooks Road / PO Box 1
Thorndike, ME 04986-0001 USA

(207) 568-3717

US & Canada:
1 800 929-9108
www.centerpointlargeprint.com